Knights of Darkness

Knights of Darkness

Jean-Yves Soucy

Translated by Alan Brown

STEWART
HOUSE

Canadian Cataloguing in Publication Data

Soucy, Jean-Yves, 1945-
[Chevaliers de la nuit. English]
Knights of darkness

Translation of: Les chevaliers le la nuit.

ISBN 1-895246-29-6

I. Title. II. Title: Chevaliers de la nuit. English

PS8587.O93C5413 1994   C843'.54   C94-931376-9
PQ3919.2.S68C5413 1994

The translation of the text was completed with the support of the Canada Council.

The publishers acknowledge the support of the Canada Council and the Ontario Arts Council for their publishing program.

Typesetting by Softprobe Computing Services Inc.
Printed and bound in Canada

A Stewart House Book
481 University Avenue
Toronto, Ontario
M5G 2E9

1 2 3 4 5   98 97 96 95 94

Knights of Darkness

The endless procession of scraggy spruce whisked by in the early light. Wisps of mist and the speed blunted their pointed branches. Here, a glimpse of a creek still brimming with the dark; or a patch of burnt forest where black, crippled trunks fled twisting by. A violet lake and – swiftly, after this break – the trees re-forming ranks. The flash of a bird taking flight. The land whizzing past with a monotonous sound. Only the sky stood still, though it too was changing slowly, altering the dark purple with pink and pale milk turning to yellow. But this was nothing compared with the sudden metamorphosis of the bush. You had to stare long at the sky to see it change. Below this dawn thronged the eternal, crowding spruce trees with their unvoiced questions. A whole world watching the train go by.

The two boys, their eyes red and their legs sore and stiff, stared endlessly out the window. Inside, a distant snore and the hissing dialogue of two old women: these sounds had been constant throughout the night with nothing else to punctuate its passing. Mother was dozing, holding their five-year-old sister Françoise in her lap. One of the child's arms dangled in the aisle.

Morning at last! All night they had strained their eyes trying to see the mysterious world outside, to spy some detail from which they could construct the unknown landscape by imagining. But they had glimpsed only an occasional blue patch on the black of night, gone before it could be named. And now the thin, pre-dawn light was revealing a country even stranger than their imaginings. A country of trees, deprived of humans. Thousands, maybe millions of spruce trees, each one like all the others, crowded together so they touched. More trees than these city boys had ever dreamed of. The train was eating up the miles and there was still no end to the forest. Abitibi was really far.

As late as yesterday, when Rémi and Robert were discussing that fabulous region their father had talked about so much, it hadn't seemed nearly as far as this. For them, living on the eastern tip of the Island of Montreal, and skipping stones on the wavelets of the St. Lawrence, Abitibi was just over there, across the big river. But here they sat, rolling northward in a train that clattered on as if it would never stop.

They were going to make a new start up there. It would be like a permanent holiday – no electricity, no T.V., no paved roads or traffic lights, no park with trodden grass and shrivelled maples, no more St. Helen's Island and taking dips in the shadow of the bridge. Nothing familiar any more. Just the fun of the unknown.

They'd be pioneers like in the movies: inventive and resourceful. But they were ready for it, leaving everything behind, cashing-in the past, freshening their minds to encounter the Abitibi. They would have to stop being children now and change their ages as they were changing homes. But now Rémi thought they might have been too daring in their talks. It was easy to make resolutions when they were safe in their old routine, but quite another thing when caged in this train that stopped nowhere, racing toward a destination from which, perhaps, no road led home.

Beneath them they heard the wheels beat a stern rhythm on the rails, the stubborn tom-tom that was the country's beating heart. Rémi didn't feel up to all this. He curled, shivering, on the seat. Weariness crept over him, but a wakeful despair came with it. He struggled to drive his imagination forward, while his eyelashes blinked against the cold window vibrating against his forehead.

They'd been told that the Abitibi region was as far away as the Gaspé. This was a known measure: a whole day's trip, leaving home at sun-up. On the way to the Gaspé there were villages with pointed steeples, farms, woods, and fields as regular as the squares on a chequer-board. You could try counting cows, there were telephone poles beyond number, there was lunch at Rivière-du-Loup and lobster bought at a roadside stand, then Mont-Joli and Matane, all in familiar order, in miles that were so many hours and distances measured by your hunger. But Abitibi! Its distance had nothing to do with that of the Gaspé: it lay in a different dimension. During the night, time had dissolved and miles had no more meaning. You'd have had to measure the way in spruce trees, the thickness of each being added to those past until you had a living wall from Pointe-aux-Trembles to Amos. But the spruce went by too fast to be counted, and in any case the boys hadn't enough numbers between them to do the job. They'd never know for sure . . .

In the middle of the green blur, a black form. A moose, it must be, or a bear. People had told them about this country and they'd looked it up in books. They exchanged a glance, forcing each other to smile. This really was somewhere else. For long minutes this thought filled both their minds, with not a word exchanged. The drumming on the tracks grew more insistent. The boys stared at each other. Their excitement was giving way to something else, and each could read in the other's face the signs of his own distress. Lost, they were strangers in their own skin, powerless to alter fate. Was this woman in fact their mother? And what did "mother" mean? Robert, who was younger, burst into sobs, which he tried to muffle. Rémi felt relieved by his brother's tears. Tears were human, more real and natural than all the spruce in the forest.

But the sound had awakened their small sister. She moved and woke her mother, who began to rub the arm that had gone to sleep from the child's weight. The woman slowly became aware of the train's movement, realized where she was, and glanced outside. Her expression, sleepy at first, grew startled. It was a fleeting surprise, and she turned at once, smiling, to reassure the boys. But Rémi had seen. He took care not to show it.

"Morning, mum."

Her attention was all on Robert's tears, and she didn't answer. Rémi took charge.

7

"It's nothing, ma, it's my fault. We were fooling and I hurt him a bit. I didn't mean to and I said I was sorry. You're not mad, eh, Robert?"

"No . . ."

"Well, don't do it again, Rémi. You're the oldest, you're fourteen. You have to be good, be an example to your brother and little sister."

"Yes, mother."

Robert didn't quite know what his brother was up to, but he played along, grew quiet, and dried his tears. Their mother tried to wax enthusiastic.

"We're almost there. I can't wait, can you? We'll see your father, and our new house. Say, you must be hungry."

The boys nodded, but the little girl touched her mother's arm.

"Mummy, I made a pee."

And she pointed to a spreading circle that stained the seat. Her mother raised her hand threateningly, thought better of it because of the sleeping passengers, glanced furtively around to see if there were witnesses, and hid the stain under the rented pillow.

"I'll just take Françoise to the toilet and we'll have some breakfast."

They ate the last sandwiches, which were getting stale, and emptied the last of the lemonade. As the hours rolled on, signs of civilization appeared. First an Indian encampment, then a few clearings with lumbermen's cabins, then farms, few and far between but enough to force back a patch of woodland. It was as if they had crossed a broad frontier, a deserted forest, and emerged in a different country. Reassured by these sights and stoked with food, the boys grew excited again, welcoming the unknown. They had become used to the drumming wheels and now were almost comforted by the sound. A village, then another and more villages, with growing frequency.

Toward noon the train slowed for a long curve followed by a slight downward slope. An endless field of soaked velvet stretched forward to the houses of a small town

8

dominated by a giant verdigris dome. It reminded Robert of a breast, the kind you see in reproductions of old paintings in the dictionary. He looked at Rémi who gave him a wink. Their mother noticed their exchange and understood, for she too saw a breast in the cupola, and she blushed, suddenly ashamed of the domes stretching the green cloth of her best dress. Her sons were wakening to life, and she felt a pang. She had dreaded this time, hoping it would slip by unnoticed. She felt guilt at being a woman, and feared these glances that had lost their innocence.

Their father was waiting for them at the station, a rusty little building with a grey cement platform. The people standing around all looked strange. The boys tried to think what it was about them . . . There was no obvious difference between these people and Montrealers, but the impression of strangeness grew and crystallized: it was their attitude, their way of walking without rushing, of tilting their heads back to look at the sky, of staring openly at travellers. Faced with these few dozen pairs of eyes, which sized him up more carefully than the thousands of eyes on St. Catherine Street in Montreal, Rémi suddenly felt awkward. He tried to put on a bold face or find something to do, but the more he tried the easier it was to spot him as an outsider in the crowd. People took their time here, even to do nothing, and his father had become like them. Rémi drew back a few steps from the family circle. Was he the outsider, then, the intruder here? The feeling that he was lost, here by mistake, perhaps dreaming, came back insistently. He didn't know the place nor the people, nor even himself. Choking back his fear, he silently said his name until it crumbled, formless. . . . Rémi Simard, Rémi Simard, Rémisimard, remiseemore, Remiseeless, remiseema . . . like a spell that didn't work. No, he was about to wake up and find himself back in the house on Hochelaga Street. Someone called his name and he was startled by the sight of his family on the platform. He wasn't dreaming. Montreal was far away and this was a place called Amos.

The feeling of strangeness continued even in the car, itself so familiar. The seats, however, had a new, acrid smell. Piled in, jammed against suitcases and packages precariously balanced, they drove down the main street: one restaurant, three hotels, a bank, a garage, and a general store with a verandah. Inside, among the traps and pots and pans, reigned a stuffed moose head with glassy eyes. And everywhere these odd people acting as if they were in a slow-motion film. Rémi searched the street corners for troops of cowboys riding into town, or a cavalry regiment led by Rin-Tin-Tin.

The car crossed a bridge over a lazy river, climbed a steep hill lined with low houses, and passed by a sawmill with its yard full of bright, good-smelling wood. Then they were out of town and there was nothing but moss, grass, and bushes. And the spruce trees were coming. Rémi was almost glad to see wild country once again.

After a lake, skirted by the road, and a few wide curves to avoid outcroppings of rock, they came to an intersection. The car slowed and turned off to the right on a gravel road. Behind them flying dust obscured the landscape, swirled into the car and settled everywhere. It had the same acrid smell as the upholstery. A few miles of this and the passengers looked the worse for it: their skin turned pale and rough, their hair and eyebrows grey. Their throats burned and Françoise cried and said she was thirsty. Their mother was sulking in secret. Her joy and excitement had faded as they entered the forest outside of town. Robert and Rémi watched saying nothing.

Then their father began talking non-stop, not waiting for answers, repeating the words that had persuaded them to come here, words that had made Abitibi sound like paradise. He rewove the dreams reality had ravelled, transfiguring the wilderness by his faith. Suddenly, as if he had ordered it, the forest drew back, and they passed two farmhouses facing one another. Had their car forced its way past a spruce barrier raised to block access to the promised land? No, the trees were never far. Driven back valiantly by little pastures where skinny cows went about their business, the spruce would crowd back at the first opportunity to the embankment of the road. Nowhere was there a large space cleared of trees. There was just enough room around the houses to graze the livestock, no more. Wherever you looked, the soft, green wall was unrelenting. Miles and miles of the same: square houses with high-pitched roofs, some green, some blue but in the same imitation brick. Small stables surrounded by mud trampled wet every day by the animals' hooves, a gaily painted rubber tire making a stingy bed for a few wretched flowers, mail-boxes all crouching at the same angle on their posts as if blown into submission by some prevailing wind, children running, children swinging, their eyes following the car in perfect synchronization. Monotony, boredom, thought the mother, who wasn't listening to her husband. And between these islets of humanity, these oases of fields bordered with tall, purple flowers, pushed the forest-desert, ever-present. The mother felt her stomach turn.

Their father fell silent, his first flush of good humour quickly dissipated. Rémi noticed a small detail, something so everyday that it had not struck him at once: there were electric power lines along the road. If need be one could follow them, as Tom Thumb followed his pebbles, back to civilization, away from this wild and dreary land. That was something to cling to among all the uncertainties.

But the car turned right again, leaving the gravel road for one still narrower.

"Straight ahead you come to Saint-Gérard. This here is our line."

With difficulty Rémi repressed a shiver. The power lines went on toward the village. Only fence posts marked this ill-kept dirt road that spoke so eloquently of the solitude around. "Our line!" You could take it all in at a glance: narrow fields, a corridor in the forest, four houses huddled there. The car slowed between two of them facing each other across the road. On one side was a pasture so filled with tall weeds you could barely see the young spruce

11

shoots re-invading the clearing. The house was run-down. The stable, half-collapsed, was almost hidden behind giant thistles.

"That's Godbout's place. He's not up to much."

Their father was pointing left. Rémi read the clumsy letters on the battered mail box. The car had almost stopped.

"Over here, there's some Russians, I can't remember their name. A man and his wife. Good people, hard working."

Rémi had only a few seconds to look, but the house, surrounded with flower beds and aspen, whose leaves trembled in the breeze, was disconcerting. Real trees, with leaves.

A few hundred feet ahead, on Godbout's side of the road, stood two houses separated by a tiny field, not much more than a yard, in which stood a single skinny aspen. Beyond that the crowded ranks of spruce flanked the road, which pressed on between them.

"Are we home?" asked Françoise.

"Not just yet," said the father, his voice faltering.

He added hurriedly, "This is Réginald's place. We're stopping here. He's invited us for supper."

"It's too early. First we see our house."

Their mother's voice was firm, but a little hoarse.

Rémi and Robert stared as they passed the house that belonged to Réginald, this cousin they had never met. The house was like all the others. Behind it, hiding at the bottom of a slope, stood a tiny stable of which only the roof was showing. And right after that came Martel's house. In his yard children were playing on the fenders of a gleaming red truck. Soon the forest closed in on the road again. How many times since they'd left Amos? At every clearing you thought you'd finished with the trees, that you had come out on a plain full of human life, like the land around Montreal, but every time you were disappointed.

Thicker than ever, the walls of green pressed in, and it made Rémi shiver to think they'd travelled all night through the woods. The impossible really did exist: an endless forest where there was barely room for man, where he had succeeded only in opening a few narrow slashes. Their mother sighed loudly, and the boys understood. Françoise felt that something was wrong and began to cry. Their father remained stubbornly silent. He barely moved his lips to announce "Méo and Blanche" as they passed a little clearing: a few acres that had been cleared a long time ago, a blue house on the right-hand side of the road, and an old log stable. As a backdrop, surrounding everything, stood full-grown spruce trees, obstinate and domineering. In a trice they left the clearing behind. Again the prison corridor of trees closed in.

"And where do we live?" asked Robert.

"Oh, not far. Two miles and a bit."

"No! Oh, not in the middle of the trees! And no neighbours. Turn back."

The mother's voice was desolate, not far from tears.

"Just wait, wait till you see."

Their father was almost pleading. Rémi, worried, looked over at his brother, who was looking distressed. The boys tended to share their mother's feelings about the trees. Forgotten were their plans to become brave pioneers.

"Just wait, wait till you see," said their father.

They all seemed to hold their breath as the branches rushed by. The car was jolting along, faster and faster, its wheels kicking up stones against the floor. The dust rolled up and in through the cracks of the doors. In front of them the air turned brighter, losing the green tinge it took on between the trees. At last, two miles later, they emerged amid fields that lay unbounded by any fence. Their father, free to relax now, slowed the car. The family was to have time for a long look. From here the road climbed a long hill that hid the landscape behind. Almost at the top the shape of a house could be seen. The roadway had narrowed to a dry-land jetty running out between seas of waving grass stirred into life by the dusty passing of the car. As they climbed the hill the landscape around them was revealed. Trees were still to be seen, but far away, far enough to be just a lacy fringe on the skirts of the paler green of the plain. They stopped near the house and everyone piled out, filled with curiosity – and with gratitude for dust-free air.

Before them an immense field sloped down toward the distant forest and, miles away, above the tips of the evergreens, you could make out the metal spire of a village church. There wasn't so much as a bush near the house. Its builders must have had a horror of trees. Its walls appeared to rise to dizzy heights above the tall grass and plantain. Rémi thought of the Ark stranded on its mountain, or a ship on the back of a tremendous swell. Behind their home the ground rose further before beginning its descent, hiding both forest and horizon. After the grass, there was the sky, right away. You could imagine a city hidden there, or at least a village or lake, or perhaps a river with sudden, splendid views, and that was a comforting notion.

The boys are exploring around the house. Farther up the road is another house, seemingly abandoned. Its windows and doors are boarded up and weeds flourish by the walls. Facing it, but a little toward the hilltop, between the gravel road and the waving grass, is a square cabin. Then the road continues, disappearing for a moment in a hollow, but rising again to slice through the forest, which is back in force.

Their mother also walks slowly around the house, stopping at each corner to put the landscape to the test. She touches the rotating pump at the well, tries the railing of the stoop, works the latch on the shed door, and kicks the steps with her heel, then returns to the car where their father anxiously awaits her verdict.

"I like it."

A deep breath. You'd think he'd been running. He wipes his forehead where a furrow of sweat has formed in the clinging dust. Françoise is chasing a yellow butterfly in the tall grass.

"Don't go too far," the mother cries.

"There's no danger," says their father.

He's coming to life now, he's gathered his family about him and pushes them inside, one by one, vaunting the virtues of the house. Abandoned for years, looted by humans, and battered by the elements, it had suffered badly, and he'd had to redo the roof, tack new imitation brick on the outside walls, put in doors and windows, rebuild the stairs, and insulate the second floor. He had placed the furniture any old way. The mother smiles and tells him where every piece should go. The floor, hastily swept, bears traces of his recent carpentry. The woman pushes at grains of sawdust with her foot and talks about a great house cleaning.

It isn't a big house. On the ground floor are the parlour, the kitchen, and what will be the parent's bedroom. Upstairs there are no partitions. The boys and their sister are separated by a curtain. The parents have gone downstairs again but Rémi and Robert stay on to examine their future domain. Between the two beds with their heads to the wall, a narrow space leads to the window. They open it. The sill is only a few feet from the flat roof of the shed. They jump down to this convenient balcony, from which they have a view of the house next door with its grey cedar shingles; the cabin at the field's edge; and in the hollow, ducking beneath the road through a culvert, what seems to be a creek. In the middle distance, camped on the slope, spruce trees hiss in the wind and stare at the boys. They climb inside and join their parents downstairs. The father confirms that there is indeed a stream in the ravine.

"This road runs through the woods to a crossing five miles away, and the other road goes to Amos. But there's not much traffic here, nobody'll bother us. And it's safe for the kids, the creek's not deep. I've seen little fish there."

This news excites the boys, and they want to go outside. They can't wait to explore the territory, discover its secrets, and invent the great games that would fill their summer. For this their room is too small. They must build a world to fit their inventions.

They unpack their things, and while the mother is putting away her pots and pans and dishes, Rémi and Robert make a timid excursion into the fields. The country isn't void of animal life, as they had first believed. The grass is crawling with insects, a field mouse is poking about its business, a grass snake wriggles furtively between two stones. In the grey of the clouds you can make out the flight of birds and hear their voices mingled with the wind. A dishevelled jay, grey and blue, comes to stare impudently at the humans. Their father lets them try the pump. Once the water comes, there's a continuous stream. Everybody takes a turn washing his face in the icy water. The children watch in astonishment as their father prepares oil lamps and pumps air into the Coleman lantern.

It was a happy reunion, with loud voices and bursts of laughter, much back slapping and many jokes. The children, who didn't know these relatives, felt a little left out. Cousin Réginald was a tall, lanky man who wore loosely laced green boots and showed a gold tooth when he laughed. He slapped the boys on the back.

"Well, sonofagum, they're almost men."

His wife Sonia, dressed and combed with an elegance that clashed with this rough place, gave them a kiss, smothering them with her powerful perfume and smearing their cheeks with her lipstick. She was tiny, a miniature woman, barely taller than they were. She laughed at the way they addressed her, repeating, "Auntie, auntie!" Her daughter Sophie was Françoise's age and the two girls promptly got in a fight over a doll.

They had barely sat down when Méo and Blanche arrived. As they were from Quebec City, the boys had never seen them either. Méo was short and bandy-legged, and swore at every second word, and at the beginnings and ends of sentences. A strong bass voice compensated for his small size. Blanche was a whale of a woman who made her husband look even punier. Her stockings were rolled down to her calves, her hair was dyed yellow, and her mouth was turned to a slash by a smear of flashy lipstick. Blanche, like Méo, was blessed with a piercing voice. Her pudgy arms were clutching two bottles to her flabby breasts. Méo grabbed them away from her and slammed them on the table.

"Sonofabitch, there's a real drink for ya. An' I'm the guy that boiled it. Straight Canadian gargle, by Christ."

He laughed derisively at his own joke. Robert and Rémi had to hold still for a salvo of resounding kisses from Blanche. Cousin Réginald sat down at the table and invited the others to do the same.

"Say, come on, eh? Sonofagum, we're goin' to have a little drink before supper."

The adults gathered around the bottles and began to dream, dwelling on the words they had said or written to each other as they prepared for this adventure. The three families had worked out the project and met with the Settlement officials. Nothing had been left to chance. The men had travelled here to have a look and again to get everything ready. Now they'd all arrived and things were going to hum. Five more years of hard work, clearing, felling trees, ploughing, and cultivating, and the Crown land would belong to them. They'd be farmers, not settlers. Now they answered to no boss; each was lord and master of his domain. That called for a drink. Méo, whom the boys decided to call uncle even though he was no relation, started telling dirty jokes, promptly seconded by Réginald.

"Go play outside, boys," said their father.

"That's right. Go see the animals in my stable," said their cousin.

Robert and Rémi went outside. They had no desire to hear the grown-ups repeating phrases about the "project" which they'd heard a thousand times from their father and told to each other until they knew the litany by heart. A boy of ten or eleven came running from the house next door.

"You the new guys? Hey. Come on and see my dad's truck."

Before they had time to answer he was leading them along the little path to his house. His feet were bare in his rubber boots and squished as he walked. The truck was new, riding on enormous tires. Young Martel was bursting with pride.

"My dad drives that. He takes me along sometimes."

They followed him on a tour of the mastodon. From the other side of the truck a girl was staring at them. Her loose hair hung in tangled locks over her shoulders. She didn't speak, her face expressionless but for a pair of suspicious eyes. Robert and Rémi noticed the small bumps pushing against her faded dress, and when the door opened and she turned, Rémi caught a lightning glimpse, through a tear in her clothing, of a little budding breast capped by a dark-brown point. His stomach was in knots and he had to breathe deeply to regain his calm.

Coming out of the house was the girl's mother. Because she was carrying a basket of washing she let the screen door slam behind her. She walked to the edge of the stoop and began hanging out her wash. Robert and Rémi stopped listening to the young Martel boy's dissertation on the art of trucking. The mother was like a vision from another world. Not that she was beautiful: her face was hardened by the wear and tear of life and had grown a trifle puffy with the years; and her nose, a shade too large, detracted from features that could have made her beautiful: her dark eyes with their moist look, and her black hair, thick and shining. Her mouth full of clothes pins, however, was less than flattering. But the boys couldn't take their eyes off her shape silhouetted against the sky. Each time her arms stretched out to hang some article, her sleeveless dress revealed the soft hair under her arms. But this was only an introduction to her cupolas. By comparison even the Amos Cathedral dome was vestigial. Her breasts, round and wide at the base, thrust horizontally between the earth and sky, defying the law of gravity and stretching her blouse until the space between the buttons gaped.

It took their breath away. They caught each other's glances and read each other's minds.

"Hey. Are you guys listening?" asked young Martel.

"Yeah, yeah, we hear you," Robert mumbled.

At this unfamiliar voice the woman turned to examine the newcomers. Her smile made friendly wrinkles around her eyes. For that second she was fifteen years younger.

"Oh. The little Simards, I bet."

"Yes, ma'am," replied Rémi, taking a short step forward and forcing himself to look her in the eye.

He went no closer for fear she might notice his face, which he felt must be flaming red.

"You'll like it here. You can come over and play with Albert and Diane. There's not much doing and it may be dull at the start, but we get along all right, you'll see."

She went back to hanging out her wash. Rémi had missed her last words, anyway. Between her legs he could see the distant branches of the spruce trees interlaced at the horizon's wall. So sure of themselves, those trees. Rémi, a little boy who'd strayed into a bad dream, was now their prisoner. Nothing existed but Rémi and the threatening trees. He was drifting, growing dizzy. Only the woman's legs were human. When he stared hard at them the wall of spruce blurred and receded. Quick. Keep focusing on the legs. Tell yourself the rest of it isn't true. But it didn't help. It merely changed the source of his confusion. He felt surges of hot shame. Suddenly the woman rested an edge of the empty basket on her hip and turned around. As Rémi struggled back to reality she stood still, watching him curiously. He looked down while she passed by to go inside. The door opened. Braces hanging down from his pants, hands in his pockets, a man came padding out in heavy wool socks.

"I'm hungry."

"I've finished. We can eat. Albert, come on in."

The man looked at Rémi and Robert.

"Nice truck, eh? Bet you never saw one like that in Montreal."

"Sure didn't," Robert hastened to say.

"See you tonight at Réginald's."

He went back in the house and again the door hit its frame with a sharp crack that hurt your ears. The brothers were left alone and walked off slowly through the small, grassy enclosure, avoiding the path. They said nothing, busy watching their step. A great toad crossed their path but they were in no mood to go after it – or do much else, for that matter. No sleep the previous night had left them prey to despair. Aimlessly they wandered to the stable.

The moment the door opened the smell enveloped them, warm and thick, new but loaded with memories. "The Gaspé!" thought Rémi. That's where it was, the other stable they'd visited, feeling like lost children in a strange land, as they did here.

What Réginald calls "my animals" consists of a cow and a stallion. The cow turns her head briefly in their direction, then returns to her cud. The horse, more high-strung, whinnies, paws his stall floor, and tosses his head. He's warm, and his coat is sleek with sweat. They close the door, which swings awkwardly on its twisted hinges. Rémi presses his nose to the fly-specked window and contemplates the skirt of the forest blurred by the dirty glass to an unreal landscape.

Robert speaks first: "Did you see those tits? Did you see that? And the black hairs under her arms. Wooow!"

Rémi is staring at a spider that has stopped at eye level on the other side of the glass, blocking a part of the backdrop. He sees the woman's legs again and dreams of her femininity, so powerful it could annihilate the threat emanating from the trees . . . He had been as helpless

20

against her power as against the evergreens. He's not yet sure whether her spell was a pleasant one, and as he thinks about it the sensation returns. Robert is still singing Mrs. Martel's praises. He was stunned by her breasts and is now describing in detail how he imagines them to be, and boasting that he'd fondle them if he had the chance. And all the while he's kneading away at the cow's bag and her teats.

Rémi shrugs. Poor Robert, he'd seen her breasts, nothing more. He hadn't felt the power that radiated from the woman, from her whole body, from her very presence. Of course he was very young, whereas Rémi . . . Someone was calling them.

In the house the party grew noisier as the level in the bottles dropped. The boys were seeing their parents in a new light. Their father makes jokes, just like other men, and, as they do, talks much too loudly. Their mother's eyes are laughing and slightly moist. Rémi is ashamed for them and finds it hard to accept the notion that they might not be unique. Robert, for his part, sees little of what's going on. Sitting on the stairs, he is staring heavy-lidded at the pump handle.

Boiled ham with potatoes, cherry pie for dessert. Supper, a formality to get over with. Tonight's party is going to be different. On the stairway where the boys are eating, plates on their knees, they feel left out of the jollity at the table, but at the same time have no wish to share it. Cousin Sonia is serving her rice wine, a transparent liquid floating above thick, whitish lees in the heel of the bottle. Rémi finds his too sweet and passes it to Robert. What with the wine and the excitement the adults are louder than ever and Robert is dropping off to sleep. He is led away to the bedroom and Rémi soon hears his snoring.

But Rémi is fighting off his fatigue. He wants to watch, to observe. For once he's not being treated like a child. What he really wants is to see Mrs. Martel arrive. Here, through the banister, he'll be able to eye her discreetly. Now the men are taking a drop of "Méo's gargle" just to settle their meal, and the women are doing dishes and putting children to bed. All, that is, except Blanche, who remains near the bottle, nursing her glass. Cousin Sonia goes to change and fix her hair. Then the Martels arrive. First the father, his forehead surmounted by a brilliantined wave, wearing a black shoelace for a tie and shiny metal armbands to keep his shirt sleeves neat. His ready smile broadens when he sees the bottles. Behind him comes his daughter, Diane. In her pleated skirt, black knee-socks and tight-fitting sweater, she is no longer the grubby little girl they had just seen: she's almost an adolescent.

Then Mrs. Martel steps inside. After a second's hesitation she moves forward, her string of beads glittering, rolling and sliding dangerously toward the gulf one could almost see between those prodigious breasts. Robert is likely dreaming of them this very minute. She's already past Rémi and has left him nothing but a whiff of perfume, quickly lost in the smoke-filled air.

A second table is set up for cards.

"Two tables, and the losers move," shouts Réginald.

Mr. Simard is to play with his niece, Sonia; Blanche with Mr. Martel; Méo with Mrs. Simard; and Réginald with Mrs. Martel. Twos and threes are removed from the pack, the cards are shuffled, partners give each other one last piece of advice, and the games of five hundred begin to the sound of continuous chatter and the clinking of glasses. There are loud exclamations, timid calls of "eight in spades" or a triumphant cry of "nine no trump," thought to be unbeatable. Comments on the game mingle with puns, teasing, dirty jokes, and reproaches. Or a harsh curse accompanies a card slapped on the table.

"That the best you got?"

The losing couples change tables. There are challenges, promises to do better, accusations of playing a chicken game.

From the back of the kitchen Diane smiles as she watches the players. The smile is fixed, a mask she has assumed for the evening. It could just as well have been a pout, and remains quite empty except when her sharp eyes land on Rémi. Provocation or challenge? He's not sure. What's certain is, she's interested.

A knock at the door interrupts the game. It's the neighbours with the unpronounceable Russian name. But you have to call them something, so they'd acquired a nickname. People said, "Dam-Bogga" and "Mrs. Dam-Bogga," referring to the old man's favourite exclamation. He is short and stocky, his white hair still streaked with blond and his face as wrinkled as a dried apple. And in the middle of this maze of wrinkles, a mouth full of teeth all brown from chewing tobacco. He wags his head happily while his wife greets the company with a timid nod. Then she pulls a bottle from under her shawl and hands it to Sonia.

"Oh. Some of your good wine. Thanks."

The old woman smiles feebly. The interruption makes someone think of lighting an oil lamp and the Coleman lantern, which whistles away giving off its pure white light. The pause is a blessing for those who want to refill their glasses and start in on new bottles. Not many choose the wine: just Mrs. Dam-Bogga and Rémi, who gets a glass from Sonia. The ruby liquid is tinged with orange in the lamplight.

The game starts up again, along with the drinking from freshly opened bottles. The new arrivals are going to sit in, which means there will always be one couple not in the game. The old woman sips her wine, barely opening her lips, and stays out of the conversation, speaking only to announce her plays in a thin, almost inaudible voice made even harder to understand by her thick accent. Her husband, not as shy, waves his arms and spouts phrases with many missing words. He fills the gaps with signs and laughter. He often uses roundabout expressions for simple things, and every second word is damn-bogga, damn-bogga. Depending on his expression or tone, the word expresses joy, surprise, disappointment, or anger.

The window panes grew lavender coloured, then sky-blue, then navy-blue. Not black, not just yet. The lamps smoked away with their oily light, the players lit cigarette after cigarette, and thick clouds stirred by gesticulating arms eddied, rose, and melted away in the heat of the hissing lantern. Rémi, his eyes puffy and his throat sore, wiped away a tear and wet his dry mouth with a sip of wine. But the wine was treacherous. He felt giddy and a little drunk. That woman smell, mixed with all the smoke. Rémi hadn't stopped staring at the women the whole evening. Mrs. Martel, whose bust projected a whopping shadow, Sonia, whose skirt crept up her leg when she reached for her winnings, Diane, lost in a fog, a lamp accentuating the illusion of her breasts. The other women didn't count: the old one, mute and fragile, was no more interesting than a chair; and Rémi's mother was, by virtue of that very title, devoid of femininity. He even tried to forget that she was there. As for Blanche, laughing and belching generously, Rémi avoided looking at her.

But he was glad not to be in bed like his brother. He wanted to enjoy this delightful somnolent state as long as he could. At last Woman was revealing herself to him through her haunting presence: woman imperfect, perhaps, but a hundred times more potent than the dream-women they showed in magazines. Did other boys feel the same spell, or was his experience unique? Would it come back on other occasions? Rémi wondered what his former friends in Montreal, with whom he used to enthuse over Marilyn's thighs, would think of Sonia's, less beautiful but very much alive. Rémi was reliving old day-dreams, his own personal films that he would roll at times to brighten up a dull class at school, and his thoughts were disquieting. Staring at Mrs. Martel, he tried with all the force of his imagination to rip open the black dress that hid her skin. Breasts, a waist, buttocks appeared to him in flashes. Sonia stood up and passed through his field of vision, interrupting his reverie. She made the rounds of the tables filling empty glasses, then came toward Rémi. He held out his wine glass, which she filled without looking, by the sound. She was staring at Rémi.

"If you're falling asleep, why don't you go lie down with your brother?"

"No."

"You're not too bored?"

"I'm watching."

She smiled and left him. Mrs. Martel was changing tables, and as she bent over, her beads spilled into that lake of shadows with the steep banks. Rémi could no longer see her legs, but he felt their presence and imagined them even more sharply.

Dam-Bogga was picking butts out of the ashtrays and packing the shreds into his pipe. He did it so naturally that no one paid any attention, even when he stuffed handfuls of butts in his pockets. Rémi stared at the adults one by one, each of them absorbed, studying their cards. He couldn't understand what passion held them there, sitting around the table for hours on end. This disillusioned him. Weren't there more interesting and important things to do than play these games that were barely good enough for dull children bored with themselves on a rainy day? He'd have liked these adults to be less everyday, to be a shade mysterious as he had imagined them not so long ago. For sure when he grew up he wasn't going to waste his time fooling with silly bits of coloured cardboard.

Diane gets up and wanders, almost strutting, between the tables, deliberately bumping an elbow with her hip or brushing a dangling hand with her thigh. The men's eyes gleam as they watch her.

"The kid's drinking," Réginald exclaims.

"A little drop'll make her not so snarky," Martel says, defending his daughter.

"Yes," says the girl's mother. "She's a big girl now."

"Thirteen."

"Poor kid. What's in store for you?" Blanche interjects in a tired voice.

"Now you there, god damn it . . ."

Méo doesn't have to finish. Blanche gets the message. Méo turns his hot gaze toward Diane.

"Hey, kid. Watch out for yer cherry. There's a couple of boys around here now."

"Méo," protests Mrs. Martel.

Laughter, free and open, bursts out loudly, except for Mrs. Simard who doesn't feel like laughing. Rémi stares into his glass. Réginald goes one better, his speech slurring, pointing at Rémi with his hand of cards: "I wouldn't trust that one there. It's your dog that don't bark that's goin' to bite."

"Réginald. They're only children. Watch what you say, eh?"

"What do you know about young boys?" Réginald asks his wife.

"True enough," says Méo. "When I was his age, now . . ."

Blanche interrupts him.

"That's right, you started too soon. That's why you can't cut the mustard now."

The laughter covered up Méo's curses, and everybody teases him. Rémi is glad to have their attention diverted from himself and uses his respite to huddle against the wall and make himself small in case a volley of wisecracks is directed at him. It fails to materialize because the game has started up again. Sonia goes to the cupboard and bends over to get clean ashtrays from under the sink. Her white thighs appear, quartered by the black line of her garters. That lasts only a moment and she is on her way back to the table, but Diane noticed the boy's indiscreet curiosity and he glimpses her mocking smile. That's going too far! Rémi rushes outdoors on the stroke of ten.

The air outside is like a damp, cold hand on his forehead. He sneezes to clear the last traces of smoke from his nose, squints at the dark, and is surprised to find that night hasn't really fallen, it's only a late twilight. The western sky is still full of light, and great streams of purple and violet clouds flow westward where they turn to orange. The sky is emptying like a sink, soon there is only a greenish patch on the enamel, and suddenly one by one the stars appear, seeds of light that germinate and bloom. Their flowers pulse in a wind too high for the boy to feel it, too high even to cause a shiver among the waiting leaves of the nearby aspen.

Cool air rises from the grass, the night grows darker and the amphitheatre with its distant wall of trees comes alive with the croaking of frogs. Bats go through their vibrant aerobatics and lightning bugs blink on and off. The frogs' music grows liquid and hampers his movements, and Rémi realizes that he won't make it to the aspen. He is more tipsy than he had thought. He stops in the middle of the field, confused by the noisy flight of creatures he can hardly see. Trying to establish his position, he takes a bearing on the Martels' house, which is mo more than a dark mass. Time passes, marked by the distant cries of night birds. Rémi remains motionless. Slowly a different universe reveals itself to his eyes, a world unknown to the sun, in which everything is possible, even affection for the spruce trees and their black lace like a band around the globe, holding together the smooth skin of the sky and the hairy grass. Rémi turns to face Réginald's house, and the light that comes crawling through the hay from its windows makes the stars turn pale. He goes back inside.

And there he is again in his spot on the stairs, trying to pierce the fog of smoke to see whose laughter it is that ends in a loud cry, whose cry it is that hiccups like a laugh. You'd need a bat's radar or an owl's eyes. He gives up, and becomes fascinated by the sinuous movements of the cigarette smoke, caressing the feminine forms that it suggests. The whole kitchen smells of woman the way the stable smelled of animal life, the kitchen becomes a woman in Rémi's hungry eyes. He gets up to fill his glass and returns to the stairs. As he passed, he was able to see the players and recognize their faces, and he turns his attention to them now. His eyes have grown accustomed again to the polluted air, and from his spot on the stairway he can still see well enough.

Joy is uninhibited, the jokes are crude, the humour at times is cutting. The glances of the women are provocative and their lips mouth silent, libidinous words. The men's eyes are greedy. The atmosphere in the room is tense, more because of the undercurrent than because of the bawdy words spoken aloud. Rémi has heard all the words in the street back home and they don't bother him. What does, is the posturing, the facial expressions and unsaid words: he feels increasingly uneasy.

What if it's all his own imagination, and he's inventing, making it all up. That embarrasses him, for his parents are there. He tells himself that these people aren't even aware of the undercurrent, that it's beyond their control. How simple-minded and disappointing these adults are! It's the first time Rémi has been a spectator in their world, seeing them together without the constraining presence of children, and he is very disillusioned. There's nothing mysterious or secret, there are no incomprehensible words, no rites or gestures into which he should be initiated. Are they really not supermen, able to perform wonders? It doesn't look like it. In fact, they're no different from himself or Robert. Every man, then, must feel the same sexual pleasure as another, or the same well-being when he eats. What about his own father? The boy shivers when he thinks of his parents and sexuality. He rejects the images. They're too true, too plausible. Could his father have a penis? Not a chance. Desires such as he, Rémi felt? No. The boy struggles against these morbid thoughts that are ruining his enjoyment. He clenches his fists and tries to think of something else. He is still looking for some kind of magic in these adults, but finds nothing. They are certainly different from what he would have liked. They are different, even, from what he thought he knew. Instead of being grave and serious folk, thinking only of how to make a better living, talking about grown-up things and problems, these people before him thought of nothing but laughing, drinking and having a good time. The more adults were themselves the farther they were from the ideal that children had of them. These men here were behaving exactly like Rémi's chums in the alley back home: the same language, the same gullibility in some, the same cowardice in others. The women were copying the style of little girls: false innocence, honeyed words, cruel remarks, glances supposed to be touching or provocative. Mrs. Martel is the enticing one; Sonia is her rival; Rémi's mother is playing the innocent who knows very well, etc. Blanche is the tomboy who challenges the boys on their own terrain; and Mrs. Dam-Bogga is the cripple or "re-tard." Diane is the one who plays grown-ups.

Rémi's gaze lingered on Mrs. Martel, who was scratching herself under one breast, causing movement in the mass of flesh. As a result he lost track of his accusatory thoughts and the judgement that would normally have followed, giving in to the giddy observation of the women, taken by their playfulness, which just now he had judged to be childish – so taken that his sex began to swell. This erection could become embarrassing. He panicked as he saw Diane coming toward him with the wine bottle. But despite his confusion he couldn't help staring at her sweater and the bumps caused by her small breasts. She moved closer, raising the bottle, and he held out his glass, not realizing that he had just uncovered his ignominy. He should have refused the wine. Too late now. His waist was at her eye level and she must have noticed the unusual bulge. To avoid looking her in the eye Rémi tried to define the faded detail of a coloured calendar picture hanging at the back of the kitchen. The weight of the wine stopped increasing in his glass and he heard Diane's footsteps as she left him. Then she turned up beneath the calendar. His eyes fled the sight of her and he tried to gain control of the situation by ignoring his body. This was when he encountered Sonia's smile, and a little farther on, the sight of Mrs. Martel's low-cut dress. But his curiosity was too much for him. He turned and looked into the depths of the kitchen, and found what he had expected. Diane was gazing at him, her mocking eyes full of laughter, her mouth opening and closing on obscene words that no one could have heard but which Rémi understood. There was sheer arrogance in her face, and Rémi felt it like a slap. He had the same raging sense of helplessness and the same wish for revenge that he had known once when a boy held him down while another beat him up. The girl held him fast on the rough stairway with supple cords of smoke and the bonds of his own tipsiness. She emanated silent challenges. She had seen, and was letting him know. Rémi was ashamed of his stubborn penis and envied Robert his peaceful sleep. Telling himself that he shouldn't have been drinking, he swallowed another mouthful of wine. She was still watching him.

His only recourse was flight. Outside he staggered a little and his stomach was making more noise than his footsteps on the ground. Somehow he made it to the solitary tree and leaned on it with one arm. He breathed deeply, shut his eyes, opened them again. A pale luminescence fell from the sky and made the grass faintly phosphorescent. He looked up. Above him an enchanting spectacle hung in space: light, pure light, light free of any source, self-producing light, shot high, and dipped, and turned in a gigantic orgasm. Out of nothing would appear a point that burst and grew to become a patch outlined in red and green. Sperm! Milt of the stars! The night was discharging great streams of it that spread and gathered around the constellations. Dizzied, he clung more tightly to the tree. The night sky? The inside of a dome. Rémi became a tiny particle floundering inside Mrs. Martel's breast. All around him mother's milk oozed from unseen glands and dribbled down upon him. The air tasted of sugar. Rémi took a few steps, trying for equilibrium in movement and some kind of self-control against the inexplicable forces that assailed him. He walked in a circle and came back to the tree. The strange lights disappeared and the stars were once more masters of the heavens, but not for long. In the northwest pale forms arose from the ring of spruce trees, climbing, stretching like lascivious dancers revealing their charms through diaphanous veils: rounded breasts, thighs, a buttock, the graceful gesture of a plump arm, broken waves like curling hair . . .

The lights took on carnal volumes, as the smoke in the kitchen had done before. Rémi tried to hold tight to the certainty of the tree, but under his hand the smooth bark trembled like a timid skin, shy but sensitive and growing warm, until it was the boy who was trembling under this arboreal caress. He laid his cheek against the trunk and shut his eyes.

Nature in Abitibi was letting him know its will, heightening the fever of this little city boy in distress. Oh, the dead asphalt and the defensive trees in town! But this tree held close the defenceless child, and in the air, motionless as it was, its head of leaves whispered and rustled.

Rémi ran at top speed toward the house and leaned his back against the inert frame wall where he could hear his heart grow quieter. In this milky night, directly under the northern lights, the aspen called him softly. And the boy went inside so as not to hear it, resuming his endless vigil on the stairs. It was no use lying down, he wouldn't have been able to sleep in any case, and besides he had to stay awake to keep his upset stomach under control. Diane was watching him with her defiant eyes, and Rémi, out of bravado, knowing he shouldn't, accepted another glass of wine. The end of the bottle. Friday night was almost Saturday morning.

"Diane, go see if everything's all right at home."

"Eh? No. S'dark an' I'm scared."

"Don't talk back. Go see if the kids are asleep."

Martel gave orders, not requests like his wife.

"I can't. It's too dark."

"Rémi can go with you."

It was his own father betraying him, pushing him at this profligate girl. He couldn't refuse, that would have been unheard-of.

"Careful in the dark corners," Méo jeered.

"Yeah, don't be long, eh? Show us your cherry when you get back Diane, won't ya?"

That was Réginald. Who else. Rémi went out behind Diane with a last piece of advice ringing in his ears.

"Keep yer hands in yer pockets!"

Why couldn't they shut up? It was bad enough without their talk. They should stop acting like young hoodlums ganging up on a boy who was down. The two went out and started off side by side, in silence. Rémi avoided conversation, but he would have sworn she was smiling. They passed the sighing aspen. The moonlight sifted down palely on the landscape. Innocently, the girl allowed her hand to brush his leg at every step. He knew very well that there was nothing innocent about her, and that she was probably misinterpreting his lurching gait, which caused his thigh to collide from time to time with her hip. He was terrified of Diane.

He waited at the bottom of the four steps while she opened the door a crack to listen for her brothers' and sisters' breathing. Then down she came again without going inside, and led Rémi toward the truck. She pushed him, held him against the metal body, took his head in her hands, and kissed him. He let himself go, foundering in a whirl of unfamiliar sensations. He had lost all hold on his surroundings, could only fall free in the bottomless abyss. It was Diane who broke the spell by ending the kiss and moving away. While he was getting his breath back, and

32

his presence of mind, she pulled two cigarettes from her belt, the paper well wrinkled, and a book of matches.

"Cigarettes!" exclaimed Rémi

"Didja ever smoke?"

The tone allowed for a touch of contempt if the answer was no. He hastened to tell the lie.

"Sure. Lots of times."

Sitting on the cold metal of the running-board, they smoke. Rémi coughs. His first cigarette. And his first, clumsy tête-à-tête with a girl. The effect of the tobacco is added to that of the wine, and no doubt that of the long and unexpected kiss; and Rémi feels increasingly uncomfortable, his movements less and less under control. He is afraid of what's to come and would gladly flee if he had the courage. How he'd love to be asleep. She's waiting for him to speak, to act. She's going to judge him by that. Perhaps she has already. Cornered, Rémi loses his head, reaches a hasty hand toward Diane's breasts, and stupidly pinches one of them. She laughs derisively. The secret is out, she has Rémi's number, she knows he is inexperienced, can imagine his state of mind, and is laughing at his clumsiness. Adding insult to injury, she gently lays one hand between his legs, and he, busy puffing on his cigarette, chokes, hiccups, and coughs. He swallows some tobacco and his stomach revolts. Rémi is powerless against the spasms of nausea that make him throw up on himself and on the ground.

Diane springs to her feet, draws back and contemplates the scene. She laughs aloud, throws away her cigarette and disappears behind the truck. All that can be heard is the sighing of the aspen and finally a door slammed shut. Rémi doesn't dare sit up, he'd like to sink into the ground, disappear into the shifting sands of his disgrace. Die! Die there like a dog by the roadside, never having to raise his head again. Slowly he grows calm again. That's better. Despite the sour taste in his throat and a splitting headache, he feels his spirit cleared of the fog that had pervaded it. Dragging his feet he heads for Réginald's house, which is buzzing with human voices and laughter. They all know already, they're waiting to have a laugh at his expense. He takes some grass and wipes his shirt and pants as well as he can. What will she have told them? That he got sick on wine? Did she blab about the cigarette, or the kiss, or the other thing she did? And if she had, how could he ever face his parents again or all those people? Rémi rubs his lips hard with the back of his hand to take off any trace of lipstick. He'd deny it. Deny everything, except being sick, they could see that for themselves.

Rémi hesitates, his hand on the doorknob. It's awful. But he has to go in. He's repelled by the world of grown-ups. They should have put him to bed like Robert. It's all their fault, all of them, and his parents too. Especially because all his watching had been in vain. Adults are only big children who think they can do what they like because there's nobody around to tell them not to. They're no different from himself, and no better. He takes a deep breath and shoves the door open. His entry is greeted by a chorus of laughter. The teasing starts, hot and heavy.

"Hey, look, he's turned green."

"He's trying to pass for a man."

"Your first jag, young feller, you'll never forget it."

"Don't worry about your daughter, Martel, he's not ripe yet."

"Here, have another glass, that'll cure what ails ya."

They're making fun of his youth, laughing at his inexperience but without spite, remembering nostalgically their own first attempts. Rémi realizes this, even in the half-saddened, half-amused glance of his mother, even in Sonia's solicitude as she washes his face. The charm of her femininity is without effect now. His father's reprimand, not too severe, the kind of thing a father says after a runaway returns, has no effect on Rémi. What hurts is Diane's smiling face. Triumphant, she crushes him with her glance, attacking the softest spot. Everybody is amused by his embarrassment, but she knows everything, and harasses him with insults disguised as smiles. She couldn't hurt him more if she took a stick to him. He hates her.

During the midnight feed, amid postmortems on the various games, reproaches and congratulations flying, Rémi goes to lie down beside his brother in the dark room. He can't sleep. Nothing will ever wipe out such a humiliation.

In their second-floor bedroom Robert woke up at nine, in a hurry to go exploring. But when he tried to drag his brother out of bed he got only abuse for his pains. Rémi didn't open his eyes until midday and didn't get up even then. The hum of the sewing machine soon stopped, replaced by the sound of the table being set. The family's life was already starting up again, seeking out a balance that would become a daily pattern. The mother was finishing arranging the house. Today she was sewing curtains and tomorrow or the next day they would be fully settled and they'd know more or less what life was going to be like in this house so far from everywhere.

Gazing at the ceiling with its open beams, Rémi thought about the others who had looked up at them as well. This house, new for the Simards, had been built, lived-in, loved by other people. For them too it had been "home." They had cleared the land and farmed it. They'd had projects and dreams, and then one day they'd dropped everything. Why? Perhaps other families had followed them, only to give up in turn. Now it's us, the Simards, fixing up the abandoned house. Funny to think that they were starting again. Children had lived here, and now Rémi and Robert were going to discover all that had been familiar to them. Was there anything, anywhere, that was really unexplored?

What had he discovered on the evening of their arrival on this line? Hardly anything new. Rémi grew defensive, sifting his memories, rejecting the ones that were disagreeable. He was afraid of hurting himself. It was like scratching a scab and opening a recent cut; but he couldn't help it, his memory was itching. So he wiped out the details and kept only a general impression. The grown-ups had disappointed him. They had nothing new to offer, and neither did the girl, who must be like the adults. Then he thought of his drunkenness, of the night, so vibrant, and the madness of the sky, and the languor in his whole being provoked by the presence of those women. Anything new? Yes, but in himself.

His mother, calling him for their noonday dinner, interrupted his reflections. Downstairs he found his brother pouting because of his rebuff that morning. But Robert could never hold a grudge for long, and he forgot all about it as they talked about exploring the creek. It wasn't until mid-afternoon that the boys were able to leave their little sister during her nap. When she was awake they were supposed to look after her. Quickly they passed by the abandoned house and ran down the slope of the road. The creek ran under it through an enormous corrugated metal culvert.

Muddy water flowed swiftly between its steep, grey banks, polished, worn, and hollowed ceaselessly by the stream. Starting down, Robert lost his footing and found himself standing in the current, in water no more than fifteen inches deep. The upper layers of the banks were of dry and crumbling clay, those nearer the water were damp and shiny. Rémi took off his shoes and pants to join his brother, and as they played, slipping on the rippled bed and exploring the meanders, Robert questioned Rémi about the previous evening. Rémi, affecting frankness, with a free and easy tone, described the endless card game, the drinks and the feeling of getting tight. He took good care not to mention his humiliation on the running-board of the truck, and his sickness. Robert wanted to hear more, so Rémi grew animated and tried to convey the wonders of the night sky in his awkward words, wondering if he hadn't dreamed it all. Robert smelled an unconfessed secret, and probed with a few questions about the grown-ups.

"What about Mrs. Martel?"

"She was there with her husband and daughter."

"Did she say anything to you? What about the daughter?"

"She talked a bit. The girl's a waste of time. She's a nasty sneak if you ask me."

Robert was thinking. His hand crushed a lump of wet clay.

"I've got an idea."

His fingers dug into the bank and came up with chunks of clay, which he dipped in the water and kneaded carefully. He piled them up, worked them into a single mass, and soon on the shore lay a shining heap of wet clay. When he had enough he began to model it, and little by little, after mistakes and corrections, an enormous breast took shape. Rémi smiled and gave advice. At last the artist capped his breast with a wide, flattened halo, and an erect nipple, then sat down beside his work, amazed and delighted.

"Isn't that beautiful? You'd think it was alive. I'm going to make the other one and then I'll come here sometimes to see them and touch them."

"Are you crazy? Break it up; you can see it from the road."

"You're the crazy one. Do you think I'm going to break that? It's too beautiful!"

"Hide it then."

"You know what? We should build a cabin in the woods. We could put it there."

"I always wanted a hide-out."

"Should it be a tree house? Or just a hut?"

"No, they're too easy to see. We should dig a lair."

"A cave?"

"If you like. Not too big. Just enough for the two of us. Let's find a good place."

They walked downstream on the creek bed. Robert, second, carefully carried the clay breast and almost fell a dozen times. They went under the road through the culvert, where the water pattered noisily over the corrugations. After a few hundred feet the stream grew deeper and the boys took to the bank where the trace of a path led along the water's edge.

"What about the bank of the stream?"

"No, the slope is too slippery. Besides, you never know who'll walk along the creek. And the water could rise. Let's look somewhere else."

On they went, Robert beginning to feel the weight of his burden. Between them and the forest, amid the brush and bushes, was a whole series of tiny, crescent-shaped ponds, whose tips pointed toward the stream, former meanders abandoned by the current, in which rain-water stagnated, covered with frogs' eggs. The banks of these pools, not as steep as those of the stream itself, were high enough to accommodate the planned hide-out. Robert and Rémi chose the third pond from the road. They could see others farther downstream. Robert deposited his sculpture on the ground. They planned their work and set about it. The soil was too hard for their fingers, so they used bits of branches. But the clay was slippery, and after an hour's work they had managed to dig only a narrow passage three feet deep.

"We need shovels, or maybe tin cans. Something like that."

"We can come back tomorrow."

They explored the surroundings of the crescent pool where their cave had started to exist. Frogs, water-lilies, cat-tails, insects skating on the silky surface of the water, others swimming under it, a dragon-fly chasing mosquitoes, a turtle going into his dive: a whole little universe cut off from the great one, isolated by a ring of alder trees. They visited other ponds, all like their own, then made their way back to the bridge. There, an oblique light revealed stones half-buried in the clay. Grey, brittle, they looked as if they had been flattened by the clay's embrace. Mysterious shapes, some like miniature animals or people, sometimes perfect discs. Were they fossils or the result of frost heaves? The round stones were the most interesting, resembling large coins. On one side concentric circles like tree rings appeared in faint relief, and on the other a flattened lacy pattern traced mysterious symbols. Rémi, delighted, caressed one of the discs. Mysterious was indeed the word, embracing at the same time everything around them. The tiny lakes along the creek: mysterious! And mysterious the sound of nature breathing . . . And the abandoned house. And this creek that came from who knew where and trickled off toward the unknown! Everywhere around them there was mystery only slightly veiled. A world to be discovered. Already the spruce trees seemed less hostile. They'd have to get to know them better. Rémi was exultant, feeling he was on the verge of a great adventure. He searched for words, but could do nothing but grasp his brother's shoulder.

With a gesture he pointed to the world around them and said with emotion: "All that, Robert, all that is ours. Even . . . the trees."

The house already looked different with curtains on the windows and the family photos that their father had just hung on the walls. During supper, happy to see that his sons liked the place and that his wife hummed a song as she arranged things in the house, he broke his usual silence and dreamed aloud, talking of the stable they'd soon build, the ground-breaking work that the Settlement service would do, the animals they'd have. Françoise demanded rabbits, "all for me." The only dissonant note came from their mother, who remarked that not a single car had gone by the whole day. No one took up her remark or even showed they had heard it. But enthusiasm flagged a little afterwards. The boys wanted to go out after supper but their mother hesitated.

The father intervened: "Oh, let them go. It's holidays, and it gets dark late. There's no danger, we're not in town here."

"We'll stay near the creek," said Robert.

Near the little cabin facing the abandoned house they found the tin cans they needed. There was a pile of them out behind. They were empty and half-eaten by rust. The winter before truckers had used the cabin as a shelter. Despite the door that hung open, the interior held its old smells. The rain, dripping in on the stove, had decorated it with fancy patterns. Amid rags and dust on the floor Robert discovered an old calendar with a faded photo of a smiling woman showing off her breasts. He whooped with delight and hid his find under his sweater, next to his skin.

"We'll keep her in the hide-out, eh?"

That evening their excavations made good progress. The access tunnel burrowed four feet into the earth, then widened out to form what would be the cave. The work was hard, and they soon tired. One would dig while the other emptied the passage. They had to rest often and spell each other off. The cave was taking shape, but they had to stop. Darkness had filled in where the earth had been removed. Below the hill the sun had set already, and the boys went home keeping to the middle of the road, not daring to walk too close to the dark of the ditches. An owl flew by, its cry as soft as its flight. Beautiful! But scary too, especially with the abandoned house coming nearer at every step, alive with shadows and strange sounds.

A musical, melancholy howl came diving through the air. The boys stood stock-still. In the distance the forest was a closed curtain against the wind. The noise grew louder, other noises joined in and fused in a heavy beating sound like a machine, some gigantic pump. Could a heart be beating beneath the grass? It was only Rémi's blood beating at his temples. The howl dove to the earth again, but farther off. The boys stared and stared, but couldn't find its source. Suddenly, very high in the air, a feather was lit by a stray sunbeam and they were able to watch the dizzying fall of the snipe. It was sure to crash. No, it pulled up, glided horizontally and then struggled up to altitude again. Only to fall again, its wing feathers vibrating in the air. And the whole business started over. The bird, elated with speed, drunk with noise and mad with love, thus measured off the spaces in the heavens' dome.

In front of the abandoned house, where every board was creaking, Rémi stopped his brother.

"You know, maybe there's some calendars in there too."

"Well, you can go and look. Not me."

"A calendar, or something else for our cave."

"Don't try. It's no good. I'm no chicken but there's a limit. Just listen to the noises in there."

"It's the wind."

"There is no wind."

"It's mice."

"Mice . . . or something else. Forget it."

"Well, I'm goin' in there one of these days. Something draws me to that house, you've no idea."

"I sure haven't."

"How can we live right beside it and not go in for a look, or not want to go in?"

"It's probably empty."

"Even if there's nothing there, it's full of secrets if we don't go in."

"Let it keep its secrets, I won't lose any sleep over them."

"I want to see."

"Come on home."

Robert moved on and Rémi caught up to him. When they arrived at the hilltop there was a reverse sunset. The fold in the earth had hidden the sun but now the boys saw it reappear, rising a little higher above the horizon with each step they climbed. Just in front of their own house, they were bathed in a coppery light. Clouds were gathering in the west: stratus clouds daubed with colours, translucent altocumulus against a sky of green. As in an animated film the picture was in constant change. Never had they seen such magic, and no doubt the same went for their parents who were outdoors watching. After a long silence Rémi mentioned the lights he had seen the previous night. Unbelieving, Robert made fun of him.

"There are lights like that," said their father. "They're marionettes, the reflection of the sun on the ice at the

North Pole. We call them trumpets, too, because they announce a change in the weather."

The sun exploded, sinking into the wooded horizon, and the light of its burning was slow to be extinguished. The family went inside long before the end. In their room the boys had trouble sleeping. In whispers they talked about their cave and the treasures they'd find to hide there. Robert went on about Mrs. Martel's breasts, the ones on the calendar and the ones he had modelled in clay. In the safety of the dark Rémi smiled at his brother's obsessions. A thought came to sober him. Diane! He tried to relive the precise moment when she had laid her hand on his sex, but instead of the memory of her gesture it was her contemptuous laughter that rang in his head. Yesterday, however, was already long gone. Why not try to forget instead of persisting in re-creating this situation? He was furious with himself.

Below, in his parents' bedroom, the bed squeaked. He heard murmurs. Rémi tried to convince himself that they weren't making love. They must be arguing, or maybe his mother was talking in her sleep, keeping his father awake and making him move in the bed. Any excuse would do. . . .

"Fun and games downstairs," jeered Robert.

"Shut your mouth."

No. His parents were different, they didn't do things like that. Rémi was sulking, and Robert tried in vain to get their chat going again. Finally, to shut out the sounds, Rémi went to the window. There was no curtain yet, and the night came in full force through the naked panes. A vague glow among the stars presaged the great ballet of the northern lights. At ground level, there was the house next door, blacker than the darkness.

"Any marionettes?" asked Robert, trying to make up.

"Not just now, but they're coming. What about going out on the shed roof to watch?"

They slipped into some clothes, opened the window with care and slithered down to the roof of the lean-to.

"It's chilly out here."

"Yeah, the air, but feel how hot the roof is. We should lie down."

On their backs, they could no longer see the terrestrial world. Nothing but stars met their eyes, nothing but the deep firmament, which was also wide awake. To keep from falling into empty space Rémi groped for something to hang on to. He couldn't get a grip on the smooth shingles. And so he had to give in and be carried off by the northern lights, which came in hosts to dart through the upper sky and run along the line of their deserted road, turn back in the west, and hang still above the abandoned house. Rémi took part in the play of these dancing-girls of light; Robert saw in them neither faces nor voluptuous bodies nor moving women, and soon went back inside. Rémi didn't notice, nor did he feel the tar shingles beneath his back. He had eyes only for this sky, which became a part of him, a fluid screen on which his thoughts and hallucinations appeared. There was Diane. The boy tried to think of something else, but her image persisted. The whole episode, so damaging to Rémi's pride, would be there in replay from yesterday. All he could do was change the ending, and the luminous lines obeyed his will. Diane's whole body appeared. She was naked, stretched out like a milky way across the vault of heaven, helpless because of the stars that nailed her down. The shifting lights were her muscles and her glowing flesh. Perseus was her glowing pubis. At the feet of a gigantic Rémi, who towered over her, she trembled helpless, her eyes pleading. Wheedling, she held out her hand toward his penis. No. Nothing doing. He lifted one foot and deliberately crushed Diana out of the Lights. The shadow of his heel wiped out the stars, jostled the aurora and finally shattered his illusion. Then the sky grew tame and the luminous meteors paled and disappeared. No longer curved, space became a bottomless abyss. The stars were no longer stuck into the underside of a vault, in orderly and accustomed constellations, but floating in infinity, each farther away than the next, until he could have plunged in and paddled among them, brushing past them as if they were so many strands of sea plants. And that was what Rémi did.

Next morning, at ten to ten, the whole family stood outside the church. Everybody stared at them shamelessly. They were outsiders, in a Sunday best less practical than its local equivalent. New settlers! The smiles were barely hidden, a mixture of sympathy and amusement. The local boys cast challenging glances at these potential rivals. A little group had formed at the entry, a gauntlet to be run. One of them, who seemed to be a kind of leader, was a little in front of his companions. He stood up to Mrs. Simard's disapproving look. Rémi, like his father, looked away. Robert arrogantly stared them down one after the other, gave a dig with his elbow to the young cock of the village walk, and went with his head high into church. Rémi couldn't understand how his brother could provoke a local boy in front of his chums and in front of girls. Such an insult could only bring complications.

But while he disapproved of his younger brother's action, Rémi was proud of him for it, and this made it easier to walk to their pew, where he collapsed into the safety of the seat. Safe, but not protected from the eyes. The adults glanced, the girls peeked and sized them up and the young men standing at the back looked daggers. Rémi saw Diane laughing with another girl, no doubt about him. Maybe she was giving details, exaggerating, though she hardly had to. She caught Rémi watching her and made a contemptuous face at him. Imitating Robert's effrontery, he turned to look full at her. He remembered the distress of Diana of the Lights the night before, but his stare was useless, she was untouched by it: tossed back her head, in fact, to look down her nose at him. And so he redirected his attention toward the priest and the mass.

After the service they stopped at cousin Réginald's place for a drink. Rémi and Robert insisted on walking on home. Three miles, an hour's walk, they'd be there as soon as their parents, if not before. They went out through the yard. The aspen looked just like an ordinary tree. How simple everything was in broad daylight. Too simple, thought Rémi.

Someone was singing in the house. Mrs. Martel didn't go to church, staying home to watch the youngest children.

"Want to go have a look at her?"

"No," Rémi replied hurriedly.

"Why? She don't bite!"

"Her daughter."

"She's not back from Mass, and even if. . . ."

He looked suspiciously at Rémi.

"What's our excuse?" Rémi asked.

"A glass of water."

Rémi hesitated. He was afraid Diane would get back from church, and afraid that her mother, by jokes or allusions, would let Robert find out about his misadventures of the night before. And what if Diane had talked and her mother scolded him? But Robert didn't wait and was knocking at the door. The woman answered, in her dressing-gown. Behind her, four children were playing on the linoleum.

"Well! The young Simard boys! Church is out already?"

"Yes Ma'am."

"Réjean . . . oh, yes, he had some things to do in town."

"Could we please have a glass of water?"

"Of course. My, you're polite. I like that."

She ruffled Robert's hair with her hand. She was so friendly, she mustn't know anything about Rémi.

"Wouldn't you like milk instead? It's a lot better than water for growing boys."

They followed her inside. She took the pitcher and bent over to fill the two glasses. They left shortly after, Rémi tugging at his brother's sleeve. Robert would gladly have lingered. He was walking in a state of elation, his feet barely touching the gravel. Rémi followed him in silence. He had nothing to say, he wanted only to sink into his daydream.

After a while Rémi sighed: "Good idea you had."

But he pursued the thought in his own mind. This morning the woman had smelled not of perfume from a bottle but of her own body. He still had the taste of the milk in his throat. He waved his arms as if he wanted to fly away. Robert mimicked him and together they became birds zigzagging in the wind, chasing each other, grazing the branches on each side of the road. The spruce trees. For the first time they saw them with pleasure. They even touched them and were stained with the strong odour of the resin. Some branches had moss in their armpits, and they slowed to a walk in search of tree trunks in the image of Mrs. Martel. Robert claimed he had found her. Rémi saw nothing but old knots where the hardened gum had transformed into budding breasts like Diane's. Her again!

On the right the forest gave way to a fallow field that surrounded the house of Méo and Blanche. The sound of voices came from inside.

"Let's spy."

Playful and lively, Robert led the way through the grass. They walked around the house and then came closer to it, crawling on their bellies to just beneath an open window. One quick look: Blanche and Méo were sitting at the table in front of an empty bottle. They seemed exhausted, as if they hadn't slept all night.

"Come on to bed, goddammit."

"Leave me alone."

"Lush."

"If ya don't like it fuck right off. Go peddle your ass on St. Catherine Street, go to the hotel in Amos, you'll find some guy's drunk enough."

"Christ, I wish I knew why I came to this goddam country to live with some old crazy. And those son-of-a-bitchin' spruce trees all round . . ."

She was crying, sniffling.

"My daughter told me. Don't go there, she said. It's a dump. And Méo's a good-for-nothin' and a lazy drunk."

"Your fuckin' daughter hasn't even got a father."

Blanche was still crying but her face turned hard. Menacing, she moved toward Méo.

"You little worm, don't you talk about my daughter. She's a good girl. An' she's better off with no father than havin' one like you."

"Your daughter, she's an ol' bag like her mother."

"Oh you sick bastard."

"It's true. Why, when she was fourteen she'd let me touch her. An' when she was fifteen I could get her inta bed whenever I felt like it."

"That's not true. That's not true. You're just sayin' that ta hurt me. It's not true."

She was howling, wringing her hands.

"You better believe it's true. Ya think she made all that dough waitin' on table? She's a whore. Like mother, like daughter."

Blanche leapt on Méo and struck him repeatedly. He protected himself as best he could but the woman was standing and had the edge. The edge of weight as well. Blanche stopped hitting and as Méo stared at her she took advantage of his lowered guard to let fly a blow that tipped back his chair and sent the man sliding across the floor to come to a stop near the leg of the stove. He didn't move.

Blanche looked at him incredulously and began to moan: "Méo, Méo. Wake up I didn't mean it."

"Gimme a glass."

He drank. She helped him to his feet and supported him as she dragged him toward the bedroom.

"Come on, dear little man, come on to beddy-bye. You'll see, Blanche won't hurt you no more."

Robert could barely hold in his laughter.

"Let's go, Rémi!"

They crept to the bedroom window but it was closed and the curtains were drawn. Robert gave a furious kick to the earthen underpinning of the house and the brothers left, restraining their hilarity until the road had again plunged between the spruce trees.

"My Aunt Blanche. My Uncle Méo. Great relatives they would have been," cried Rémi. "Did you ever see anything so funny as that?"

"Méo, dear little man."

Their bursts of laughter echoed right and left as they took off at a gallop down the road. They weren't even raising dust as they ran. In the endless corridor the echo was loud and lingering.

They shouted "Aunt Méo!"

"Uncle Blanche!"

The sounds, distinct at first, mixed and grew unintelligible, a diminuendo wail ending in a modulated "oh-oh-oh-oh" or a weeping "anche-anche-anche." The boys trotted along in the racket and played with the echo until the bottom of the long hill that was dominated by their home. Tired now, they dragged their feet as they climbed through this grassy desert parched by sun. As they had no key they had to wait outside for their parents. At first they sat on the back steps but soon moved to the shade on the lean-to side.

"We need a ladder to the shed roof. That way we could get in our window."

"Robert, you're a genius. What's more, we could get out at night if we felt like it."

"At night! Are you kidding? I don't like that idea too well, not with that house over there."

Robert pointed to the neighbouring house. But his arm stayed pointing, as if he were paralysed. His mouth hung open and he went pale. Rémi looked toward the house, saw nothing and gave his brother a shake.

"Hey. What's wrong with you?"

"Th . . . there . . . There was . . . something moved. Somebody."

"You dreamer. There's nobody. I didn't see a thing."

"I did. Like a man. Or worse. I tell you that house is haunted. And you want to go out at night?"

"You know, I think you're crazy. At night, O.K. you may be scared, I'm not brave neither. But at noon, in broad daylight? Didn't you know ghosts melt in the morning? And you're the guy who's never afraid of anything."

"I saw something, I'm not crazy."

"A cat."

"If cats grow that big around here . . ."

"Well, let's agree you saw something."

"I did."

"It didn't float through the air?"

"It moved, and it went in the house."

"Let's go see."

"Hey! Hey!"

"We'll look from away off. Get some stones."

"You don't catch me going near that shack."

"You're a scaredy."

"Listen, Rémi, show me a guy bigger than I am, I'll fight him. An' I won't run away from two, because I know how to handle it. But going there to meet god knows what? No, sir."

"Okay then, let's hide in the shed and see if he comes back."

They're pressed hard against the wall peeking out through cracks between the boards. A cool thread of air plucks at their lashes, and time goes by. Just as they're about to leave the shed they see a shape dart away from the house and, crouching, head for the young spruce growth not far away. Open-mouthed, the boys watch for a long time after the branches have again become immobile. They hear a car approaching, undoubtedly theirs.

"There! Did you see that? See, I wasn't dreaming."

"Sure, but that was no ghost. A ghost would have stayed inside."

"A man of the woods. Maybe an Indian."

"I don't know. A prowler. Maybe there's a treasure in the house. Who knows? But that ghost of yours isn't very brave. He must be a relation of yours."

"Lay off, eh?"

They jostled each other a little as they went to meet their parents, but there was no need to warn each other not to mention the mysterious intruder.

Rémi went upstairs to change from his Sunday suit. He was dressing in front of the window where he could keep an eye on the house that so intrigued him, when he saw a movement beyond the creek. A shape emerged from the thicket and climbed the hill, disappearing in the foliage at the crest. Whatever it was had been walking right in the middle of the road. Rémi wasn't afraid, for he was sure it was a human being, beyond a doubt the creature they had seen a short time before.

After dinner Rémi got permission from his parents for himself and Robert not to go to Réginald's, where there'd be a repetition of those interminable card games. As soon as they were alone the discussion began. Robert would rather have gone with the parents, and that made Rémi angry.

"I'm not too keen to go to the creek with you-know-what prowling around."

"That's the whole point. I saw it again."

"Where?"

"On the road, past the bridge. A man, running away."

"You think it was a man?"

"Let's go look at the tracks."

"Mmmm. . . ."

"We can just look, from a distance."

Before they left, Robert armed himself with a club.

"It's not that I'm scared of a man, but you never know . . ."

In front of the abandoned house Rémi stopped.

"I'm going to look around."

"No."

"Just to see if there's any tracks in the grass. You don't have to come along."

Rémi led the way through the tall hay that had invaded the former lane. The house looked like a sick man, with the rotten teeth of the verandah, its eyes patched and its mouth gagged with boards. Its grey siding had dark stains beneath the rusty nail-heads. Rémi circled the house at a distance, staying in the sunlight, distrustful of the shadows. Close by he heard Robert's steps accompanied by the tapping of the stick.

They came across the tracks left by the fugitive, barely perceptible in the grass, which was already raising its head again. The prowler had ripped off one board from a window at the back. No doubt he had intended to force his way in, but the arrival of the boys had driven him into hiding in a corner of the building from which he had emerged to take refuge in the spruce woods. It had indeed been a man, and Robert's courage returned with this certainty. But as Rémi advanced with measured step toward the window, his young brother stopped in his tracks. It was ridiculous to follow this madman. Rémi, his heart beating like a drum, laid one hand on the sill and, holding his breath, put an eye to the dusty pane. Nothing. Too dark. Slowly his eyes grew accustomed to it, and he saw a table, some chairs, a side-table, farming tools, trunks – and everywhere an incredible hodgepodge of odd objects, hanging on the walls, lying on the furniture, or scattered on the floor. It would be a long but exciting job to identify them all. There'd be a surprise a minute. And there must be other rooms, no doubt equally crammed. Quite tempting for a thief.

"Rémi? What's there?"

"Nothing. Just furniture and stuff. No ghosts."

"Oh, no. But at night."

Past the creek on the slope rutted by many rains, accumulating sand here or baring rocks there, creating a kind of tormented geography, the prowler's traces were easy to see. Half-way up the slope they emerged from the brush and followed the road to the top. In his footprints you could see the pattern of his soles. Robert measured: barely bigger than his own foot.

"Well, now we know. Hey, look at this place, wouldn't it be great for playing with toy trucks? You put a road here with a bridge, and dig a tunnel through there . . ."

"Come on. We haven't time for kids' games."

"We don't? What have we got to do that's so important?"

"Explore. We should follow his tracks. And that way we'll get a look at the other side."

Robert went first. He walked carefully, getting a good grip on his stick, ready for anything. They climbed the last few metres on all fours and checked out the deserted road for a long time before standing up.

"He'll be a long way off by now."

"We can go a little ways anyhow."

They followed the trail, eyes alert, ears cocked, until the tracks disappeared in the forest. Impossible to see them now. They might as well give up. They were resting for the walk home when they heard a distant sound: a hammer on stone, or stone hitting stone. In fact they were both too tired to go and see what it was, but neither wanted to pass for a coward.

They walked beside the trees and the sound came nearer. It was not as far away as they had thought. Somewhere in the woods, a little to the left. They crawled on the moss between the trees. Ahead they could see some movement, despite the screen of needled branches. And a sound came with each brusque movement. They crawled a little farther. A man was kneeling on a rock, hammering at it for all he was worth. Sparks and rock dust were flying, his clothing was in tatters and patched in many colours, his hair and beard were long and white. He was frail looking, which reassured the boys. He had his hammer, of course, but there were two of them, and Robert had a sturdy club.

The man succeeded in breaking off a piece of stone, picked it up, and cried in a tremulous voice, "Rich! Rich! I'm rich!"

Then he grew calm, stared longer at his discovery, shook his head and tossed it away.

"Some day I'll be rich. Some day."

And he began hammering the rock again.

Robert murmured, "What do you call that?"

"A prospector."

"Funny guy. Let's talk to him."

They walked toward him, no longer trying to stalk him silently. But the man neither saw nor heard their approach. Robert touched him on the shoulder with the tip of his stick. He gave a start, dropped his hammer, turned, squinted at them, and flopped down with his stomach covering a rock that he tried to hide.

He shouted, the words tumbling out, "You're robbers. But you're not going to get my gold! This is mine, it's my rock, my gold. I'll die before I give it up."

"We're not robbers," Robert protested.

"No," said Rémi. "It's more like you're the robber."

"Me a robber? Me? Me? All this is mine, here. It's my gold. I'm no robber."

"Well, what were you doing in the empty house?"

"House? What house?"

"Across the creek."

The old man sat up on the granite rock, slowly, as if he needed time to think.

"Oh, that one. Across the creek of the curse."

"Right. You went there to steal."

"Are you sure you're not robbers?"

"No," said Rémi, sitting down.

It was going to take a lot of quiet and patience to get this man to talk, and even then it might be nonsense.

Rémi went on. "We're not robbers, we're just going for a walk, having fun, the way kids do."

Robert was staring at his brother. What was getting into him? The man was alone, weak, and frightened: you had to be tough and make an impression on him. Poor Rémi, he had no feeling for battle. If you sit down beside your enemy you give him an advantage.

"Kids?" said the old man, incredulous.

"Sure. And we wondered why you were trying to steal from the old house."

"Me steal? Never. Listen, I search for gold, and I find it."

"In the empty house?"

"No. In the rocks, under the moss, wherever the genies are hiding. What I was looking for in the house was a hammer. Mine's not much good any more. Look."

Robert snatched the tool the old man held out before Rémi could get it. It was a funny-looking hammer, with no claws.

"That's a prospector's hammer, for breaking stones, setting free the gold, getting rich!"

"What good would that do you, being rich?"

"You must really be little kids if you ask a question like that. Being rich is . . . is being rich!"

"Where do you live?"

"Oh, I know. You just want to find out so you can come and steal my gold. I ain't goin' to tell you."

"We don't want your gold. What would kids like us to do with a bunch of gold?"

"That's true what you say."

"Is it far to your place?"

"Over that way, in the alder bush. It's a log house. I ain't goin' to show you where."

He started hammering away at the rock again. Under the blows of his hammer the black, red, and white grains turned to a greyish powder, which crunched beneath the steel. A horrid noise. A chip with cutting angles flew off and the man carefully scrutinized the mineral secrets thus revealed.

"Why do you say there's a curse on the creek?" Robert inquired.

The prospector stopped his work, hesitating as though reluctant to talk, but his eyes, delighted, belied this pretence.

"Because . . . Oh, you'd never believe me."

"Sure we would. Even before you start."

"Now don't tell a soul. I don't want no problems."

He looked furtively around into the underbrush and lowered his voice.

"That crick is under a curse because it's a graveyard."

"A graveyard!" the two shouted in unison.

"Yes, the clay's a coffin."

Robert went pale, thinking of the cave they were digging. What if they'd unearthed a corpse. Dead bodies, a haunted house; for sure the country had a curse on it.

"Who are the dead ones?" said Rémi in a voice that trembled slightly.

"The dead? He wants to know who the dead are. Why the genies, that's who. Genies condemned to death for what they did. They're changed into grey stones and buried in the crick bed. You dig there and you'll find them. Sometimes you see where the water uncovered them. Round stones, covered with secret signs, and others like little crushed bodies. If you touch them you're cursed as well, bad things can happen. And if you break them the genies get away, and I'd just as soon not think about what could happen then."

He peered at the boys to see what effect his tale had had on them. Robert was paralysed with fear. Rémi was wondering if the man was making fun of them or if he actually believed his nonsense.

"Genies?"

"Aha. You don't believe me, eh? There's lot of genies here. I know it for I've been meetin' up with 'em for fifteen years."

"You've met some?"

"Mostly they live at night. But even in daytime they take on all sorts of forms to show themselves. And they like to play tricks on you. Sometimes it's worse, and they'll try to kill you. You're walkin' along and *Crack*! There's a stone under your foot that makes you fall, or a dead tree falls down and almost gets you. Why does the tree fall? Who gave it the push? At night the genies dig up their gold and have fun. I can hear them flyin' around between the trees and runnin' on the moss and shouting. Just watch out for the genies, don't go near that cursed crick."

The old man went back to hammering rock. Robert, who didn't know what to think, looked questioningly at Rémi. His brother's calm and a discreet wink reassured him.

"Listen, will you?" Rémi began in a grave voice, slowly getting to his feet. "He and I are genies."

"Genies."

The old man found it hard to believe.

"Yes. Could you hear us coming?"

"N-n-no."

"We came floating through the air."

The man was speechless for a long moment, then got to his knees, mumbling, "Genies, what do you want from me?"

"We just want to tell you, one thing: don't ever cross our creek again, never, not even by the bridge. If you do, our curse will follow you, you'll be changed into a tree and that'll be the end of your search for gold."

The old man hid his face in his hands.

"I promise, I swear it. Never go to the crick. Never."

"Very well."

"Can I . . . can I still look here for gold?"

"Yes, if you don't go near the creek."

"What about gold? Have you hidden hereabouts?"

"Lots of it. Keep looking."

Taking advantage of the prospector's prostrate position, Rémi hauled Robert away, and they disappeared in a second through the spruce trees. They were on the road again. The old man must have leaped to his feet and danced for joy. They could hear him screaming, almost singing, "Rich, I'll be rich. Gold. Lots of gold!"

His hammering started in again with a vengeance. The boys slipped away and didn't stop until they were out of range of his hearing. Then they rolled on the moss and Robert pounded the earth with his fist.

"It can't be true. It can't be true!"

"Genies."

They were still laughing when they came to the creek. The creek with the curse on it. After some hesitation Robert asked, "Look, you don't believe that stuff, eh? About the genies?"

"Ha ha ha, good old Robert!"

"Don't laugh at me. Do you believe it or not?"

"Come on, of course not. That's crazy, all of it."

"But you know, those stones in the creek, there's something funny about them."

"Sure, but that doesn't mean they're genies, dead genies. Do you want me to tell you the story of Bluebeard?"

Robert shrugged. Rémi went on: "Listen, the old guy's nuts. Just look at him . . . And he took us for genies, genies that hide gold in stones."

"He believes in that so much it's almost true."

"Creek of the Curse. That's a good name. I like it, there's mystery about it."

"You don't believe in mysteries but you talk about them."

"There may be a little truth in what he says. Mysteries exist all right, and it seems to me this is a good spot for them. But his stuff about genies, that's a bit too dumb. I always think a mystery is more complicated, more of a secret. Genies? Pooh! The only genies around Cursed Creek, that's you and me."

That afternoon they managed to finish excavating their cave. Robert dug very carefully for fear of finding "something" buried there. But he tried to keep his brother from noticing the lack of ardour in his work. The vaulted chamber was three feet high, five feet long and four wide. With rags and water they polished the walls. Then, with great ceremony, Robert set up in one corner the breasts he had modelled, as he thought, on Mrs. Martel's. Already as it dried, his work was cracking, and he rubbed it down with water and smoothed its skin with his hands. And uttered insanities as he did so.

The sun was descending and, as it grew dark in the bowels of the earth, they came out. They were going to need some light in there. Rémi pondered the problem as he sat on the heap of excavated earth that now rose to overlook the pond. Birds were singing in the reeds.

"What do you think? Is the old guy going to find gold?"

Rémi shrugged. Good question. And why did the prospector want so badly to be rich with nothing but all those spruce trees to impress! What was he going to do with all that money? Try and find out.

"We could spy on him, follow him at a distance. See what he does. Where he lives."

"Aw, Rémi, what's the use? He's crazy anyway."

"He's no ordinary madman. Living all alone? How? And what's he live on? Where does he come from, the old guy? What did he do before? That's what I'd like to know. Why does he believe in genies? And he does believe in them, I'm sure of that."

"I don't believe in them, but I don't like that whole business."

"Chicken shit, piss your pants."

"Laugh all you like, what do I care? Come on, Rémi, what do we know about this place? It's not Montreal any more. People along this line are always just walking away from their houses, there must be a reason. Look at those trees. They could be hiding anything."

"That's what I like about here, everything's possible. What hides in Montreal? Some guy that wants to grab your ass, or a gang that wants to beat you up."

"Yeah, we knew how to deal with them. But how can we defend ourselves here?"

"Who says we have to? I don't see any danger. There's lots of things in the world that you don't see right away, lots of signs you have to learn to read."

"That scares me. It's best to leave the hidden things the way they are."

"You have to take your time discovering them. That way you get the riches, you're the strong one . . . Maybe that's the gold the old guy's looking for!"

"No. He's looking for yellow nuggets you can weigh in your hand and see them shine. I understand him, that's the way I am, too. I'm happy with just the things I can see and grab in my hands, that's all I want. Just what I can see and touch."

"What about all the rest? Hey. Think of searching, finding, getting, and knowing invisible things. Being hunters of mysteries. Sure beats football! Look around you! Can you see us playing the games we used to in Montreal? We have to make up some new ones now!"

"You're never satisfied with what you got. You always want something bigger and better."

"Suppose it's a game. We become mystery hunters. The cave is our hide-out, the secret place where we start our expeditions."

"And how do we go about finding mysteries?"

"I don't know. Believing's more than seeing. You have to look through things, everything becomes a sign, you try and read it. I suppose daytime isn't so good for searching. It's too bright, everything's too normal."

"You don't mean . . . I wondered when you talked about a ladder for getting out at night. . . ."

Robert was thinking about the abandoned house, the menace of the spruce trees, the wide, deserted fields, wondering how it would be at night, walking on the clay studded with coffin-stones!

"Don't be such a scaredy-cat."

"You really want us to go hunting at night?"

"Yes. Night-time is different. The day we got here, during the party at Réginald's, I went outside. Everything was talking to me, Robert. The grass, the trees, the stars. I couldn't understand them but I heard. And last night on the shed roof I saw the sky was full of signs."

"You're crazy!"

"And you're a yellow-belly."

"I'm not scared of anybody."

"But the dark, eh? Scared of the dark?"

"Yes, and I'm not ashamed of it."

"To tell you the truth, so am I, but I like it all the same."

"You can go look for your mysteries by yourself."

"But I need you along. It's too much for me, but the two of us. . . ."

"No."

"O.K. I'll go out by myself at night, but just don't ask me about it. If I find something I'll keep it all for me. And if I don't come back it'll be your fault. Don't expect anything from me or think I'm going to play your kid games in the day time. You can play with Françoise."

"Coming up here we got to be friends. We said we'd share everything."

"That means danger too! What about adventures? Have you given that up? And why should we be scared, the two of us? We can hide, we can look, we can catch people doing things, nobody's going to know. But we might find out just about everything. When you know things, you're the master. Wouldn't that be something, being master of the night?"

"A bit, I guess, but . . ."

"Never mind the buts. Listen, tonight we're going to our cave, nothing else, just for a start. Try it once and then we'll try something else tomorrow if you feel like it. If you're not too scared. If you are you can stay at home and I'll still be your friend, I won't mind."

"Well, all right. Just once, to try it. . . ."

They sat watching the sun slip obliquely toward the trees. Rémi was glad of the silence, it gave him time to think of the words that had just come to him, from God knew where, and measure the phrases that he had invented, sounding them for unknown meanings. Robert, for his part, looked no farther than their implications for his daily life. Everything was going to be subject to his brother's crazy ideas. Around them the breeze had fallen and all was still. Except, of course, for the sighing of the spruce trees, the rustling of the reeds, the song of the creek, the buzzing of the insects, the frogs' splashing, and the cry of the birds.

They made their way home. Past the abandoned house.

"That house!" Robert was trembling.

"That house, indeed."

"We should make a detour so we wouldn't see it."

"A house full of mysteries, I'll bet. And so far away."

"Close enough for me."

"No, it's far because of all the things we don't know, far away in our own courage. I swear, Robert, I'm going in there."

"Not me. The very idea of going past it tonight. . . ."

"You won't be alone."

"Makes no difference. I'd burn it just to see the last of it."

"Don't ever do that. I want to get the best of it first."

"Sometimes I wonder why I listen to you at all. Why do I go along with you, you damn dreamer?"

Their parents weren't yet back from Réginald's. The boys improvised a ladder with spikes driven in at the angle of the house and the shed. Tonight it would be easy to get out without being seen.

"Robert, go and get a candle and some matches."

Rémi tiptoed into his parents' room: what if he uncovered secrets here? That was the last thing he wanted. Therefore, no drawers would be opened. By chance the tobacco and cigarette papers lay on the dresser. Clumsily he rolled a cigarette then joined Robert again.

"Here's a candle. Should we make swords? Not that I'm scared, but it would look good."

"No, sticks. That's how I imagine a master of the night, with a staff like a shepherd."

In a little rucksack Rémi stuffed the candle, the matches, a jack-knife, two sandwiches, some apples, and the cigarette. They hid the bag and the staffs in the grass near the shed. At last the rest of the family arrived. The boys described in great detail an afternoon spent playing Indians down by the stream. Their father, beaming, pointed out to their mother how much better the quiet of this country road was for the boys than the evil influences of the town. After supper the whole family moved outside to watch the fall of evening. The father was moved to revive his dreams yet again, and in the glancing light great crops of hay and oats shot high, cows appeared, grazing behind a field of potatoes, they could almost hear the ritual sounds as the chickens made ready for the roost. These were good dreams, rich and full of life. You didn't have to stretch your imagination much to see farm buildings taking shape. But the black flies began to grow aggressive and they took refuge inside from the swarms. The lamp bathed the kitchen in its silent light. The boys, having nothing better to do, went up to bed. Their little sister was chattering softly behind the divider. Their parents came to kiss them good night, then went to their own room.

Rémi counted the time as it passed slowly through his head. He was feverishly impatient to be out in the night, staff in hand, not yet as master of the night, but as her pilgrim. When he thought the hour had come and all the house was sleeping, he touched Robert's shoulder. Robert had been pretending to sleep.

"Come on."

"Listen, I'm. . . ."

"Piss your pants, piss your pants." Rémi hissed.

"Couldn't we put it off till tomorrow?"

"No, now, right now, or you'll never be a master of the night."

"I'd rather. . . ."

"I'll go to the cave by myself, I'll break the tits."

Robert sat up, threatening, "If you do that, we're never going to be friends again."

"When you want something you have to defend it. Come on, just for a while. We'll look and come right back."

"Well, O.K., but just this once."

Having recovered their staffs and bag from the hiding-place, they waited at the bottom of the ladder for their eyes to grow used to the dark. Rémi was trembling with excitement. Slowly the dark grew penetrable, the fields appeared, and the abandoned house reared up majestic with its shadowed gables, impressive with the towers and crenellations it acquired from the tricks of starlight. An impregnable keep, self-enclosed, blind, defended, perhaps, by some malevolent creature. "Only what's precious has to be defended," Rémi said to himself. He'd have liked to lay siege to the house at once, ravish its secrets, but his courage was not yet up to that. He'd have to wait through his apprenticeship in more subtle secrecies: the house was such an obvious challenge.

Robert said gruffly, "Well let's get going. The sooner we leave the sooner we're back. It's cold out here. I'm for bed."

Rémi took the lead and his brother followed until they reached the road and the feel of pebbles underfoot. A faint luminescence, seeming to come from the earth itself, transformed the road into a wide waterway. The house was beside them, and for a moment it had them pinched between its shadow and that of the cabin opposite. The Creek of the Curse was high, its darkness overflowed its banks, filling its course with thick and stirring shadows.

"Wait up, Rémi, not so fast, eh?"

"Slowpoke."

They head downstream. The footing is irregular, sometimes slippery, sometimes crumbling. They trip over unseen, unexpected shapes, bushes grasp at them as they pass, and they often need their staffs to keep their balance. To their right the forest murmurs – or is it the whining of the mosquitoes attacking the intruders? Robert is frightened; he thinks of the underground dead and their gnarled fingers breaking the surface to catch at his pant leg and draw him from his path. Afraid of being left behind, he holds on to Rémi's jacket.

"Tremble, oh Creek of the Curse. The masters of the night are here."

"Not so loud. Are you crazy?" Robert whispers to his brother. "What's got into you? They'll hear us!"

"Who's 'they'? We're miles from anywhere, we're the only people here."

"Yeah, people. You said it. You said we'd hide and watch. Then you go shouting. That's not the deal."

"They have to find out who's boss."

"They?"

"Sure, all the ones hiding in the dark and watching us."

"Rémi, damn you, you're trying to scare me; you just got me here to make fun of me. If you did, just you wait, I'm goin' to smash you one you won't forget."

"I'm not fooling. We're being watched. But you mustn't be afraid. We're the masters. They're the ones who have to shake and shiver. If that's not enough for you, go on back. I'm not keeping you here."

"Damn you, I'm never coming again."

"Stick with me Robert. The two of us are stronger than anything, stronger than fear. Look, we're almost at our hide-out."

In the crescent pool the frogs are singing their heads off, out of rhythm, out of tune. The moon, a great overripe fruit hanging in the trees, rises, and climbs rapidly up the sky, drying out and shrinking as it goes. The stars cannot compete with this overweening light; but storm clouds frizz their fringes in its silver. Somewhere a bird cries out and goes to sleep again. At times the noise of the mosquitoes drowns out the frogs.

"We've been watching for a while now, Rémi. What about going home?"

"Too soon. Don't give up so close to the goal. Follow me."

Rémi crawls into the narrow cave, where the humidity is deadly cold, bumps into the back wall, and curls up.

Robert arrives after him, whispering, "Rémi? Rémi?"

"I'm here, where do you think? Make yourself at home."

They can't see each other. Not even a hand in front of their eyes. Where they are there is no space, no wall, no ceiling, no up or down, it's as if they were floating in a world that was its own womb. Only their breathing tells each one that he is not alone.

Rémi's voice is solemn: "Robert, do you want light?"

"What makes you talk that way? Sure, light the candle."

"Quiet. This is a ceremony. Robert, do you want light?"

"Er . . . yes."

"As you wait for the great light, receive this one as a symbol."

He scratches a match and sticks the candle into the clay. They are blinded, their dilated pupils contract. The flickering flame lights their faces from underneath, shadows dance in this space that has no angles.

"Robert, do you desire to become Master of the Night?"

"Yes."

"Are you prepared to submit to trials to reach this high rank and bear this name with dignity, always searching out mysteries, unveiling them with respect, and keeping all their secrets?"

"Well, uh . . ."

"Say yes or no."

"Yes."

"Repeat after me. In the bowls of the earth . . . I die and am born again, and I am about to go out into the great night . . ."

"Not so fast."

". . . into the great night . . . to begin my search . . . taking no rest . . . respecting the rules of the Order . . .

following the rites and the trials . . . climbing one by one the steps of knowledge."

After a pause Robert whispers, "Where do you get these ideas?"

"Repeat: I, Robert, promise . . . to keep silence about the Order . . . and I ask to become a Knight of Darkness . . . If ever I go back on my word . . . may the unknown forces crush me . . . and the shadows swallow me."

"What trials?"

"I'll let you know. After your two tests you'll be a knight, and then after long service and other tests you'll get the title Master."

Robert doesn't know what to think. Everything is so out of the ordinary. The phrases he repeated. Night in the cave. The cave itself. Rémi snuffs the candle and pushes his brother toward the exit. They blink at the near daylight from the moon: not the crude, empty daylight of the sun but a vibrant, living half-light. As if the night had opened itself to the eyes of the initiates.

"Take your staff, pilgrim of the night, and come silently."

They make their way to the bridge, climb the slope, and follow the road with its crushing escort of dark trees. A long walk takes them to where they saw the prospector; then they turn back to the stream.

"There. That was your first trial."

They sit down, their legs dangling over the stream.

"Where did you get this idea, Rémi?"

"It's not just an idea. I know you have to be initiated to have power over the night. I just feel it."

"Are you initiated?"

"No, I'm getting initiated same time as you. Have a sandwich."

"Oh, yeah. Walking makes you hungry. Can we talk regular now?"

"Whatever you like. But nothing's regular at night."

"You know, just now on the road I almost wasn't scared. Only when that animal ran across, my heart hammered a bit."

"An animal. Or whatever it was. We don't know. We're going to have to learn to know the night."

"What's the next trial?"

"Eat. Get your strength back. You'll see."

A cool breeze flows over the countryside, with warm cross-currents in it. The black flies have disappeared. Rémi leads Robert toward home.

"Are we going back already?"

"Silence."

Rémi has put on his solemn voice again and Robert responds with respect. In front of the haunted house they stop.

"Not that!" says Robert.

"Don't make a sound, we're not far from home. The last trial: go to the door of the haunted house, knock, and come back without running."

"Not on your life. Count me out."

"You are free. If you leave now you will never be a Master of the Night, nor even a Knight of Darkness."

"Just knock and come back?"

"Yes. I'll go first."

Rémi, gripping his staff, advances alone toward the darkling wall. If he had chosen the other side he would have been helped by light from the setting moon, but it had to be the front door so that he could show the house he was unafraid, and that some day he'd dare go in . . . He comes near, the shadows swallow him up and he disappears before Robert's anxious eyes. The house attracts Rémi like a magnet, and his staff leads him too slowly for his taste. He goes up the squeaking steps and puts his weight on the creaky platform floor. His heart beating fit to burst, he stretches out his fist and hammers three times at the boards nailed across the doorway. He takes a step back. There is a thin echo from inside, like the sound of running feet. "I'll be back, I'll be back," his mind shouts soundlessly.

Robert's turn.

"Go ahead."

"Nothing happened? I'm scared."

"A knight conquers his fear, or learns to like it."

Robert is there and back in no time. He didn't run, but it was a near thing. His face is shining as if from sweat.

"There."

"Good for you. You beat your fear."

They return to the bridge. Rémi makes his brother kneel and touches his shoulder with his staff.

"Because you passed your trials without flinching, Robert, I dub thee Knight of Darkness. You must choose a woman who will be your Lady, your thoughts and deeds will be for her. Who is she?"

"You mustn't ask that."

"Robert, I dub thee Knight-of-the-Lady-with-the-Big-Breasts. Arise, Sir Robert. My congratulations. Now it's my turn."

Rémi kneels and Robert repeats the ceremony.

"Who will your Lady be?"

"The princess of the haunted house."

"She doesn't exist, it don't count. Pick a real woman."

"She exists all right. Baptize me."

Robert hesitates a second, moved in spite of himself.

"Rémi, I name you Knight-of-the-Princess-of-the-Haunted-House."

"Thanks. That's a nice name."

Rémi gets the cigarette from the bag, lights it, coughs and passes it to his brother. They take turns puffing, they smoke without inhaling.

"It's strong but it tastes good. Where'd you get it?"

"I rolled it myself."

"That's the first time I ever smoked."

"Not me."

Rémi fell silent, thinking of the scene by the truck. He'd been on the point of touching the girl and undoing her clothes and she wouldn't have stopped him, that was certain. It would have been a wonderful first time, coming after an evening of intense desires, but he'd given up at the last moment. And the girl had a chance to laugh at his inexperience. Every time she'd looked at him after that had been an insult. And her mocking smile in church. And all the things she was probably saying about him. He hated her anyway, and now that he was devoted to his own princess he mustn't go regretting a missed opportunity.

"What are you thinking about, Rémi?"

"Oh, nothing. Just looking at the night. It's ours now."

"What are we going to do with it?"

"Find out all about it, live in it. Search for mysteries and conquer our Ladies."

"Conquer Mrs. Martel? Are you drunk?"

"Knight-of-the-Lady-with-the-Big-Breasts, I promise that you will possess your Lady. The night will give you the power if you are worthy of it."

"Well, I can think about it anyway."

"No, Robert, believe, and fight for it. Come on, let's go in."

They stopped for a moment on the shed roof.

"Look at the sky, the marionettes, and the ring around the moon. We have to learn how to read these signs. Look down below. That's our domain."

"Even the haunted house?"

"The castle of my princess."

"Ha ha! Her I've gotta see."

"You have little faith. You'll see her some day. When I've rescued her."

"Poor old Rémi!"

"Are you glad to be a knight?"

"Sure. But what about tomorrow?"

"Tomorrow we'll go out again. You're coming, eh? No tests or trials tomorrow. We're going to start discovering. First of all, our line, who lives along the road. We'll see how different it is from daytime, we'll spy on people."

"Oh, great! The Martels, too, eh?"

"Sure. Get a good rest. Sleep in tomorrow. We've got to be in good shape."

"I'm going to bed. Aren't you?"

"I'll just stay here for a while. Leave the window open."

Rémi sat down and watched for a long time as the moon shifted the shadows on the abandoned house. The wind rose and the waving grass silently battered the castle with pale, moving lights. "You'll get nowhere," Rémi muttered. "Only I can rescue the princess." It seemed to him that the bright graffiti of the sky confirmed what he was saying: a powerful thrust of northern lights suddenly hung still above the castle, then whirled and quivered over the building, shaking it. The meteor disappeared. Now Rémi was sure of his mission. The moon fell quickly now toward earth, white at first, then golden, copper, rust, and red in turn. It plunged into the trees and was extinguished. The frightened stars resumed their accustomed places, menaced only by the erratic course of a bluish planet. The gleam on the grass was gone.

Already ten o'clock. Their father had left for Amos just after breakfast, taking Françoise along. He's supposed to meet the Settlement people about grants for farm buildings, animals and machinery.

Robert and Rémi have decided to make some improvements to their cave, the main one being a niche where they can set up the clay breasts, which take too much room on the floor. They head down toward the creek. Their house is already out of sight. They'd heard a car approaching but had paid no attention. But it's stopping at their place. From the sound they know it's not their father back from Amos. Who could it be? Should they go home and see? No, they decide to go on despite their curiosity. Just as well, the car's driving off. No. It's coming their way. They back toward the ditch as a white Volkswagen pulls up beside them. A priest gets out.

"Hello, boys. I'm your parish priest, Father Ricard. We're laying some turf around the church with the help of the children of the parish. I wondered if you'd like to join us. You look like healthy fellows and we need all the strong arms we can get."

"Yes, well . . .," Rémi started.

"Your mother agrees. You'll get to know the other children in the village."

"Well, you see . . .," Robert began, showing his fishing pole.

"Do this for our Good Lord. Fishing can wait for another day."

Robert sends Rémi an imploring glance, but Rémi feels unable to say no. What reason could he give that would justify refusing?

"We'll go."

They hide their tackle down the slope and get in the car. Robert in the back and Rémi in front beside the priest. He drives fast and the pebbles fly up against the floorboards. Behind them a long trail of dust rises and is carried sideways by the wind across the fields. The abandoned house, made insignificant by their speed, their mother waving, the forest, Méo's retreat, the Martel house swarming with children, cousin Réginald trying to hitch up his stallion – it's all gone too quickly, as in a dream. What a busybody this priest is – forcing them out of the security of their country road, ruining a beautiful day. . . .

Suddenly the driver jams on the brakes. The car skids and comes to a stop across the road after almost tipping over. The priest is in a rage, he slams into reverse and backs up to the fence in front of Godbout's place. He bursts out of the car. Near the fence is a cardboard box and sticking out of it a crucifix, the head of a statue, and framed holy pictures. The priest rescues the crucifix, rubs it lovingly against his cheek, then brandishes it at arm's length and howls, "Godbout! Godbout! Godbout!"

A man emerges from the house and leans against the wall, crossing his legs and hitching his thumbs behind his wide braces. He smiles.

"Yeah?"

"Godbout, you're in for damnation. Throwing out religious articles this way."

"I told you to get that crap out of here."

"Infidel."

"Priest."

"You deny the religion of your fathers."

"Jehovah is my father."

"Without the church there is no salvation."

"Without the church, no collection, you mean, eh? You don't care a hang if I'm damned or not for your pack of lies. As long as I put a dollar on the plate and pay my tithes. How much'll you take to leave me be?"

"You don't know what you're saying. The evil one inhabits your soul. You live in evil, you *are* evil incarnate."

"No, I love creation, Jehovah's world."

"You lie, you hate mankind."

"I hate mankind, yes, and you above all. But I love the true God."

"We must not live by hate. Hatred is death. You are not alone on this earth, Godbout; there are others, your brothers."

"I don't give a shit about the others. Let 'em believe in the all-powerful Jehovah and maybe they'll be saved. I'm gettin' saved on my own, let the others do the same or go hang. To hell with them. They'll be damned, Ricard, and it's goin' to be your fault, the fault of your Holy Virgin and your holy host, and your saints."

"Your Jehovah is the Devil himself."

"Look here, in the Bible. It's all written down. The only true religion. You, you're an idol worshipper. A pagan."

"Godbout, you understand nothing. You're playing with things that are too big for you. Some fast talker comes along and you believe all you hear. You read a book and think you're intelligent all of a sudden."

"A book? *The* Book. That burns your ass, eh Ricard? That I'm a little smarter than the others?"

"You think you're better because you waste your time listening to short wave, reading the Bible and God knows what crazy stuff. A little knowledge is dangerous when you're not prepared for it."

"You're scared of me because I got half way through my classics course, you're scared I'll tell the others what you are: a bloodsucker living off the poor's last pennies. Exploiter."

"Godbout, repent. You know not what you say, poor wind vane. Today you're a Jehovah's Witness, tomorrow you'll be a communist. And after that? Turn off your cursed radio and live like a normal man here in Abitibi. Work, occupy your soul."

"Oh, shut you, you make me laugh. I know what's going on elsewhere, in other countries, even Russia, but specially in Rome, Babylon of the popes. You try to keep us ignorant, you're up to your neck in it with the bishop and the Member of Parliament and the Settlement office. It suits you right down to the ground when people are suckers. Well, Godbout won't swallow that no more! And from now on you'll have me to reckon with, I'm going to bring the Good Word to everybody and convert them to the true God. That'll be the end of them fattening you up like a pig, you'll have to do a man's work if you want to eat."

"You'll end up in jail."

"You there, if you was in Russia, you'd have been in jail long ago with the rest of the bloodsuckers."

"Poor fool, what do you know about goings-on behind the iron curtain?"

"What do I know? The Russians have already launched a ball in the sky, with a rocket."

"Foolishness. Don't come spreading your evil words and lies among my flock. For you'll have me to reckon with as well. Truth and time are on my side."

"That's enough. Go waste your time someplace else."

"This is my parish."

"This is my home. And I'm a son of Jehovah."

"May God forgive you. I'll pray for you."

"Right, I'm praying for your salvation too, so you'll give up your idols and worship the true God."

The priest picks up the box of "idols" and stows it carefully in the trunk at the front of the car. He drives off jerkily, in a rage. On the front step Godbout, his hands a megaphone, hurls inaudible imprecations after them.

"You didn't hear anything, did you, children?"

"No, father," they lie.

"Good. That man is the demon incarnate. Let us pray for him."

And for the rest of their drive the priest recited the rosary, through clenched teeth. Robert and Rémi gave their listless responses.

At the church a real sodding-bee is underway. The week before good black earth had been spread on the grounds and now the children are laying squares of turf. They're being cut from the field behind the church and brought out in wheelbarrows. There is more ground to be covered than one might think at first glance. Three teams – one to cut the turf in regular squares, one to man the wheelbarrows, and one to lay the grass – are commanded by a young straw boss. The priest pushes the Simard boys in his direction. It's the boy Robert had jostled in front of the church the previous Sunday.

"I have no time for introductions," says the priest. "You'll get to know them as you work."

The workers, all village children between ten and fourteen, stop and stare at the newcomers, but the priest sees that they are all back to work before he disappears inside the church. The young foreman, arms akimbo, jerks his chin at Rémi.

"You there, go lay turf. The other one, take a wheelbarrow and get to work."

The day is steaming hot and after a half hour Rémi is wet to the skin. It's not easy. Working on your knees, you have to even the earth, flatten it, take a square of turf, and fit it exactly so there are no gaps. His back is sore, but the worst part is being surrounded by silent hostility. Nobody speaks to him, they all look sideways at him and murmur behind his back. The foreman doesn't let Robert out of his sight. Hands in his pockets, he follows him to the field, follows him back, hustles him, gives him orders, and makes unpleasant remarks. Each time Robert comes back with his load the foreman seizes the opportunity to stand behind Rémi and watch him. Is he making faces? Perhaps, because when he's there the children round about whisper loudly and giggle. Rémi looks down at his work and says nothing. His greatest fear is that Robert might explode and the whole thing degenerate into a brawl.

A girl manages to edge near to Rémi, as she works. Soon they are laying sod silently, side by side. Their next squares of turf are going to part them again. Everything could be all right if one of the village kids spoke. Rémi doesn't dare be the first to talk. He barely manages to get a look at her. She's not bad. Almost pretty. But she is the one who's going to speak. She leans her head closer, her face is very near his, and her eyes are smiling above her freckles.

"Are you the sissy?"

Rémi is about to sink into the ground. She stares at him with eyes that pretend innocence.

"I mean, the kid that doesn't know what to do with a girl, so scared he gets sick?"

Under his arms and knees the earth is trembling. Rémi wishes it would really open up and swallow him. Around him are mocking faces, jeering smiles, restrained giggles. A trap! They couldn't have heard what she said, therefore they must have known in advance what she was going to say and were watching him to see the effect. There is no effect. Rémi freezes, not knowing how to react or what to do. What shame. He's humiliated in front of everyone, intentionally, with malice. The laughter at his predicament grows more open.

"Come here a moment, Rémi."

It's Father Ricard standing in the doorway of the church. His appearance breaks the infernal circle from which Rémi had feared he would never escape. Looking at no one, he hastens to join the priest who has withdrawn inside the church. The door closes on laughter from outside, which echoes long over the empty pews. A stingy light descends through imitation stained-glass windows. The priest leads the way, his footsteps silent, while Rémi's shoes make a frightening noise. They pass around the altar and take a side door to the vestry. The priest waits for him and pushes the boy toward a table where there is a model of the church and its surroundings. He speaks with a velvet voice.

"Do you see this marvel? The church, in its lovely simplicity. Here, we're putting down grass today. Later we'll have flower-beds and here a grotto of Lourdes with illuminated statues."

He lays an arm on the boy's shoulder, pulls him closer and holds him there as if to point out features of the model with greater ease. Rémi is too surprised to react.

"There, we'll have a walkway going through an arch toward the cemetery. We'll plant trees, set up the fallen gravestones, improve the lawn, and plant more flowers. On one side will be the stations of the cross, and here a portable altar for processions. I want to create something beautiful, a beauty that will speak to the simple souls of the people here better than words can do. But I need help, and the children of the village don't work with much enthusiasm. They don't understand. If you wish, you can be my helper. In you I sense a soul that loves what is beautiful. You could motivate the other children and inspire them. This is a great work that we would undertake together, and then later we would start on something else: a parish hall with a library, cultural activities, a Boy Scout movement perhaps. Together, you and I."

He takes Rémi's chin in his hand and turns his face until they are looking in each other's eyes.

"You certainly have a sense of beauty. Don't you want to help me, become my partner?"

Rémi is stiff with embarrassment, too astonished to resist the constant pressure that holds him inexorably against the worn and shiny cassock. What should he do? Struggle? Shout for help? With the others outside who would turn the thing into a riot and make him look like a fool? Rémi was hating himself for being a weakling, never able to make up his mind. Robert, now, would have already done something without weighing the consequences.

A tumult outside broke the spell. The priest drew back, excusing himself "for a moment" and disappeared out the side door that led to the presbytery. Rémi blessed his luck and ran back through the church and out the front door. No one was left in the work area, but cries and shouts came from the side of the church. At the corner Rémi peeked around to see what was happening: Robert, his hair flying and his nose bleeding, broke away from the crowd and approached him rapidly, head high. Rémi fell in step with him and together they marched down the main street (in fact, the only street, or, strictly speaking, the road that ran through the village). No one followed them and they walked on in silence until the last house lay behind them. In front of them the grey road with its perspective of telephone poles thrust its vanishing point across the flat countryside. Rémi needed no explanation.

"I hope you won, at least."

"You bet. When the priest pulled us apart the other one never got up. He was bleeding."

"Bunch of idiots."

"I'm not goin' to that school."

"And I'm not goin' to mass."

"It's not that I'm scared of them. They're idiots, that's all."

"And the priest's a fag. He tried to make a pass at me in the vestry."

"What did you do?"

"Played dumb. But look: I snitched these on the way out." Two votive lights in their tinted glass. "They're great for the cave."

"But listen, the priest. . . ."

"I'm sure of it."

"The guy I beat up must be his pet."

"I guess so. Foreman. Ha Ha!"

Rémi, imagining the battle, feels better. Robert had wiped out the insult that he, Rémi, had suffered. The heat grows more oppressive. Insects crackle in the hay. A car passes and the boys continue, coughing, through a fog of dust. Their mouths coated, their throats dry, they can't even manage to spit. The three thirsty miles to the cross-road seem endless. The sunlight is crushing, and they seem to advance at a snail's pace. At last: the cross at the intersection. In vain they search for a scrap of shade and then continue on their way. They won't find any shade until after Martel's house. Should they stop a minute at cousin Réginald's for a drink? The image of a water glass, sweating cold, spurs them on. Already they're at Dam-Bogga's place.

Across the road, from his front stoop, Godbout shouts "Hey! You the priest's little jerk-off pets? You finish your job already? How's the pay at Ricard's place, eh?"

Robert, furious, picks up a stone and lets fly at the mailbox. He connects, the tin rattles, and a little paint flakes off. The initial J is no longer visible.

"Why you goddam little pipsqueak!"

The boys stick out their tongues and run, for Godbout is after them.

"Wait till I catch you!"

Their cousin's house is too far away. Godbout will have them before they get there. They double back and dive into Dam-Bogga's place, scramble over the fence, and find themselves facing a great black dog. They're cornered, but Godbout turns and goes home.

"I'll get you another time, you little bastards."

From the corner of his house, doubled up laughing, his eyes almost slits, Dam-Bogga gestures to them to come in.

It's like entering a different country. First, the house is surprising: it's not covered with imitation brick like all the others on the concessions. It has the same shape – a cube with a steep roof – but on this base the man had done some elaborating. Unsquared logs had submitted to the builder's fancy, curving outward to form the eaves, twisting in flattened arches above the windows, interlaced like clasped fingers at the corners. The wood has the patina of age and weathering. Between the horizontal timbers the caulking, enriched with dust, makes a home for moss. The house is alive: verdure and flowers hide the foundation and flourish in the window-boxes. On the roof, hairy with grey mosses and pink with mould, the shingles curl as if they were not of cedar. In the yard there are many small buildings constructed with the same fine taste. Fences of branches, woven in a repeating pattern, join the buildings, making enclosures where chickens, pigs, and sheep live their animal lives. Even the manure pile looks neat, as a precious asset should. Everything is orderly and clean. There's a garden swing, with two facing seats and a lath roof. And a sound that mixes with the animal noises: aspen, birch, and hazel trees stir the air with their supple branches, and from all those tiny leaves comes a sound like the flight of a flock of birds. Dam-Bogga lives in a country very far from Abitibi.

The feeling of strangeness is even stronger when the boys enter the kitchen. In the half-light heavy with good, unfamiliar smells, the woman is embroidering. She gets up and opens her arms in welcome, laughing softly. The words she says to her husband are brief but weird as the mumbo-jumbo of a magic spell. At Dam-Bogga's reply she blushes, looks across at Godbout's house and rushes to the little shrine, where a votive light burns before a statue standing between two icons.

She touches a blessed branch and crosses herself. At once her good humour returns. She hugs the boys, then, seeing the dried blood below Robert's nose, drags him to the sink and scolds him gently, laughing as she washes his face.

"Ya ouverena, shto ty pooralsia, malrchichki vsye odinakovyie, vsye poskorei mujikami stat khotiat. Ouj skolko ya rezbitikh nosov nautiralas."

Rémi takes the chair offered by Dam-Bogga, who points to Robert: "Village? They not like settlers. Not good, village. Here good. Very good."

The room is homey, warmed by its varnished woodwork. A harmonium stands sleepily in the corner under braids of onions and bunches of dried herbs losing powder from their leaves. Bottles of pale-coloured preserves line the shelves and sausages hang from a beam. A great pot is steaming on the stove. The whole place is redolent of comfort, food, and peace.

"Godbout bad man. No fear God. Not good."

"What makes him bad?"

"Devil in him!" exclaims Mrs. Dam-Bogga, slapping the table. "Before, good fellow. Work hard. But . . . hee hees! Wife run away with Settlement Inspector. He mad, gets nasty."

The woman lays her rough hands on the table polished by use and far too big for two.

"Ouj kohetchno oni ne obedali, zdes poiediat. Skaji im. Doust siadout. Skaji im."

"You eat here," Dam-Bogga translated.

"No, thanks. Just a glass of water."

"Not water. Milk. Good cows, good milk."

The woman understands and brings two cups and a pitcher. Timid and reserved as she had been at Réginald's place, here in her home Mrs. Dam-Bogga is lively and at ease.

"Vyieti leta vsye maltchichki vsegda golodnye."

Paying no attention to the boys' protests, she slices bread and spreads it with butter that runs before the knife. She also brings a kind of cheese in soft, humid, tiny rolls. "Good, no?" the man asks. "Every thing make here, bread, cheese, butter."

The woman watching them wolf their food, nods contentedly. The man seizes the excuse to go to the cupboard and bring out a bottle. He pours himself a small glass of liquor with some herb embalmed within it. His wife casts a glance at him that is half reproving, half anxious. But he says, *"Radost moia,"* and she nods, smiling, understanding that he's celebrating this small joy of their visit. He lifts the glass to eye level, smiles in turn, very broadly, knocks back the drink at a gulp and groans with satisfaction. He sets down his glass and goes to the harmonium. His finger points quickly to a frame filled with photos showing boys and girls in cap and gown. His voice is full of emotion.

"Children in city. Doctors, engineers. Not settlers. Nice blond children, like my country."

He's beaming with pride. The woman's eyes take on a dreamy look, and she wipes away a tear as she comes to herself again. Dam-Bogga sits down again.

"Like it here?"

The boys, their mouths full, nod vigorously.

"Good country. Hard country. Work hard, country give. I make hay in front your place. You help me?"

"Sure!" Robert exclaims.

The woman pats his head.

"You know all the people here?" Rémi asks.

"Yes, all. Thirty years we here. Work, raise family, work, do everything. Children in City. Rich. Education. Thirty years happy. What want know?"

"We met an old man in the woods not far from our place, on the other side of the creek."

"White beard? Long hair?"

"Yes."

"Ha ha ha. Old madman. Prospector before. Now crazy. Breaks stone, looks for gold. No be afraid. Not dangerous."

"We're not scared of him. Where does he live?"

"Old cabin Saint-Dominique way. Don't be afraid. Not like Godbout. He dangerous. Stay away."

"We have to go now. You can count on us, we'll help you with the haying."

"Good Simard boys."

The woman says something to him and disappears up the groaning stairway.

"Just wait," says Dam-Bogga.

She comes back with two jackets carefully folded, one in wool with coloured checks and the other in buckskin with fringes down the sleeves. Rémi tries on the buckskin and Robert the wool and they parade before the delighted eyes of the old woman. She imagines her sons are there again.

"For you."

She laughs at her own accent, then, giving them a bottle of her black current wine, adds, "For your modder."

Out on the road again, turning their backs on Dam-Bogga's leafy world, they find themselves back in Abitibi, on the sideroad with its silent barrier of spruce that shuts out the world. Mrs. Dam-Bogga stands watching them for a long time, and her husband has to console her, because she begins to weep for no reason once she is back inside the house.

Réginald calls out to them and they join him. He smells of horse, sweat, and work and his soaking shirt clings to his skin.

"Sonofagum! It's too hot to work. I'm unhitching. Where are you fellows coming from?"

"The village."

"Ha ha! Robert. You had a fight. Over a girl?"

"Heck, no just a dumb guy."

"That's it, my boy. Show those assholes in the village who's boss."

"They know it now."

"You walked all the way? Goin' home now? Why don't you come in a minute, take a rest."

The black stallion pulls angrily at the long halter rope tied to the aspen in the yard. He whinnies and paws the ground.

"Hey, sonofagum, I showed him a thing or two today. He's a stubborn bastard, he's vicious, he kicks and bites too. But he's met his match. He'll soon get used to the whipple tree. By winter he'll be quiet as an old nag."

Rémi smiles discreetly. In this latest confrontation the horse no doubt had been victorious again. The house smells tempting. Sonia is making a pot of boiled vegetables.

"Hey, we got company! Are you all by yourselves? Walking in that heat. Sit down, you're going to eat here."

"Thanks, I'm not hungry," Rémi replies.

"Well, I could eat a bite if it's not too much trouble," says Robert.

"Eat, sonofagum. Fightin' makes you hungry. Keep it up. Kids have to fight. You just stay the way you are, don't let anybody tread on your toes. Hey, Rémi, I'll bet you're quite the fighter too!"

Rémi knows he's being kidded.

"I get other people to fight, that's smarter."

"It's sure not braver," says Réginald.

"He's right," says Sonia. "You've got to be smart, not brave. You've got to make other people do the work for you in this world if you want to get along. It's that or be a slave."

She's defending Rémi. Réginald gives her a cold look and for a moment a silent, deathly duel crackles in the air between them, incomprehensible to the boys. Rémi, pretending not to notice, lays his jacket and the bottle in the stairway.

"What. A bottle of wine! Gettin' ready for another jag, eh?"

With this little joke Sonia defuses the atmosphere. Though Réginald laughs his head off Rémi decides not to be angry at him.

They take their places at the table. Robert is facing the window and Rémi understands why his brother wanted to stay: he's not hungry, but he wants to get a look at Martel's house. There's washing hanging on the line and no doubt the woman will come out any moment to take it in. While the others eat, Rémi sips at a cup of weak tea. Robert is sneaking glances out the window. Sonia is feeding the little girl and Réginald is talking with his mouth full.

"So uncle went to town this morning."

"Yep," says Rémi.

"He took Méo and Blanche along. You can guess where the two o' them's goin' to spend the day."

"Where?" asks Rémi, out of pure politeness.

"At the hotel gettin' drunk, just like you did the other night. Ha ha ha!"

"Réginald, don't talk like that about Blanche and Méo."

"Hey, sonofagum! These little guys have eyes. They know, they understand. They're next thing to men!"

"That's true, they're real little men!"

Robert has stopped chewing, his eyes are sparkling: the neighbour woman is taking in her wash. Réginald, at first perplexed quickly sees the light.

"Aha, Robert! I caught you. So, that's how it is, eh? You like those tits of hers, eh, ma Martel's, eh?"

"Yaaah!" gasps Robert.

"Well at least, sonofagum, you're not ascared to say what you think. But it's true, she has a great pair of knockers on her. And look at those gams!"

"Réginald!"

He looks mockingly at his wife.

"Jealous, are you? You got no reason. Your own aren't so bad, ya know."

And he rejoins Robert in their occupation as voyeurs. The neighbour woman goes about her work, unaware of being observed.

"Hey!" shouts Réginald. "There's the daughter. She's a sex-pot just like her ma."

"I like the mother better," says Robert.

"What do you know about it, sonafagum? That girl's goin' to be quite the woman, let me tell you. Eh, Rémi? Diane, there?"

"Don't know."

"Hey hey hey! You're the sly kind, you are. Th'other night there you go outside with her, dead drunk, I'm darn sure somethin' went on."

"Réginald," Sonia says in a crisp voice in which anger is not far off. "What's got into you today? That's no way to talk in front of kids. And our daughter!"

"The little one? Look at her, sound asleep in her chair. And these boys, they're no kids any more. If they don't know now, it's time they learned. At that age, now I. . . ."

"Yes, we know all about that."

Sonia takes Sophie in her arms and carries her into the next room, which has a curtain for a door.

"Réginald, would you come and pull down the covers?"

"Rémi, away you go, you're closer than I am."

Rémi gets up, trying unsuccessfully to disguise his haste. The curtain in the door flails like a wing. In the half-dark Sonia is whispering, "Pull the covers back."

He lifts a corner of the wool blanket. His elbow brushes her arm, their skins touch for an instant and strange waves weaken his knees and turn his legs to butter. Sonia leans over to lay down her burden. Her odour submerges Rémi and sets his temples throbbing. She tucks the little girl in, lays a hand on Rémi's shoulder and guides him toward the doorway. He's certain everyone can hear the crashing beat of his heart.

"About time," Réginald cracks. "I was just about to go see what's goin' on."

He laughs at his own joke and Rémi turns red. Oh, he hates himself for showing his feelings over every little thing.

"That was good," says Robert by way of thanks.

"After a good meal, a little drinkie. How about a little creme de menthe, boys?" Réginald asks.

"Réginald. They're not used to drinking!"

"Rémi is. And I'm sure Robert would like a drop."

"Sure, I'll have a drop."

"See what I told you? Get the bottle and four glasses." She gives a glass to each of the drinking buddies.

"Careful, now, it's pretty strong."

"Call that strong?" says Robert.

On his second glass, Réginald rolls a cigarette, stops, looks out the window.

"Mother Martel has her washing in and young Diane's on her way over."

Oh, no! thinks Rémi. Not her. He tosses back the rest of his drink and holds out his glass to Sonia.

"I might have a little more."

"Come on, take care, Rémi this is very potent stuff."

"Give him some more Sonia, it won't hurt him. Aha! You want my tobacco too, eh? Would you look at him roll that, Sonia. I told you they were gettin' to be little men!"

Happy in the middle of the cloud he is exhaling, Réginald finds it great sport to watch the boy roll a cigarette. A real little man, as he said himself just now. Robert is surprised. He doesn't understand the sudden change in his brother's attitude. Even the tone of Rémi's voice takes on authority.

"Here, Robert, roll one."

Sonia looks worried.

"Boys, don't be in too big a hurry to play grown-ups. Enjoy your own time."

"Oh, when I was their age I was workin' like a horse for my old man."

"You're still working like a horse. Nowadays they're better off getting an education."

Réginald feels attacked.

"What have you got against workin' with your hands? That's a man's work, the only real work. Earn your bread by the sweat of your brow. It's only fairies wear white shirts and push pencils."

"May be, Réginald, that may be, but your fairies are doing O.K. getting other people to work for them and putting the money in their own pockets."

"What do you know about it? A woman's good stayin' in the kitchen and lookin' after her kids. It's up to the man to do the hard work."

"They do the hard work, and they curse, and they drink and they run after girls, is that it?"

"That's life. Woman in the kitchen . . . and in the bed, ha ha ha!"

"Réginald!"

"Nothing to stop us doin' it in the afternoon, the kid's asleep and it's too hot to work."

Sonia is unable to answer. Someone is knocking. Without waiting Diane Martel comes into the overheated kitchen. Rémi avoids her eye, but puffs harder on his cigarette and blows the smoke higher. Sonia points to Sophie's chair.

"Sit down. Have some tea?"

"No, but I wouldn't mind some of that."

She pointed to the bottle of green liqueur. Sonia gives up, shrugging her shoulders as she goes to get a glass. Réginald thinks it's funny.

"This afternoon we're goin' to tie one on, all of us, an' then we'll all go to bed together."

"Not enough men," says Diane.

"There's three of us."

"You call them men?"

She jerks her thumb at the Simard boys. What for the others is nothing but a joke is a cutting insult for Rémi, denial of his virility. Oh, he'd like to beat her up. His fists would send her flying. Maybe some day he'll strangle her to make her swallow her rotten insinuations.

Robert merely says, "Listen, shrimp, I don't waste time on ones like you, I send them to get their mother or big sister."

That did it. The girl is flabbergasted, her grin frozen on her lips. Rémi stares at her triumphantly as if the witticism had been his invention.

"Don't you think that's enough, now?" asks Sonia angrily, offering Diane a glass. "Let's change the subject. That's no way to talk at your age. And Réginald, you let them do it! You egg them on. You should be ashamed! This isn't a tavern here."

"You, you're nothing but a spoil-sport. Get off your high horse. At their age you'd already bust your cherry. Don't try to say different, your brother told me so."

"Don't go too far. That's enough of your foolishness. This bottle's going back in the cupboard."

"Just keep your hands off that goddam bottle, will ya? Take a drink instead, it'll loosen you up. You're worse than an old maid."

Robert laughs. Diane runs her tongue sensually over her lips, looking provocatively at all the males in turn. Sonia slumps onto her chair. She knows it's useless to argue. Réginald is off and running and nothing and no one will stop him until the bottle's empty. Anything she says will be turned against her, will only make things worse. She knows about the touching of knees beneath the table, and she sees Diane ogling and challenging the boys and even Réginald openly defying her. But she will not make a scene, not even a remark. This would give Réginald a chance to floor her with an insult. The young girl is telling a very daring joke about a wedding night. Everybody laughs loudly except Rémi, who is concentrating on his third glass. When he looks at Sonia he understands her distress and turns away again. She can't count on him for an ally, he is as powerless as she is, tied hand and foot by the memory of his humiliating moment that night by the red truck. Diane is no doubt just waiting for him to provoke her so that she can make a fool of him.

Diane is being friendly to Rémi as if she were giving him a chance to redeem himself. But he's suspicious, and ignores her. Robert and Réginald are giving her enough attention as she sits there fluttering on her chair. Rémi can't forget Sonia's sad, defeated eyes. Oh, if he could only call up a frightful anger that would shake him out of his stupid reserve and embarrassment, an anger that would blind him and burst the bonds of reason and restraint, he would turn the table upside down with all the glasses and the bottle, upset the chairs and their occupants and rush out through the screen door. Get out, never again set eyes on this kitchen of her tears. But first he would spit on Diane, punch his brother in the nose, knock out Réginald, and place a consoling kiss on Sonia's forehead. Oh, if he could even get up now and leave, saying nothing!

Sophie is waking up. Sonia, shaking off her lethargy, picks her up and takes her out the front door, hiding with her body the scene of jollity at the table.
"Carmen! Carmen!"
Her neighbour appears at the door of the next house.
"Carmen, can I send Sophie over? Keep her for a while? Don't look for Diane, she's here."
The other woman acquiesces with a wave. Despite the distance she got the message: she also has a man and some bottles. Sonia would have liked her to call Diane home, but she won't insist. She goes back inside. She goes back in though no one notices her return, and she sees the kitchen in a mess, the plates piled in the sink, the ashtray spilling over onto the table and the smoke rising in the sunlight. She hears a conversation of drunks and the dirty jokes she's known for an eternity. Is this her life? She runs into the bedroom and they can hear her sobbing hopelessly. Rémi jumps up but freezes in mid-flight, embarrassed at his reaction.
"Right, go and console your cousin a bit."
Rémi doesn't budge. A joke? A trap? A serious suggestion with no malice aforethought? He can't tell from the tone.

"Get in there, sonofagum, pat her on the shoulder, tell her she's a danged old fool. Get goin', you little fucker."

Réginald punctuated his order with a blow on the table that made the glasses ring. This time he means it. Rémi goes into the bedroom and, from behind the curtain, hears others joking in the kitchen.

"Don't worry, that one's not dangerous."

Laughing, Réginald replies to the girl, "Never mind those two. Come on over here, you little devil. Sit down here between Robert and me. We got things to talk about."

Then there's nothing in the kitchen but laughing, giggling, and the sound of liquor being poured. As Rémi approaches the bed his cousin's sobs make him forget the rest.

Sonia is curled up on the turquoise chenille bedspread, her face hidden in her hands, her dress riding half-way up her thighs. The protruding line of her hip makes her waist seem even slimmer, and one arm is pressing a breast against the bed. Rémi is ashamed about noticing such things at such a time, and disapproves of his own thoughts. He hesitates half-way across the room. Partly excited by her pose, but disconsolate at her sobs and hiccups, he is filled with compassion and real tenderness; yet he can't forget Réginald outside, and the possibility of his bursting in. Fear, always fear. Fear of Réginald's tongue, fear of going back to the kitchen, fear at the woman's grief, fear of being caught in the middle, of not finding the right words, of not being up to the situation, fear of his own fear. He goes nearer. Her misery is so far beyond anything he has ever seen that he can't help being fascinated. The way you're fascinated by an injury, in spite of yourself, even knowing in advance that you'll be shaken by what you see. Oh, the pretentious wish to heal.

He lays his hand softly on her shoulder, touching the skin of her neck, fancying that this may be how to calm her tears. But the sobbing, stopped for a second by her surprise, only starts again with greater violence. Rémi lets his hand stray to her hair, and tries to think of nothing at all, to be no more than a presence. He sits down on the edge of the bed and Sonia turns toward him a drawn face where streaming tears have left a silt of make-up. Her reddened eyes are pitiable, and her mouth, white teeth biting at her lower lip, is frightening. He tries a smile that turns into a poor grimace. Sonia, her cheek against the boy's thigh, is swept away by fresh waves of sobs. He feels very childish in the presence of this adult grief, very much a boy who is ignorant of women's lives and finds himself for the first time a spectator of such sorrow: not a furtive tear that's no more than a sign of sensitivity, but a bruising, rushing torrent, uncontrolled and savage. Rémi, moreover, is a poor lifebuoy at which to grasp, for despite his compassion he can't help feeling her tears wetting his thigh through his pant leg and her burning breath curl on his skin. He can no longer even control the beast that writhes between his legs with no sense of the moment's solemnity. Rémi is ashamed of his undisciplined body. He would like to be far away, never to have become aware of this tragedy, still to be a carefree little boy. Yet he cannot go. If only Sonia doesn't suspect what a despicable comforter she has! She takes his hand, presses it between her own and holds it tight to her heart as if to slow its irregular gallop. He can feel it beating wildly against her rib cage and at the same time his thumb and wrist are directly against the weight of a breast and its soft flesh. Stranger to pity, his penis swells. All the blood has fled from his brain to gather in this shameful organ. Mad desire flashes across a mind devoid of thought: open your hand, grab her breast, feel it, knead it. . . . Shame, Rémi Simard, shame on the bad Samaritan. No, no, no! Rémi struggles fiercely, beginning to weep first silently, then aloud. Sonia, when she realizes this, sits up, takes the boy's face in her two hands, wipes away his tears with her thumbs and kisses his reticent lips. Rémi is close to fainting: this breath heavy with mint and burning, this taste of salt from her cheeks, her insistent mouth, these eyes, so close to his, with tiny drops caught in their lashes.

He understands, or thinks he does: all she wants is someone near her, a human contact, a communion, however fleeting, between two souls. But even that is too much, and Rémi bridles. He's afraid of losing his head, afraid of Réginald appearing through the curtained doorway, afraid of yet another humiliation in front of Diane. Sonia has no ulterior motives, her only desire is a moment of friendship in a wretched life, but Rémi refuses. He calls reason to the rescue, reminds himself of the princess of the haunted house to whom he owes fidelity. All in vain, his insides are throbbing monstrously. Ocean depths yawn before him, he has lost his hold, the struggle becomes futile, he gives up and burrows with his lips in the curve of her neck. She begins breathing heavily. And he shuts his eyes against the oncoming waves.

"Rémi, Rémi. . . ."

"No, Sonia, keep quiet, just let me come. . . ."

"Rémi! Rémi!"

It's Robert calling. Rémi gets up quickly, pushing her slightly.

"Rémi, come on."

Rémi is standing beside the bed, avoiding Sonia's eyes, until she turns on her stomach, also to avoid his. He moves toward the doorway, trying to hide his swollen crotch. At the curtain he stops. His guilty face must be a complete giveaway. Guilty of what? He has no reason to reproach himself, except for his desires. Réginald's order to console Sonia was only partly obeyed. But he is red with shame and will be accused of what did not happen. Yet aren't his soul and his feelings those of a guilty person?

"Rémi!"

To hesitate longer is impossible. He must take the plunge, rush out through the curtain as if hurling himself into a fire. Diane has left, cousin Réginald is dozing in his chair. Robert, who has already picked up their new jackets, is hiding away the tobacco he has filched from the table. Rémi relaxes. He has nothing to fear. He taps Réginald on the shoulder.

"Huh? What?"

Réginald wakes with a start, shakes his head, lifts up the empty bottle, and smiles.

"We're leaving now."

"Well, that's all right, kids. Sonofagum, don't breathe a word of this to your parents."

He sees them out and hooks the screen door after them, shouting through it, "Come again."

Robert heads directly for the road. Rémi lingers for a moment. He can hear voices from the bedroom, low voices punctuated by shouts. He rushes off after his brother. He hates them all, Réginald, Diane, Sonia, even Robert, who's singing to himself.

"Shut up, eh?"

"Lemme alone, I'm O.K."

"Drunk."

"Drunk. And what about you? You, the big brother makin' me drink and smoke! What does that make you?"

"Nothing!"

Robert sings on and Rémi hangs his head. He's hurting. A moment ago near Sonia he'd felt like a superman, and in fact had been nothing but a weakling crushed by his own lack of will.

At the roadside, in front of her house, Diane stands holding a doll. She watches their approach with a pout of disdain. Robert looks her up and down.

"That's right, go play dollie. That suits your age."

"Oh, you, you're his brother, all right. A real pair of scaredies."

"Go and change yourself, your diapers smell of pee."

That makes her furious and she throws the doll at them. Rémi catches it on the fly and makes off with it.

"Give back my doll."

"Cry!" orders Robert.

"Give me my doll."

She really seems to want it back. Rémi decides that it's all her fault, the things that are happening. She's the one who made Sonia cry. And the gossip about him, Rémi, in the village. It's a great chance for revenge. In a rage he rips off one of the doll's arms and throws it on the road.

"No! Don't do that."

For once he has the upper hand over her.

"Here. Here. And here."

He tears off the other limbs and throws them at her, then, before her horrified eyes, separates the head from the body and tosses the trunk in the ditch. Robert stops him as he is about to get rid of the head as well.

"Keep that for a souvenir."

"Yeah, you're right. Good day, Miss Martel."

"You'll be sorry, Rémi Simard. You're going to pay for this, both of you."

They look back frequently to make faces at the girl, who is still standing there. Then the spruce trees hide them from the hate in her eyes. They plunge into the corridor of the road, hugging the south side for shade. Suddenly Robert calls a halt.

"I can't go on. I'm getting dizzy."

"What d'you expect? All that drink, and the sun."

"How'd it be if we opened the bottle of wine."

"No. D'you want to come home drunk?"

"No, but it'd be fun to be like we were back there. Everything seemed funny. And I'm thirsty."

"It's not far to the little stream. We can stop there."

Robert begins to whistle, stuffs his hands in his pockets, and zigzags along kicking pebbles. Rémi is thinking about Sonia's tears. For a moment, there in the bedroom, she was transfigured, no longer the ordinary, workaday wife of Réginald, putting up with his faults and submitting in silence to the burden of her work, but distant and superior, of the same blood as the princess, Sir Rémi's Lady. He would like his as yet unknown princess to have a body like Sonia's. He imagines her, small and slender, speaking some unknown tongue, which he, however, would understand as one understands the meaning of tears. With her the doughty knight of darkness will know no internal struggle, but will let himself be carried away by the whirlpools of voluptuousness, or rather will hurl himself into their midst with all his might. And the princess will have Sonia's body: well-turned legs, white thighs, rounded hips, and slim waist, breasts in good proportion, a warm neck, and kisses sweet as wine. Sonia's body, in short, but not her face. The princess will have an unusual face, one that couldn't be confused with any other in the world.

Not far off they can hear the trickling of the little stream. They can't feel it's cool air yet, but they have word of it from the scent of marsh marigolds, the vibration of a half-submerged branch of dogwood, or the chirping of a pair of cedar waxwings.

What if he'd chosen Sonia as his Lady, instead of a hypothetical princess, as Robert had chosen Carmen Martel? No. He had no right to doubt the existence of the Lady of the haunted castle. And anyway Sonia lacked mystery. True, she'd revealed something about herself when she was crying, but maybe that had been just Rémi and his own emotions. . . . When she was younger, before living with Réginald, Sonia could no doubt have been a Lady. But not now that life had snuffed out the dream in her.

On the road just ahead a fat bird clucked, a spruce grouse, almost black with a bright red brow above his eyes. He was afraid, but hid it well, striding high on his toes, his throat swelling and his tail displayed. He was trying to impress them. . . . Robert picked up a stone.

"Let him be," Rémi ordered.

The cock, head high and nodding with each step, his glance threatening, advanced majestically. Under his ruffled feathers he was trembling with fear, and as soon as he neared the trees he crouched low, pulled in his neck and trotted quickly away beneath the branches.

"I could have got him," said Robert, put out.

"Why kill him? He was funny, he reminded me of you."

"Pff!"

They kneeled on the wet moss in which the tiny stream ducked out of sight and reappeared, spread out in a pool, slipped over a rotten log, and went on its way again. They drank on all fours.

"Hey, I forgot to ask you: do you love her? Our cousin, I mean."

Rémi was surprised.

"Her? No!"

"But. . . ."

"I don't love her. She's nice, that's all."

"And in the bedroom there. . . ."

"Nothing happened in the bedroom. She was crying so I consoled her."

"Consoled lots of women, have you?" Robert asked, half-incredulous, half-mocking. "How do you do it?"

"Nothing to it. It's easy."

"What did you say to her?"

"Oh, I don't remember. A bunch of things."

He wanted to change the subject.

"What about you and the Martel kid?"

"Nothing. Réginald didn't either, but not because he didn't try. She's not shy but she's tricky."

"I hate her. I mean it. Look."

Rémi brandished the doll's head, holding it by its kinky hair. "A trophy of war!"

"You know what, Rémi? Let's keep it in our cave. Are we going there tonight?"

"We may be too tired."

"And you said we could spy on people."

"That means more walking. Are you game?"

"We can rest tomorrow. Today's like a feast day: I had a fight, we got drunk, tonight we can drink the bottle of wine, and I've got the tobacco I stole from Reginald."

"O.K. We'll run around all night being knights. I'd like to see what happens at Godbout's place."

"And Martel's. Gee, it's great being a knight."

96

"And it's going to get better. We're going to win our Ladies."

"Yeah? I wish I knew how."

"Everything in its own good time."

They're lying on their backs, hands behind their heads, watching the sunlight filter through the sharp needles. The green light is tinged with the thick odour of spruce and the silky smell of crushed fern. Between these, barely perceptible, an earthy hint of broken mushroom. The spruce trees are friendly, their branches fanning out to make a conical roof. Rémi is reassured by their presence, and notices that on closer acquaintance each one is different. Robert has been asleep for a short while and now his brother follows his example.

They are awakened by the voice of the spruce grouse, the cock they had seen before, now marking off his territory and showing his discontent at their invasion of it. The tree shadows have turned. The bottle lying in the icy water awaits their pleasure. They return to the road. A car is coming, they can hear the flying gravel hitting metal. It's their father. He picks them up, and their little sister, her dress smeared with ice cream, gives them a joyous welcome. Their father asks about their unkempt appearance and they say they've been working all day for the priest. And the man walls himself up in his usual silence. He seems worried.

Their mother is in a bad mood. She spent the day bored and alone; the gasoline motor of the washing machine had refused to start, the pump lost its priming, in short, nothing had worked as it should. She hasn't heard a human voice, including her own, since morning, and to add insult to injury there was the dead screen of the T.V. set staring at her. What could be more ridiculous than T.V. in a house with no electricity? The mother declares she's had it up to here living like a savage. During supper the atmosphere is tense, and the boys need no urging to take their little sister outside to play.

They were sent to bed, even before sundown. Françoise went to sleep without waiting for the end of Robert's story. There was the muffled sound of talk from the parents' room downstairs, sometimes with a word that could be distinguished. The tone seemed sharp. Robert was snoring. Rémi opened the window, knelt with his elbows on the sill and leaned out. The fires of sunset caressed the cedar shingles of the abandoned house. Dusk seemed to ooze upward out of the earth and already lay deep in the hollows. On the hilltop, behind the Creek of the Curse, the spruce were bronzed, and just above them a thin spear of cloud turned violet. The slight breeze seemed out of breath, perhaps because of the sounds it bore along: the trill of the red squirrel, the hammering of the woodpecker, the cries of night-birds waking, and all the other unidentifiable noises, songs, complaints, murmurings of plants, the grating of horizons where the sky bears down with all its weight, the age-old stretching of the bones of earth.

The night was coming, his darkness of the Knight, and that was so much more important than human problems. Rémi watched a long time as a red fox trotted up the road, ears pricked prudently forward. It stopped, seemed to stare at him, then slipped off into the tall grass and disappeared among the tress. Rémi turned back into the room. The murmurs and louder words were still there, though he tried not to hear. Grants, settlement, problems, solitude, loneliness.

It was too much. They might have the decency to whisper. The boy didn't want to know about family business, nor even that it existed. And now his mother was crying! That made her a woman! Right now she must be a little like Sonia! No! She was his mother, nothing else.

He opened himself wide to the outdoors, closing himself off from the life within the house. An owl, dazzled, landed clumsily on the roof ridge of the house next door and his claws rattled on the shingles. He smoothed his feathers, took a few proud steps, turned to look east, and showed his great, round eyes in which you could read his impatience to be off hunting. His throat trembled and his *who-who* filled the sky pricked with stars so pale that they were outshone by the lightning-bugs in the grass. The owl sailed off on his silent wings, and a whole string of bats scrambled from the eaves into the air, scattered, and melted into the grey light.

The doves of the princess! Her messengers! Not for her the white birds of peace, proud daytime birds, high-flying. For her, what else but these black beasts with their erratic, nocturnal flight! Mammals, thought Rémi, winged monsters with pointed teeth and giant ears, night monsters, the only creatures that could follow the Knight in his wanderings and bring a message to him. Rémi could see himself riding fearless through the dark, a bat perched on his wrist. What a sight! His soul cried out toward the house of shades.

"I heard, princess. It is I, Rémi, your knight. I am coming, I'm coming, only be patient, I will set you free and you shall be mine, sweet princess."

A bat came dodging above the shed, swooped just in front of the boy's face and disappeared with its sound of flipping pages. The princess had heard and understood!

It was quiet downstairs now. Rémi put his ear to the floor. His father was snoring. His mother must be asleep. Should he do the same thing? He was tired, but his excitement was stronger than his fatigue. He shook Robert with one hand and gagged his mouth with the other.

"Not a sound. Get up. The time has come."

"Eh? What?"

"The night is here. Silence. Get dressed."

"I'm tired."

"Up, lazy one. The night awaits us."

"Tomorrow."

"No, now, oh Knight-of-the-Lady-with-the-Big-Breasts! Adventure calls us. Listen!"

"It's an owl."

"The cock that crows for the aurora borealis. Come, we are going to see your lady."

"Okay, I'll get up. Quit shaking me, eh?"

There they are, back in the grass wet with evening dew, picking up their staffs and rucksack and heading west. Venus emits her tranquil fire and, on the right, the Big Dipper already lies horizontal, slowly tipping backwards. The earth is cool but the air is warm, even hot in places, like the breath of some great dragon. The great, supple body of the night crushes the road in its folds, and its flank is teeming with life, insistent, loud, hurrying to perpetuate itself before the dawn. In the midst of this racket the passage of two humans is hardly noticed. The spruce trees part to let the road go by.

Rémi begins talking loudly.

"Tremble, beasts of the night, fear for your secrets, genies, the Knights of Darkness are upon you. The earth shall open to divulge the treasures of its bowels, the air shall be torn like a veil. Have patience awhile, sweet princess, the doors of the castle shall give way before my courage. Bow your head, O night, be quiet and submissive: the knights are here, the silent conquerors."

"Silent, he says, and he's talking his head off."

"There are words that are like silence. Are you afraid?"

"No. And not just because there's two of us with sticks."

Méo's clearing. The house is a dark, lifeless mass. The inhabitants are asleep or, more likely, absent. Suddenly an incredible crashing noise emerges from the hedge of firs. Branches crack and break, there is a swishing, silky sound and a shape appears. The boys freeze where they stand, their fists tight around their clubs. An immense animal is coming their way. A horse? More like a mule. A moose! With a surge of his back muscles the animal climbs out of the ditch, and his hoofs clatter on the pebbles of the road. He stops, caught in the net of smells emitted by the two boys. In his great eyes are stars, and a bluish light that runs to his tear-ducts. Rémi, his heart already beating madly, jumps a foot when Robert touches his arm. Robert's face is so pale it is fluorescent. The moose snorts to clear his nose of human smell, and Rémi is frightened. They have to do something.

"Attack. Come on, Robert!"

Their staves hum as they whirl around the boys' heads, the animal is tense and a muscle flutters in his thigh. The knights attack, howling, and the moose takes off in a spray of gravel. In two bounds he reaches the bush, and there, in his element, he disappears with scarcely a sound. The boys are standing on the exact spot where he had been. In the air a trace of his presence hangs, a subtle smell that recalls the zoo. Rémi leans on his companion, his knees trembling. Robert is jaunty, but he's breathing hard.

"See? We're stronger than anything!"

"I wasn't scared, just surprised. But the moose was surprised too. And he was scared, strong and all as he is."

"Just wait till I tell them about this. A moose, and right up close. No more than fifteen feet."

"What do you mean, tell? Tell who? You're not allowed. We can't tell other people the secrets of the night."

"That's true. We wouldn't be able to go out after dark any more."

"Don't worry. You'll see, it's more fun to know and tell nothing than to go boasting about everything. And the fun lasts longer."

"Are there things you hide that way? Even from me?"

"Er . . . no, I tell you everything."

At Martel's place only one lamp is lit, and it's turned low, but at Réginald's there are intense white rays beaming from the windows, projecting far into the dark before growing weak and ineffectual. Things are happening at their cousin's place, and that's where the boys decide to go. On all fours they crawl up beneath one of the kitchen windows. As they might have expected, a card game is on. Réginald, Sonia, Carmen Martel, and Dam-Bogga are playing. Sitting out the hand, Méo and Blanche await their turn to replace the losing couple. It's the usual ritual: exclamations, the deal, glasses of liquor, clouds of smoke rising to the Coleman lantern. This is a weekday party, not as lively as Saturday games. Not much fun to watch. Rémi draws back, pulling Robert with him.

"Why? I want to watch!"

"We'll come back."

They cross ploughed land where the twitch-grass roots lie like shiny, thin worms, and they come to Godbout's place. A hay-rake abandoned to rust and weather provides a hiding-place. On the other side of the road a light flickers. It's the candle that's keeping Mrs. Dam-Bogga company as she waits at home. Invisible, her black dog barks as he patrols his land. He has smelled the intruders. They advance in a crouch, hugging the wall. They must be careful, there's nothing but a mosquito screen over the open window. They risk a peek. The man gets up from his rocking-chair, which continues to rock and squeak. He shakes his fist in the direction of Dam-Bogga's dog, which is still barking.

"God-damn whelp! One of these days I'm gonna shut your mouth for good."

He knocks his pipe against the cast-iron stove and the ashes fall like black now in to the grey dust on the floor. He fills the pipe again, lights it, and begins marching up and down the room.

"It must be time. Shut up, you god-damn dog!"

He fiddles with the knobs of his radio: hissing, crackling sounds, beeps and modulated wails, sometimes strident, fill the air, and at last a voice, quavering and distant, announces news in an unfamiliar French. The man sits down, listens attentively, punctuating the revelations from the world at large with blows of his fist on the arm of his rocker, or a volley of spit directed at the floor. Music follows the voice. Godbout goes back to pacing up and down the kitchen, cursing as he goes. He goes as far as the door, comes back to the stairs, stops exactly where there is a squeaky board, and returns to the door again: a bear in a cage, or a prisoner in his tiny yard. His footsteps leave a trail in the dust, as if it were snow in winter. The boys quickly adapt to his movements, hiding when he comes from the door and faces them, and rising to watch him as soon as the board has squeaked and he has turned away.

Godbout doesn't pay attention to the music. He repeats the snatches of news that he remembers and recites them like a legend with infinite implications, interrupting this with comments and curses, mixing up the stories and thus creating new events even more horrible than reality.

"A sputnik! They've launched a new balloon in space, a new star of steel. Yesterday they were talkin' about it. That's the end, the trumpets will sound the world's end, the iron curtain will veil the sun, the end! The end! Terrible, terrible! Ha ha! Wonderful! Jehovah the all-powerful will save the just. I'll be saved, and Ricard will perish with his canaries and goldfish. Ha ha! And you too, you bitch, you'll die like the she-dog you are. You'll die, your guts will rot, a corpse among corpses."

He stops facing the wall in front of a photo whose glass is broken and can no longer protect it. He spits in the face of a woman already badly stained by tobacco juice. He paces up and down again, vociferating, cursing, calling on the furniture to witness the truth of what he says, raging, shouting, threatening the pope and all his bishops, damning the cabinet and all members of parliament. Finally, out of breath, he stops once more before the photo of his former wife.

"God damn you! I gave you the very best and what did you do with it? You wanted to ruin me, you plotted with Public Works to make me lose the contracts and my bulldozer. And I lost them. Don't tell me it was the election, and a new party in power, it wasn't that at all. I knew you were goin' behind my back with those people in Public Works. Just jealous. All of you were jealous of my success! I should have killed you that time, I was too good to you. I wanted to give you a chance to reform. I was a silly bugger, believing the priests. Feed your hog more, he'll shit at your door. Fuckin' whore, an' it's your fault I went broke on the job. You turned their heads when I wasn't lookin' and played the sweet innocent in front of me. You musta laughed when you and your pimps had me licked. Jealous, envious bitch! You knew you were guilty an' you wanted to drag me down to your own level. Sure as hell it was you set fire to the buildings."

He spits a great gobbet before proceeding. "Oh, that was a good slap I gave you! But not hard enough, I was taken in by your bawling. I was too good, I listened to your excuses. Yeah. Jealous, was I? Sick, was I? Imagining things, eh? How could I doubt your love, right? But time proved me right. I wanted to give you the benefit of the doubt because of the teaching of the false God. I brought you out here with me to help you, free you from temptation and cure your soul. We could've been happy on this lot but you screwed me again, you run off with that dumbbell inspector, the only man ever come here. I guess he got a surprise when he found out what kind of a shit-pile he'd ended up with. Thought you'd hurt me, running away, eh? Ha Ha. But I was the winner, the insurance paid up. And then I found the true God and I understood what had happened to me. You were the devil's tool, and sought my ruin. I was Job and you were my boils. Your tricks turned back on you, I'm saved and you shall perish, you rotten whore, you priests' carrion."

Godbout goes back to his radio and twirls the dial until he finds a voice. It is speaking in a singing language, full of vowels. He listens as if he understands, as if concentration could reveal the sense of the words. Suddenly his face lights up. "Roma!" He's caught a word.

"Roma, Roma, the Vatican, fornication and corruption! Den of the apostles of Satan. May Jehovah crush them all with his just wrath. Let him send them to everlasting death and damnation with the Russians, the Germans, the civil servants, the English. And the Chinese, and the others, and Ricard's settlers. And you too, you cow!"

He lights his pipe for the tenth time, cocking an ear toward the speaker. For a long time he continues listening to the newscasts, to the world destroying itself a fragment at a time. Robert gives a tug to Rémi's sleeve and they go back across the ploughed field.

"Crazy guy!" murmurs Robert.

"Not too bright. I wouldn't even like to give him a scare."

"He's the scary one."

A door slams at Réginald's place and a shadowy form appears on the road. It's Dam-Bogga coming home. They crouch down and the man passes, plodding. The dog starts whining softly but stops when his master speaks to him. When the sounds tell them that Dam-Bogga and his pet are in the house, the boys slip off to Réginald's place. Rémi looks up at the night and the beauty of its stars twice as large as usual, throbbing, it seems, quite close to earth. A great bird awakes, flaps its wings, and goes to sleep again. It's the aspen tree in the yard. In the stable the horse whinnies. He too heard the moving wings of the tree-bird. Again the door slams and voices are raised. Rémi crouches low. Mrs. Martel is going home alone by the little path. The tree gives a start as she passes, but does not wake completely. She is not quite alone. Other footsteps on the road echo hers. She says, "Good night!" and Méo and Blanche reply from the road. The boys hear them talking as they grow more distant, talking to keep each other company, so as not to think of the dark around them. The night's silence closes in again like wavelets subsiding in a pool. "All the others tear the dark as they pass with their smell or their noise or the light of a lantern. And pass is the word, they're scared of the night, they don't live in it but hurry through it. Only Robert and I live there. And we send out no waves."

At Réginald's the light goes out. Robert makes the first move and his brother follows. By a wide detour that takes them past the stable, they head for Martel's house, the only one with a light on. The truck is not in the yard. Carmen puts water on to heat and settles down to darn socks. Heavy shadows make her breasts stand out even more than usual. Rémi joins his brother close to the bedroom window. "She's in the kitchen." "Her husband must be away working with the truck." "Rémi, I want to see her when she goes to bed. The blind isn't right down, but the window's too high. I jumped up just now and hung onto the sill, but my fingers slip an' I can't hold on. Go on your hands and knees and let me stand on your back." "And what do I get to see?" "The main thing is for me to see her. She's my lady!" "That's true. Have it your way." They have to wait. Robert keeps an eye out for possible movement in the house and waits for the rising shadow she'll make when she stands. Rémi, feeling left out of the coming events, has turned his attention to the spaces of the dark. What a sweet world it is, bathed in night! The souls of things ooze out through their surfaces and dissolve appearances, and everything takes on its true aspect, so different from that of daytime. "She's making a move," Robert whispers. The woman goes to look at her sleeping children, then comes downstairs again, and carries the lamp into her bedroom. "Down!" Robert orders curtly. Robert climbs onto his brother's back and his eyes just reach the space between blind and sill. With a big towel over her arm she comes in carrying a basin and a large jug of steaming water. She sets them down near the lamp and goes to shut her bedroom door. As she returns to the basin her hands fumble behind her back to find the zipper. Robert stamps with anticipation: she's going to undress to wash and he'll be able to see it all! "Hey, stop walkin' on my back!" Rémi complains. "Shhhh!"

"Is she in bed yet?"

"Shut up. I'll tell you in a minute."

Carmen faces the mirror. He sees her in half profile and, in the glass, almost full face. She's in her brassière and slip, stark white in the yellowish light. She lets her hair down and it flows over the curves of her shoulders. She tosses her head and the hair flies behind her back. She soaps her face and neck, raises one arm, and the black bouquet of hair in her armpit opens and spreads. Robert hasn't eyes enough to see everything at once, body and reflection, the graceful line of her back, her slim waist with barely a ripple of fat above the elastic of her slip, her belly which, one surmises, must be flat, her chubby bottom. And above all her breasts, which more than fill their little bonnets seamed in concentric circles. They bounce with her every movement, and Robert's inner life shakes and shivers with them.

"Quit kicking or I'll dump you."

"You do and I'll choke you to death," Robert growls.

"What's goin' on?"

"Later, later."

Carmen Martel unhooks her bra. Robert's breathing has stopped and his heart is racing. His hands clutch the rough wood of the sill. In the mirror two haloes stare at him like giant owls' eyes. Rémi, gritting his teeth, submits to his brother's trampling. At each brief respite he wonders what on earth Robert is seeing. What can she be doing that has him so excited? His shoulders and back are already sore, his neck is stiff, and his tendons are twitching. Rémi doesn't mind doing a favour but he can't hold out much longer. At last, after an interminable wait, Robert jumps down in the grass and runs off whining like a wounded beast.

Rémi straightens up with difficulty, tries out his stiffened joints and limps off behind his brother. It takes him a while to gain his stride, and he doesn't catch up until the edge of the forest, where Robert has tripped on some bushes and is lying there, weeping.

"Robert! Hey!"

"Oh, it hurts. It hurts! Oh, if you could have seen how beautiful she was. I couldn't even tell you!"

"How was she?"

"Naked, stark naked. Her white skin. Her black hairs. I'll never forget that."

"Well, tell me, eh?"

"I don't want to talk about it. She's my Lady."

"You're right. It was better for only you to see her."

They remain silent for a long time, then return to the road. They're opposite Méo's house and through the uncurtained windows can see two shadows at the table, busy drinking no doubt.

"Want to have some fun with them?"

"No, Rémi, I need a drink first."

"You're as bad as the two of them."

On the road, between the trees, the air seems to be warming up, growing stifling, full of the irritating whine of mosquitoes. Robert is speaking softly about Mrs. Martel and his voice is weary.

"What more do you want?" asked Rémi. "You saw her naked. Aren't you satisfied?"

"Sure, it was great! But the more I think about it, the less I can see how she'd be interested in me. What am I to her, eh? A kid, just like her own."

"You're going to win her, just wait and see."

"Winning means forcing her, I can't do that!"

"No, it's seducing her."

"It's being the master, a winner."

"No, Robert. You get the right to seduce her by making an effort, making the right kind of efforts."

"Yeah, know-it-all. Who did you ever seduce? Anyway, you've got to be a hypocrite for your system. Just like you. You get to be the master because you're bossy."

"Imagine she sees you coming and she wants you, she kisses you and makes you feel you're special and she says, I'm yours. Wouldn't you like that?"

"Sure, but that's never going to happen. It's a dream. She doesn't even know I'm alive. But if I used force, I'd be sure to get something."

"The trouble is, you've got no faith."

"I've got my feet on the ground."

"You do? Look down: can you see your feet? Can you see the ground? No."

"That's because it's dark. I can feel it."

"You just think it's the ground. A flea thinks the same thing on a dog's back. You think that what's under your feet is the ground and not an animal's back, though you can't see it, but you don't want to believe in a dream. I'm telling you, Robert, at night, dreams are as real as the solid ground."

"Force. . . ."

"You and your force. It's far weaker than patience. What about this force of yours? With her build, ma Martel could take you to pieces and throw you out in the garbage. And she wouldn't even be out of breath, unless she died laughing. You wouldn't like getting laughed at, eh? The only way to win her is my way. Real strength can't be seen and it makes no noise. It's all in your heart and head."

"Well, how do you want to start?"

"I don't know yet. We've got time, time and the dark."

"I hear the stream. Let's run."

"That's right, Robert. Run, don't think."

They slake their thirst. The water has a faint taste of moss, of black earth, of roots. They recover the bottle of wine. Robert pulls the cork with his teeth. To escape the mosquitoes that swarm in the underbrush, they go back out on the road. There they take turns drinking long draughts of the cold nectar from the bottle.

"Robert, let's go to Méo's and scare them."

"Great!"

They take their time on the way, and when they reach the clearing the bottle is half empty.

"Look at those lightning-bugs. That gives me an idea. Let's catch a bunch of them."

"I'm hiding my stick and the bottle here. Can you remember the place?"

In the grass they quickly capture a good number of fireflies, which shine between their closed fingers. They slip behind the house and huddle by the little log stable. There's a strong smell of molasses and alcohol. The still must have been working the last few days. In their palms the boys crush the bugs into a phosphorescent paste. Rémi paints his brother, giving him shining eyebrows, two small horns on the forehead and a line down his nose, a little beard on the chin.

"Open your mouth, show your teeth."

He smears light on the incisors.

"Wow! You'd scare Frankenstein. Go out in front near the window where they're sitting. I'll toss a stone on the roof, you hammer on the glass and show your face. I'll make more noise back here and you can make your getaway. Meet you at the bottle."

The stone hits the chimney and bounces down the shingles. Rémi dashes to the door of the house, Robert raps on the window pane and howls are heard from within. Rémi rattles the front door and takes off for the stable. Another stone hits the roof and rips loose a shingle that rattles to the earth. Robert explodes in a whinnying, jeering laugh, Rémi laughs with him and the clearing resounds with their mockery. Silence reigns inside the house. The boys meet in front.

"Let's get out of here. I can't stand any more," begs Robert, holding his sides.

"Just a second, here's the kiss-off."

Making a megaphone of his hands, he shouts, "I am the master of the dark. I shall return. I love the stink of alcohol and sin."

And they stampede off so that their laughter can safely explode. Robert collapses on the road and Rémi holds himself up by the branches of a spruce. They laugh until they can laugh no more for aching ribs. Almost calm again, they march off singing:

Onward march, onward march
Soldiers of Christ on guard,
Onward march, onward march,
Soldiers of the Lord.

After another drink of wine Rémi does his version:

Onward march, onward march,
Knights of the dark on guard,
Onward march, onward march,
The darkness is our Lord.

They both adopt the new version, adding a comical or irreverent note at will, singing of the charms of Carmen Martel or recalling the fear they put into Méo and Blanche. Their shirts stick to their backs and the sweat attracts the black flies. The boys run to escape them, but in vain: they are there in swarms as soon as they stop. They drink, and heat and fatigue added to the wine produce a delightful euphoria. By the time they reach the edge of the forest their gait is rather uncertain. Here the trees disappear, leaving the broad desert of grass that swells upward into the hill. The moon is on her throne above the horizon, and in her velvet light they go forward as if on a heavy carpet. With a thousand precautions, holding back any expression of joy, they pass their own house. After the abandoned house, which Rémi salutes with a deep bow, they caper along to the bridge at the Creek of the Curse. Between its shining banks the light runs as thin and turbulent as the water itself.

Following the creek, Rémi boldly calls to the genies, "Up, you cowards! Come up, dead genies, hidden genies,

genies of our gold. I command you to come and lie down at our feet."

"They're not goin' to come. Wait, I'll dig one out."

All Robert's fears have vanished. He goes down the steep clay bank, feels around blindly and comes up with a hard, round stone.

"Got him."

"Bring him up."

Rémi takes it, cleans the surface with his fingers and raises it to eye level to decipher its lacy signs.

"Wretch, your masters are about to do you an honour of which you are not worthy."

"Should we break it?"

"No, Robert, we'll put it up in our cave."

Soon they're near the pool, in front of the round mouth of their grotto. They plunge into the bowels of the earth, or rather are swallowed by them. The stub of yesterday's candle lights up their den and they go over the inventory of their possessions: the heel of a bottle of wine, the two votive lights swiped from the church, the genie in his stone coffin, the package of tobacco, and one doll's head. Each thing recalls an action or a special moment.

"It's getting crowded in here."

"Let's empty the bottle, that'll be one thing less."

"Robert, we've got to dig a cupboard."

Rémi goes out and returns with their tin can. Finally their cupboard looks like a niche.

"Like in church, where they put the statues."

"Imagine Ricard's Virgin in here."

"Yeah, Robert, we need our own Virgin, different from the others. We'll do one out of clay, the way you made the tits."

They collect clay from the stream and by the flickering candle-light patiently mould a woman's body. The saints have draped robes; this one will be naked. The saints have nothing feminine but their faces; this one shall have exaggerated charms, enormous buttocks, a vulva half-way up her belly, heavy, pointed breasts. More from weariness than inspiration, Rémi decides to stick the doll's head on the statue's shoulders. The effect is startling: an angel's face on a demonic body.

"Fantastic!" Rémi exclaims.

The round stone marked with strange signs is imbedded in the floor of the niche. "An altar-stone," Rémi reflects. The statue is put in place, legs wide apart, one foot on each side of the stone that serves as a pedestal for a votive light. That light is now lit with some pomp. It sheds a reddish glow around it and a white beam upwards. The flame trembles as the boys breathe, and flickering shadows give the clay body life and movement.

"You'd think she was dancing."

The goddess twists and weaves. Only her head is motionless.

"I love her," Rémi murmurs.

"She's moving for us. She loves us."

They finish the bottle in two swallows and light a cigarette. The cave is soon full of smoke. Robert laughs for no good reason, staring through the acrid mist at the black virgin's wriggling body. He leans over and, despite the flame of the votive light that scorches his chin, plants a kiss on her still-damp belly.

"That was good, Robert. I'm sure she liked that."

He coughs.

"Great Goddess, made from the blood and earth of the creek, protect the Knights of Darkness and crush their enemies."

"Protect the knights," Robert repeats.

"Let them discover mysteries. Give them strength and courage. Guide them to win their Ladies. Crush their enemies."

"Amen."

They meditate for a moment.

"I'm going to find her a flower," says Robert. I've got to get out of here, I'm choking."

They clamber out. Robert takes off his clothes and jumps in the little pond. He splashes around, terrifying the frogs and crushing masses of eggs in their gelatine womb. He breaks off a water-lily, rinses the winebottle and sticks the flower in it.

"Here, Rémi, bring that to our Virgin," says Robert. "I'm goin' back in the water."

Rémi, on his return, strips as well and jumps in the water, shouting, "Shut up, you drunk!"

They wrestle and shove, wreaking havoc in the frogs' retreat.

"Dare you to catch me."

Robert dashes off through the elders and dogwood bushes, Rémi at his heels. It's exciting to run in the dark. They utter guttural cries, groaning like beasts, calling and taunting each other. Never mind the stone that hurts a foot or the twigs that scratch a thigh or the dead branches that slap at an arm or cheek, they run right to the foot of the hill where the rows of conifers begin. The first branches open before their rush and whip back after they pass. Running in the underbrush where the ground is coated with soft moss and rough lichens, the boys begin to love spruce trees, learning how friendly they are. Trees with leaves are stubborn and never give in. But spruce trees bend and let you through, with only a murmur as they close again. Once you've passed two or three of them you're safe: they hide your passage with an innocent air: "Nobody went this way!" Their branches are soft and even their needles are supple. You'd think they would prick you, but no! They bend and leave the feeling of a caress on your skin. Like a hand on your stomach, your hips, or your back, like fingers on your thigh, your arm, or your cheek.

At the top of the hill the boys regain the mad pace they had lost in the climb. They stumble as they run and the spruce trees push them this way and that with sweeping gestures. Laughing and choking, they emerge on the road, where the sharp stones bring them to a halt. Facing them are the impassive moon and, below, a whole section of the forest singing. In the sea of spruce there's an entry, pierced by man, no doubt, but unused and filled, in time, by aspens. A melody of water mingles with the rustling leaves.

"Want to go on?"

"Let's go."

They cross the road, hopping on tiptoe, push through the fringe of elders and are back among the aspen. Female trees. A schoolyard of happy girls, loud-voiced, excited, with here and there a larger adult, well-behaved and severe. The trees grow silent when the boys come, then whisper behind their backs. Hostile, they try to prevent them from passing and a detour is necessary to avoid their treacherous branches. Rémi slaps one on the trunk as he goes by. The tree's leaves chortle, with much disdain but also a touch of pleasure.

"Imagine, Robert, going at these with an axe!"

They are stunned and a little fearful at even entertaining the idea. They laugh loudly to cover up.

"Robert, listen, will you?"

It's the trickling sound of a distant waterfall, good to hear when your body is covered with sweat and mosquitoes.

"Come on, let's have a look."

They follow a zigzag course, pushing at trees that resist and catching at a young sapling that gives in ungracefully. After they are gone the class of young aspen buzzes with discontent. The boys pay no attention. They're concentrating on finding the waterfall. What they find is stagnant water. It has risen onto the moss and bathes the feet of the trees, and, as they progress, grows deeper. And they come to a clearing in the forest where pale tree stumps point to the sky. On the other side of a felled tree, its leaves still green, extends a wide, still pond.

"What's that?"

"A beaver pond, I guess. Yes, look, over there, it looks like their dam."

They walk around the little lake and cross the narrow mud causeway. In the middle, a thin trickle of water follows the overflow and spatters down among flowers and leaves, colourless in the night. They had thought they'd find a great cascade: illusion of the dark and the echoing woods! Rémi rips a branch from the dam. Its bark has been gnawed at and the tips are bevelled to a point. "This must empty into the Creek of the Curse. Let's follow it."

They wander for a while, then reach their creek well above the bridge. They make their way down the slippery stream bed, sometimes at a walk, sometimes at a tear-ass pace, whipped by the water's muscles. The frogs, who moved back into their kingdom while the humans were away, maintain a prudent silence on their return. The boys' euphoria has disappeared and a great weariness takes over. They pay their respects once more to the Goddess. Rémi touches her belly, which the flame is gradually drying. The statue is showing cracks. She is fragile, he reflects, and they'll have to take good care of her, often starting her over.

"Robert, tell our Virgin what you saw in Mrs. Martel's room."

Like a litany the boy recites the forms and movements of his Lady. In the light his hands model those things for which words fail. He grows excited. To show, and to remember, he carves on the ceiling, with the pointed stick stolen from the beavers, the lines of his Lady's body. Threads of darkness cling to the crumbs that line the furrows of his drawing, making it stand out.

As they crawled out the moon was setting fast. The haunted house was silent, despite the strengthening breeze. Not a squeaking board was to be heard, not a scratch on the shingles, not a whistle from the cracks in the gables. As if the house felt threatened. Rémi was saddened by this. He would have liked to go there and reassure the princess, but Robert dragged him home. It was only as they climbed the spike ladder to their room that they realized how tired they were. They had trouble clambering over the roof's edge. Robert opened the window, listened for a second, and went in without a sound.

"You coming, Rémi?"

"Hand me out my buckskin coat."

"Haven't you had enough? I'm dead, I'm falling asleep, and I've got a headache. You know how late it is?"

Rémi wrapped himself up and leaned back to watch the silent, deserted house in the slanting light. Nothing, no one was awake there, it was a house of the dead. The princess? He called her softly, inaudibly, waited a long time, but she didn't appear. Slowly his body grew stiff, and he was acutely aware of every aching muscle: here it was a cramp, there a painful twitching, a trembling like a nervous tic, a sensitive knot. Or he would feel a stretching or stiffening of tendons. The breeze was growing stronger every minute. The distant spruce trees had begun a hissing sound, and the grass was rustling, the house of the princess groaned. A great wind now swept across the hillside, heavy with dust, twigs, and leaves. The night grew more dense, lit with a flash of sheet lightning and was dark again. Swift, frightened clouds scudded past the moon, which seemed to flee. Then it was submerged. In the north, one last star blinked its signal and all the sky was hidden. The wind was still rising, whipping at the fringes on his jacket. The castle whined.

Then a violent scream split the night. Rémi was up with a start. He stared and stared but saw nothing in the blackness. What animal was powerful enough to utter such a cry? And there it was again, hoarse and bestial, prolonged into a strident howl. Rémi trembled. The house had grown quiet again, though the wind had not let up. The princess and her chateau were afraid. For a third time the animal clamour overpowered the wind and lashed Rémi like a whip. He felt the cries were addressed to him; some giant creature had hurled down the gauntlet. He was terrified and apprehensively scanned the crest of the hill, expecting to see some giant or monster head appear. Had he not upset the genies and provoked the secret forces of the dark. In the constant roaring of the wind he sought the echo of a heavy step. Nothing came. The enemy had issued his challenge and was waiting somewhere in the depths of the dark. For a moment Rémi regretted having invented his order of knighthood and venturing on to unknown ground. What if he went to bed, as if nothing had happened? Robert would never learn of his lapse. But he himself would know, and that would turn his chivalry into a mockery or a game, nothing more. What about his oath? A shingle flew off the haunted house. The princess! She was counting on him and he had almost taken to his heels at the first threat of danger. She was to be the monster's victim. If it was challenging the Knight, this was because only he stood between the monster and its prey.

Despite the fear tying his insides in knots, and partly because of that fear, Rémi climbed down from his vantage point. On the ground he found his staff, a silly weapon, no doubt, but he would fight if it cost him his life, and the princess could be proud of him. He carefully walked around the house and stopped to try and see something. Nothing there. He waits, and there is the voice again, menacing, insulting. Rémi advances through the tall grass that whips at his legs. Above, torn clouds hurtle across the sky. The wind is cunning, bearing treacherous grit that gets between your teeth. The heavy air makes breathing diffi- cult, and an invisible arm is tight around his chest. You'd think the elements were in league against him. None- theless, he marches toward the hilltop. On his left the ranks of spruce bend under the gusts and whimper calls to prudence. Prudence! The time for that is past, now is the moment for daring and courage! And something is driving him toward his meeting with the enemy. Pride, perhaps? It seemed that knights had been very touchy about questions of honour. The boy's brain blacks out at times, he has an

118

after-taste of alcohol, and his stomach is rebellious. Holding his staff horizontally before him to break the squall, he tries to concentrate on the notion of a battle. That's it, he must think only of struggling, fighting, vanquishing!

At the summit he stops and stares into the dark. Below, five hundred paces away, he sees it. Disguised as a poplar tree, the monster rises to a dizzy height. There's no mistaking it, it's certainly the evil beast. Disguised or not, he can hear its frightful breathing. Rémi is terrified, discouraged. The enemy is standing upside-down, legs in the air. From the crotch of a black cloud a titanic member descends to deflower (O monstrous debauchery!) the parted thighs of the poplar. A sacrilegious fornication that discharges floods of wind. What can a poor, small Knight do, alone with his staff, to stem the lechery of the elements? But Rémi marches on.

At closer range the illusion is shattered. Stripped of its bark, like a dead, decapitated trunk, a shining, rigid log is plunged into the fork of the tree, raising ripples of bark. The beast is roaring at the boy who has spoiled its little game, and the wooden penis is transformed into an elongated head in which woodpeckers have carved innumerable eyes. The thighs have turned into what they had always been: arms raised up with hundreds of knotty fingers. The beast lets out a frightful cry designed to terrify the enemy. So this was what Rémi would have to fight against! And he must take great care, for the beast is a thing of deception and illusions. But now it must give up this hollow pretence of being a tree, passing for a poplar with a bark of diamonds: Rémi will not tread in its cunning trap.

He is close by it now and the monster has still not moved. Is it so sure of itself? What can Rémi do? Rip at it with his nails, bite it, beat it with his naked hands? He makes his rush and twice the staff falls on the hollow-sounding trunk. Whistling, a branch falls down and crashes at Rémi's side. Others follow, and Rémi hugs the trunk to keep out of harm's way. Aha! Defend yourself, will you?

So you didn't like my little beating! (Probably only its pride was wounded, for its armour seems capable of warding off any blows.) Rémi is exhausted, Rémi is cold. He must rest a moment. No! He has to fight! It's the enemy who's trying to make him think of rest. Another cunning trick. Hitting with his staff hurts his hands, so Rémi hugs the trunk in his arms, without being able to encircle it completely. He pushes, shoves, squeezes, pulls. No use. His muscles risk snapping like strings but the poplar barely shivers. Rémi strains in a fresh effort to down his adversary. In vain. His arms have gone slack, a sour after-taste of wine rises to his mouth and his vision blurs. A pause. He lays his cheek against the rutted bark. The tree cries out again and Rémi's blood runs cold. He should be grasping, attacking, but he is totally exhausted. He looks up to see the whole body of the trunk and suddenly the magic of the tree world is upon him. Before he can react the images attack him, powerful, violent and obscene. He tries to drive them away: almost succeeds, he thinks, but weakens, and before his eyes the monster becomes flesh. In the crotches of its branches tufts of lichens wave. Stumps of branches stand erect, licked by the wind. Open forks pulse lasciviously. The trunk is nothing but a gigantic, writhing pile of bodies, a totem pole of all the boy's hallucinations: breast shapes where the tip of a sucker makes the nipple, buttock bulges where great branches join the trunk, mammiform gnarls, thigh-like curves, beckoning branches, winking knots, thick lips. Rills, cankers, frost clefts – the bark has a thousand vulvas where Rémi's fingers wander. At his belly a crack opens, softened by a touch of moss. His fingers penetrate to the tree's heart where soft fibres throb. Without a thought he pushes his penis in it, grips at bulges on the bark, and thrusts forward. In spite of the pain, in spite of irregularities that scratch his tender skin, he mounts the leafy creature. The monster grows excited, the trunk pushes against his belly and aids the coupling; and while the boy groans in an orgasm of agony, the poplar utters an interminable cry that vibrates in the air and earth.

Rémi collapses on the ground. He is vanquished. Then he leaves the place, bent beneath the weight of shame and desolate with failure. His staff is dragging behind him, the wind jostles him, mocking, the grass entangles him; and as he reaches the crest of the hill the tree-monster howls its victory cry. Rémi ducks into the cut-grass and crawls a few feet to be out of sight of his triumphant enemy. He weeps a while. The sky is growing heavier again, the clouds hang low, the gusts become violent and Rémi shivers. He sets off again and reaches his room without looking at the princess's castle. Bed, at last! Sleep, and forgetfulness . . . The princess must be sorely disappointed in her so-called knight. Now she is at the monster's mercy. Dawn must be near, but no birds wake to announce it. Only this whining southwest wind that knows no rest, and the cries of dead things that protest it. Oh, to find a sleep that's deeper than death, to waken days later having forgotten this defeat, forgotten even knighthood, the dark and the princess! To become just a small boy again with no superhuman oath to keep . . .

Sleep came at last, crawling with nightmares. Trees, trees, and more trees. The outraged aspens in their school-yard, girls with pointed breasts and smooth cheeks, teachers with opulent chests despite their nun-like virginity, they all pointed at him with threatening branches, him, the impious invader, the disturber, the tool of evil. They screamed for vengeance. He scattered them with a gesture and they giggled with a rustling of pleated skirts, but their call had been heard by the monster poplar who hastened to them with giant strides. The spruce trees warned Rémi and he had time to flee. His feet slipped, however, and he made no headway. The avenging tree drew near. In vain the spruce trees lamented, begged, protested; the poplar turned a deaf ear and, leaning over, scooped up the boy in its claws and raised him to the heights where clouds rubbed past. The aspen surged together again and demanded his punishment. The tree-monster, holding the boy helpless by one foot, swinging and shaking him, trampled on the castle of the princess, then, standing in the ruins, tore Rémi's limbs off one by one and tossed them to the delighted aspens. The boy's still twitching trunk was salvaged to serve as a dildo, with which the monster penetrated its oozing clefts, Rémi's head plunged into swollen lips chapped by some shameful malady, his face crashed into rotten wood, and his nose filled with the smell of mould. At last, howling with joy, the tree hurled this poor body slimy with sap high into the air filled with the cheers and laughter of the aspens. Rémi was falling endlessly, but the spruce held out their soft arms to catch him. They missed, and he plummeted to the earth, crashing into the cave and crushing the Black Virgin. Paralysed, Rémi saw a tree approaching, whose tangled branches formed the features of Diane. She had come for the kill, followed by the other tree-girls. She lifted one foot dripping with roots and it was the end. Her foot came down, the rootlets stifled him filling his eyes, his mouth, his nose; he was suffocating and the weight was breaking his rib cage.

Rémi woke with a start, his heart pounding, his breath catching. His mouth still had an earthy taste. He went to the window but the drama was over. Heavy rain blocked his view and even the house next door was invisible. Perhaps it had disappeared with the princess, through his fault and weakness. He slept badly for a strange slice of time.

His mother woke him. It was still raining.
"Ten o'clock. Are you all right, Rémi?"
"Sure. "I'm just tired. The rain . . ."
"Of course. Sleep till dinner time, we'll eat about noon."
After she left he glanced out the window. It should have been daylight but everything was a dull grey. There was no colour, no light, no relief. And the rain trickling down the window distorted the outside world. Perhaps it no longer existed. Rémi slipped off to sleep until midday, and this

sleep, at times almost penetrated by the sounds of the household, brought him rest. Robert was sitting on his bed, speaking softly. "Hey! Was that a night!"

"Yep."

"It was great. I can't believe it."

"Yep."

"You don't seem too happy about it. What's wrong?"

"Nothing. I'm still tired."

"Did you go to bed after me?"

"Just a bit."

Robert doesn't insist. He goes downstairs again. Through brief breaks in the storm Rémi is relieved to glimpse the shape of the castle, unsubstantial though it is and half obscured by driving rain. His princess is still there! But the beast, too, is there, waiting for the propitious moment. He has no appetite for dinner. He rocks glumly for a long while in the rocking-chair without being able to drive the tree-monster from his mind. Screwing a tree! How could he have given in to such abrasive sorcery? He's guilty of a great crime and can confess to no one. Even Robert wouldn't understand. Will the princess forgive him? The enemy is devious, full of magic tricks and evil charms, but that is no excuse. Nothing, no, nothing can justify defeat. Perhaps . . . perhaps it's not too late to act? Rémi gathers his courage and talks himself into a properly aggressive state of mind. An hour later he announces that he's going out. His mother finds this unreasonable, but he insists that he'll "go crazy if he stays cooped up."

Protected by a slicker and rubber boots, he goes out in the driving rain. In the shed he finds the axe he wanted, heavy and sharp, the one his father keeps for himself. The ideal weapon. What do future scoldings matter? The urgency is great!

The wind is still there in force, wild as an animal. To make headway Rémi must push his way through the repelling elements. They mustn't slow him down, nothing must slow him. At the top of the hill he sees the monster in the same place, big as ever, touching the low ceiling of the clouds. It's daytime, but such a gloomy day that much of the night's mystery remains. Far from being frightened by this, Rémi feels strengthened by it and calls on the Black Virgin as he presses on. The hoary poplar, seeing him approach, trembles with rage. The nightmares of yesterday flash through the knight's mind but cannot weaken his determination. The combat will take place, and death is the only possible outcome. Rémi stands for a moment sizing up his adversary, staring it down despite the flood of rain across his eyes. Twice the tree utters its war-cry, but Rémi is not to be deterred.

At last he moves nearer. The beast waves its arms in a frenzy and hurls down a dead branch, easy enough to dodge. Rémi rushes at the trunk. The monster whistles in the clouds, each of its eyes becomes a vociferating mouth, spitting its venom. Rémi draws back a pace and raises the axe. He hauls off for a harder blow, which he aims at the vulva he had known hours earlier. The axe bounces harmlessly off the hard bark. But the whole tree resounds from top to bottom. Plaintive or jeering? With the next blow the blade bites in and sends chips flying. Again, again, again. Soon there is a deep cut and the chips are brown and corklike. The beast at bay throws down a few branches in self-defence, but the wind bears them away. Rémi is protected, he's standing close to the trunk. Despite his fatigue he chops away and the loosened scales are strewn on the ground. One good blow and the steel is into the sapwood. The tree shivers, touched in its tender flesh. There's a sinister cracking and a sound like an avalanche: the great ligneous phallus, which doubles as a head, breaks off and tumbles down, dragging branches with it. Rémi ducks and the log falls wide, bursting in an explosion of rotten wood. Aha! The beast doesn't hesitate to mutilate itself when cornered.

"Aaaargh!" he grunts. "I'll get you, you bastard."

The axe falls regularly now, and the chips fly and hide in the grass. The wound is bleeding copiously, but that may be nothing but rain washing out the cut. In the tree's hollow belly things are coming loose and falling. Death is approaching the monster, and it knows. No more projectiles are launched and, since its decapitation, its voice is silent. Suddenly the axe caves in the thin abdominal wall and enters the belly. When the axe is withdrawn a trickle of brown and yellow dust follows. Rémi thrusts his arm into the breach. The tree is hollow, to a far greater extent than he had realized, and the flesh is thin beneath this breastplate. Now Rémi is sure he'll win. Stubbornly he chops at the wound, from which its plant entrails escape at every blow. The belly gapes open, but the monster is tough. Rémi is growing weary. The axe slips from his hands, its shaft wet with rain. He leans back on the tree without even picking up the axe. The wounded monster can do no harm now and will never get back its strength sufficiently to prevent the kill tomorrow. Rémi will be there.

Homeward he goes. Already the sting of yesterday's insult is fading, the ignominy of his fornication forgotten. The princess has nothing to fear, nor need she doubt that her knight can defend her, despite his weaknesses. The axe, carefully wiped and oiled, is back in its place. Not a trace. Rémi returns to his rocker. He smiles to himself, and, for little Françoise who climbs on his knee, softly sings the lament of the "handsome sergeant and the young girl of sixteen." His mother, busy at her saucepans cooking supper, sings with him. In another corner of the room Robert is leafing through the Dupuis Frères catalogue. Rémi knows exactly which section holds his attention.

Their father had gone to Amos again that day and wasn't expected for supper. It was barely six o'clock and already it was getting dark. By the time their father came, at seven, it was pitch-black and the storm had turned to a tempest. From the car came Réginald as well, and his wife and little daughter. It was really a good idea for them to come visiting. Weather like that made you feel like company. The table was cleared away and ready for the card game. The newcomers told about the roads, and how there were washouts and great puddles at the low spots. Réginald's big laugh at times drowned out the thunder that rolled across the roof. The grown-ups sat down at the table and, for the first time since she came in, Sonia glanced at Rémi. Oh, just a glance, and he didn't see it. The game began according to ritual, punctuated like all their games by teasing, laughter, and stories. Nothing for the boys to do but wait for bedtime.

Suddenly, above the howling wind, they heard a sustained and distant growl that approached, passed the house, and took over the whole sky. Like a fiendish cavalcade in the clouds. Then came the flash of lightning and a crack nearby. They stopped to listen. There were marching boots and clashing blades, the shock of arms and cannons firing. A superhuman war was shaking the whole concession. Réginald spoke because no one else did.

"That reminds me . . . no, I'm not goin' to tell you, you'd think I was drunk."

"Let's hear it."

"Sure, tell us, we'll soon see."

"Well, today, I saw Méo and Blanche. Walking. In the rain. Goin' to the village."

"They must have been in a hurry."

"Listen, sonofagum, I'm not finished yet. The best part is why they went."

He paused impressively. Looked around. Let them wait for it. Then:

"They went to confession."

Astonishment, discreet laughter, incredulous exclamations. Réginald was knocking himself out. Then:

"Yep, yep, they went to confess. Them two. In that weather! Sonofagum."

"What got into them?" asked my father.

"That, uncle, is even funnier. And harder to believe."

"Out with it, Réginald."

Robert winked at his brother.

126

"Can you imagine . . . oh, sonofagum, this is good. Listen to this. Last night their house was attacked by demons. A whole pack of devils, and their leader was the Master of the Night, no less!"

To Réginald's great disappointment, no one laughed.

"Their devils come out through the neck of a bottle," said Mrs. Simard.

"That's for sure, auntie."

"Drunken foolery," the father said.

"Imagine," continued Réginald who had paused while dealing, "imagine the devil runnin' on the roof, and faces with horns at the window, Jesus! Sonofagum! And the best part was, Satan, he called himself the Master of the Night, he talked to them and threatened to come back. They didn't sleep a wink, and this mornin' off they go to confession."

"That'll keep the priest busy the whole day!" exclaimed the father.

For a few minutes they joked and speculated about the confession. A particularly violent thunderclap rattled the window panes and the dishes in the cupboard. Suddenly silent, they looked outdoors. All around the hill flickered one flash of lightning after the other. The night took on a bluish phosphorescence, invading the room on its three windowed sides and dulling the brilliance of the lantern. The thunder now rolled continuously, punctuated by crackling explosions. And the rain drove down and the wind moaned against the walls as it attacked. You'd have thought the house had been ripped from solid ground and was flying like a leaf in the storm. The two little girls were crying, and Rémi went to sit with them.

"I never saw the likes of that!" said the father.

"All hell let loose!" joked Réginald.

"Don't say such things. It's no laughing matter."

"Sonia's right," said their mother. "We'd be better to say a little prayer."

"Have you got a branch from Palm Sunday?" asked Sonia, visibly impressed.

The mother shook her head. Réginald was dealing.

"Right," he said. "A little prayer, everybody for himself. Aunt, you'd better pray that I'm going to give you a good hand. This is the one that wins or loses. Oh, yes! We should have a thought for Méo and Blanche. They must be scared to death. Even if the priest gave them absolution, their state of grace musta lapsed already, ha ha!"

Robert, from his corner, spoke:

"What if that business about the demons was true? You never know!"

"Wait a minute, little cousin. Don't believe everything you hear. Those devils were seen because somebody was drunk. Méo and Blanche had a drink at our place and then drank more at home. Sonofagum, with the skinful they had, they likely saw nothin' but a lightnin'-bug. Eh, uncle?"

"Hmm. Where there's smoke there's fire."

"Hey hey! Not so fast, eh? Just outa curiosity I took a look around their house. What did I see? Just a little look, 'cause I don't believe that stuff. It's true there was a shingle came off the roof, but their house ain't so new any more. And there was a moose track, fresh as you please, just thirty feet away, he must have made a little racket. And drink did the rest."

"Don't forget, Réginald, the devil does exist."

"Aunt, the devil is a bunch of old nuns' stories. Our father knew all those tales, enchanted fiddles, the devil at the dance, the witches' sabbath, the will-o-the-wisp, the werewolf, ghosts and goblins and the devil in form of a horse. Dad had seen him, too, but only when he came home sideways in the cutter. Your play, aunt."

"I pass."

"Me too."

"Nine in hearts, sonofagum."

Réginald picked up the cards, looked at them, and made a face. Lightning struck nearby. The blinding light was followed by an intense flash, and a shuddering of the

128

whole house. Françoise and Sophie, terrified, begin to cry again. Rémi herds them away from the windows and invents a game for them. A hairdresser's salon, with dolls for customers. Sonia smiles at him, and so that he sees it, mixes up names on purpose.

"Rémi, I mean Robert, you're right. Maybe there's some truth in Méo's story."

Rémi's glance meets hers for a second, but he looks away so as not to alarm her. He wants to show her by the way he acts that nothing really happened in her bedroom.

"Let's not talk about the devil," said Mr. Simard. "It scares the kids."

"Sure enough, uncle. But that bastard, he can carry me off if I don't make my nine in hearts."

"Réginald, don't talk like that."

"Sonia, you listened to my old man's stories too often. And you dream too much. Come down to earth."

"I'm down to earth. I've got no choice."

"Come, we're supposed to be having a little fun," said the mother, trying to keep the peace. "And with a storm like this on!"

"Some storm," said the father. "I thought I'd seen everything, but this beats all."

"Oh, I just thought," cried Sonia, "Carmen Martel's alone with her kids. She must be scared, the poor thing."

Robert leapt from his chair as he heard this and went over to the window to look out, as if that had been his intention all along. Mrs. Martel, alone in this hurricane! Horrible! If only he were with her he could comfort her, say all the things that would reassure her, caress her into forgetfulness.

He'd march into her house and say, "Follow me!" and she'd go where he led her. They'd go out and dare the storm, and the darkness would make him twice as tall. Arms and fingers outstretched, illuminated by the flashes, Sir Robert would not refuse the struggle. His voice would growl louder than the thunder, bidding the elements to be calm. From his fingertips, lightning bolts would leap to break the lightning in the clouds. All the powers of the heavens would pounce upon him, but he, with courage as a breastplate, would laugh at their efforts. And in this titanic battle the earth itself would tremble. Finally, his words and gestures charged with the powers of the night, Robert would throw open the secret gates of the air and lay the tempest low; and the wind would come to lie at his feet like a repentant dog.

The woman, terrified by the combat, looks at him now with admiration and gratitude as he returns to her side. She falls to her knees, rips open her bodice, and offers her bosom to the victor . . . With a final rattle the enemy breathes his last flame to light up these inestimable breasts. Robert graciously lifts her to her feet, blankets her in his shadow, and bears her off into the forest filled with beds.

The window is alive with grotesque faces. Robert draws back from the photons' whip. Should he go to her, defend her? He wouldn't really know how to fight the storm and she wouldn't be reassured by the presence of a boy. In the first place he'd have to walk three miles in the hurricane to get there. They'd never let him go out, and, what's worse, he'd never get up the courage. Running around the country under the stars with a brother for company was one thing, but going out alone in weather like this on a washed-out road among all the demons they'd just been talking about – he'd never make it. He could talk common sense to himself all he liked, insisting that thunder was only thunder and a washed-out road was still a road, that he knew the trees, and that he and Rémi were the only demons around, but he was still paralysed by a visceral fear.

What a humiliation. His Lady is in distress and he refuses to come to her aid. He would like to win her, though he only half believes the promise of old dreamer Rémi; but here, the first chance he gets to shine before her, he flinches. Out of fear. But had he not sworn a kind of oath? Damn his habit of getting dragged into all sorts of wild adventures by that Rémi. Sir Robert indeed. Does Rémi guess what's going on in his head? To hide his thoughts Robert stares out the window, despite the electric arcs that burn his retinas. He can see almost to the horizon. Nature is madly prodigal of its energy in an attempt to produce an ersatz dawn, a bastard of night and day, a dawn of horror. The road, pale blue in the darker field, leads off toward the navy-blue fringe of the woods' edge. Above it looms a lavender sky with yellow patches. From time to time all light goes out for a fraction of a second, only to burn and crackle more intensely afterward: forked lightning that leaves a luminescent trail, other flashes that are almost straight, but mostly shimmering sheet lightning hung over great segments of the earth.

The father is serving beer – beer fresh from the village, still cold, a rarity on this line where there's no such thing as refrigerators. Rémi has succeeded in keeping the girls busy and making them forget the fury of the elements. He gave them the start and their imagination is doing the rest. Now he's listening to the storm beating at the walls. Was the princess, barricaded in her castle, trembling with fear? Did she even realize that her knight had fought the tree and that he now was full of anxiety on her account? She was no ordinary woman, but she must share some feelings with the run-of-the-mill female. After all, right here in the Simard's kitchen, two women were scared out of their boots in spite of all the company they had.

The little ones were put to bed in the parents' room, and though the grown-ups were so near the children were still frightened of the shouting monsters outside the window. Robert, taciturn and glum, lay down beside them to still their terrors, and went to sleep before they did, snoring through their chatter. Rémi made himself some tea and took up his observation post in the rocking-chair, staring at his cousin's back. He saw the curve of her neck, her shoulders, her arms, her waist, and her buttocks pressing on the chair. He invented other faces for her, and even tried her with no face at all, making way for the future! But her shape, her size were exactly right for his princess.

The evening drags on, boring as all these card-playing evenings are. Luckily the boy's head is more spacious than any kitchen and inhabited by creatures livelier than life. But finally weariness drives him upstairs to bed. One last look outside at this unheard-of spectacle. The window pane is chattering with a broken sound. The storm hangs over the castle next door. It is resisting the attack, opposing its boards black with rain to the fiery meteors of heaven. In the flickering light you can see objects as clearly as in the dawn: the young fir trees, the dip at the Creek of the Curse, the cohorts of spruce. Rémi thinks of the prospector, who must be cowering at the notion of the genies' malediction; and of the beaver pond, which must be overflowing; of the flooded creek ripping out the flat stones in its banks. He wonders if rain is getting in their cave. Has the Black Virgin melted? Is the tobacco soaked, are the cigarette papers still good?

The storm rolls by and throbs above the creek and over the hill. The princess can relax, the danger's over. The detonations and rumblings diminish, chased by the wind. Rémi's corner of the world is plunged into darkness. Soon there is nothing but an intermittent light on the horizon, and a growling sound in the distance. The turn of others to tremble. Suddenly the downpour stops. The wind is still there, regular, monotonous. Rémi opens the window.

A far-away rumour speeds down the path the storm had slashed in the sky, a rumble as from the approach of a low-flying jet. It's a violent gust driving before it an atrocious lament of wounded things . . . The whole earth groans – stones, grass, trees, dwellings, and animals as well. Like a cry of deliverance. The roof trembles under the trampling of the west wind, the curtains fly around his head and the abandoned house makes its voice heard in the night. Suddenly there is a frightful cracking noise, a long drawn-out tearing ending in a dull, gigantic thud. Even the wind is shaken. It comes from behind the hill, and Rémi understands, clenches his fists and waves his arms. The monster, the enemy, weakened by the axe, has just joined the fallen.

Victory! Victory! Victory! The knight's strong will has vanquished the unspeakable beast. Rémi is exultant. He would like to shout for joy but doesn't dare. He never will, no one will ever know how deep he sounded his courage or what limits he passed! No, but the princess knows. She alone can hear the mute clamour of triumph raised by her faithful knight.

The wind makes off to chase the storm beyond the world's edge, and a strange calm moves in. After the din they'd been subjected to, animals and things drink greedily of this silence nothing dares to break. The world holds its breath. Even after long moments you hear nothing but the last drops trembling and the rustle of grasses straightening out their creases. The clouds break, a star appears and a timid bird tries a single note. The trees shuttle their branches.

Rémi stretches, and his muscles beat him to sleep. In his mind one thought dances: I won! I won!

At the back of the cleared land, behind Méo's house, a pathway made years ago by men, but adopted and maintained by animals, winds through the alders. The marshy soil is riddled with hoof prints. Réginald, watched by Méo, Rémi, and Robert and assisted by his uncle, is setting a noose of steel wire at the right height and according to the rules of the brotherhood of poachers. Robert tugs at Rémi's sleeve and they leave before the others, heading across fallow fields littered with the remains of cleared trees.

"I wasn't going to say anything, but I got to. Yesterday . . ."

"Well, out with it!"

"I sinned yesterday."

"Ha ha! Run and see Father Ricard. He'll scrub your conscience for you."

"Don't laugh. It's serious."

"Look at him. It must be something awful!"

"I broke my knight's oath."

Rémi whistles and stands still.

"How'd that happen?"

"During the storm, when I heard Mrs. Martel was alone and scared. I should have gone there."

"Maybe . . . but it wasn't easy. Our parents wouldn't have let you go."

"Are parents stronger than duty?"

"No."

"I could have sneaked out. Rémi, the reason I didn't go, I was scared."

"That's serious."

"If I'd been with her – I know, this sounds dumb – I think I could have found the right things to say, I think I could even have fought the storm. But I was scared of the road, scared of going there. I imagined I went there, I took her out with me in the rain, and fought the storm as she looked on. That was great! Lots of noise, fighting, and light. The greatest battle in my life. I was tall and strong. I won; I crushed the wind and put the lightning out. Carmen Martel admired me."

"You dreamed that last night?"

"No, when I was looking out the window in the kitchen. Then I went to bed like a coward."

"Why, Robert, that's fantastic!"

"You think so?"

"When you went to bed it was all done."

"I told you, I day-dreamed the whole thing."

"Do you think you fight with your hands? Against another boy, yes. Not against the storm. You can't grab the magic forces of the night in your hands like a weapon. It all has to go on in your head. But it happened."

"I don't understand."

"Look: your body stayed in the kitchen. But your knightly spirit went to join up with your Lady's and took it with you right into the heart of the storm, and there you fought and won. Listen, Robert, do you realize that just after you went to bed the storm stopped short? I didn't know why at the time, but I wondered about it. I tell you, everything got quiet all of a sudden. An' now I know why. You'd beaten the enemy!"

"Who, me?"

"You bet."

Robert stretched his arms, his fingers spread wide.

"You mean, I was stronger than the thunder?"

"You – and the night."

"Me, calming the wind. Just like Jesus."

"There's no more Jesus. Here on this sideroad, there's only the two of us, two knights, stronger than anything."

"Too bad Carmen Martel doesn't know that."

"Hey! A Lady isn't just anybody. Her spirit went with yours."

"She knows about my battle?"

"Sure she does. Maybe she doesn't remember it, but it's in her, and one fine day it'll pop up in her memory just like that, for no reason."

"Oh, that's great! I was scared I wasn't a knight anymore. But Rémi, how did you find all those things out?"

"Find out, find out! You don't have to find out to know. You make things up, because you have what they call a revelation. All that stuff you learn in school, it didn't just drop from the sky. Somebody invented it once upon a time. How do you know it's true? I know everything's true that I invent, because it came into my head all by itself and it explains everything and it's logical and every time the way things turn out proves me right."

"But what if you were wrong? Rémi, what if you were wrong about the knights?"

"I can't be wrong. You have no right to doubt! The two of us, we'd be nothing without that."

"Hey, quit pushin'!"

"You don't understand. I don't want to be like the others and live the way they do. I want terrific things to happen to me, more and more terrific. I don't want a dumb life like our parents have."

"You shouldn't say that!"

"But it's true. What kind of a life have they got? Working, eating, bringing up kids, playing cards. Where's the mystery in that, eh? I'd rather live like that crazy old prospector. If I was sure I'd end up like Réginald I'd kill myself right now."

"It's hard for us to tell about adults."

"Oh, Robert, come on! What have they got to teach you? Look at them, they're no better or smarter than we are. And their life's just routine. Robert, our life is never the same from one day to the next. Look, yesterday I had a big battle just like you did."

"You had a battle too?"

"A fantastic combat. Just like the old knights. You should have seen it! The other night when you were asleep I went to fight off a monster that was threatening my princess's castle. It was terrible, he was winning and he could have killed me; I just got away in time. So yesterday afternoon I took dad's good axe and this time I gave the monster a deadly wound. I heard him dying all through the storm last night."

"What kind of a monster?"

"Enormous. Terrifying. Big as a five-storey house and arms like tree trunks."

Just as they get to Méo's house the men catch up with them. They all go in and sit down around the table. The bottles are on it already.

Réginald thinks that's funny.

"I see the booze is stronger than the devil."

Roméo leaps from his chair and pounds the table with his fist.

"God damn it, I ain't scared of no divil."

"Oho! You strut like a gander while the sun shines, but after dark . . .," said Blanche, tidying her hair.

"That's no cause for the divil to git mad."

"The priest's coming to exorcise the house, and he gave me a blessèd branch from Palm Sunday just to tide us over."

"I told you to throw that god-damn thing out. And if the priest comes fussin' around here I'll beat the shit out of him. It's us goin' to suffer afterwards."

Mr. Simard smiled and Réginald put on a mock-serious air.

"I sure hope you didn't go to confession, Méo. The devil don't like that."

"I made a false confession, if you want to know."

"You shouldn't have done that," Blanche simpered, "you know we live a bad life, eh Méo?"

"Aw, speak for yourself!"

Roméo turns to Réginald, paying no attention to Blanche. But she goes over to him, lays her hand on his shoulder, and speaks in a voice trembling with half-repressed rage.

"I tell you, I'm fed up living in a bunch of trees like a savage," she said. "My daughter was right. I want us to get the hell outa here. An' I'm fed up with you, too, you goddamn drunk, you're makin' me into one just like you. I'm a Catholic. I want nothin' to do with the devil."

Méo turns arrogant, trying to provoke Blanche and make her break the calm she has affected since she went to confession.

"Fuck off, then. Go, go, I'm not keepin' you. Go get together with your daughter. The priest's goin' to be glad to pay your train fare. Go back to your old beat on the street. Blanche rides again! No such luck. You'll stay here because I've got my veteran's pension comin' in every month, and you like it, bein' with me and drinkin', havin' nothing else to do but drink. You're a rubby just like me."

He watched to see the effect his words would have. Blanche was breathing hard. Finally: "I'm goin' over to see Sonia."

She went out without speaking again, but her hand was trembling as she reached for the door knob. Roméo burst out laughing. Robert and Rémi exchange a look, a smile in their eyes, while their father and their cousin, uncomfortable at the turn of the conversation, hasten to change the subject.

"I'm goin' to town tomorrow if anybody wants a ride."

"Again? You're always goin' to town, uncle! You must have a girl down there."

Rémi finds the joke less than funny.

"Well . . . you know Réginald, I may have made a mistake."

"What? What kind of a mistake, sonofagum?"

Rémi and Robert are all ears. Méo goes out for a leak.

"Coming here, I mean."

"Hey, uncle. Sonofagum, we're just gettin' started. It's not even a month. . . ."

"It's true, though. Look at that land of mine. There's so many weeds it'll take years to get a good crop. I'd have to put up buildings and buy stock and machinery. And the bit of a grant I get from the Settlement people isn't going to do it. And you've got to live till the money starts coming in. I have a family; I've got kids. The little money I had when I got here is just meltin' away. There's not enough woods on my lot to make it worthwhile lumbering. Where it wasn't stripped off it was stolen. There's nothing left but broken stumps and scrub this high."

Rémi is hanging on his father's words. Robert's eyes have narrowed to slits. Méo comes back and begins a mute dialogue with a bottle.

"So what are you goin' to do, uncle?"

"I've done it. I took a construction job in Amos."

"Well, that's not so bad. At least you can stay alive while you wait."

"That's the way she goes. All very well to dream, but you have to live too."

Rémi has a very strange feeling. He tries to find arguments against his father's plan. The only thing he could say would no doubt bring a smile of incomprehension: all very well to live, but you have to dream too!

"I see what you mean, uncle. Take me, now . . ."

"With you, Réginald, it's not the same. You've got your land ploughed, there, you have a little stable and a cow. You have a good stand of timber and a horse to get it out with."

Réginald hesitates, then empties his glass.

"Even at that . . . you know I had debts when I came here. I haven't finished paying for the black horse or the cow. They're startin' to get pushy, I'm gettin' letters . . . I'm living off the grants an' I could get caught in a squeeze."

"What are you going to do?"

"Like you. Get a job. And this winter I'll go on unemployment insurance. I'll cut some trees on my lot. That'll bring in enough to pay my debts and have some cash for next year."

"Well, this winter . . . we're moving into town. Drivin' back and forth morning and night makes no sense. Staying out here would be no fun for my wife. All by herself, no electricity, she'd go crazy on me."

Rémi sees the room tilt and turn. The chair, the floor, the walls blur and turn soft. Leaving here? He doesn't even feel his brother's hand on his arm, nor see Robert's anxious expression. Leaving here! Leaving their concession road! It was impossible, insane. He still has things to do here. No, this must be a bad dream.

But his father was still talking.

"I start work next week. Just time to rent something in Amos. But it's hard to find anything, especially in summer."

All Rémi's projects are going up in smoke at this little word "leaving."

"Well, well. Sonofagum!"

"You can all leave, all of yez, I don't give a shit. I'm stayin'. No rent to pay, no expenses hardly, my cheque's enough for eats an' smokes an' booze. That's the life."

"But if you don't get some crops in, Méo, the Settlement boys'll take away your lot."

"I don't give a fuck. Till then I'm O.K. After that, we'll see!"

Rémi was no longer listening or paying attention to his brother's silent appeal. One word was tumbling in his brain, too quickly for him to catch it and analyse its meaning for him. This was a day of mourning. A day twice cursed. Getting out of the car Rémi had had another shock: a man was ripping off the boards that had barricaded the doors and windows of the house next to theirs. Stupid! This act of liberation should have come from Rémi and no other. And then only after he had passed the most impossible of tests.

Their mother told them that this man owned the house, that he was a professor who had dreamed of pioneering for a few years, then returned to teach in Montreal. Every summer he came back to his house, brought it to life for a few weeks, felled some trees, and cleared a bit of land. When he retired he would come here to stay. She'd heard all that from Martel, who had driven the man here.

Rémi took off across the fields toward the hilltop. As soon as he was out of sight he flung himself to the ground and gave way to his despair. The grass was still wet. He pounded the earth with his fists and sobbed his heart out. His whole universe was crumbling. Even the earth to which he clung seemed to tumble. His princess's castle! The house of shades couldn't possibly have an owner. Such things can never be possessed, and even when you think you've made yourself worthy of them, you're violating, stealing them: they're never really yours. And here was this man, ripping off the boards, letting in the sunlight fatal to shades and spirits, chasing the mystery out with the musty smells. The man was an impostor. No scrap of paper could grant him such rights. Should he go and fight him, kill him? Too late: the princess was most likely wandering about already, lost in the sun's glare. And Rémi was going to leave. Dreams all turned to smoke in daylight, they evaporated like dew in the sun. And yet, Rémi had not failed in his duty, he had followed the rules and fought the good fight. Robert too. So where did the bad luck come from?

Rémi rose and walked toward his dead enemy through the brambles and wild oats. The tree had exploded in its fall, the stump was split at the base, many branches were broken. He climbed onto the reclining trunk. It was a tree, that was all. Just a poplar with rough bark and many knots and, toward the top, pointed diamond markings. Just a tree blown down by the wind. There had never been a monster here, any more than there was a princess in the abandoned house. Those were illusions born of the darkness and of Rémi's brain, and of his thirst for marvels.

He returned to the hilltop where, by turning, he had a panoramic view of all horizons. There was no corner, not even the boy's heart, where mystery could burrow, there was nothing that could not be named by a word. The world around stood revealed as it really was, the true face of things unfalsified by night. But it couldn't be true! The night was so honest, and what lived in it was so powerful! It must be the sun that falsified everything. At night the earth was a great body; by day, under the light, its flesh fell away, you could see the skeleton with its scorched bones, and all became simplified, visible at a glance. Rémi recalled what he knew of night-time; as soon as dusk fell, powerful muscles of shadow rippled and swelled, the bones of earth took on flesh again and you could walk in a web of nerves, a labyrinth of veins and arteries, clusters of fibres and tendons . . . and then, nothing was simple any more.

Leave this place? Where again could he find nights like those on the sideroad? Leave the land before he had half explored it, to live in a big, middle-class village in a house like all the others, rubbing shoulders with ordinary boys, growing like them again, having been a knight only in his own head, having loved creatures of fantasy only and fought against nothing but monsters of the mind . . . Leave, and lose this universe that was his alone, cut to the measure of his dreams, be shifted off that thin borderline between childhood and adulthood. Be forced to choose. Submit.

If only people could do as much as they would like, Rémi said to himself. Everyone dreams. Coming here to settle where so many had failed, making a big farm prosper in this wild land – that was a dream, too. Why did grown-ups give up their dreams at the first obstacle? Why hadn't they the courage to defend them, and the will-power to see them through? Robert and I wouldn't give in that easily, he thought.

But life went on, very real, very ordinary. Their father was looking for a place to live in Amos, and Robert and Rémi were sulky with each other. They went to bed at night like good boys. Like good boys they helped Dam-Bogga with the haying, tramping the millet grass on the wagon like boys on any farm. They split firewood and piled it inside, played with their little sister, went to mass with their parents. But there was no joy in their hearts and very little in their expressions, just enough to put up a front. The neighbouring house was busy with the life of Professor Savard, whom they didn't know because he kept to himself like a hermit. The late nights at Réginald's place were monotonous sessions in which the boys watched their elders behave like children. Sonia's body and Carmen Martel's bust had lost their charm. The women now cast no spell more powerful than that of their cheap perfume. The boys avoided their cave of clay. And two weeks went by.

It happened in the night between Friday and Saturday. Robert and Rémi were awakened by their father, who was very excited, talking low and quickly. The moose had been caught in the snare and Roméo had finished it off with a rifle shot. Their mother made them drink hot chocolate as they dressed. Then they were on their way. The car bumped along at a great rate, and phantom branches on either side seemed to part to let them through.

The Simards joined Méo and Dam-Bogga with his black dog. They trooped off behind the lantern, the dog frisking around his master. At last they arrived at the snare. In the brush, by the light of a second lantern, Martel and Réginald were walking around the giant animal lying on its side. Rémi went up close to examine it, felt its fur, under which the hide was still warm, and touched the soft muscles. Its protruding eyes reflect in blue and green. They turn the moose on its back, and while the others hold its legs apart, Simard and Dam-Bogga cut open the hide at the chest and make an incision running to between its hind legs. Then they let it down on its side again. From the open belly a smell steams out, and the guts rumble. The men's shadows gesticulate behind them and the yellow lantern light carves deep lines in their facès. Dam-Bogga is grasping in the guts with his bare hand. Sorcerer of a bloody rite, he pulls the innards toward him, and they pile up on the earth with a gurgling sound: the rounded heart, the slippery mass of liver, the pink sacks that are the lungs.

It's beautiful and ugly, and terrifying. A mystery to which the boys are almost admitted. At last a mystery, after the dullness of these last days! The skull cracks open: splinters of bone, spurting blood in the lantern light. Dam-

Bogga officiates, lifting out the fatty brain, cutting and tearing off the tongue. He fumbles in the heap of organs and picks out the heart, the liver, the spleen and the kidneys, stuffing them hastily into jute sacks. The boys are to bring them at once to Blanche, who is waiting. They have to find their way in the velvet dark.

"Wait!"

Dam-Bogga removes the animals testicles and adds them to Robert's load.

"The balls. For me."

He laughs. All the men laugh. Mr. Simard is the first to grow serious.

"Not so loud! Somebody could hear us!"

"You're kidding, uncle! Out here? At this time of night?"

"Sure," said Méo, "Christ, we got nothin' to hide."

"Nothin' to hide?" Réginald guffaws, "Nothin' but a moose poached out of season and a still pissin' moonshine."

"So what, eh? So what? I'd just like to see the son-of-a-whore that'd bother my ass around here!"

"What would ya do, Méo, sic Blanche on him?"

Everybody laughed at Réginald's joke, even Dam-Bogga who was usually so discreet.

"You guys make me laugh. Always asking permission for everything, always scared of everybody. When I was in the army, god damn it, we didn't ask permission to kill somebody. I'm not scared of nobody. I've got my Lee Enfield under the bed, it's the same one I had then. It killed that there moose; think what it'll do to a man."

"Army, army, you've been talkin' about yer army for the last fourteen years, Méo."

Roméo grew serious all of a sudden.

"You got no idea. Just no idea."

And his eyes grow distant, forgetting the time and place. The father pushes the boys toward the path.

"Anyway, boys, take care. If you see a car on the road, hide. If you meet anybody, run here and tell us."

"You're worryin' for nothin', uncle."

"We can't be sure. You're not going to get lost? You're not scared? Do you want a lantern?"

The boys only laugh at their father's questions.

Rémi leads the way. The night is as black as the new moon, which, somewhere up there, is giving no light. The stars have the sky to themselves and are making the most of it. Robert follows his brother, careful not to trip. A damp warmth filters through the jute, soaks through his shirt and trickles down his spine. Rémi leans his cheek against the saturated sack. The notion of being smeared doesn't trouble him, he needs this contact and the blood on him. A great exultation takes over, as it did when he was a knight. Far from the lantern the dark becomes gradually penetrable to their straining eyes. The darkness, friend and accomplice, is around him. Rémi breathes in the night and at every breath gains strength. Joy is not quite in him yet, but he feels it nearby: the night indeed is real as it ever was. His thoughts rush by, his ideas tripping over each other, seeking some evasive coherence. It has to come soon, the house lights are ahead. And there is a kind of explosion in him. Everything is simple, so easy that he hadn't understood. Leaving for town, and the professor profaning the castle: these are his trials! Terrible trials over which he will have to triumph. There is surely a way, there is always a way. He only has to find it, perhaps invent it. Yes! He must defy fate and break the reality that suffocates his dream. Arise, sir knight!

They detour around the decrepit little log stable in which the still snores softly to itself.

"You go ahead, Robert. I have to take a leak."

The house door slams and he can hear Blanche's voice indistinctly. Rémi is alone. He drops his burden. A way, there has to be a way! The task that faces them is super-human. Breaking and defeating the tree-monster was easy. Dominating the storm and making it cease, that was nothing. But how can you change the course of events, get into people's heads and change their thoughts and desires? Courage was not enough to chase the intruder from the castle or prevent the family's departure. This was a new challenge and called for different means. Rémi kneels and impulsively plunges his hands in the sack, kneading and grasping and stirring the organs. This moose is surely a sign, a message sent by the night which has to be deciphered.

"Rémi. Are you dead or something?"

"Coming."

A person can't even think in peace . . . and he'd been so near the answer!

In the bright kitchen Rémi sees himself, covered with blood, his hands slimy. Blanche washes and cuts up the soft pieces, grunting with delight at the thought of eating them.

"Yum, yum. Fried with onions. And this one, thin slices smothered in brown gravy. Oh, if I only had some mushrooms!"

The boys return to where the men have just finished butchering the carcass. Each quarter is wiped with a rag and wrapped in cheesecloth to protect it from the flies. They bury the remaining innards and leave the hide for the time being. Méo will come tomorrow to scrape, salt and stretch it. In single file, their lanterns prudently extinguished, they make their way slowly back to the house. The black dog leaps around, sniffing avidly. It takes three trips to move the meat.

The quarters are suspended above the water in the wide, deep well that supplies Réginald's stable. The meat will age there in the cool air until it is properly hung. Then it will be divided up and eaten, preserved or salted, as the owner desires. With the boys' help, Blanche has carried the offal to Réginald's place, where a good fire is burning in the wood stove. Mrs. Martel arrives, Mrs. Dam-Bogga too, her arms full of herbs, spices, and several bottles of her wine. The windows are thrown open because of the heat and the pump squeaks for a long time as hands and arms are washed free of dried blood.

This unexpected bonus must be celebrated! The four women are busy: Sonia is preparing a stew, Blanche and Carmen are slicing the pork fat, onions, and potatoes, Dam-Bogga's wife is concocting seasonings and mixing sauces. It's really too hot. The men go outside, taking bottles and glasses with them. Beside the woodpile near the house they improvise their sitting-room: logs and chopping blocks for seats.

"Jesus, that's a great night. What say we make a campfire."

No sooner said than done. They tear off strips of birchbark, collect chips and sawdust, make a pile of split firewood, and in no time a splendid fire is burning, lighting up happy faces. Out come the corks. At night, at a time like this around the fire, Robert and Rémi are full-fledged men and have the right to a glass filled with amber flame.

"Oh, man, that's good whisky."

"Sonofagum, you said it."

"After this you get a taste of what I cooked up."

Each one, taking his time, taking it easy, has his turn at the bottle and pours as he pleases. There is no more ownership, no holding back. Men sitting on the ground around a fire lose their civilization fast. Rémi doesn't rush. Slowly he savours the heady, burning liquid on his tongue, lets it trickle hot down his throat and into his stomach. Unlike Robert, he is not trying to get drunk. Robert is on his third glass already. The men are talking loudly, talking nonsense, laughing for no good reason. They're all possessed of a great joy.

Sonia calls them in to eat, but they want to stay outside. Frying-pans, pots, and plates are brought along, the women sitting off to one side so that the sparks and ashes don't get in their food.

"A little of everything for everybody. Can't be fussy sittin' outside."

The plates go around, overflowing with dark gravy in which black, brown, and red meat is floating. A hand is held out with one of the dishes. It passes close to Rémi's face. Strong, wild, forest smells steam up from it. The boy's nostrils flare, and catch a woman smell as well. He doesn't want to know who passed him his plate nor to see her face. Perhaps the night itself is serving him. He places the dish on his knees. He is not hungry. Mrs. Martel gives Robert his share and rubs his cheek to remove a drop of encrusted blood. The boy empties his glass at a single gulp and sends a drunken, ecstatic glance to his brother who replies with a nod: Yes, Robert, your Lady knows about the storm.

Everybody has been served. The pots are covered and set near the coals to keep them warm. Second helpings are ready. The women are scattered among the men and all are eating, stuffing themselves rather, guzzling and groaning with pleasure, talking with their mouths full, paying no attention to the gravy running down their chins, nor to any vestige of manners. And every mouthful is chased down by a gulp of liquor or a glass of wine.

Strange: Rémi cannot recognize the familiar faces. The night, the glow of the embers, the feeling of the moment transfigure these beings. He isn't hungry, but thinks that he should eat. Tender meats, soft or fibrous flesh, secret herbs that crackle between his teeth, oily vegetables, every mouthful has a different taste, and with the animal's flesh it's the smoke and breath of the others and a bit of the night that he's chewing and getting down. Even with no appetite, he eats because he has a rule to obey. A ceremony is under way in this strange atmosphere. All of these very everyday men and women, unknown to themselves, are following a ritual. Never have they broken with their daily habits to this point: eating outdoors in the middle of the night, around a fire, their food a meat that is strange to them. They have left their civilized masks behind and sacrificed their sleep for this improvised feast. Improvised? Rémi doubts it. He thinks it was intended and has a meaning. The moose was caught in a snare that stank of man for thirty yards. He could have avoided it. What force, then, drove him to sacrifice himself? A burnt offering that the darkness presents to men so that her knights may stay near her? She'd have other ways to keep them if she wanted. No, it's more likely a sign to the knights themselves. She has to awaken her two boys who were shrinking from their trials, and perhaps at the same time give them a hint about the means to be used. Rémi feels a great joy bubble up inside him. He's on the right track. There are too many coincidences to call this chance.

First of all, the death of the moose. The fact that the boys were wakened. The walk in the dark with the sack of still-living organs on his back. And now this ceremony beneath the stars. A covenant! An alliance! Rémi must take communion of the moose's meat so that the sacrifice may not be in vain, but especially to gather strength and wisdom from it. He ends his meal by washing it down with wine.

But first, with a gesture that he hopes looks harmless, he raises his glass to the light. Some of the guests at this feast of love are starting an after-dinner drink, others are having seconds. Stories and jokes make the rounds. Laughter, shouting follow. This is a real feast, surpassing by its spontaneity a hundred Christmases, drawing spirits and imaginations out beyond their range. The world could just as well not exist around them, all that is real is the sputtering fire and its plume of sparks, and the joy of the humans grouped elbow to elbow within its cocoon of light.

Someone strikes up a song. It's Roméo, his cracked voice squeezing out a verse that should shock the women, but they only laugh and nudge their companions. Réginald gets up and improvises a jig to let off his excess good humour. The others clap to cheer him on and the stars tremble. Sonia takes off her shoes and joins her husband, twirling and whipping up her dress, which sets the fire to sparking in her breeze. The dancers grow frantic, chasing around and over the flames. For a second the leaping makes her skirt fly high, revealing the white light of her thigh, with its dusky secrets.

Godbout, wakened by the din, is out on his front stoop bawling at the top of his voice and demanding a little quiet. His only answer is a chorus of angry shouts, mocking cries, insults and blasphemies, which add to the din. He does not reply to the invitation to "come on over and get your nose blown." Instead, he goes inside. Everybody enjoyed the incident. Eyes shining, they're stretching out the evening, making the night last. Alcohol and wine run in profusion, voices are growing gravelly, speech is thickened, movements become uncertain. The women have turned languid and their shapes seem more filled with curves. Rémi drinks very slowly, but without interruption. He has reached a degree of well-being at which he would like to level off. He has forgotten about his trials, knowing that tomorrow he will seek for and find the meaning of this nocturnal feast. Robert is flat on the earth, dead drunk and still as a log.

Mrs. Dam-Bogga sings in her own tongue a lament with endless verses. No one understands a word but you can guess that the song is sad and gay at once. The words make a sound of leaves rustling in the wind. There is a pause, during which the waves of emotion settle. Then all together sing the old songs until there are no more, and they have to fall back on church songs and hymns. Rémi's lips form the words but he's staring into the fire and dancing with the bodies that twist and wriggle there, diaphanous forms that take shape and change continuously, always new, always different and more lovely.

Their voices hoarse from drink and smoke, the men fall silent one after the other. Soon only Sonia and Carmen are left singing together. They hum the *chansonnettes* and love-ballads that were popular when they left civilization. As they rediscover the words, evoking a past so recent, their tired faces become bright and vivacious once more. Their glances are a caress. Blanche is watching them, smiling dreamily. Méo's sleeping head is on her lap and you could imagine that she made the beginning of a tender gesture. But the move is quickly repressed. She drinks and her face grows hard again. Réginald is hiccuping and mumbling. Mr. Simard's head is nodding, nodding, he naps as it lolls forward, wakes with a start, jerks back his head, smiles, and nods again. Martel is staring at the fire. His only remaining gesture is mechanical. It consists of raising a glass from his knees to his lips.

Dam-Bogga and his wife leave without saying a word. She leans her head on her man's aged shoulder, and he puts his arm around her waist. On the other side of the fire, facing Rémi, who looks on discreetly, the two women are still singing. Their voices soften, and their lips close at the same time on the word *amour*. Sonia is pressing against Réginald, who doesn't react. She begins to drink. Carmen tickles her husband's ribs, teases him with light, deliberate caresses. She whispers in his ear and succeeds in dragging him behind the pile of cordwood, twenty paces from the fire. Soon little staccato cries are heard, as if someone were trying to catch her breath. Réginald sneers. Rémi is embarrassed, not knowing whether he should leave or pretend not to notice. Luckily his father is asleep, or it would be even more embarrassing. And even luckier that Robert is out cold and cannot hear the woman's cries of love. Sonia is weeping silently in her glass. But perhaps it's only the firelight reflecting in her eye, an illusion that the fire is running, dropping. Rémi is sick, sick and sore. He detests Réginald. Why doesn't he move? Why doesn't he look after this woman with the passion flaming in her cheeks? Rémi remembers . . . his mouth in the curve of Sonia's neck. He looks at her intensely until she raises her head. She should know that he understands, that he's suffering for her, with her. And that this is all he can do. Then, magic of the night, their glances touch and meet above the flames and he knows that she heard him.

Réginald shakes his uncle and drags him off. You can hear the slamming of the house door, then the car door. Blanche staggers to her feet, pulls Méo up, and, half carrying him, goes on her way. Everybody leaves without taking leave of the others, without saying good night. There is nothing to say. A muffled cry comes from behind the cordwood. The coals of the fire splutter and explode. Martel passes like a sleep-walker. Then Carmen in turn crosses the lighted stage and goes off calling softly . . . No one is left around the dying fire but Sonia and Rémi who avoid looking at each other, and Robert, snoring and wheezing. The woman stands up and Rémi watches her melt into the darkness. The screen door slams shut as it always does. The boy drinks what is left of his wine. His cousin Sonia has come back.

"Your father's asleep in the car. I don't think he can drive. If you'll help me we can put Robert to bed."

Rémi gets to his feet, his head turning, his legs shaky. He takes his brother's shoulders, Sonia takes his legs and they carry him inside. They move slowly because of the shadow crouched on the earth, concealing possible obstacles. Rémi's eyes are on the ground and his mind is working wildly. There are no witnesses now. Would the inevitable happen? Would Sonia not force him into action, somewhat against his will? Would he not fall victim to his own weakness, when present developments demanded that he remain a faithful knight? His fear takes on tremendous proportions. Sonia's hard breathing is not due to Robert's weight . . . and the sudden pull on their inert burden . . . was it a signal to attract his attention?

He pushes the door open with his foot, and the spring buzzes as it stretches. In the bedroom they lay him down beside little Sophie.

"It's a double bed, you could pile in beside them. It's all we've got, there's no sofa or armchair."

"I'll go outside, I won't fall asleep."

She stops him in the doorway, her hand on his arm. He guesses that her mouth is open to speak, but no word comes. So much the better! Her hand draws away and he pushes the curtain aside, hurrying out. His father is sleeping on the front seat of the car, his feet sticking out the open window.

Rémi is alone again in the bowl of light that pulses feebly above the embers. The air has grown cool and the ground is ice-cold. For a moment he waits anxiously, half-hoping Sonia will reappear. The door wouldn't slam if she held it. She could come out on tiptoe, holding her skirt so that it wouldn't make a sound. But the grass is stiff now and would crunch underfoot. To combat the cold and loneliness of the half-light, Rémi pokes the fire and throws some wood on the naked coals. The fire flares up and the boy curls on his side, his back protected by a spruce log. All odours have fled the plates scattered on the ground. He wants no more wine, he is contented to be with the night, talking to the night. The air, heavy at times, weighs on the fire, which collapses. The flames gather strength again, break upward and shoot high, sparks flying.

Rémi is still searching for the meaning of this feast. The night wanted to revive his courage and his faith, that was certain, and it had happened. Did it want to show him a way out? What way? Time after time he went over the evening and considered the various elements, analysing them, trying to recombine them in a hundred ways. His head heavy, his eyelids tired, his mind ran in circles: a sacrifice, the sacrifice of the moose, a feast, a covenant, a communion, an alliance. Only one way out. Of all those taking part, only he had known it was a celebration. This was the important point. If the night could so suddenly change people's behaviour without their knowing, make them leave their usual path without seeming to do so, it would also know how to change the course of events and work on the wills of men, still unbeknown to them. Neither Robert nor Rémi would know how to make it through the trial: but the night would know! In place of their courage, her secret strength. It only remained to know how to use that strength, and first, where to find it. Sacrifice and feast: these were the keys.

In the joy of certainty that victory can still be his, Rémi turns on his back, looking up at the stars, no longer searching, neglecting the fire, which has burned down to coals and cooling cinders. The night closes in, healing the wound of light. Rémi allows himself brief naps, clenching his fist to prevent some thread of thought from slipping away. He sleeps by fits and starts and wakes at widening intervals, only to work out a cramp or succumb to a stronger shiver. Even then, though, he opens his eyes just for a second, noting that the night is growing paler in the sky, and darker on the earth, like silt settling in troubled waters. A little pink, a touch of milk-white, and yellow on the tree-tops; the first bird songs in the nearby forest, the invisible dew, and the aspen gurgling, stretching, yawning, cooing. The breeze winnows the ashes and uncovers the heart, still red, of the sputtering embers.

Dawn broke over the cooking pots and plates scattered among the logs lying in rough semicircle, revealing a freezing boy, too tired even to shiver. Rémi got to his feet and went to join his father in the car. On the way his foot rolled on a bottle – a twelve-ouncer of brandy with an unbroken seal. He picked it up, hid it under his armpit and made himself comfortable on the back seat, his nose, as he went to sleep, tickled by the dusty plush. He barely noticed afterward that the car was moving. Robert was shaking him. They were home.

It was after midday. They must have looked strange: Françoise was staring at them with amused astonishment. Their mother was about to start shouting, but held back because of the children. She pulled her husband into their bedroom to settle accounts with him. Rémi climbed the stairs and flopped on the bed, plugging his ears. He wanted to hear nothing of the argument. He stubbornly refused to consider them as altogether human, with human weaknesses, desires and peculiarities. That made it almost inconceivable that they should quarrel. He knew quite well that this was irrational, but he persisted in seeing his father and mother as parents and nothing else, even if it meant being illogical and robbing them of part of their personality. After all, if it was inevitable that they act like other humans, the least they could do was conceal the fact, as they had always done.

He stretched out on his bed, then, hoping to go to sleep and hear nothing. But the house was old and the partitions thin. Despite the mental barriers he raised, he caught snatches of speech, things like "you don't just go and sleep anywhere like that, I was worried sick" or "that's a fine example for the boys" or "dragging them into bad situations." The father defended himself feebly, talking about the moose, how they butchered it, how the whole thing was unexpected. And anyway the kids were tough, a night outside wouldn't do them any harm, just a bit of fun. The mother wasn't worried about their health; it was their morals. The father had drunk too much in front of the boys and been a terrible example. And, she added, the adults in these parts were not the best of company.

The mother complained and wept. Here she'd been, alone with the little one, so scared she couldn't sleep, and there they were having a party. That's how it always was. He never thought about her, he was nothing but a selfish beast. The house was a gloomy trap she never got out of. If he was going to start again like in Montreal. . . . Rémi held the pillow over his ears and began to count the tongue-and-groove boards of the ceiling. On each side, where the ceiling followed the slope of the roof, there were twenty-one. In the middle, where it was horizontal under a tiny attic, he counted fourteen. Then he tried to locate the nails under the thin coat of paint. The conversation downstairs moved out of the bedroom and, in the kitchen, became harmless again.

They called him to eat. Robert was coming in from taking Françoise for a walk. At the table, Rémi examined every detail of the big room, and the landscape through the windows. Would he really have to leave all that now? Here you felt as if you lorded it over the whole word, or as if you were sailing, with the earth parting around the house, as water in the pictures parted around the ship. This was the ark, poised on the mountain after the flood. To begin barely to know this new country and have to leave before penetrating its secrets, leaving and taking with you forever the impression of something half-done – no! That mustn't be!

After supper Robert went to bed. But Rémi had urgent things to do. He sat outside facing the great field of grass that sloped up to the sky. He knew that the line where the millet touched the clouds was not the end of the world, it only looked that way. Afterwards the land dropped off again toward the forests and, most likely, other houses. And behind the hill, toward the bottom, where the dampness makes moss grow instead of hay and the second growth of trees starts to reconquer the land, lay the remains of a great poplar. It wasn't just a tree destined to lie and rot: that illusion came in sunlight. But by the light of the moon you could clearly see where its bones emerged through the wounds, piercing its wooden muscles.

He was searching again. Again his brain began to buzz and Rémi gave his imagination free rein. Images, phrases, words rushed by, dissolving, forming again, disappearing, returning: the ark, Noah, the wine, the feast, a sacrifice after the flood, the flood, sin, Cain and his altar, Abraham sacrificing his son, the fatted calf, Tintin with the Incas, the pyre of the Sun Temple, the high priests and their brilliant robes . . . Rémi walked off, waving his hands in nonsensical gestures. Yes, a sacrifice with offerings. To invoke. . . . A victim, sacrificed like the moose. Blood. Fire. Rémi was destined to become officiating priest in honour of the night, so that she could turn loose her supernatural forces. Conclude a pact. Rémi searched his memory in vain, and it became quite obvious that there was no appropriate ceremony. He would have to go ahead and invent something, then, hoping for luck, or by interminable trial and error arrive at success – or defeat and departure. He dragged his feet in the grass, and the grasshoppers fled with sounds like dry pods exploding. Cain had offered up the fruits of the earth, Abraham his son and his sheep; in the mass it was bread and wine. Material things, not words but symbols. He'd have to follow that line for a start.

A car drove up and stopped at the house. It was Father Ricard, who got out as Rémi's parents came to greet him. They were calling Rémi. Several voices, in unison. He turned back, and the priest led him toward the road.

"Such a nice day, we could take a little walk."

They walked side by side. Rémi tried to keep his distance, but the priest drew closer with every step. The professor was watching them as they passed. The father was now quite close to the boy, and laid his hand on Rémi's shoulder. He sneered! "Ha. That one!"

"The professor?" Rémi asked, keeping his voice down.

"Yes, Savard. He's a blasphemer. In all the six years I've been in the parish he comes up here every summer and never sets foot in church. Another one that thinks he's so smart he can get along without God. Ah, they're in for a nice surprise!"

"What if they were right!"

"Rémi! You don't believe what you're saying! You don't think that?"

"No. Just a bit."

"Look up at the sky at night, with all its stars, it will speak to you most eloquently of God. And all nature testifies to God having passed by, like the print of his own feet."

"I look at the stars every night when there are no clouds, and I know nature hereabouts."

"Well?"

"Well nothing."

"My, you're terrible! But in you I can recognize the searching soul, the superior, questioning intelligence. That's good, we must not take too much for granted. Nothing is that evident. But you must take care not to grow sceptical. There are certain limits to permitted doubt."

They had reached the creek.

"Goodness, this is a steep hill! Perhaps instead of climbing farther we could go and sit in the shade there, in the underbrush."

"Naw, it's full of black flies. Let's sit here on the bridge, in the sun. The wind blows them away out here; they don't stick too close."

Perhaps the priest understood the allusion, for he didn't sit down at once beside Rémi, but strolled on a pace or two.

"Why I wanted to see you . . . talk to you, I mean, the other day in the sacristy when we were rudely interrupted. . . . Are you listening?"

"Yeah, yeah."

"You know, my desire to make the surroundings of the church more beautiful, as you saw from the model, has no material motive. The people of the village look upon my plan as an investment to increase its real estate value. No doubt you would judge my enthusiasm to be most childish."

"No."

"Ah, how well I had sized you up! A soul of the elect! This renovation project is not only dictated by the love of beauty. If you must know, I have ulterior motives. This is only the first step in a master plan I have for changing the world. By the world, I mean the village. A very simple first step, easy for my flock to understand. I want to teach them what beauty is and then encourage their taste for more, their taste for learning to create beauty. In the process they will acquire a taste for learning as such. When we're that far along, my plan is well under way. In winter almost all of them are idle. That will be the time for their education. First they must be instructed in Christ and his law of love; their faith must be made more profound. That is my vocation, my profession. But I want to go farther than my ministry demands: I want them to enjoy the fruits of history, of French, of mathematics, agronomy and even –

why not? – the social sciences. Awaken their minds, broaden their horizons!"

"And what good will all that do them?"

"Make them grow, prepare them to take the step that follows. Then I want to develop their civic spirit, their feeling for the community, arouse a taste for the calculated risk, and channel all this toward a single goal: change the village, change it profoundly. Change its way of life, bring happiness to all. My villagers could go far if they were given a push in the right direction. The village, small and isolated as it is, suits my plans perfectly. It is a long-term design, but I have the time and patience for it. I conceived and perfected my project while I was still at the seminary, long ago. This is why I accepted the cure of souls in this parish of settlers. I am prepared to devote the rest of my life to it. I have come to know my people very well and in them I have discovered the budding of a new world. I would be sinning if I did not help these buds to flower, I would be a bad priest. What I want to do is almost revolutionary – a social and economic revolution, a revolution through love."

The priest was staring down the road, following his dream. Rémi stood up.

"Stay where you are! You haven't asked how I intend to do all this!"

The boy sighed, and asked, wearily, "Well, er . . . how are you going to do it?"

"That intrigues you, doesn't it? You'll see, it's well thought out. All the means I bring to bear for developing community life will lead to a co-operative village: everyone owns everything, and everything belongs to all. We take our destiny in hand, we refashion our lives according to our needs. I can easily see through what is going on elsewhere. We are moving toward a secular world. I would like to prevent my faithful flock from being torn at a later date between the demands of a temporal world and those of life everlasting. I want everything to be integrated and harmonious. There shall be a time for prayer, a time for study, and a time for work."

"Just like in a convent!"

"Yes, you've guessed it, Rémi! That's it, like those monasteries of the Middle Ages that were self-sufficient and influenced the life around them. The co-operative village is easy to create. It's being done elsewhere, but what is lacking there is the spiritual dimension. One need carry out only an initial collective project and people will see its advantages and begin inventing new ones of their own accord. First, we communally exploit for our own benefit all our neighbouring forests. We build a sawmill of our very own, and we cut, sell, and transport our own lumber. Then we acquire a store, we plan the farmers' production and diversify it to supply the essentials to the villagers. Handicrafts will spring up spontaneously, re-inventing techniques as we require them. We export goods, the savings and capital are put to work for us, and there are no longer rich or poor, only men equal before God."

The priest was getting carried away, he was excited and drunk with his own words. He waved his hands, and images of prosperity and happiness flashed through his imagination.

"This community existence contradicts everything life has ever taught us, but despite this I am sure the success of our village will spread. The results will be there to see, and the idea will make its way. This is how, while changing the village, I will change the whole world."

The priest grew quieter and looked down at the stream. He was thinking. Then his hands began to flutter again and his mouth gaped. He was about to start dreaming out loud again. Rémi, in a voice that he tried to keep neutral, asked, "Why are you telling me all this?"

"You are the first person I have ever mentioned my project to, and the only one I'm counting on because I feel that you understand my aspirations. Have you forgotten that I already asked for your help?"

"No."

160

A tired "No . . ."

"Before you decide to help me, you should know that it will not be easy. Nothing important ever is. For my part, I shall have to shake up my compatriots' traditional lethargy, struggle against their apathy and defeatism, their lack of ideals and their laziness. And there will be traps and snares set by those on the outside in whose interest it lies that nothing should ever change. So many people take advantage of the situation. They won't give up easily. And if, as I hope, you decide to help me, you will have to get accepted in the village, and that's not as easy as it sounds. You and your brother have already noticed a certain mistrust of outsiders."

"Oh, villages, I never did care much for . . ."

"Tut-tut! Don't play the little big-city snob, Rémi Simard. Village life is not as slow and deprived as some might think. The fact that one is not as free as in a big city has its advantages. Each person watches the deeds and gestures of the others, everyone knows everybody else. This creates certain barriers that make exemplary conduct compulsory, certain constraints that harness selfishness. The moral climate in a village is healthy, far more so than in other places. There are fewer excesses, fewer acute problem situations. Fraternity already exists here in a larval state. The obstacles I shall encounter will not come from the village, but from the concession roads. Ah these sideroads! They are the refuge of the individualist, the home of the egoist. People out here live separated from each other, each for himself. Each house is the navel of the world. Is idleness the father of all vice? Solitude is much more so. The tragedies and ignominy of our country regions come from the life of the concession roads, far from the parish church spire. Every man takes himself for a lord and master. Outside his own fence the world does not exist."

Rémi was tossing pebbles into the stream, where their circles turned to ovals in the current. He was tired of listening to the priest go on and on. He too had an important project of great urgency, and it called for preparation.

"Rémi, are you listening?"

"Yes."

"This road is the worst one. It is the thorn in my foot that causeth me to limp, my earthly purgatory. I know, too, from what my predecessor told me, that this is nothing new. To my great relief it grew almost empty, and here it is filling up again! Godbout came four years ago, then it was Martel two years back, and this year it's your outfit."

His eyes rolled heavenward.

"What parishioners I have here! Godbout – an apostate, a heretic, an unbeliever, next thing to anti-religious. As for Dumb Buggy, his house. . . ."

"Who?"

"Dumb Buggy. That's the nickname of the Russian who lives across from Godbout. Quite a harmless nickname. Haven't you seen through his tricks? I mean, his house is a temple. Oh, he and his wife are good people, they are generosity itself, but they are living in error and sin. They are pagans who neglect Christ for the saints. Images, statues, icons, they worship all that. And your cousin? A half-irreligious, half-unbelieving blasphemer. Martel: lukewarm, perhaps quite cold. And his wife, on the pretext that she has children to look after, is no longer practising. Roméo and his Juliette, better known as Blanche! The only thing blanched about her is her name. A fine pair of superstitious fools! They are living in blasphemy, sin, debauchery, alcohol, and infamy. I've heard some marvellous stories from them! Even I, who thought I had heard everything, even I was startled! But my ministry obliges me to secrecy. And now we come to you, the Simards. What do we find in your case? Catholics by habit, devotion without conviction. No, no, do not protest. Luckily distance keeps you from the evil influence of the others. Your weak faith would be no defence. And now, to that fine collection of Christians we must add Professor Savard. No doubt the same calibre as the others."

"Yep, that's our line, all right."

"That's your line, Rémi. Evil dwells here. You want proof? The devil does not hesitate to show himself. I am convinced more sins are committed in these six houses than in all the rest of the parish."

"And you don't know everything, father."

"I don't doubt that, little Rémi. I don't doubt it! Poor innocent soul thrust by life into the midst of evil!"

He ran his fingers through Rémi's hair.

"But never forget your confirmation and solemn communion: you are a soldier of Christ. With your brother you must pray for the conversion of the sinners. You're going to help me bring the gospel to this line. You know, Rémi, this is a veritable mission field, just like Africa. I'm going to be the missionary and you will help me."

Furious at the man's hand on his head, Rémi got up suddenly. His glance took in the hill and its scattered spruce, the muddy creek, and, on the other hill, the two roofs in profile against the endless blue. Behind him he was aware of the cave of clay with its black goddess who saw the priest as a laughing-stock. That gave him all the daring he needed. He pointed to the horizon with a sweep of his arm and searched for solemn words: "I belong here!"

"Rémi!"

"I'm with this line and against the rest."

He ran away down the road, shouting at the top of his voice, without looking back, "I'm a pagan!"

He found Robert in the kitchen.

"Has the priest gone?"

"No. He's coming. Where's mom?"

"Gone shopping with dad and Françoise."

"Lock the door, Robert. We're goin' to hide upstairs."

They lay on their beds and Rémi gave a brief report of his conversation with the priest. Ricard arrived, knocked on the back door, shouted, knocked louder, circled the house, craning his neck to see in the windows, rattled the front door, and came back to the rear door, which he attacked with a vicious boot.

"Rémi, Rémi! Open up Rémi. Answer! I know you're in there. Open! Rémi! Rémi!"

The boys laughed silently. At last the priest had had enough and went on his way.

"He's gone, Robert. Want to go out?"

"Not on your life. I just got up to eat. I'm going back to bed."

Rémi went out. He needed to find his own silence again, wipe out the priest's words and get back to his real concerns. He scoured the countryside, filling his sack with whatever might have meaning or importance in a ceremony still to be invented: rotten wood from the poplar-monster, insects, a snake, plants, flowers, branches from bushes. The fruits of his search were piled in their cave. In front of the entry he levelled out the heap of excavated earth, and on this flat space prepared a pyre of dry wood, a big pyre that would burn high. Working like a beaver, he transformed the banks of the pond into a place worthy of the great solemnities to come, and while he was going home for supper he tried to imagine rites appropriate to the evening's ceremony. You don't go sacrificing just like that, point-blank, without a certain decorum. The officiating priest must recite formulas and prayers. Of course, not prayers like those in church. It wasn't the Jesus of light that Rémi was about to invoke, but an unknown god who had no name, perhaps a multiple god or one with no definite form. The god that was Night.

After supper, Robert, who had been sleeping almost the whole day, wanted to play. He didn't understand the serious, reserved attitude of his brother, or his mysterious airs. Rémi suggested that they go for a quiet walk along the road.

"What's got into you, Rémi?"

"Tonight the knights go out."

"Where to?"

"Don't ask too many questions. You'll know soon enough."

"Come on, you and me tell each other everything. That's what we agreed on. If we don't it's not fair play."

"It's not play at all, Robert. It's very important, very serious. Tonight there is going to be a ceremony beside the Creek of the Curse. I can't tell you any more. You'll see for yourself."

"How do you know?"

"I decided on this ceremony. It's to keep us from moving to Amos."

"Aw, that's silly. You don't believe a ceremony can. . . ."

"We're talking about the survival of the knights! And the professor has to disappear from the princess's castle."

"And the ceremony's going to. . . ."

"Right. A kind of mass. I was inspired. It'll work, don't worry. Just like the other night when you stopped the storm."

"Some kind of mass?"

"A terrible, frightening ceremony. We may not come out of it alive."

"Hey, don't try to scare me!"

"It's just a warning."

"We'll stay together?"

"Yes."

Night came at last, their parents slept, and the boys were able to go to their retreat.

"We're going to make a fire!" said Robert, surprised.

"Yes. Give me a hand."

From the cave they brought out the stones, the plants, and the jars in which the insects were rattling, and the other jar in which the snake lay curled – all the things Rémi had collected earlier. Robert was more and more puzzled.

"Don't ask questions. Just wait. Here's the statue. Set it up there against the bank. Be careful with her."

They set the goddess up facing the pyre with the offerings at her feet. Rémi lights the votive candle and they roll cigarettes. Rémi opens the small bottle of cognac stolen that very morning.

"Take it easy with the stuff."

Rémi smokes and tries to appear calm, but he is burning with impatience, counting the passing moments, which are far too slow for his taste. He's waiting for midnight, the time he judges propitious for his task. It will be Sunday, as well, the day of rites. Rémi would not have felt right about officiating on a Friday or a Monday. The boy is deeply moved and fearful at the same time. When he thinks the time has come he takes another pull at the mickey and stands up.

"Robert, you are to follow me and do what I say without asking questions."

They remove their clothes. Rémi lights a torch which he had made a few hours earlier by sticking a roll of birchbark in the split of an elder branch. Holding the flame at arm's length, he leads his brother down to the stream, plants the base of his light in the clay bank, goes into the water, and submerges completely. Robert does the same.

"Come here so that I can baptize you."

"Are you crazy?"

"We have to be baptized tonight."

"You know, Rémi, we shouldn't joke about stuff like that."

"This is no joke."

Rémi cups his hands in the water and holds them over his brother's head. The water drips between his fingers and onto Robert's hair.

"Robert, I baptize you in the name of the Night and the Black Virgin."

"What am I supposed to say?"

"So be it."

"So be it."

Then it's Robert's turn to be the baptist, and he feels no desire to laugh, as he had feared he would. The light

166

dancing on the water of the creek, the thickening shadows all around, even the gesture of his raised hands – all these combine to inspire the fear and respect that only come from the proximity of a sacred mystery. From the bank they take handfuls of clay, work it into a muddy cream, and rub it all over their bodies.

"Everywhere!" Rémi orders.

They become black on the side where the shadows lie and almost silver where the light strikes them, shining and earthy as worms. The taste of earth is in their mouths. Nature is silent and attentive as the procession of the clay men goes by, their skin cracking at the joints. Not a cloud in this moonless night, only stars like so many votive lights in a temple with a giant dome. Rémi kneels, torch in hand, in front of the Virgin with the childish head. He bows.

"Oh, Black Goddess, deign to preside over our sacrifice. Intercede for us with the Powers, so that they accept our offerings and grant our wishes."

And he bows deeper still until he kisses the earth. The torch, its bark almost consumed, sets fire to the pyre. The dry wood catches fire and at once the flames leap high, high in the still air, a pillar pointed by the perspective. A breath of air and it becomes a tree with red and green roots, its trunk twisted like a malformed cedar, spreading out into transparent wreaths of foliage, covered with brilliant flowers that give off their ephemeral pollen.

"Kneel, Robert."

As Robert falls to his knees, Rémi stretches tall, holds out his arms with fingers spread in the air as high as he can reach, grasping. His projected shadow covers underbrush and moss, lying flat on the earth. His eyes search the stars, dancing in the smoke like sparks. He feels himself growing taller, taller, like a giant. It is as if strange forces were pulsing through him: forces from the air, caught by his antenna-arms and running down his muscles to circulate with his blood. Other currents rising from the earth through his bare soles to his legs meet those of the air in the region of his belly where they mingle rowdily after their rude collision. Rémi has become a hyphen between air and earth, the place and organ of their coupling. He feels full of a power that frightens him, and he suddenly realizes what he has released is too much for him. But he can't go back. His gestures, the least movement of a hand, a palm turned upward, are no longer ordinary but have taken on a solemn beauty and grandeur. Robert no longer knows his brother, whose face in the firelight has become a frightful mask.

"O Powers of the Night, here we are before you, humble supplicants. We, your knights, are in need of your magic. Receive our offerings."

Rémi goes to get some victims.

"O Night, we are your servants. Here is a feather torn from a bird by the storm that Robert calmed. Here is a part of the bowels of the monster I slew. Receive them in the smoke of the fire as proof of our identity. We are indeed those we profess to be."

He raises the feather and the wood and throws them to the flames. Another trip from the statue to the pyre. Each time, objects are presented in language that Rémi tries to make ceremonial.

"To you we sacrifice this branch, still green, of the shivering aspen, and a perfumed branch of black spruce."

"We sacrifice the flower, which will bring no fruit, and the root that longs for earth."

"We sacrifice the singing grass, and the caterpillar that will never be a butterfly."

"We sacrifice this mushroom born in one night to earth, and the dragon-fly with rainbow wings."

"We sacrifice this bread, which no one shall eat, and this snake twisting with fear. May all these nourish you."

Rémi has become excited, his voice as he officiates betrays growing panic. When he has exhausted his supply of objects he stares around him wildly, finding nothing. But his celebration is incomplete. The things he prepared in advance are not enough. He has to go further. He takes the small bottle of brandy.

"We will take communion with alcohol."

He gives some to his brother, drinks from it himself, and pours the rest on the fire, which flares up noisily with a soft blue flame.

"Drink with us, O Night, and be merciful. May your ears hear our voices."

A bat, flying out of nowhere, zigzags into the flame, cries out, and falls in the fire with a sputtering sound.

Rémi is exultant.

"Robert! Did you see that? It's a sign. It worked. Come on."

And they begin to dance around the pyre, staggering a little. From their throats comes a guttural chant and their feet stamp out the rhythm. The brandy gives them inspiration. They wave their arms, leap and twist, and their movements fan the flames. After a time Robert sits down again. Rémi has become feverish. He must find something else; he must push ahead quickly before the Powers grow tired and leave. But his means are exhausted. Exasperated, the high priest turns his back on the fire and faces the night, which by contrast is so dense that the eye cannot pierce its wall. And Rémi, at the top of his lungs, shouts, "Beelzebub, Satan, demons of the dark, come out! I order you to come close and listen!"

He must go on, he must invent. But Rémi knows nothing of sorcery, neither its formulas nor its ritual. The only words he knows apart from everyday speech are those of the church, Ricard's religion. And so he howls out a whole litany of blasphemies.

"Stop!" screams Robert. "Have you gone crazy?"

Rémi is out of breath but frantic, and hears only the words he is vomiting out. He is weeping.

"Holy powers of hell, come to my help, come and share in the sacrifice. And you, the dead, rotting in the earth, come and pray with us."

He darts at his rucksack and grasps a rosary and a St. Christopher medal lifted from the dashboard of the family car. He brandishes these, jeering.

"Look here, forces of evil, see what I'm offering!"

Robert pleads in vain for his brother to stop. He is terrified and trembling.

"Shut up, Robert, or I'll damn you. Fire and the devil will eat you up right here."

He swings the objects of piety above the flames.

"Demons of the night, receive these poor offerings: a rosary and cross, and a bearded saint."

With a new string of blasphemies he hurls them into the fire. He removes the round stone from beneath the feet of the Goddess and tosses it into the coals. The stone, damp as a sponge, bursts open with a click.

"Take also the damned soul of this genie which I have set free."

Rémi turns back toward the night and strides alongside the pond.

"Come, show yourselves, come close, I feel you hiding there. I see your glowing eyes, your pale flesh of the living dead. I hear you, scaly monsters crawling out of earth. I smell you, fantastic vultures sailing on velvet wings, I can breathe your sulphurous breath. What more do you want in exchange for your help? Say it, speak. And you, Beelzebub, grinning across the creek, with your sex standing up like a tree, what more do you want, great Master?"

Rémi leaps up and down, talking to the trees, and his madness creates hideous faces between the branches, shapes that dance a saraband on the frontier between the night and the firelight. Robert, terrorized and paralysed by panic, is hiding his face against the earth, sobbing. He wants no more of the night nor of the priest's insanities. Rémi scratches the drying clay from his chest, rolls it in a ball and flattens it to a cake between his palms. He turns back to the fire, elevating this disc with its imperfect contour.

"I consecrate the black host, fruit of the marriage between water and earth. *Per omnia saecula saeculorum.*"

In the glowing fire a mouth opens and consumes the host.

Feverish, Rémi falls to earth and weeps, as much from exhaustion as from loss of his powers. Suddenly the night grows brighter. Lifting from the horizon a multitude of auroral flames shoot upward to join at the zenith, where they melt into an opaque mass. The night turns pale. This sphere of shifting lights is the final sign: the sacrifices have been accepted.

It was eight o'clock. Their mother had a hard time waking her sons. Rémi, washing his hands, saw that they were still smeared with clay. The bath in the stream had not taken everything off. No doubt other stains remained elsewhere, under his clothing. Sunlight flooded the kitchen and from the ripening grass rose the song of birds. It was going to be a beautiful day. Lunch was a happy feast, but the boys did not share the mood. The mother didn't understand.

"Did you two have a fight?" They shook their heads.

"Just look at that lovely sunlight! Even that . . . no?"

She was making fun of their glum faces. She must be happy about something.

"We're lucky to have such good weather. Don't you remember, we're going to Val-d'Or today?"

That seemed to leave them cold.

"You don't care? You're hard to please. But I have more good news for you, I didn't tell you yesterday. Your father found a place to live in Amos. We're moving!"

Despite his expressionless face, Rémi was dismayed. Robert was staring at him with an angry, reproachful look that seemed to say, "See, all your fooling around yesterday got us nowhere. It may have done us harm."

Their father was laughing.

"That's not the way to make them happy. They know already we're going to move, and I don't think they like it. If you want to see their faces change, tell them *when* we're moving!"

"D'you think so? Well, it's not right away. The house won't be free till mid-September. In the meanwhile we stay here. Your father's going to drive to work every day."

Rémi couldn't believe his ears. He said it over to himself just to be sure. Mid-September. Mid-September. His heart was beating hard against its rib cage. The rest of the summer here. He wanted to shout. But all he did was smile.

Robert spoke: "That's great."

He stole a glance at Rémi, full of admiration. He no longer resented yesterday's madness, their goal had been achieved. But Rémi was paying no attention to Robert. Tranquilly, selfishly he was savouring his joy.

They were supposed to go to nine-o'clock mass and afterwards pick up Réginald, Sonia, and Sophie to go to Val-d'Or. This didn't suit the boys too well. They protested that they'd rather stay home and enjoy the splendid day. Their parents hesitated, uncertain about leaving their sons alone. Rémi tipped the scales by pointing out that if they stayed there'd be more room in the car. Otherwise eight people would have to pile in, and it was a long drive. The boys had to promise not to play with fire and to be careful near the water; not to go too far away or too deep in the forest; to beware of strangers and keep the house locked. They promised. They would have promised anything. After a little more negotiating they were allowed not to go with the family to mass at nine. Instead, they would walk there for eleven. The walk didn't deter them, and they would take along a snack to eat on the way home. (Rémi had no intention of walking all those miles. All he wanted was not to hear Father Ricard saying mass and not to take part in that ceremony during which his day-dreaming would only be filled by the one last night beside the Creek of the Curse).

As soon as they were alone in the house they shouted for joy. They had no words to express it, all they could do was laugh and punch each other. They poured their hot chocolate down the sink and replaced it with coffee laced with moonshine. Then they sat outside.

"Rémi, I never thought it would work."

"It had to work. Everything's possible at night, and I saw signs of the alliance yesterday."

"What if it was . . . just a coincidence."

"Robert. You're not doubting. . . ."

"Listen, it was yesterday afternoon when they got the place to live, and they found out then we'd move in September. We're the only ones found it out this morning."

"But it was thanks to the Night, Robert! Thanks to her. She knew we were going to have the ceremony. And maybe they didn't find the apartment yesterday. Maybe it happened last night, in their heads."

"You mean it's not true?"

"Oh, it'd be true just the same. The apartment, the move, even if they didn't go there yesterday. The past would be changed."

"Hey! A little complicated, isn't it?"

"Even if you don't understand, don't doubt. You're not allowed."

"Anyway, don't try those crazy tricks again. That was terrible what you did, and the stuff you said."

"I had to do it. I'd do it again if I had to."

"I was scared. I'm not ashamed to say it. Real scared. You didn't see yourself; you were so changed, awful looking. And those devils and the things you were describing, did you really see them?"

"I don't know if they were real, but I saw them."

"I hid my face in the ground and I could feel the earth shaking. Even when I had my eyes closed I could see shadows moving."

"I was scared too, Robert. You can't imagine. But it was worth the risk."

For a long time they sat sipping their coffee and watching the play of a wind that was too high for them to feel. A plover skimmed the grass, then climbed, crying killdeer, killdeer. . . .

Robert stood up.

"I'm happy, that's for sure. We're spending the summer here."

"You bet. Same here."

Blows of a hammer echo in the woods, and the ascending scale of a nail being driven into a board sends shivers through the grass. The haunted house! All the glory of the day fades for Rémi, and his joy is tarnished. Since he found out that the charm worked on his parents he has been wondering anxiously if it also worked on the professor. He had put off finding out the answer to his question, preferring hope to a demoralizing certainty. And now the intruder is sending him a message with the sounds of his activity. The ceremony had, then, been no more than half successful. Would he have to start over again with his sacrifices and blasphemies, set up a new ceremony and risk his neck again with the dangerous forces of evil? The thought makes him physically ill, and he dumps his coffee in the dust where Françoise had stuck a few wilted flowers, her "garden" where her doll received visitors. He goes inside, with Robert on his heels.

"Where are you going, Rémi?"

"To bed."

"What? It seems to me that even if you're tired you have to celebrate good news."

"I hurt all over. I'm dead."

Robert can't figure it out, and this only makes Rémi more impatient. He feels alone, misunderstood by his brother, who, as a fellow knight, should know better.

"Hell, if I'd known I'd have gone to Val-d'Or! You just drop me and go to bed. But when you need me, eh, I follow you, even when you're having dreams like a madman."

Before lying down, Rémi stops a second before the window, just to have a look at the house next door, one good look before asking himself if it would be worthwhile celebrating another sacrilegious mass. Should he wait for a new sign from the Night, or drop the whole thing and enjoy his summer in this wild land? Forget that he was a knight for a short while, that he came close to mysteries and lived in a night-time that was more real than day? There's no such thing as a knight with no Lady to serve and conquer. And it was probably bad form to change Ladies in mid-stream.

The hammer is still ringing, and Rémi at first doesn't grasp the meaning of the boards that are once more barricading the windows. In the lane that goes from the verandah to the road two suitcases are standing, like black dogs lying in the tall grass, waiting. It takes a few minutes for Rémi's stunned mind to draw the obvious conclusions.

"Robert! Hey! Robert!"

Robert arrives on the run, trips on the stairs. Maybe his brother's dead or dying, or there's a fire. Something like that. Robert is all pale.

"What's up? What is it?"

Rémi smiles broadly and points to the window.

"Look."

Robert rushes over but sees nothing odd. The sky, the trees, the hill, the grass. . . .

"Damn you, what kind of a trick. . . ."

"Trick? Look at the haunted house, dummy!"

Robert also takes a while to grasp what's going on next door. Then it's an unbridled round dance of wild Apaches. The covers fly from the beds, the pillows fly at the walls, the curtains bite the dust. Never mind, they'll pick it all up. For the moment nothing matters but the flight of the intruder, chased out by the magic forces let loose by the two knights in their nocturnal ceremony. A feeling of infinite power fills their hearts. The princess can now come back to a castle as dark and silent as she could desire. Everything will be as before. The quests will begin again, and the service to Ladies, the expeditions – with knights who have grown through the trial they just experienced. Rémi falls to his knees.

"Let's pray."

"Are you all there? Who do you want to pray to?"

"The Virgin."

"After what you did yesterday? It makes no sense."

"The Black Virgin, our clay goddess. It's not enough to ask, you've got to thank as well. If we don't, she could drop us next time."

"Yeah, but . . . just like that, in broad daylight?"

"You're right. She probably sleeps all day and only listens in the dark."

He gets up.

"We're going to our hide-out right now. Her temple. It's always dark in there. Anyway, it's Sunday. That'll do for a mass.

"Rémi! Don't joke about those things. It may be just a bunch of lies the priests tell, but you never know, and it's bad enough not going to mass without making fun of it. If it turned out true . . ."

"What if it was the truth, Robert? That wouldn't change anything for us. Somebody said you can't serve two masters. You've already chosen yours."

"I chose nothin'!"

"Oh, yes you did! Every time you do something, you're choosing. Because at the same time you're saying no to something else. When you pray to the Black Goddess you refuse the other gods."

"Well, anyway, it's likely not true, all the stuff they taught us."

"No, Robert! It has to be true. If Ricard's Jesus isn't true our Virgin can't be true either."

"You have to choose? There's no other way?"

"You have to choose without fear! My truth is as true as Ricard's. His is all hearsay and mine's imagined."

They're outside near the shed watching the neighbour, who seems to be waiting for someone or something in the shade of the verandah.

"Come on, I want to see what he's like."

They cross the field. Ever since he arrived they've seen him only from a distance, as he never visited the Simards or, for that matter, anyone else. Rémi hadn't dared go near the house, out of respect for his old dreams. Today it's different, everything's different.

"Good day, sir."

They can't see him very well for the bright sunlight. But he stares at them for a moment with a severe expression.

"You're from next door?"

"Yes. Are you leaving?"

"Yeah. I have to give summer courses this year, I can't stay any longer. Too bad, looks like a nice summer. But don't you take advantage of my going away to get into my house."

"Oh, we wouldn't do that! We never went in before."

"I know. And just as well, too. This house isn't an ordinary house. You might almost say it's haunted. The ghosts know me, so they don't do me any harm. But if they found a stranger in there I wouldn't give two cents for his life."

"We know it's haunted. There's noises sometimes at night."

"Noises? Are there . . . does anybody come sneaking around my house?"

"No. There was a man one time. When he saw us he ran away. Nobody ever came since."

"I suppose it's not so bad having neighbours after all. There's a lot of looting up and down these lines. They rip the doors and windows off empty houses and take any furniture that's inside. They even tear out cupboards and sinks. Listen, I know you won't want to come too close because of the danger, but you could keep an eye on my place. And if anybody comes, scare them off or tell your parents, eh? Like soldiers on guard duty. And next spring, if you've done a good job, I'll bring you both a present from Montreal. O.K.?

"Yes, sir."

"Promise me you'll be good guards."

"I promise," said Robert.

"Me too," said Rémi.

"Great. I'm going to give you a little something right now. I'm going to tell you a secret. Do you like fishing?"

"Yes sir!" they replied together.

"About a mile past the creek, on your left as you're headed, you'll see an enormous dead birch. You can hear it before you see it because there are always woodpeckers at it. Between the road and the tree it's full of brush and alders and raspberry bushes. But they don't amount to much, maybe twenty feet or so. You go through that. Just at the birch there's the start of a trail. You climb through the spruce and the outcropping of rock for maybe a thousand feet. Then it goes down pretty steep through the ferns. And you come to the prettiest little lake you could ever imagine. Oh it's a lovely place! Quiet. There's not many trout left, but there are lots of catfish there, and big ones."

"There are?"

Robert remembers the lake near Laprairie where their father took them fishing sometimes, casting over a curtain of reeds for pretty little catfish, their skin so smooth, almost black on their backs and creamy white on the underside. You had to be careful of their three whiskers, and they took a long time to die out of water.

"That lake isn't well known. Keep it a secret."

"We won't tell."

"Listen, is that a car coming?"

"I think so."

"That's for me," said Professor Savard, glancing at his watch. "Right on time."

The boys watched him put his suitcases on the back seat and slide in beside the driver. The dust hung in the air for a long time before settling on the aftergrowth in the fields. Rémi was silent, almost choking with emotion.

It would soon be eleven o'clock, time for high mass. Their nostrils and eyes just out of the water, their green bodies camouflaged in the green scum of the stagnant pond, the frogs were contemplating the world as it was reflected in their golden-irised eyeballs. Rémi and Robert were tidying up in front of their cave, burying the ashes with the remains of the sacrifice, small, shrivelled things, hard to distinguish from the wood coals. And all that was only yesterday. Yet it seemed so far! In fact, it was always that way: in the sunlight, memories of the night before seemed old and quite unreal. And in the evening grew plausible again. Then it was the day's turn to become like a dream that fades as you wake. Rémi felt that he led two parallel lives.

"What are you thinking?" Robert asked.

"Nothing important."

Rémi captured a frog and carried it into the cave. With the votive lamp lighted the Goddess came alive for her knights, looking as strange as ever with her child's head and woman's body. They knelt, and Rémi recited a thanksgiving prayer, opened his jack-knife and, holding the frog in one hand above the idol, disembowelled it with a sure hand. There was no cry, just the sound of punctured organs. Blood and juices splashed the face, shoulders and breasts of the statue.

"Why did you do that? It's horrible."

"Robert, don't blaspheme! That was a sacrifice, a mass for our Goddess. To please her."

"How do you know she likes it?"

179

"It's a sure thing. She's the opposite of Ricard's god who loves life. She loves death. The priest's god is god of light and the sun. She's the Goddess of night and darkness. And she likes vice and evil, just the opposite of the other one."

"Do we have to do bad things for her?"

"Don't get excited. Bad, bad, that's nothing serious!"

"That's not what we were taught."

"Sometimes you're a real fool. Believing everything they tell you, in school and everywhere."

"But . . . we're the ones who made her!"

"Sure, we made the statue, but I think it was the Goddess who found us. She could even have made us come from Montreal so we could invent her."

"That's not possible."

"You don't think so? Do you dare to doubt the Goddess of the Night?"

Robert looked fearfully at the clay idol. A drop of blood created a curling smile, shining at a corner of her mouth, and dark milk dripped from the point of a breast.

"No, I don't doubt her."

Skinny fingers brushed the boy's hair as if in an approving caress. He ducked, terrified. His hesitant hand touched a root that had pierced their cave roof and hung there with its pale radicles.

They recited more prayers. Then Rémi tossed the frog's corpse outside, its nerves twitching after death. The boys decided to carve further niches at the base of the dome to accommodate the provisions they had brought. They had taken advantage of their parents' absence to filch candles, matches, a knife, and some tinned food. Their excavations gave them the idea of decorating the hide-out. Robert gazed at the image of Mrs. Martel that he had already made, and felt the urge to produce a vast fresco depicting him, Robert, making love with Carmen Martel in all possible positions. He went to work, carving with the knife point, occasionally adding relief with small bits of clay which he wet with spittle to make them stick in place.

"Terrific," Rémi approved, admiring the roof.

He too decided to draw his fantasies. He depicted the ceremony of the night before. He himself, the high priest, was throwing into the fire a giant serpent, which twisted itself into agonized coils. Robert, kneeling, was holding the Goddess's statue at arm's length. All around them danced horned monsters with pointed teeth and demons with cloven penises to match their cloven hoofs. Then he scratched in all the images that crossed his mind: sketches of organs and members, intimations of erotic scenes, Diane, flat on her back, bound and spread-eagled. He punctured her body repeatedly with the thorn he was using as an etcher's needle, finally leaving it sticking under one breast, where her heart should be. A drop of moisture squeezed out and dripped along the murder weapon. Beside the Goddess's niche, where the curving wall was almost vertical, he sculpted in relief a body that was inspired by Sonia's. He took great care with its proportions, and tried to draw clean, uninterrupted lines. And he succeeded in drawing a desirable body. But it was not really his cousin that he was drawing, and he omitted the head. He was waiting to see the face that belonged to his princess.

Their parents came back from Val-d'Or in high good humour. At last their mother had been able to go out and forget the sideroad and the wild countryside. They had driven past the house they'd soon be living in. The move was all she thought about now. Having running water, electricity, radio, T.V., neighbours and a phone! Oh! Back to civilization, forget the last few months as if they'd been a bad dream. The thought of this would sustain her through the rest of the summer and transform even those few weeks into a kind of vacation, as if they were roughing it a little in a summer cottage.

Rémi went to bed late, his eyelids heavy and burning. All during supper he'd had to fight to stay awake and not to show the fatigue he felt but would be unable to explain to his parents. He wanted only to lie down and let every muscle go to sleep, feeling his body sustained by something other than its strength. He looked forward to a deep sleep, dreamless, tainted by no dissatisfaction with himself. He had barely slept since the death of the moose, and so many events had been crammed into so little time! Just before dropping off he managed to drag himself to the window and see the castle of the princess melting into the night. The house was empty now and would certainly remain so until the emanations of the intruder disappeared. Then the princess and her court would come in procession to their abode. As soon as he was sure that she was there, Rémi would go to meet her.

A whippoorwill flew past, uttering its name . . .

The days and weeks went by. For Robert and Rémi, thanks to their dream and to the darkness, the frontiers of their sideroad disappeared or were pushed back until they embraced a whole universe. Distance lost its meaning, and the knights' quests could not be measured by time: they lasted a second, or perhaps an entire night. One leap and they were at the other end of the concession line: or after three hours of running they had not completed their exploration of ten spruce trees.

The castle of the princess began to come to life again with its creaking sounds, its complaints, its mysteries. Rémi resisted the temptation (which was tinged with excitement and fear) to lay siege to the sacred place. He told himself that he wasn't ready yet, he must pass other trials to prepare himself for this one, like a sword whose steel was cleansed of its impurities by fire and use. The summer dragged on through torrid days as the crickets sang their hearts out in the grass; interminable days, squeezing the night in their vise. The air, heavy with pollen, grew visible. The light was gold dust, the whole landscape shimmered under the sun's merciless caress, and the horizons grew uncertain. The earth swelled, grew rounded in the heat, soft as an overripe fruit. The spruce tips lost their thrust, the tangled grass lay still, a bird tried its song but after two notes was still, exhausted. And it was not yet noon!

There were quick, violent storms, too sudden for the clay to absorb the rain. Saturated moss gave off surplus water that split into a thousand silver trickles, a filigree in the dust, and came together in watercourses that furrowed the sand, little streams that cut the gravel, torrents that slashed out their own canyons. Moraines, eskers, muddy meanders, sandy bays, alluvial plains, deltas, a whole miniature geography across which the flow of mud carried off plants hairy at both ends and rolled already-rounded pebbles before plunging into the abyss and splashing at last into the silt-filled waters of the Creek of the Curse. The creek, in turn, was swollen by a hundred such tributaries, and, at its flood, filled the culvert at the bridge, backed up, and formed a lake that threatened to overflow and take everything with it. Along with the wind, the sun came and greedily sucked in this moisture. You'd have thought the sun was a voracious butterfly on a flower. The wind pretended it was a bee and hummed along the slopes where the water had caused little wash-outs. The cloudburst had washed the dust from all the grass and cleaned the leaves and the air. For several days the world was renewed, with strong and virgin odours.

Then there were days during which drizzle alternated with a slow and glacial rain. Summer became a memory and the whole Abitibi landscape grew as dull and gloomy as it was in fall. On those days Mrs. Simard felt very far from Montreal, and the whole household had the benefit of her sullen mood. On those days you had to stay indoors and make up games that didn't last too long, for you were always running to the window. At last they had had enough, and roofed by stiff raincoats, went off across the fields where their footsteps caused water to spurt sideways. Despite their rubber boots and oilskins they were soon wet and shivering.

When the weather was fine the boys went on the hunt as soon as it was dark. They became creatures of the shadows, learning to find their way without seeing it, developing another sense, like a kind of bat's sonar, a sense of hearing that, far in advance, felt out not only concrete things but mysteries as well. They learned to navigate by the North Star and to estimate time by the Big Dipper, almost turning on itself in a celestial pirouette. Thanks to a book that Blanche gave them, an old dog-eared book that smelled of must, with faded, clumsy illustrations, they came to know the names of things and animals. They could name the plants, tell the difference between a house martin and a sand swallow, identify the great horned owl that patrolled the air above the road at dusk, and not confuse it with the hawk-owl who had his nest in a tree where the forest had burned. The bird that had its territory along the Creek of the Curse was called a striped owl; and the one with his nest in the grass, near the poplar-monster defeated by Rémi, was a marsh-owl. They often saw him in the morning in the air, above the hill with its beard of millet, casting a last cold eye over the world before retiring. He would scold the soaring kestrel steeped in the early sun. These flowers in phosphorescent pink turned out to be the Canadian rhododendron, and those beside the catfish lake were purple pitcher plants. As you learned to name each thing, each animal, you became its master, you almost possessed it. It was exhilarating, and the boys spent a good part of their time on this inventory of the world. The book showed the constellations. The stars were not just points of light strewn haphazardly in the sky. Cunning lines joined them to form fabulous creatures: Pegasus, the Dolphin, the Dog, the Serpent, the Bull: the book populated the firmament with fauna the eye would never have discovered. This pleased Rémi, confirming certain suspicions. Nothing was simple, even things that seemed so. The boys repeated the names of the stars aloud, names full of music: Vega, Arcturus, Deneb, Aldebaran, Cassiopaeia. But there were certain inhabitants of the dark about which the book knew nothing, those nameless beasts whose presence could only be guessed at from certain noises, or from a fleeting glimpse of their wan, lambent forms.

The night is scary. To know this, one need only to have heard on a single morning the mad joy of the birds who, happy to have survived, sing loudly of life to the sun. But darkness was the lot of our knights, and fear walked with them, not yet become a friend, and barely tamed. Often they ran through the countryside and came home only at dawn, chased by the light. Thus they took possession of the whole country, learning its hidden corners, knowing the course of the smallest stream, and where the cedars (rare in these latitudes) grew in pungent groves and gave protection to secret homes beneath their branches. They knew, too, where the wild cherry hid the peppermint odour of its sap, and where the air was filled with clinging black flies and the piercing song of the mosquito and the smarting bite of the midges. Some of their expeditions had to be broken off because of the insects. These occasions only made the others more pleasant, the nights of cool mists when the sluggish mosquitos retreated, leaving the air to the breathing of the trees and the panting of the boys, delighted at last to be able to run free without interference.

Their travels sometimes took them far from the road, even past the back line of the lots a mile away. Beyond that there was forest and more forest. The black stumps of a burnt-out patch lined up in close formation or in ranks bristling with the most varied arms, and barred all passage. The knights would charge, stick in hand, and in the course of epic battles, vanquished many of the enemy. The slightest oddity, a twisted tree, a strangely shaped bush, could trigger endless adventures. Robert and Rémi were drunk with the freedom of their nights, despite imaginary threats and the real dangers of cutting rocks and stabbing branches.

The knights had no objection to keeping an eye on humans. They loved to terrify Méo and Blanche, or simply to hide and watch them frighten each other, or quarrel or get drunk or have a slanging match or a fight and finally fall into each other's arms. No, it was Roméo who would fall into Blanche's arms, sinking into the gulf of that flesh with its folds and counterfolds, absorbed by this crushing mass of fat that now screamed obscenities, now wept and lavished cooing words, ridiculous in both its moods.

Martel's house attracted Robert with a special magnetism, particularly when the red truck was not in the yard. Often Carmen's lingerie hung on the line, panties trimmed with lace and brassières that held the form of the breasts they served, skirts shiny from rubbing. Robert would lay his cheek against these things of cloth, sure that in the odour of damp wash there were traces of female effluvium perceptible to him alone. Nose in the air, he breathed in deeply, excitable as a male in rutting time. The print of a shoe in the dried mud beside the stoop called his fingers to explore its contours, and images in his head exploded and drove his heart to beating faster. A ray of light would escape beneath the blind and the boy would run to it like a butterfly to its doom. He would peek voraciously, desperately: a body floating free in a night-shirt, the shape of a foot or a shoulder and his dreams were fed for the whole day that followed. Sometimes the fleeting vision of a naked body would reward his patience. Then, his senses on fire, Robert would run off grinding his teeth, to disappear among the trees.

Godbout was always good for a show, and Rémi and Robert always laughed themselves sick as they watched that lighted screen, his window pane. Imprecations and maledictions rose up to fill the kitchen, threats and insults rained down. Godbout strode up and down, grabbing at the empty air with his clenched hands. The sight of this man, a prisoner of his own contradictions, soon became monotonous and even painful. Each time the boys went away filled with rancour, saddened at seeing so much squandered energy. Godbout talked about a crusade he was about to launch against Ricard, a holy war to free the people of Saint-Gérard and lead them to the true Shepherd, and chase out this traitor in the pay of the English and "those in power." The boys felt attracted to this noble cause, but they didn't trust Godbout and especially didn't believe either in his clairvoyance or his steadfastness. He would never get beyond having projects. "Like Ricard," Rémi thought.

On the other side of the road, Dam-Bogga's country was rustling with all his leafy trees, a forbidden domain. But it was not the undefended frontier of his fragile sapling fence, nor the barking of the dog who had become their friend, that held them back. It was more like an occult power, but one opposed to that of Night. Was it the strangeness of the perfumed air or the flickering of the votive lamp near the blessed branches? Or just the air of moral confidence and material prosperity? Dam-Bogga's domain, his fattened stock, and the very fact that he was still there were in such contrast to the rest of the Abitibi concessions! Most of them were poor farms that had seen the passage of several successive owners. Whatever the reason, the knights lost their special powers in the land of Dam-Bogga. Only in daytime, as very ordinary boys, did Rémi and Robert approach the house of the flowered wood and allow themselves to be spoiled by the old woman or listen to Dam-Bogga himself explain the secrets of animal life, the coupling, the births and deaths. He spoke willingly, if not easily, and told the story of each of the neighbours' houses: who had built it, why the owners left, who had come after them. He listed the evils that had befallen almost all of them, and Rémi began to understand why there was so little cleared land. Quarrels, misunderstandings, poverty, hunger, suicide, suspicious deaths, and, above all, the paralysis that follows the death of hope. Perhaps Ricard was right when he spoke of a settlement of the damned.

When all the lights were out, and sometimes earlier if there was nothing to be seen, the boys would slip off to their hide-out. The walk up the dark road gave them a chance to exchange impressions and ask questions about the goings-on of the adults. Then, in the safety of the cave, its walls covered with engravings, new rites were invented, as they were at humanity's dawn when learning had just begun. The Black Virgin was their confidante and accomplice, listening without flinching to the most blasphemous obscenities. The insidious perfume of the evil deeds her knights admitted to having committed in her name floated in the air, headier than the incense of all the churches.

During these weeks there were some long evenings when cards were played, sometimes at Simards' or Martels' place but most often in Réginald's house. These parties were held on Saturdays or Sundays, by unspoken agreement. Sometimes events or a sudden inspiration would spark a game on a week-night. It was the grown-ups' only amusement on the line, and none of them would miss it for the world. Cards were more than a game, they were almost a passion, a bitter struggle in which each tried to compensate for his failures in daily life and the frustrations encountered there. They could play a daring game, taking frightful risks, staking everything on one play, lose with the good grace of a gentleman or win and have an illusion of power. "Chicken in life, big wheel at cards," Réginald had said to Méo, not suspecting that the same applied to himself and all the others. Rémi, watching the adults hold their cards close to their chests like precious objects, seeing them think of nothing else, reflected that these evenings were not genuine meetings. They didn't come to see each other and talk, but to try to beat the adversary. Cards, a game? But look how seriously they play! To the point of forgetting everything else, and even blotting out each other. The boy concluded that the only real get-together had been the night the moose was killed.

Robert and Rémi came along on these parties, though no one ever suggested that they play, and they would have had no desire to do so. They knew that despite their parents' ban, the atmosphere would loosen up and they'd soon be offered a drink of wine or spirits, and that afterwards they would manage discreetly to have a second. The trick was not to show your real condition. In the smoke-filled room the boys were on the look-out for the women, their perfumes and the heat that they gave off. Their falsely innocent expressions disguised an alertness that missed no vision of feminine charm, however fleeting: the shadow in the middle of a neckline, the flash of a thigh above the stocking, the soft contour of a leg, or simply the cloth curving around a breast or a hip, or clinging to a buttock. There were other things that a taste refined by habit came to appreciate: a flashing eye, a tongue swiftly passing over a red lip, the velvety down that powder makes visible on a cheek, the fall of hair on the neck's curve, the full gesture of an arm, or the play of the lamplight that would project on the wall a great-breasted shadow or a callipygous silhouette. It took no more than this to send off at a gallop minds already befogged by alcoholic vapours.

One Monday there was a trip to Amos for the boys. They went with their father to register in the school of the Marist Brothers. As soon as the formalities were over, their father went to work. The boys had to put in time until evening. Seeing that they would be bored, their father gave them a dollar each, telling them to explore the town and eat at the restaurant, not forgetting to be back at the car for six o'clock. They walked for a long time, not talking much, thinking sadly of the move. Amos had its old town, with frame houses. That was where it grew lively, around the stores, restaurants, and hotels. Behind the cathedral boarding schools and seminary were grouped. At the opposite end of the town were the fine houses with lawns and trees and flowers. Then rows of more modest houses, two storeys high and with several apartments. Then came the fields, the road to Val-d'Or and the cemetery hill. And the railway by which they had come to this new land.

They found the house they would soon move into, inspected the resources of the neighbourhood, spied on the people and children to get a notion of them, measured how far it was to school. It was a really small town. There weren't even any alleys where you could play out of sight of adults. September. The word was a threat to Rémi's dream. For Robert, a rebel against books and discipline, it meant a nightmare.

At about two, in a former bus transformed into a restaurant, they ordered hot dogs, French fries, and orangeade. On their right was the automobile bridge, on their left the steel railway bridge. In front, across the brown, wax-smooth water, beyond a desolate park and promenade, houses were scattered on the face of a long hill.

Rémi felt the need to get his bearings, for this visit had disconcerted him. Robert was silent. He too must be suffering. This town, which reminded them of their life in Pointe-aux-Trembles but had none of its advantages, was so far from their sideroad and its spruce forest. They'd cease to be all-powerful knights and become ordinary boys again. And not even that. For they had changed, they had known freedom, they'd tamed the Night and the sinister woods. Transplanted to Amos, chivalry made no sense. Yet the Night had promised them so much! Mirages? Castles in the air? Nonsense inspired by solitude and isolation? And what about the Ladies they wanted to conquer and possess? Time, it was time they lacked, time was going to ruin everything. Weeks were flying past and the castle was still inviolable. And Carmen was still inaccessible. Something had to happen to trigger a change.

Robert, who seemed to be thinking the same thing, said hoarsely, "Too bad."

"Yeah."

"We have to do something, Rémi."

"Yes, but first we need a sign."

"What?"

"I don't know. Something that's going to seem meaningless. We have to keep wide awake, keep an eye out. I know, tonight we'll read the stars."

For several nights in a row the boys were on the look-out, but no message came. Rémi stood with his back to the boards of the haunted house, held his ear to the wall and waited. But all he heard was the life of aged wood and old abandoned things. He didn't dare go in, perhaps because he secretly suspected there was nothing there to find. But he often lay on the roof of the shed, looking up at the sky. Then he saw nothing but the heavens: the earth had disappeared. The firmament was no longer a dome, and Rémi suddenly grew conscious of the depth of space and the relative distance of each pinpoint of light; and he felt like a passenger on a little travelling planet. Even the wind was cosmic. At times the moon would rise and elbow its way through little, fleecy clouds. The skin of the sky became the heaving flank of an immense steed, whose steel-shod hoofs trampled the trees and Night foamed at the mouth.

Time passed, and the sun shortened its course up to the zenith and the night grew longer by the same amount, nibbling at both ends of day. Toward September everything speeded up. Only yesterday the hayfield had been full and fluffy, well-stuffed with the wild oats and their bearded heads, the supple timothy hay with its hairy grains. All these feathered head-dresses when touched by the air had given goose-flesh to the fields. The grains drew birds down and the birds gave a voice to the meadow. The stems would bend with the weight of chaffinches, goldfinches, cowbirds, hanging there like fat fruit, a delight to see. But in August! The heavy air leaves its traces everywhere, flattening all around like the bed of a gigantic moose, and the crushed hay, having lost its suppleness, will never stand again. A morning with a taste of fall: is it the wind or the dying grass that has a rough side and makes this rasping sound?

Réginald had no luck training his handsome stallion, despite the hours he spent on the task. One was as stubborn as the other, and their contest ended in a draw. Nothing worked: gentleness, shouting, and whipping were equally useless. Réginald's dream of earning money by lumbering faded. But his discouragement lasted only a few hours. He had the knack of landing on his feet like a cat, only to invent new dreams and make them, by the use of words, truer than reality. This was how he had drawn the Simards and Roméo into this god-forsaken concession. Now he decided to sell his stallion, which was not completely paid for, and "make a buck" by going in partnership with Martel to truck pulpwood. They made arrangements with a lumber company and were to begin the first week in September. Martel, who had always had trouble meeting the payments on his truck, saw himself rich by Christmas, or something like it.

It was Dam-Bogga who bought the stallion for a song. The whole line turned up the day he took possession of the animal. They wanted to see how he would get on with this unruly beast, which Réginald's strength had been unable to control. It was a chilly Saturday morning splashed with milk-and-honey light. As they left the house Simard said, "Smells like a day for hunting." And at ten they were still shivering, down in the hollow where the frosty air clung to the earth.

Dam-Bogga went into the stable alone. He refused all offers of help. Outside, Réginald, the Martels, parents and children, Méo and Blanche, Rémi and Robert and their father – almost the whole line – listened to the sounds coming from the stable. There were snorts from the horse and the sound of pawing hoofs. No shouts or curses from the man, nothing but a monotonous murmur. Everyone waited impatiently for a shout, a protest or – why not? – a cry for help.

Réginald was smiling. He had his money, and would never go back on the bargain. He was sure that the buyer (he'd warned him!) wouldn't be able to break in the horse. Oh, wonder! Here's Dam-Bogga in the doorway, stepping down, leading the black horse, which follows in a mist of odours, blowing clouds from his trembling nostrils, stretching his muzzle toward the crowd and sniffing. One hoof paws at the wooden threshold, he tosses his head, and great ripples of nervousness run back along his side. He whinnies and refuses to come out. Prudently they all retreat, even Réginald, who's grinning now. If the stallion takes the bit in his teeth his new master will flutter like a rag at the end of the halter rope. The little man turns to face the horse, grasps its nose and talks softly to it until it grows quiet. The audience goes "Oh!" and "Ah!" and Réginald stops smiling. When Dam-Bogga walks away again he has no need to pull on the tether. The horse comes along of its own accord. Everyone marvels: can he talk to a horse? The two climb the slope; the curious onlookers keep a respectful distance from the hoofs.

Rémi, arriving at the top of the slope, sees Diane, who has been watching the scene. She has put on her mocking face for him, and he replies with a stare of pure hatred. Unable to keep up the confrontation, he turns to look at the horse, still docile, still following. Diane is walking behind him, whistling a snatch of a *chansonnette* to make sure he knows she's there. He's in a rage. Oh, if she were a boy! He'd pound her with such pleasure. Now he understands Robert's taste for a scrap. But how do you take revenge on a horrible girl like Diane? She's right on his heels, he can feel her breath. She even walks on the heel of his shoe, trying to make him stumble. A real burr! But he strains hard and lets a resounding fart. As the sound fades away the girl falls back behind him. Rémi hears Robert beside him laughing derisively.

The pebbles rattle under the horse's hoofs, he's started prancing. From the field behind Dam-Bogga's buildings comes a long whinny. Dancing, the horse advances again, his hindquarters swing, his front feet paw, and you'd think he was floating on the dust he kicks up. Never had he seemed so handsome or so powerful. Réginald turns red, and everybody whispers that Dam-Bogga has a way with animals.

Robert tugs at his brother's sleeve, murmuring, "What's she after anyway, the little bitch?"

"I don't know. She's sure a pest. She's a pimple."

"Why don't you pound her?"

"Well, she's a girl."

"Dummy!"

"And her dad's here. Ours too."

"Wait for your chance and let her have it. Don't worry about her bein' a girl."

The two horses keep calling to each other, and Dam-Bogga needs all his science to hold the stallion.

"Jesus! If you ask me that mare's in heat."

Réginald is already regretting his deal. The stallion is not so bad, he even seems spirited and admirable. Perhaps he hadn't known how to handle him. When you watched Dam-Bogga it seemed so easy. He should have kept the beast. Even if he couldn't tame it, it could have made money. Réginald could have let it out to stud. "Let's say twenty dollars a service, there was money to be made. There's lots of settlers around here would be glad to have him sire their colts. Another chance I missed."

The procession arrives in the yard. The calling between the two horses has become an endless lament. In the meadow, still gleaming with dew, the big mare, muscular from ploughing many fields, leaps with the agility of a calf. Her ponderous, placid air is gone, you can see her yellow teeth in a grimace of laughter and hear the earth resound like a drum under her pounding hooves. Someone runs to open the gate, and Dam-Bogga leaps to one side, freeing the stallion, which bucks and gallops off. He catches on a fence post in passing and rips it away. Now he's in the hayfield. He has no intention of grazing, all he wants is to race flat-out screaming his desire. Clods fly up from his feet. Then he arrives near the female. They rear up on their hind legs, clap their front hoofs together, fall to all fours and smell each other. They chase for a long time around the field and through the bushes, leaping gracefully over ditches. To the female's plaintive invitations the stallion replies with lugubrious, guttural sounds. Rémi is fascinated. Everybody is fascinated, even Réginald. Dam-Bogga is beaming, and invites them all inside for a celebration. At the window his wife is beckoning. There is room for all in the big kitchen. While her husband serves the drinks, the old woman brings coffee to the table, which is already decorated with cookies, pies, and cakes. The boys hope to see a bottle of wine opened, but have to settle for coffee made from roast barley corn and the consolation of many cakes.

Someone asks Dam-Bogga what he plans to do with the horse.

"Nothing."

"You won't break him to harness?"

"No."

"Raise colts? Put him out to stud?" asks Réginald anxiously.

"No. Dam-bogga. I just keep him for look at. Beautiful horse. Vojdelemmia strast."

No one understands this decision to own the handsome black stallion without putting him to work. After all, he has to be fed. A horse that doesn't earn his oats you might as well feed to the foxes. The old woman lays a hand on her husband's shoulder and he pats it gently.

"Dam-bogga! Don't need work any more. Children grown up, got jobs. Got hay and wood and food, lots of food. No work to do. Dam-bogga! Need nothing. Much work here before." He shows his hands. "Lived, brought up children, now old. Land can rest; Dam-Bogga can rest.

Sit on swing with wife, watch beautiful black horse. That is good rest for Dam-Bogga."

He nods his head, smiling. Rémi understands: this is the passion for beauty that Ricard talked about. Réginald breathes in noisily through a corner of his mouth. He's going to say something.

"It's true the land isn't very good around here."

"And the climate," adds Martel with a knowing look.

"Must be patient here," says Dam-Bogga. "Lots of years, lot of work, then make money. Before, you could do that. Not now. Have to buy everything dear, dam-bogga! Before, do everything yourself, can wait till land starts to pay. Not no more. When I saw you come, dam bogga, I say no to my wife, no good. Others came, they gone now. Can't live off lot now. Have to work in town, earn money, farm at same time, raise animals, clear ground, plough. After long time can live off land but never rich."

"It's true what you say," said Martel. "But I got over my idea of doin' all that. I stay here because you live cheap. I got my truck for makin' a living. I'll never farm my lot."

"Me neither," Réginald chimes in.

Rémi sees that his father sits with bowed head and says nothing. Perhaps he was the first to have seen the obvious. He's already working in town, about to move there. A fine dream has gone up in smoke and for the rest of his life he'll be at the mercy of his bosses. Rémi understands. He too has dreams that show signs of crumbling on contact with life. Can it be that he is so like his father, so near to him? Suddenly Rémi discovers that the pedestal on which he had placed his father had unobtrusively collapsed some time ago. The boy is now facing the fact. His father turns out to be a human being with limitations and weaknesses. And Rémi still loves him, perhaps even more than before.

Rémi went out and Robert followed. Outside, the music of the horses in love filled the country air. To see the animals they went around the stable to the fence near the manure pile. Diane was there. She hadn't been in the house. She'd stayed out to watch the horses. She was so absorbed that she didn't notice the arrival of Robert and Rémi. At the far end of the field the black stallion was covering the mare. Robert made Diane jump. "Like to be in their place, eh?" She smiled, shrugging. Robert whinnied like a horse. The girl jeered.

"You a stud? Not if you're like your brother. . . ."

Rémi boiled with rage.

"You'd need a bull, a cow like you."

"Ha ha. Call me names, Rémi, that won't help you any. You're a sissy."

Rémi grabbed her arm and twisted. She persisted in her arrogance.

"Big man, eh. Go to it, don't mind me. I'd like to see just how far you'd go."

"Cut it out," said Robert. "Here's the priest."

It was indeed Ricard's little white car that came buzzing down the road leaving an enormous plume of dust behind it.

"Wonder where he's going." said Rémi. "He drove right by, didn't stop."

"Maybe Méo's," Robert suggested.

"Maybe your place," added Diane.

She started laughing. Rémi let go her arm.

"Yes, he's going to your place. I'm sure he'll have some things to tell your mother. You're going to get it, both of you. Ha ha."

"Why? What do you mean?" said Robert, baffled.

"Yeah, what the hell have you been up to now, you little bitch?"

"Aha. I'm not telling. You'll find out."

The two boys moved toward her, threatening.

"You better talk."

Just then there was a sound of voices leaving the house. The girl felt safe enough to look superior again. Robert saw red and jumped her, put his arms around her waist and threw her down beside the dung pile where a puddle of liquid manure had collected. She fell square in the middle of it and sat there splashed and stained. She stared at them without a cry or a complaint, her eyes filled with hate. Robert went off, laughing softly. Rémi stood sheepishly, wondering what he should do.

"Get going, fat-head. Want to join me, eh? Oh, sorry for me, are you? I don't mind sittin' in the shit. See me smile. I've got back at you already. Dung-piss is nothing to what you've got coming."

She stuck her tongue out at him. Robert was calling and Rémi ran to catch up. He was intrigued by the girl's stoical attitude, but terrified by her threats. What kind of story had she made up? And what did the priest have to do with it?

Their father was still hanging around at Réginald's place. Rémi had stayed outside to think. There were so many things he and Robert could be accused of. But nobody knew about them. Could she have caught them at some of their activities? Had she spied on them in the night? Unlikely. Only they, the knights, dared brave the dark without a flashlight or a lantern. She must have made up some lie.

But what? She seemed so sure of her vengeance. Or was she bluffing? She walked past along the road, saw him, threw her head back and began to whistle. God, she was filthy. The yellow dress blackened from waist to hem, her bodice spotted with stains, her arms and legs dark brown, she walked with a determined air and stopped in her yard by the steps. She turned toward Rémi and waved. Then she began to cry and call, "Mummy, mummy" in a plaintive voice. Mrs. Martel rushed out and stopped, astonished.

"Who did that to you?"

"Nobody," she answered with a sniff. "I fell in the manure. I was looking at the horse."

"Stay out there; you stink; you're disgusting. Wait, I'll be back in a second."

Rémi detested the girl, but he could only admire her courage and nerve. She wasn't a tattle-tale and she did her own dirty work. It would have been simple to tell on Robert, but that was too easy for her taste. She would get revenge her own way. And anyway she considered herself already avenged. Rémi continued weighing all the possibilities but found nothing plausible.

On the way home they met the priest's car. He waved as they passed. In fear the boys went in the house. They'd gladly have wasted time at their cousin's to put off the fatal moment. Nothing happened for the first few minutes. Their mother acted just as usual. Their parents did go into the bedroom for a discussion, but nothing filtered out of their conference. The boys might have thought they were getting off scot-free but Rémi felt that some kind of scene was about to break. He shared his feelings with Robert, and they stayed away from the house the whole afternoon. Time passed, and the threat seemed to fade. Robert had doubts about his brother's intuition: Diane had been pulling their leg. And their parents could have had a hundred reasons for a discussion behind closed doors. And the priest's visit might have been routine, or to see Rémi, or something else so ordinary they couldn't even guess at it. Robert almost thought they were out of danger.

There was a certain tension around the supper table. Rémi hunched over his plate, expecting a dressing down any minute. Instead of the expected storm came a harmless remark by his father.

"Father Ricard wants to see you both in the vestry before eleven o'clock mass tomorrow."

"We'll be there," Rémi hastened to reply.

"He hasn't much time between masses, you'll have to be on the dot. I'll drive you there."

"No need," said Robert. "We'll leave early, lots of time."

"No, no I'll take the car."

Rémi didn't insist, so as not to provoke some evil still in gestation. Robert took the whole thing too lightly for his brother's taste. They discussed it in their room, where they had taken refuge from their mother's saddened face and their father's stricken look.

"You're fussing about nothing, Rémi. To hear you talk there's always some threat in the air, stuff like that. You dream too much."

"And you don't think enough. Did you get a look at their faces?"

"What can the priest know about us?"

"Whatever Diane told him."

"Stuff she made up."

"Comes down to the same thing."

"If it's not true it's easier to defend ourselves. The only thing Ricard can have against us is that we didn't go to mass."

"You think he noticed?"

"If he thinks you're so cute, Rémi, could be."

"This is no time for jokes."

"I'm sure he's going to talk about his projects and ask us to help him. Some kind of foolery like that. You're making a mountain out of nothin'. I wouldn't help him. I'm no sucker; he's not going to exploit me and make me work like a slave for nothin'. Godbout's right sometimes. But if it's because we didn't go to mass he wants to see us, what can we say, Rémi? Our parents aren't going to be very happy."

"We deny it. We swear we went and he didn't see us. We swear on the Bible if we have to. They'll believe us."

"On the Bible? You don't mean it?"

"Pff. It's only a book. Ricard's religion isn't ours; it has nothing to do with us."

It was a quarter to eleven when their father let them off beside the church. He didn't drive away until they were inside. The priest led them along to the vestry and began his preparations for the next mass. Robert was fascinated by the model of the church and grounds.

"Don't touch. Go and sit down."

200

The priest stared at them in silence while he donned his alb.

"Have you guessed why I had you in?"

"No."

"Say, 'No, father.'"

"Yes, Father."

"Well, since I have to dot your 'i's for you. . . . A charitable soul with your salvation at heart has informed me that you do not come to church, that you do not attend mass. Thus, that you are living outside the sacraments."

"Charitable soul!" exclaimed Robert. "A little spy, you mean."

"Be quiet. Do not display your evil mind in my presence. And don't defend yourself by accusing others. I was saying that this person. . . ."

"We know the 'person,' as you call her. So what?"

"Wretched boy! Are you not aware of the implications of your words and actions? Poor creatures, still so innocent!"

"And we want to stay that way," said Rémi, who had to show off a little before his brother, though in a voice that was less than self-assured.

"And you are aggressive toward me, your priest, the vicar of God!"

"Your god isn't the only one," said Rémi.

Ricard whirled on him, choking with rage. A button flew from his collar. He pounded with his fist on the model church, causing bushes and hedges to fly to the floor. He almost screamed. "I believe in God, the Father almighty, maker of heaven and earth, and in Jesus Christ, his only begotten son. . . ."

He could go no further, his voice cracked with emotion. He controlled himself, and his convulsed face recovered its natural colour, but quickly turned livid.

"Poor young things, the evil has advanced farther than I had believed. I do not hold this against you, I know who is speaking through your lips. But never fear, I will save you, you shall be exorcised, I will redeem your sins at the cost of my own life, if that must be. I always desired a martyr's death, and I dream of the early church when men died rather than abjure their faith, marching to death with a hymn on their lips. I am a poor, weak man, little worthy of my ideal. But I will suffer martyrdom if need be. Father, bring this cup to me. I shall not falter."

Ricard moved toward them, hands clasped, eyes staring upward. He spoke in an exultant voice.

"My children, thanks to you, and thanks to the misfortunes afflicting you, I have been awakened. I had begun to doze in this too-comfortable cure of souls, I dreamed of leading my flock uneventfully toward our Father by building material constructions. But the Lord has sent you to me as a sign: this is the century of the crusades! I shall save the two of you first and then reconvert the others. The celestial legions shall be my helpers in this holy war. I must be pitiless, and to those who refuse to yield I shall apply the order, believe or die!"

Ricard was close to the boys now, and his bulging eyes, his haggard, wild appearance terrified them. Robert stood up, but could not escape. He was concerned. The priest calmed down a little.

"Be not afraid. I am excited, but only because I see clearly for the first time the mission that has been vouchsafed to me, and this is most stirring. I am your friend. I am going to restore the purity of your little souls until they are as beautiful as your little bodies. Pray with me, renounce Satan and all his works."

"We don't know your Satan," Robert protested. "We don't want to know, either."

"Silence! I know good and evil! You shall listen! I can recognize his voice in yours, and I know the origin of the evil that has possessed you. It's Godbout. That is where you went on Sunday instead of being present at the holy sacrifice. That damned soul has contaminated you with his false, bewitching words!"

"Not true," said Rémi.

"I know it, I have been told."

"Yeah," jeered Robert. "And she made it all up."

"Did you come to mass?"

"No," the boy admitted.

"Then the rest is also true."

"No."

"That will do. We have not much time. I can see the foul influence he has on you. He is the one who has poured evil into your defenceless hearts and turned your spirits away from Mother Church. How else could it have happened? Ah, what a terrible thing! I can see his great sacrilegious hands on your chaste bodies. That unspeakable creature! What he must have made you suffer! It breaks my heart to think of it, I can imagine indescribable scenes. Ah, what a pity!"

Ricard opened his eyes again, fresh from his visions. His hands were trembling.

"We never talked to Godbout."

"That is untrue, Robert. You are lying without even knowing you lie. You are possessed! Something else is speaking through your lips. I do not blame you. But only Godbout could have turned you away from God this way."

Ricard held his head in his hands and fell to his knees.

"Oh, what a task awaits me! Lord, come to my assistance!"

The priest meditated, staring upwards, and remained for a long time as if in ecstasy. Robert and Rémi looked at each other, flabbergasted. He was mad. Or drunk. They should run. But the man was barring the way out. They'd have to go the other way, through the church, where they could already hear the faithful assembling. Rémi felt that he had got into an unbelievable situation. It was all absurd! Ricard finally rose to his feet and seemed to have returned to normal. He continued to apparel himself for mass.

"My children, my poor children, God will help me. I have already spoken to your mother and made her understand the gravity of the situation. I cannot conceal the fact that your conduct shattered her, broke her heart, and made her weep. She asked me to save your souls. I promised to do so, and I shall do it against your will if need be. We must start at zero. You must go to catechism as you did so long ago. Each day you will come here to receive my instruction in the only true faith, that of the one God. With me you will find the Faith again!"

He stared at them with astonished eyes, caught up by the work he was called to perform. It was so much more difficult, but so much more rewarding spiritually, than beautifying the church grounds. Rémi made a face for his brother's benefit. Robert, without weighing the consequences of his act, and following his instinct and the all-powerful desire to preserve his freedom, opened his zipper and flopped out his penis.

"There, start saving me."

Ricard turned green and moved away, unable to speak, holding onto the table. He was about to collapse, have a fit or an attack of some rare and prestigious disease. There was a knock at the door, and Robert hastily zipped up his fly. A boy came in, the former straw boss, who doubled as altar boy.

"I came to get ready for mass, father. Father? Are you all right?"

"Yes, I'm . . . better now."

"We have to hurry, father. We'll be late saying mass."

Ricard turned to the Simard boys.

"Go sit in the choir. And stay there till the end of the mass or your father will hear about it."

They went leisurely out followed by the curious gaze of the young altar boy who was buttoning his cassock. They sat by the wall near the altar, stared at by dozens of pairs of eyes. The nave was almost full. Rémi avoided looking at the congregation. Robert, more rebellious, stared back at those who stared at him, one by one, until each lowered his gaze or looked away. Only in the second pew was there someone who resisted this confrontation: Diane's pinched lips could hardly conceal the beginnings of a smile.

Robert nudged his brother and whispered, "The slut is there, she's laughing."

"Little bitch."

"Wait till I get my hands on her; she'll laugh then."

"Shhh! Not so loud!"

"Rémi, what are we goin' to do? What's going to happen?"

"We'll talk about it. Shut up, they're looking."

The priest makes his entrance and the faithful stand up. On his way past, he checks to see that the boys are indeed where he sent them and begins the usual rites. Rémi stares fixedly at the corner of the altar. On his right he feels the stirring of a shapeless, multicephalic beast. He cannot forget its presence. It fidgets, coughs, scrapes its feet, and makes a thousand unidentifiable sounds. He follows its movements without intending to, like a robot: he sits, kneels, mumbles Latin words he doesn't understand. Then Ricard climbs to the pulpit and his resonant voice electrifies the crowd. Even Rémi is shaken from his torpor. Quite a sermon, this, not so much the words as the tone and the voice, now breaking with emotion, now trembling with rage. No one can remain indifferent, you are moved, exalted by enthusiasm or crushed by guilt, you share his anger, you feel called to perform a noble task, and at the last you want to applaud or weep softly over your miserable fate. Tremolos, flights of oratory, well-calculated pauses, effects inserted at the most telling place – Ricard has become a great preacher.

"Yes . . . my heart bleeds today. My brethren, my dear brethren, Evil has taken its place among us." (The altar boy looks at Rémi and Robert, and many of the faithful follow his gaze.) "Evil, I said. Not the sin we all know, grave sins, which God, however, pardons easily because of his infinite mercy, knowing that we are weak, not the sins that absolution can wipe out. No, not this sort of sin, but in fact true abomination, the terrible and blasphemous evil inspired directly by Beelzebub, the evil that denies divinity itself and the omnipotence of God, denies the Church of

Christ!" (In the nave there are expressions of shock and others of incredulity. Again the faithful turn their glances to the boys sitting in the choir.) "And this evil, my dearly beloved brethren, this evil is contagious!"

Ricard had almost shouted. He stops to allow those who were startled to grow calm again, and during this time the diminishing echoes fade away.

"This evil is contagious and might well contaminate the whole village, like gangrene. This evil, which comes from Satan, is brought among us by one person only, a former believer from this parish who has fallen under the power of the Demon. This evil can be communicated to others. Already certain young souls have stumbled." (This time the whole congregation looks toward the boys. Rémi sits down. Robert, who remains standing, thus shields him from the eyes of the curious.) "They are the first victims," the priest continues, "tomorrow there will be others, your children, perhaps yourselves. Heresy lies in wait for all of us! Not for nothing is it said the Evil One is cunning. He knows how to go about it, he knows the words that can seduce, and the speech that brings the sleep of the conscience. Is he not the old Tempter, the same who tried to make Christ fall?"

Again a pause allows his words to sink in.

"This sick limb may need to be amputated, but first we must try once more to cure it. I need the help of all of you, and your prayers and presence. Partake now of the holy sacrifice so that we may triumph more easily. Rather than continue this sermon – for I know you all understand the urgency of the situation – we will say ten rosaries together, begging the holy Mother of God to make us into valiant soldiers of Christ. Please kneel. Hail Mary, full of grace . . ."

The response flows back to him, full of fervour. Then he continues to celebrate his mass. At communion time Robert, as a sign of defiance, goes to the rail. Ricard passes him by without giving him the host. Rémi is near the end of his rope and can hardly wait to run away as fast as his legs will carry him. But before the *Ite missa est* the priest speaks again:

"Last Sunday's collection brought in thirty-three dollars and forty-six cents. Do not go home immediately after mass. A procession will leave here for Godbout's place to pray for his salvation and exhort him to return to the straight and narrow way. This procession following the monstrance is to give you the opportunity to affirm and temper your faith, and at the same time to show the Demon the kind of opposition that awaits him. I want to see all of you with me."

There was some shuffling around in front of the church steps before the order of marching was arrived at. People shunned Robert and Rémi as if they had the plague. Accordingly, the priest himself placed them near the head of the parade, in plain sight. They trudged off through the village. At the very head marched the altar boy. The lace of his surplice whipped in the wind and he swung his censer enthusiastically, though as an economy measure the incense had not been lit. Then came the churchwarden who had taken the collection, carrying a crucifix stuck on the end of a pole. Next was the priest with the monstrance, its golden rays flashing in the sun, another churchwarden with the holy water and the aspergillum, and then Robert and Rémi, who were marching out of step. Not far behind was the crowd of the faithful, the numbers swelling as they emerged from their houses just out of curiosity and ended up joining the retinue, most often from sheer idleness. The farther back you looked from the head of the parade, the less devout was the expression of the marchers. At the very rear were the young, covertly smoking and whispering jokes. At times the sound of prayers and hymns drowned the noise of feet on gravel. A car stopped, and the occupants got out to kneel in the dirt of the road, but not before spreading a handkerchief to protect their Sunday best. They crossed themselves as the Eucharist went past and drove on only when the last joyous, tag-playing child had gone by in the wake of the praying adults.

There was a halt at the crossroads just where "the line" began, and they recited a whole rosary there. Ricard was jubilant. A great cause, he thought to himself. Gather them together in a great cause. Then the procession moved off again. Godbout on his stoop was rocking away, watching the approach of the monster. And indeed it was a monster that crawled nearer, its pointed head on a long neck, its body undulating, and its restless tail of youngsters twitching idly. Godbout's surprise soon changed to amusement. It was too much, seeing these imbeciles trudging in the dust they had kicked up and sweating under the implacable sun. But when he saw the priest and his followers stop before his house, Godbout forgot to smile and leapt to his feet. He shook his fist. Ricard raised the monstrance and the faithful bowed their heads respectfully. Godbout spit on the ground: a shiver ran through the crowd and a cry went up spontaneously, especially from the young.

"Jehovah's Witness!"

"Pagan!"

"Ought to beat him up."

"Beat him to death."

Ricard turned toward his followers.

"No, no, we must not blame him. He knows not what he does. Let us rather pray for the salvation of his soul, so that he may remember his baptism and his confirmation. Hail, Mary, full of grace, blessed art thou amongst women. . . ."

Without making a move, Godbout heard out a dozen Aves. In her kitchen Mrs. Dam-Bogga was kneeling, praying and trembling. When silence fell again after the Amen, Godbout began to laugh as loud as he could.

Ricard shouted, "Repent!"

"Repent, yourself!" says Godbout.

"Look at this host, our Saviour's body. Fall to your knees, weep and implore. God in his infinite mercy. . . ."

"Okay, sucker! Don't you know that God, the only true God, Jehovah, is laughing at your antics? Just look at you, all tricked out like a medicine-man! And the rest of you,

you poor dumb bastards, can't you see that this fake is making fools of you? He sucks out your money and takes you in, and you follow him like a bunch of sheep. Why don't you wake up?"

"Listen not to the voice of the Evil One," howled Ricard. "Pray! Sing with me to efface his blasphemies. 'Victory, thou shalt reign, O cross, O our salvation. Victory . . .'"

The faithful intoned the hymn after the priest and it was in vain that Godbout bawled till he was blue in the face: not a soul heard him. Raging, he disappeared into the kitchen. Ricard, passing the monstrance to his altar boy, who took it respectfully, armed himself with the aspergillum and the portable holy-water basin. He began to sprinkle the fence, uttering certain Latin words. He pushed open the gate and advanced a few steps, sanctifying the earth before him with generous motions of the sprinkler. The house door opened and a stifled cry arose from the crowd, which retreated in panic. The priest remained stock-still, his arm raised in the air. Godbout had a gun! He shouted to make himself heard but he could have whispered, so total was the silence.

"Back up! Get back! This is private property. First one to walk on it, priest or no priest, I'll shoot him. I'm goin' to kick your asses all the way home, you poor bunch of suckers."

When the first moment of stunned surprise had passed, some of the men on the road grew agitated. Their eyes were full of hate and anger. Ricard didn't move an inch. Godbout raised his shot-gun and fired into the air. The terrible noise of the explosion was followed by a hail of pellets on the roof of Dam-Bogga's barn. Godbout seemed determined. He reloaded. The crowd shrank back, murmuring. They had numbers on their side, but concerted action was impossible and each one felt powerless by himself. Some had backed up as far as Dam-Bogga's gate, where the black dog was showing his teeth and growling, adding to the confusion. The shot-gun's one eye wandered over the crowd, which retreated farther. Ricard's arm and its weapon, the sprinkler, slowly dropped, and Ricard, with three prudent paces, regained the road. Godbout fired again, this time just over their heads. There were cries and some panic, and many took off in the direction of the village. The procession, now a shapeless mob, retreated in disorder. Only the priest, Rémi, and Robert remained facing the house.

"Come, my children," the priest said softly.

They remained silent and made no move.

"Fuck off, you filthy priest!" Godbout screamed.

"I am going away to pray for you. Your impiety will lead you into crime."

"Git outa here with your tame sheep, you god-damn canary."

"You are the damned one, Godbout. You've refused salvation."

The crowd stopped a little way off to wait for the priest, and out of curiosity as well. It divided to let Ricard head the procession again. The two boys were left on the road, their arms hanging at their sides. Robert picked up a stone and hurled it with all his strength toward the villagers. At the same time Godbout fired in the air again.

A voice wailed, "I've been hit in the head, I'm bleeding. He's shot me, I'm going to die."

The mass stirs and reforms its ranks. They help the wounded man along and the retreat is under way. Despite the priest's exhortations there is less spirit in their song and prayer since their defeat, and perhaps the long miles ahead in the dust and heat have something to do with this as well.

Rémi heaves a long sigh. Godbout turns towards the boys, his shot-gun ready.

"Come here, you guys."

Robert grabs a rock and threatens to throw it. Godbout smiles.

"Come on in."

210

"No," says Robert.

"You little bugger, I'm gonna shoot you."

He looks nasty. Moments go by and nothing happens. The man softens.

"Come on in, I won't hurt you."

He lowers his gun. The boys look at each other. Robert throws away his stone and they go in the lane. Godbout precedes them into the house and hangs his still-loaded weapon behind the door. They know his kitchen well from looking through the window, but are surprised by its smell, a mixture of tobacco and wood smoke; and a certain sound: dust and sand crunch underfoot.

The man sits down in his rocking-chair, and the boys sit too, without waiting for an invitation: Robert on the bench by the table and Rémi on a step of the stairs, not too far from the door to the outside world.

"What were you doin' in that procession?"

Rémi reflects that it's as well to be on Godbout's good side.

"They forced us to go along."

"How's that? They forced you?"

"Because we didn't go to mass," says Robert.

"The priest told our parents," Rémi adds. "And he decided to convert us."

"That son of a bitch, that black-robed bastard!"

"Could I have some water?" Rémi asks.

"Go ahead. There's the pump."

The boy works the pump-handle and sulphurous water emerges. He's so thirsty that he doesn't mind the dirty glass.

"When I think of that Ricard forcing people to believe in his false religion! Don't let him push you around, boys!"

"We can look after ourselves," Robert boasted.

"Yeah, but you don't always know what you're up against. Don't believe everything you're told. They'll all tell you a pack of lies just to suck you in. Just look how many religions there are in the world. Hundreds of 'em. I know it, I've done some reading and I have a short-wave radio.

I know what's happenin' everywhere. Everybody invents religions to catch suckers with. But the only true religion lies in the service of Jehovah."

"Ricard says his is the only one, too," Rémi advances timidly.

He regrets his words, for Godbout leaps up from his chair. He doesn't move toward the boy but toward the shelf where his Bible is lying. He shows it to them.

"It's written in the Bible: Jehovah! Even the Catholics approve this book, but they twist it to make it mean what they like. And then they invent those pagan goings-on."

Godbout sits down again, the book on his lap.

"I'll just tell you why Ricard wants to convert you two. To exploit you, the way he does the others. Because, my boys, there's two kinds of people on earth, the wolves and the sheep. The wolves take their time to think and don't believe all they hear. They don't let themselves be exploited, no sir, and they don't believe other people's better than they are. The sheep, those damn fools, they swallow everythin'. They're afraid to take a risk, and they get led around by the nose. Not much choice in life, you're a wolf or a sheep. Young fella," he turned to Rémi, "which one do you think I am?"

"A wolf," Rémi hastens to reply.

"Yer right, I'm a wolf. And that cousin of yours alongside, what's he?"

"A wolf." Robert makes a wild guess.

"Wrong. Just because he talks loud and swears a lot, and he's big and has a strong arm? That's not what makes the wolves. That cousin of yours believes everything they tell him, they could take the shirt off his back, he'd give in, he'd bend. Now, Ricard, there, he's a real wolf, he's no ordinary wolf, he's one that turned out bad, his power went to his head. He's become an exploiter. He lives off the village, that fine flock of sheep. Now, they're scared of everything, the priest, the bishop, the Settlement Office, the scalers, the shanty jobbers, they're scared of the storekeepers, the English, everybody that talks loud. Oh, you've got no idea how innocent they are! A peddler sold thirty sets of plastic dishes last year in Saint-Gérard and nobody needed them at all."

"Well, I don't want to be a sheep," said Robert.

"You're right, my boy. But you've got to learn. Learn! That's the secret. I had two years at classical college, I know Latin and history, and that's why Ricard's scared of me. Because I'm educated. They try to keep us ignorant. That's the best way to make sure we don't grow up wolves. Sure, they teach us things, but they're useless things, false things. The teachers, the priests, the brothers, they're all goin' to hide the truth from you. They stick together, the wolves protect each other. You there, at the table, do you know Korea?"

"I never heard of her."

"It's not a woman, it's a country. A few years ago, you should remember that, there was a war there. Some Canadians went there and got themselves killed. You never heard of that? You're not the only ones. There's not a sonofabitch in the village knows about it except the priest. You may say it doesn't affect their lives, but that's just an example. It's the same for everything else. They vote Grit or Tory and they don't know why. They vote for the last wolf that told them the prettiest lie. You've no idea how bad things are in the world. There's wars you never hear about, people dying by the thousands of hunger and sickness. Nobody knows about it. Me, I hear it on my radio. I hear the news from Montreal and Paris and London and Washington, even Rome. Sure, they're tellin' lies too, but not all the same way, and when I average them out I get pretty close to the truth. Do you know there are starving children?"

"Sure," Rémi replies. "I give to the Sainte Enfance."

"Ho ho! That's a good one! Ha ha! That's funny. You poor kid, they got a new pope not a year ago, oh boy! What a celebration! Well, that big splash, they paid for it with your money and the money of the other suckers that give to them. Your little Chinese didn't get a cent out of your quarter. The end of the world is nigh, and no man knows it."

"The end of the world!" exclaims Rémi, who's pretending to be interested.

"Yep, the end of the world! The Russians – there won't be one of that abominable race left alive, not even the guy across the road. Why, they launched those sputniks! A sputnik! A ball up in the sky! And now they're talkin' about sending up a man! But they won't have time. Man has escaped from the earth God gave him to be his lot. Their sputnik is the angel with the trumpet. It is there to announce the end, we're all going to find ourselves in the Valley of Jehosephat before long. There they will separate the wheat from the tares. Jehovah will save a few of the just, and the rest – Gehenna, into the fire!"

"So that's going to be soon, eh?" asks Rémi, wide-eyed.

"Very soon. If you like, boys, you can have a chance of being saved. Stop goin' to church and come to see me often. I'll teach you the true religion. I'll show you the God of justice, Jehovah!"

"We'll sure come back," says Robert.

"Yeah," said Rémi, going him one better, "I want to be saved. But right now, we've got to go."

"That's right, away you go. But you come back, I'll save you."

From the road they saw Dam-Bogga coming back from his barn. They waved, but he seemed not to see them. Their feet dragged as they walked. The sun was at its strongest.

"Do you think Dam-Bogga's mad at us for going to Godbout's place?"

"I don't know," said Rémi. "Maybe. Ha ha! Godbout! A wolf with his teeth falling out!"

"Ha ha! That's right! Hey, that's the second time today somebody tried to save us!"

"Don't talk about it, Robert. I was trying to forget."

Diane, sitting on the stoop with her baby brother in her arms, watched their arrival. When they came to the nearest point she stuck out her tongue. Robert wanted to take care of her, but Rémi held him back. This was not too difficult, for the last thing Robert wanted was to make an enemy of Carmen Martel.

"Hey! You looked real smart in front of the Church. You'd make a couple of dandy priests!"

They go on without answering her, and when they are out of sight, between the trees, Rémi leaves the road and collapses on the moss. Robert wanders around breaking the tips off branches. Rémi is in great distress. True, he has escaped from Ricard's clutches and the hostile crowd, but that was only a momentary respite. The priest will return to the attack. And have an easy time of it. Their parents are on his side. Their parents! Now he remembers: he'll have to confront them shortly. Questions, reproaches, supplications, sermons. All that from their mother, their father content to nod his head. Rémi tries to switch his thoughts to another track, because a phrase of Godbout's has floated up in his memory. The wolves, the sheep . . . and Rémi's father is a sheep. He feels disloyal having such thoughts. It's as if he were insulting his father. To escape from this line of reflection he tries to imagine how to get out of the trouble stirred up by Diane. The sequence of events is too big and complicated for him, and he sees no solution. But he must react. Sheep? Son of a sheep? Could it be hereditary? Never!

Robert is in an aggressive mood, suffering from having had to hold it all in. To feel normal he needs a good battle, and lacking one he collects stones and bombards a sapling until it's in shreds. Then he sits down beside his brother.

"Don't let it get you down. We have to fight."

Rémi shrugs.

"I tell you, Rémi, fight!"

"Against what? And what with? We have to go home now. What's going to happen there, eh?"

"It won't be fun, that's true. Unless . . . unless you find something, Rémi. I was counting on you to have a good idea."

"I can't even think."

"Let's walk slow. Don't get nervous. And think all the time, think! Find a solution!"

"All very well for you to say!"

"Listen, we're both wolves, we're not tame sheep. Let's not change now."

They walk in silence, Robert leaving Rémi to his thoughts. It's getting hotter all the time. The earth is cracking like a cake in the oven. The road is as long and drawn out as a desert track. Yet life is abundant in the ditches and the brush. Under the spruce trees lies deep shadow, but you don't notice that because of the blinding light on the gravel. Nothing is real but the dust, the burning pebbles and the vapours that create mirages in the air, surfaces like water that retreat as you come near them. Rémi dreams of a road that winds beneath cool branches, occasionally curving around a high rock, full of surprises at every turn and sudden views of luscious landscape. Instead, the little road is straight as a die, as a stretched cord, and the trees, hardly thicker than telephone poles, create an endless perspective with nothing to interrupt its monotony, a distance that wears down your courage, where the weakest ray of Abitibi sun can strike down and turn the path into a Saharan furnace.

"I've got it!" Rémi exclaims.

"An idea?"

"Yeah, we have to attack, the way you said you have to do in a street fight. We're goin' to accuse the priest. Not defend ourselves, attack! Our parents are going to believe us if we both say the same thing and keep a straight face. We've got to act, play innocent, and even cry if we have to."

By the time they reach home the meal is long over. The family had waited for them a while, and then concluded they were eating at the presbytery. The parents talk about this and that, avoiding the subject that troubles them. They are obviously ill at ease. Rémi judges that the time is ripe.

"Go play outside, Françoise. I'll be out in a minute."

His mother understands and holds her arms out to the child. "No, we're going to have a little nap now, eh, Françoise? An after-dinner nap?"

"Yes, mummy. My doll!"

The mother is back in a moment.

"Did you eat?"

"No."

"No? O.K., sit."

She gives them potatoes that are almost warm and some roast meat with fat that doesn't run. The father takes a cup of tea but doesn't sit down at the table. He shifts to a chair by the window looking out on the road. Rémi speaks with a voice intended to sound repentant.

"It's true we didn't go to mass on Sunday."

"You know . . .," the mother begins.

Rémi goes on, not letting her speak.

"But we had a good reason, mum. The time we went to work around the church he got us into the vestry, and there . . . there he tried touching us . . . Robert and me."

Robert, his mouth full, looks up at his parents with eyes enlarged by emotion and nods agreement. His young face radiates frankness and honesty. He's not afraid to stare down his father and suffer his mother's horrified expression. Rémi goes on, trying to use childish phrases.

"We didn't want to, we fought him, and we said we'd tell you. . . . Then the priest got mad and threatened us, he said he'd call the police . . . and he said we'd lose our farm lot here, so we ran away and we didn't say anything to you so he couldn't hurt our family."

His throat blocked by a sob, Rémi pauses. The silence is heavy. He goes on.

"We knew we're not supposed to stay around bad company, but he's the priest. So we didn't go back to mass, because we didn't want him to catch us after, we were afraid of what he'd do to us."

Rémi is so at home in his new role that he begins to cry. Robert takes over.

"He talked to us today and we were scared. He was getting ready to say mass and putting on his robes. He pushed me into a corner and I struggled but he's the strongest and here . . . he touched me here."

Their mother opens her mouth on an "Oh!" which she has to swallow. The father is counting the tea leaves in the bottom of his cup.

"I told him to stop," says Robert, "I said it was a sin. He just laughed and said we should come to see him every day in the presbytery because he told you we used to go to listen to Godbout, the Jehovah's witness, and you wanted him to save us from sin. He was laughing. He said he'd have time to take us in hand. I said we weren't coming back because he was a bad priest. It's true he's a bad priest, mum. He scares me. Mum, I don't want to go there any more."

The shattered parents don't know what to say. Rémi decided to score a point.

"I just wonder how he can bear to say the mass, blessing the host just after his hands were doing bad things to Robert."

His mother is trembling all over. She controls herself with an effort, but her voice is hoarse.

"There are black sheep in every walk of life. You mustn't judge by one. Even if there are bad priests the church is holy and true."

"I know that, mum. But we don't want to go to Ricard's mass any more. I couldn't take communion, I'd think about what his hands touch."

The mother's stomach heaves.

"Disgusting!"

Their father has come over and touches her arm. She pushes him away.

"No, it's true, he's disgusting! Trying to corrupt my children! I'd like to go to the bishop."

"For god's sake don't get into that!" their father begs. "Those people all know each other, they stick together. We're too small to make trouble, we'd just get sat on."

The mother is growing calm again, but her voice is hard.

"In any case, we're not going there to mass any more. I'd be thinking the same thing about the host. And just let me catch him around my kids! You should do something, René."

"We've just got here. Let's not make trouble. We're going to Amos soon, and in the mean time we can go to mass somewhere else or listen to it on the car radio."

Rémi feels that he can make his last play.

"What's more, it's not true about Godbout. We never even talked to him, except once he shouted crazy things at us and we threw stones at his mail-box. It was the priest invented all that so he could get us into his presbytery. It's true we skipped mass, but we were scared. We went down by the stream and kneeled and prayed. We asked God to forgive us. I'm sure he understood. We didn't want to be in sin."

"My poor dears! You did well," their mother said. "And if ever anything like that happens in the future, tell us, even if you've been threatened. You'll be going to the Brothers' school. You never know where there'll be rotten men. But you mustn't judge the institution by that. You're old enough to understand: you're going to meet shameless people all your life, wherever you go. Some day you'll be able to handle that yourselves. In the mean time, always tell us."

"I want to be like Maria Goretti."

The parents smile sadly. Damn that Robert! Everything went perfectly, and here he could ruin success by going too far. Rémi nudges him discreetly, and when he still doesn't understand lets him have a sharp kick on the shin.

A car was coming. Long before it arrived they recognized Father Ricard's Volkswagen. Robert glanced worriedly at his brother, who sat there stunned. The mother, seeing this interplay, took it for a distress call. She clapped her hands decisively.

"Him! He's got a nerve! Never mind, I have a few words to say to him."

"Let's not get excited," says their father.

"Excited? Excited? Simard, you damn yellow-belly, you mean you wouldn't put your fist in his face? Okay, stay here. I'll give him what for!"

She goes out to wait. Rémi and Robert skitter upstairs and open the window to the yard. They're all ears. The Volkswagen door slams.

"Rémi, what's going to happen? He'll defend himself."

"Shhh. You know she won't listen to him. She believes us."

With crossed arms and a determined air, the mother and her anger block the way to the house. Surprised, Ricard stops at the bottom of the steps. She towers over him.

"Mrs. Simard . . ."

"Don't tell me anything. I know it all."

"Ah! They told you!"

"Yes, I know everything, you pig."

"Mrs. Simard!"

"Don't Mrs. Simard me. You're a false priest! You vulture!"

"Madame, please, be calm, I pray you. . . ."

"Instead of praying me, go and confess and change your life."

"Madame, mind your words! You are speaking to a priest, your priest. I am consecrated!"

"Consecrated to evil. Disgusting man."

"I don't understand your attitude, there must be a misunderstanding. If you would only explain. . . ."

"You want me to draw pictures? You want me to say words to excite your diabolical mind? You want a play-by-play of your sin?"

"Madame, madame, be calm, let us talk like reasonable beings. . . ."

Beside herself, she drops all politeness: "Don't come any closer, damn you! Put down your filthy paws. Get out! Do I have to call my husband?"

"I'd just as soon, if *he* has his head on straight!"

"I'll have yours, you bastard! I'll tear your eyes out."

She moves forward, all her claws out, full of the wild courage of a female defending her progeny.

"Get out, pig. And never come back here."

"Madame, do you realize that. . . ."

"And don't ever hang around my boys again!"

He retreats as she advances, tries a last, feeble protest; but one hand claws his face. That's quite enough for him, he whirls around, scampers to the car, shuts himself in and, just to be safe, locks the door. He stays for a moment, contemplating the fury who's shaking her fist in his face. When he doesn't go, Mrs. Simard's anger flames up again, and she begins to gather stones. Clumsily, she bombards the car. The fourth stone hits the target and the priest takes off like a storm. The gears complain when, on the road, he pumps the clutch without mercy.

From the window the boys stick out their tongues. Rémi slaps his brother on the back and whispers, "We got off lucky. We're saved. They won't make us go to the village any more."

"Did you see him take off with his dung-balls rattlin'? We'd make good actors, eh, Rémi?"

"Yeah but let's not ruin it. Keep the game up, don't make liars out of us. Let's go down."

In the kitchen their mother, still livid, is washing the dishes. The plates are rattling.

"You shouldn't have," says their father. "You went too far."

"And you said nothing at all! You never say anything. If they stole your car you'd never yell stop thief. I don't understand you."

"Oh, come now. . . ."

"No, it's true. You'd let them steal the shirt off your back. You're just like your father. He never spoke up either."

"What good would it have done? Nobody listened to him anyway!"

"All he had to do was shout. No, he made new land. He'd take a new lot, your father would, and build a house on it and a stable. And when he could have been somebody people'd listen to, he'd sell. And start all over again farther away, and never say a word."

"He never said much, but he did a lot. He opened up whole parishes."

"And where did that get him?" He died as poor as Job and nowadays his parishes are dead. He opened up land? You were born at the neighbour's place! And what did he leave you? When I married you, you had a poor thin cow that didn't last the winter. That's what your father got for never opening his mouth."

Simard shrugs and mumbles something or other before retiring behind his silence again. Rémi is suffering from having heard this conversation, especially because his lies are partly responsible for starting it. To quiet his mother he goes over to the sink.

"We'll finish the dishes, mum."

"He's never comin' back, is he?" says Robert.

"No, honey. Don't you worry."

The boys are doing the dishes. To still the atmosphere and relax everybody, their father suggests, "What about a little spin over to Amos. We could have supper at the restaurant."

"Oh, yes!" sighs their mother.

"We," says Rémi, "we'd rather stay here. We'll have fun. And we can make our own supper."

Their mother hesitates, and Robert chimes in, "We don't open for anybody. And we'll be careful with the fire."

"That way we could leave the little one with Sonia and just the two of us go," suggests their father.

The mother reflects.

Father adds, "Then afterwards we could go dancing at the hotel. There's an orchestra at the Relais."

"That would be nice."

She hesitates for a second only, just for the looks of it, for she needs to get away and forget the children and the line.

"You're sure, boys, you don't mind staying?"

"Come on, you know that's what you want!"

"Dad's right. Go ahead, mum. We'd like that."

The mother smiled, already thinking of the band and the dance floor. Rémi thought, she deserves it.

As soon as the parents have left, the boys collect the butts from all the ashtrays, glean a handful of tobacco and a little ash into the bargain. They pour two bottles of beer into another container. Surely their father doesn't know how many empties he had. They lock the door as they were told to do and hurry to their hide-out. There, by the water's edge, they drink the warm beer and burp noisily. They laugh. They have every reason to laugh. Their freedom of action is once more complete. They are laughing at Father Ricard, and how they outmanoeuvred him, and at their mother's reception of the priest. He must really wonder what's going on! Two consecutive bloopers for the missionary in search of savages, the crusader in search of a holy war! The boys are triumphant. They were victorious and always will be. Let Diane play her dirty tricks and try to ruin them; she'll run into a blank wall. After all, she has to deal with two wolves, better still two knights who are smarter than the wolves. At the mere thought of the girl Robert grows furious and recites the humiliations she has coming to her, using all the insults that he knows. Rémi just spits on the ground.

The beer loosens Robert's tongue, and he takes the trouble once more to describe his Lady's charms, not as you'd recite a lesson but with vivacity, with pauses and exclamations, and words that make visible the woman's motions. He doesn't know it, but he's talking to himself. Rémi isn't listening: he's thinking about his parents. His father behaved like a sheep just now. Again. Rémi resents his being like this, and doesn't even feel guilty any more about having such thoughts. They're true, aren't they? The only times his father talks, it's to describe dreams and projects in which he himself may not even believe. Does he raise his voice to defend or condemn or blame or congratulate? No. To tell you of some insignificant piece of news, worn-out phrases used by people who barely know each other. On the rest, the important things in life, nothing. Rémi would like him to say, just once: "You're growing up," to prove that he sees his boys getting to be men and approves of it. Rémi would like him not to be afraid of showing love, or at least to have a try at friendship. The time with the moose, you could have hoped that would come. It was a great chance. But a lost one. Yet it wouldn't take much, a little phrase, a word, maybe only a gesture. If you can't be a superman any more, why not try to be a chum?

The boys crawl into their cave where the humidity is busy inventing smells. Hair roots have grown down and broken some of the drawings, adding life and mystery to certain others. They repair their work where necessary and carve out some new scenes: their mother striking the priest with an axe; Diane, backed against a stone, transfixed by the monstrous member of the black stallion. Before their black Virgin they celebrate their Sunday service. Then they go out and lie in the sun, and sleep. They are awakened by the fly and mosquito bites that go with the evening.

Their parents do not return until nightfall, their father carrying a sleepy Françoise. Rémi and Robert go to bed at once and their parents also retire. When the household is finally asleep Rémi gets up. The day had been too rich in happenings to let it end so tamely. He wakes Robert, who grumbles and tells him to go to hell. Rémi whispers in his ear, "We're going to see Mrs. Martel!"

Those are the magic words. Robert leaps out of bed and is ready in no time. The night promises to be cool. They put on their jackets. The evening dew has given back some suppleness to the wilting grass. Only the dry pods of the vetch explode underfoot. The stars, decked out in their spear-point petals, spend their feeble light on the pebbles of the road, which still smell of sun. The sound of an unseen animal follows them in the field. They aren't worried by it, they just grasp their clubs a little tighter. There are so many things that are more frightening than a mere animal. Farther on, in the forest, they sniff out the presence of something. . . . Something is walking ahead of them on the road, always at the same distance, just where you can't make out anything clearly in the confusion of black and dark blue. Is it leading the way? Is it their guide? Or is it running away from them, but not too fast, as if it were curious? Afraid? No! Aren't they knights, the masters, of whom everyone is afraid? The presence finally fades away with no more noise than at its coming. Light is streaming out of Méo's windows, shadows are moving in the kitchen. Then comes Martel's house, all lit up, and Réginald's with only a night-light. Everything is already dark at Dam-Bogga's, and Godbout's lamp has just gone out. Every house is closing out the night.

The boys approach Carmen Martel's house with caution. Suddenly loud voices send them plunging into the brush. Somebody's starting a car: the starter labours, the pistons pump, and the machine is singing. A glaring light floods the road, the truck appears around the corner of the house, bumps along to the gravel, and turns. The beams of the headlights sweep the sleeping trees and dazzle a jack-rabbit, who freezes. The motor grinds up and down as the gears change and soon the red tail-lights disappear in the distance. A door slams. The boys get up and creep to the wall of the house. Robert is jubilant. With her husband gone he imagines he has the woman to himself. He pulls Rémi along as far as the window of her bedroom. Disappointment! The blind is down, nothing is to be seen.

"Damn!"

Rémi secretly smiles at his brother's chagrin. Silently they climb onto the front stoop and kneel so as to have their eyes at the exact level of the window, which is protected by a flimsy tulle curtain. Diane, in a night-dress of washed-out pink and with her feet tucked under her, is rocking as she reads what looks like a photo-romance.

"A stupid love story," murmurs Rémi, "that's her style all right!"

She's alone. No, her mother is coming back from the bedroom, she too in her night-shirt. No doubt she had just put it on.

"Think what I missed!"

Robert's voice is sad. The mother and daughter are talking, but for the eavesdroppers it is only a mumble. Carmen Martel is walking up and down the kitchen in her backless slippers, waving her hands, laughing. Then she picks up the steaming kettle and goes to the sink. Diane joins her there. They wash their hair: first the mother, then the daughter. Carmen, her arms raised, goes at Diane's hair with a vengeance. Diane seems to be complaining, but her mother continues vigorously.

"Hey! Isn't that nice, now?"

For a long time the boys stay watching how the women dry their hair by the stove, then curl it, and file their nails and paint them with red nail polish. The daughter too! Carmen's movements, airy and unconstrained, reveal a freedom that the boys had never seen when her husband was around. Diane is no longer the little girl who gets put to bed early: she has become her mother's companion and friend, almost a woman. You'd almost say that both of them are celebrating a kind of liberation.

"Should we knock?"

"Do you feel all right? You're crazy."

Rémi drags his brother right to the road, pulling on his sleeve.

"We're going in!" Robert orders. "At least I am!"

"No!" says Rémi sternly.

Robert begs: "Come on, don't be a piss-cutter."

"You're a darn fool, Robert Simard! She's goin' to wonder what we're doing out so late. The word'll get around and then we won't be able to go out when we want to. And Diane's there, can you imagine how it'd spread?"

"Rémi, I'd like to go. She's not in bed, she'd ask us in and we could talk. . . ."

"Yeah. You could say. 'Carmen, I love you!' Eh? What would you say to her?"

"Nothing. I'd just listen to her, and look."

"You know what," says Rémi, "we knock at the door, we go in, we knock out the kid and I'll hold the mother while you rape her."

"God damn it, don't laugh at me!"

"Okay, okay, go sit down in there and make fish-eyes at her. She's the one who'll laugh at you. You have to wait, it's not time yet."

"It's never goin' to be time. And I don't believe in your stuff about knights and Ladies. Not any more. And I never did."

Rémi grabs him by the collar.

"Robert! You've no right to doubt that, you've no right! You're a knight, and don't forget your oath or terrible things could happen to you."

"I'll never get Carmen Martel."

"Believe, keep at it, show that you're worthy and she'll be yours. You don't just walk in and say 'Yoo-hoo! Here I am!' and she falls into your arms. That's not how it works."

"Then what the heck should I do?"

"I don't know, Robert. But don't lose hope. I don't know how, but she'll be yours. Faith is stronger than anything. Look, we got out of all our scrapes! I suppose you'll have to pass other trials, or win a great fight."

"I want it right now. I'm ready to fight, I'm not scared of nothing."

He dances in a slow circle, brandishing his club. Then he laughs softly.

"Faith! Ricard has faith, and so has Godbout. Where does it get them? They're only poor bastards. Win Carmen Martel? I'm not asking that much, I've got my feet on the ground. All I want is to see her, watch her, have lots of time to watch her, be in the same room sometimes. Then I can dream."

"You'll have more than a dream, Robert."

"You swear?"

"Yes."

"Ha ha! Old Rémi's a fool! You tell me things you don't even believe!"

"I believe it. It's going to come."

"How? When? Eh? Tell me, when?"

"That I don't know. You have to wait for a happening and keep ready. A sign."

"You an' your signs. Where's it goin' to come from? A tree? Or a bird? A voice from the clouds?"

"Laugh if you like, but I feel there's something like intending behind what happens. Everything has a meaning, nothing happens for nothing."

"No, Rémi, it's chance, nothing but chance. We're the ones that decide to do this or that, or not to do the other thing, to go or stay home. What happens afterwards is just luck."

"No, we're on a trip, and we go where we were always supposed to."

"No, no! I don't like that, I'll never agree. I decide about me, nobody else. Because I'm young I still have to pretend to obey, but it won't be for long."

"And what about being knights, and the rules?"

"I'll accept that because I feel like it. But even there . . ." He stops and listens. "Hear that? Something's walking behind the house."

"Don't try to change the subject."

"I tell you, I heard a noise."

"It's the wind."

"Somebody walking."

"Wind. It's the washing flapping."

"You think? I'm not so sure."

"Then come on an' look, you pig headed. . . ."

It turns out to be the wash line swinging in the wind, not enough to make the sheets whip but enough to make them go swisssh, swisssh and sound like something walking in the tall grass.

"Would you look at this tit-sack!" Rémi exclaims.

Robert is shocked. He punches his brother in the ribs. "You don't say things like that. It's no way to talk about my Lady."

"I'm sorry," says Rémi penitently.

Robert reaches out and almost religiously strokes the contours of the cups that have kept the form of breasts.

"Why don't you take it, Robert?"

"Steal it?" The boy is astonished and hurriedly withdraws his hand. "You're not serious!"

"That's not stealing. She's got others, she's just giving you this one. In ancient times ladies gave their knights a scarf or something like that, and they'd fasten it to their lance. I saw that in a movie about Lancelot in Montreal."

"Can you see me parading around with a bra on my stick?"

"Only after dark, when the knights go out."

"Do you think. . . ."

"Sure, go ahead, take it!"

Robert delicately takes down the brassière, touches it, almost caresses it. He is very moved, and his imagination is off at a gallop. He ties a strap to his cudgel and goes off holding the pennant at arm's length. The wind swells out the cups and brings them to life with the wind's life, filling them with airy curves. Robert bears proudly the favour of his Lady, and Rémi, following in step, is only partly amused by this. They veer off into the forest and its rank turpentine smell, and reach home after a long march through a night in which they are not alone.

On the shed roof Rémi asks, "Where's the brassière?"

"I have it."

"We should have hid it."

"I'm goin' to put it under my mattress and sleep on it."

Robert lifts up the window and slips into the room.

"I'm goin' to stay here for a while," says Rémi.

"Do what you like. I'm goin' to dream."

Rémi leans back against the wall, stretches his legs and stuffs his hands in his pockets, for it's cold when you stop walking. The night is unusually calm, the sky is empty apart from the stars, which float immobile; no moon, no northern lights, no clouds. And on earth, not a sound, no animal's cry, not the whisper of a breeze to set the trees humming. In this dense silence the gurgling and splashing of the distant creek are audible. The princess's castle, darker than the rest of the night, seems dead. Nothing but the sleep of wood and nails, of chairs and cupboards and things . . . and dust. The whole house is lying in the same lethargy as the princess herself. A kind of spellbound sleep. Only the kiss of a true knight. . . . But when?

"A sign. . . ." Rémi begs, "Send me a sign, lovely princess, so that I can be courageous and join you there at last. I'm not ready yet, not pure enough! Let me know! A sign! The time for me to leave is almost here. Be quick!"

He lies waiting for a long time. Nothing happens but the gliding curve of the constellations. Then, stiff with cold, he admits defeat and goes inside. Cold! And only August!

The sun is lighting up his bed, its light still timid and full of the drags of night. Rémi awakes to the double sound of hammering: first that of the hammerhead on nails, then the less metallic echo returning from the trees. Suddenly, even before his eyes are properly open, Rémi thinks of the professor who said he owned the haunted castle. Robert was watching him wake up.

"Guess what."

"I give up. The professor?"

"No. We've got new neighbours."

"Where? Who?"

"He's thinking about the castle, which must belong to no one."

"Come and see. This is funny."

In no time Rémi is at the window, his elbows on the sill and his head sticking out. Nobody at the castle, but across the road there's activity around the cabin. Méo is there, and Blanche, and two men whom he doesn't know. They're having a real building bee. Méo is on the roof, and Blanche, half-way up the ladder, is handing him shingles. One of the men is tacking tar-paper on the cabin wall.

"Well I'll be damned!" Rémi exclaims.

"Mum says they're friends of Blanche. Seems they're settling in for the winter."

"In the cabin?"

"It doesn't belong to anybody. But did you see what the other guy's doing! He's sewing!"

"I'm getting dressed. Let's go and watch."

Rémi is a little anxious, at the same time as being delighted by this change in their routine. In no time they're on the road in front of the construction site. Méo is swearing like a trooper at Blanche who, he maintains, hands him the shingles wrong way around on purpose.

The man repairing the wall waves with his hammer.

"Come on, kids, nobody's going to eat you."

Blanche growls at the newcomers, her teeth clenched. "Just keep your hands off, by god. They're my nephews. If I catch you. . . ."

She does the introductions.

"Robert, Rémi. This is Frank Pizza. This is his chum, Richard."

The said Richard peeks up and smiles, then goes back to his sewing. In his twenties, blond, wavy hair, a thin face with a light growth of soft, golden down, he works with delicate, harmonious gestures. His limbs are slender and his fingers are nimble with the needle. The other one, Frank, is his complete opposite. Rather stout, his brush-cut hair bristles in the wrinkles at the nape of his neck, a stocky neck supporting a bovine head. His chiselled lips are made thinner by a fine moustache; his eyes, small and round like a pig's, are shifty and fleeting. An animal! And the thick rug overflowing from his back via his shirt collar, and his hairy arms and corpulent body accentuate this impression. He makes Rémi think of some heavy brute.

"Hi, kids. Good looking boys, eh, Richard?"

"They're angels!" Richard enthuses.

"Angels my eye! Get those arms! The build on them, too! They're almost men. Makes you think, eh?"

Blanche cuts in. "Frank, don't you forget they're my nephews. Just lay off."

There's a moment of silence, quickly filled by Méo's laughter. He doesn't even look up from his work. Blanche has taken Frank aside and they're whispering together. Richard gets up.

"Come on in and see our palace."

They don't follow him, merely sticking their heads in the opening, which as yet has no door. The inside has been cleaned.

"Hey, there's only one bed," says Robert, feigning innocence.

Richard's blushing like a shy girl, but Pizza, outside, slaps his thigh.

"Only one bed! Only one bed! That's a good one. Ha ha ha! I must remember that one."

Richard goes back to his sewing and the boys do the tour of the place, inspecting the work in progress with a pretence of fascination.

Pizza asks Rémi, "Want to give me a hand? You hold the tar-paper and I'll nail it. That way we can get to know each other."

"Uh, my uh, mother's waiting. . . ."

232

"Yes, yes, she's waiting for him now," Blanche insists.

From her tone Rémi gathers that he'd better leave. He hails Robert, who's watching Richard stitch a hem. The fragile blond tosses his head and a lock of hair flies back.

"Do you want me to show you how?"

Robert waggles his head.

"That's women's stuff. Sewing! Jeez!"

Richard is miffed and goes back to his stitching. Rémi is getting impatient.

"Well, good day all."

"'Bye, kids!"

"We're neighbours now, we'll see a lot of each other," says Frank.

As soon as they've reached a safe distance, Rémi exclaims, "Neighbours! We're gonna have to watch our ass."

"You said it. That Pizza's hungry."

"He looks dangerous to me."

"Not the other one. I had a good look at him. He's a real girl! I don't know, it's how he moves, his skin and his eyes too. And yet he's a guy."

"That's what they call effeminate."

"How come there's guys like Pizza and him?"

"Some kind of a sickness, maybe? How can you tell?"

"Like the priest, Ricard."

"Well, him, we're not really sure about him. Maybe he only seems that way. Or maybe he wants things but doesn't do anything."

"Same difference. He doesn't like women, he's scared of them. I noticed."

Méo, Blanche, and their friends were coming over at noon for dinner at the Simard's, so the boys had to eat earlier than usual. Their mother set up an extra table and the guests arrived: Blanche wanting to help serve. Méo talking loudly, Pizza taking up a whole side of the table with his elbows and his smell, and Richard, who sat down shy in a corner.

"Are you French, Mr. Frank?" Robert asked.

"French from France," Blanche confirmed pompously.

"What didya think, French from China, ya fool woman!" Méo grumbled.

For the first time in his life Robert was showing an interest in France, drawing Pizza out. Richard kept an eagle eye on the procedure. He grew red with jealousy and then pale with anger. His pancake face and his furious eyes were too funny for words. Rémi had to turn away to hide his grin.

After the meal Méo took a bottle from his haversack. He filled some glasses and the men rolled cigarettes. Rémi offered to help his mother with the dishes. Blanche took the hint and offered as well, followed by Richard. Mrs. Simard turned down all offers, but Richard insisted and came over to the sink.

"I'm going to dry," said Rémi.

And he joined Richard, who was already up to his elbows in the sink. The mother poured herself a cup of tea and sat down. Méo seized the opportunity to pour another round. Rémi's hands, as he dried, occasionally touched Richard's when he passed him a plate. Such soft skin fascinated him. In a woman it would have been agreeable, but in a man it was upsetting. The boy felt that a powerful emotion was vibrating in Richard and he played upon it, amusing himself by provocation, as his brother had done with Frank. This time it was the fat man's turn to rage. He even forgot to answer Robert's questions, with eyes for only Richard and Rémi.

The visitors sat on for a while before returning to their work. The glaring sun must be making their task no easier. The boys took up position at the corner of their shed to watch.

"I guess we stirred up a family spat!"

234

"Serves them right; they make me sick. Pizza stinks and he's got bad teeth. The other one looks like a half-assed girl."

"Richard isn't so bad."

Robert stared at him, wide-eyed.

"You're kidding, eh, Rémi?"

"Sure! If you want to know, I'm glad they're here."

At supper time their mother warned them about the newcomers, in guarded words because of their little sister, but mostly because of her own shyness.

"Boys, I don't want you hanging around our new neighbours. Just stay away from them."

"Why, mum?" asked Robert.

"Because. They're not nice. And we don't know them."

"They're friends of Aunt Blanche's," he protested.

"They seem O.K.," said Rémi.

"Did you get a good look? You're still too young to judge. Believe what I say. You know, those men aren't normal."

"That's true!" exclaimed Robert. "The one called Pizza stinks."

"It isn't that, Robert. Father Ricard . . . Remember what I told you about bad men. Our new neighbours are like that. If you hang around with them they'll teach you bad things. Vice. They're vicious men."

"Oh, that's terrible!" said Robert.

"Yes. Flee them like the plague. And if they ever bother you, you tell me."

"I promise," said Rémi. "We'll be careful."

He wanted to put an end to the conversation. With a look, he let Robert know this, though the younger brother could have gone on for a long time quizzing his mother, making her blush with embarrassment. She was visibly happy to put an end to the chat, and to leave the kitchen and look after Françoise.

Then their father arrived, with stories and news from town. The gossip was a kind of slow introduction to their future life in Amos. This interlude, when he came home with a breath of life from the small town on the Harricana, was the happiest time of day for Mrs. Simard. And every evening brought her a little closer to their move and her final farewell to this imprisonment in the wilds. Less than a month to freedom! Especially because life here was becoming unhealthy for the children. First the priest, now these two men . . . and Méo and Réginald weren't exactly good examples either. So many dangers threatened her little angels! It was worse on this godforsaken line than it had been in Pointe-aux-Trembles. Unless. . . . Unless she's been blind in those days . . . But she quickly banished this thought. A mother's heart makes no mistakes, and she was certain her sons were not corrupted. On the contrary: their innocence was obvious and did her heart good.

The father had ordered a phone for their future home and it would be installed when they moved in. Their mother took to dreaming whenever she heard the word. Phone, T.V., radio, electricity, running water, neighbours, nearby stores. Civilization, instead of this hole. Living! When her husband complained, ever so mildly, about his fussy, ill-tempered foreman, she stiffened visibly. There was a price that had to be paid for comfort and easy living. When her man went on with his complaint she cut him off, "You're well paid; that's the main thing."

The new neighbours were taking some fresh air on their doorstep and the lantern inside filled the doorway with a murky glow.

"What say we light a candle and get undressed in front of the window," suggested Robert. "They wouldn't get a wink all night."

"No, that's going too far, we could get ourselves into trouble."

"How?"

"They could take us serious and they'd be on our backs the whole time. We'd better just stay quiet and keep out of their way."

"Aw, come on! We can get a laugh out of them; what can they do to us? If they bother us we'll tell our parents. If they blame us, our mother'll show them where to get off. Don't you remember Ricard? That was fun!"

"No, it wasn't really fun. We got off lucky that time. And when I think about it I feel sorry for the priest. I don't want to start up anything else like that."

"Gee, you're dumb sometimes."

"No use lookin' for trouble."

"Hey, they're going."

Pizza is swinging the lantern. Their feet move in darkness, but all around the strollers a wreath of light wobbles along the road. They walk past the Simards' house. So they're cowards! Fat and tough-looking as he is, Frank is afraid of the dark like all the others. That pleases Rémi.

Robert is already asleep, or pretending. Without waking him, Rémi climbs out and lies down on the roof of the shed. There he feels like a captain on the poop deck of his ship, or a shepherd in Christ's time observing the march of stars, or, best of all, a knight at the top of his castle's highest tower. And there, far below in the plain, is the castle of the fair lady of his heart. Suddenly a thought disturbs his mind: these new neighbours, so close to the Lady's castle, could spoil everything again. The mystery, so slowly moving back into the haunted house, might disappear for ever this time, or take so long coming back that Rémi would have gone already. Was he never to know his princess? Unthinkable! Without her, all the knights' quests become absurd. Unless the arrival of Pizza and Richard was a sign, the call from the princess for which Rémi had been waiting.

He took hope again. He climbed down to the ground and stretched out a hand for his club, but changed his mind. It must be with empty hands, unarmed, that he went to her. He walked forward in the knee-high grass. The evening had brought sleep to all the insects that hummed there the day long. He was not close to the house, which seemed to hold its breath. Through the cracks between the boards, the window panes, because of the black behind them, turned to mirrors that reflected stars. The house was closed in upon itself. Rémi touched the boards with a hesitant hand, laid his palm flat on them, trying to feel whether the building was an empty shell or a place of life. His lips against the wood, he murmured, "Princess, it's me, your knight. I've come to set you free. Tell me what I should do! Tell me if you need me."

He waited for an answer that did not come. There wasn't even the creak of a board; the house and its occupants had no voice. Yet he felt their presence, the princess and her followers, cowering behind the panes, their eyes on him. Why wouldn't the princess speak to him? Because of her courtiers, afflicted with fright and hatred, terror and jealousy? If Rémi succeeded in getting inside, would he meet other obstacles? That would explain her silence. He felt the beating of his heart, felt his anxiety grow, felt panic overwhelm him. He fancied he heard a step in the field behind him. Perhaps shades were moving 'round the house to catch him by surprise. The wall would open and swallow him and the princess would be powerless to defend him, now a prisoner of her servants who preferred to see no change. Rémi forced himself to remain still, talked to himself so as to stay calm, and, to avoid the appearance of flight, slowly, slowly backed away, turned from the house and walked off with a regular stride. He had a firm grip on his fear.

The impression of a furtive movement made him look up. First he saw two falling stars, then another, and another, all in the same part of the sky. This was unusual; but after a brief wait, further streaks of light ripped at the dark. They kept falling, two, sometimes three together. Then there was a calm, and Rémi thought he had been dreaming. One second there had been a shower of light, like the explosion of fireworks, and then the sky and all its stars became immutable again. The circus started again, and Rémi stood, his head thrown back, watching the firmament gone mad. He was exultant: this was the sign for which he had waited so long! The princess was calling him. Wild with joy he rushed out in the midst of the fields and trees. He leapt over invisible obstacles, whirled his arms like windmills in the air and ran, holding back shrieks of joy. The earth rose under him and Rémi came closer to the sky until he could hear the crackling of meteorites and see the exploding stars at arm's length. He had become a cosmic knight, and on the hill, in the night of the Perseids, he danced and danced like a fool of the gods.

Robert couldn't fathom the serenity and confidence of his brother. Rémi put on mysterious airs as he told Robert to wait till evening, he'd understand then. The neighbours finished fixing up their cabin. That afternoon Dam-Bogga brought their luggage on his wagon hitched to the mare. His wife was with him, and on their way back they stopped at the Simards'. The mother made a great fuss over them, because they were her favourites of all the settlers on the line. Mrs. Dam-Bogga, all smiles and bows, accepted a cup of tea but wouldn't have a cookie, while her husband took a glass of brandy, licking his lips frequently with satisfaction, sipping slowly. He asked permission to cut the hay in the Simards' fields, since they were leaving. The mother replied that she would have to speak to her husband, but could see no objection.

Dam-Bogga accepted a second glass, and passed on the news that people from Saint-Dominique had found the old madman dead on the road. The crows had eaten his eyes, and animals had opened his belly. Terrified, Françoise began to cry. Mrs. Dam-Bogga scolded her husband and took the child on her knee, murmuring a song. Dam-Bogga made his excuses to the mother.

"Don't worry," she replied. "But who was this man, anyway?"

"He used to be prospector. Went crazy. Lived in cabin a few miles from here. You know him, you boys?"

Rémi, to his mother's astonishment, quickly replied, "Yeah, we saw him once, down by the creek. So he's dead!"

"All alone dead on road, damn-bogga. Found three, four days later."

"He had no family?"

"No. All alone in cabin. Not many cars go by. He could have stayed there weeks."

"Poor fellow, that's awful," she said.

"Oh, better like that. Crazy man. In his hand, holding iron, little shining stones. He thought gold. He knew better, but went crazy. In cabin found piles of money, everywhere."

"Tonight we'll pray for him."

"Yes," said Dam-Bogga. "Best thing to do."

Rémi saw in his mind's eye the old man they had terrorized. In particular he thought of the time when, coming back from the lake the professor had told them about, they had extorted from the old man the treasure he had about him. These nuggets now served as a floor in the niche of the black goddess, and according to Dam-Bogga they were nothing but worthless iron. Rémi shivered to think he and Robert could have discovered the body.

As soon as he thinks his parents are asleep, Rémi pulls his brother out of bed and leads him outside.

"You're going to explain now," says Robert.

"Easy. The princess spoke to me."

"Go on."

"Yep. And tonight I'm going into that house."

Robert protests. "Don't do it!"

"Now's the time."

"Look, over there, they're still awake."

240

"I'm going in the back. They won't see."

"Wait, what's your hurry?"

"There's a hurry all right. Before they do it."

He points to the cabin, where the lantern is lit.

"I don't like it, Rémi."

"Then lump it."

"It's an old house. There's rotten planks, you could hurt yourself."

Rémi fetches a hammer and a wood chisel from the shed. Robert, carrying both clubs, follows his brother. They stop fifty feet behind the house, which now hides them from any possible view from Pizza and Richard's place.

"Rémi, forget it."

"No, I tell you I'm going in tonight."

"I'm not goin' in."

"I don't want you to, neither. I have to go alone. You stay out here."

Robert, relieved, sits down in the grass.

"If you need help, just call."

"I won't."

The younger boy makes a last effort to dissuade his brother.

"What good's it goin' to do you? We could go there in the daytime and maybe find interesting things. What can you see in the middle of the night?"

"Interesting things! You know what I'm after!"

"Rémi, that's just a game. We both know there's no princess in that old house."

"Don't say that. My Lady exists, and I'm goin' to find her. If I don't there wouldn't be any more chivalry."

"You should have done like me: choose a live person you can see."

"My princess is there."

"Do what you like, then."

"I'm not asking you to do anything, Robert. I'm going in. You can go back to bed if you like."

"I'll stick around. You might need me."

With his chisel and hammer Rémi approaches the house. From the foundation to the attic comes a protracted creaking, like a groan. The wind? Rémi feels damp, a chill draught runs like ice-water along his spine. He shivers. Notices that he is casting a pale shadow. Turns around. Above the trees hangs a slim quarter-moon with a twisted halo whose phosphorescence fades off into the sea-blue sky. He can hear the light descend to the earth and grate against it before it disappears. The alder leaves shimmer, the spruce needles cast back a pale reflection. And the grass echoes the sky with its lactescence as diaphanous as diluted mist. The night is fragile, and the lightest noise resounds like the inside of Ricard's church. Rémi moves on again, toward the house and its island of shadow. His steps are noiseless, but it seems his heartbeats must be audible right to the Creek of the Curse. Out of breath, his legs about to give way, he reaches the wall and creeps along it to the window. He musters all his courage and easily rips off a board covering the opening. He slides his chisel between the frame and the sill and pushes down. The window resists, he applies all his strength, and a crack appears where he can insert the chisel farther. Something is holding the window, which gives just a fraction at a time. At least there's a space where the hammer can fit, and Rémi presses down the handle with all his might. Suddenly the window slides upward and Rémi finds himself sitting on the ground. Up he gets and can now raise the window farther, his muscles trembling from the effort, until it sticks again.

Puffing a little, he shoves his head carefully inside. The breath of the house, hot and dry, comes in his face. Rémi waves to his brother, who is watching, and without further reflection makes the plunge. His head goes in easily, and his chest, but he's stuck at the buttocks. Some unidentifiable object clatters down with an unwarranted racket that echoes through the whole house. He shuts his eyes to keep his self-control. He's not about to back out now after all the weeks of waiting, not even with fear tying knots in his innards. He wiggles, and makes a little progress. Outside, his feet flap wildly until his buttocks slip inside, and his body, overbalanced, flops into the house. Arms outstretched, Rémi lands in a cloud of dust and lies still a second listening to the silence drown out the pounding of blood at his temples. His survival instinct would send him scurrying home, but he forces himself to lie there on the rough planks until the dust settles. He coughs, as much out of nervousness as from the stuffy air, and he opens his eyes wide to dilate their pupils so that he can make some sense of the dark. Objects gradually take shape, vague masses, rather mysterious. The faint light from outside is not enough to give life to many of the objects. He touches – and with his fingers sees – a chair, and crawls on his knees, exploring with his hands: what's this? A table leg. With its help he stands up at last, walks blindly, tentatively, and trips on a rocker, which keeps rocking for a time as if someone sat there. He waits for this noise to cease, listens for others that do not come, and tries to guess where any vengeful spirits might be lurking. But no such welcoming committee materializes, nothing but the silence of the furniture and other objects, nothing but the odour of old wood, mould, and dust. "Perfume of a tomb," thinks Rémi, shivering. He forces himself to react against the fear that threatens to submerge him. "It's me, princess, your knight! Just me! Don't be afraid. . . ."

He lights a match. The sudden flame dazzles him at first, but it shrinks to a small blue fire that allows him to see the cast-iron stove with its enamel panels, the pots and cupboards and the yellowed, framed pictures on the wall, a table, some chairs. At the back there's a tangle of tools, axes, sickles, rakes, a cross-cut saw, a scythe, a bread-bin, jute sacks. On the wall hang harnesses whose cracking leather seems about to crumble. Rémi blows out the match, which was burning his fingers, and total darkness closes in again. The room, disturbed for a moment by the flickering light, is quiet once more.

It seems to him now that dozens of pairs of eyes are staring at him, eyes that belong to all the objects he had just seen. He is more embarrassed than frightened, but because he can not stand the sensation any longer, he takes the butt of a candle from his pocket and lights it. The flame blinds him and trembles in his breath. He lifts it over his head. There they are, all those objects, and it's true that they have eyes. Each thing has its own face, a kind of personality, almost a soul. You can feel that each one is aggressive, rebellious, or timid and fearful. Some seem to be hiding, others are brash and pushy. They seem to crowd in upon him, and he advances a little to escape. But it is not so much the visible objects revealed by the light that bother him: it's the dark masses, the obscure corners, the moving shadows that hold his attention. He imagines the horrid threats that they conceal: monsters, ghosts of the dead, indescribable horrors. Rémi feels cornered. His heart is beating like a trip-hammer, he can feel a vein pulsing in his wrist, he's sweating and shivering at the same time. Anything is possible in the dark, and any frightful thing could rise against him from the next room. He moves ahead among the dancing shadows. Something has moved behind him, a skeletal claw is about to grip his shoulder. He doesn't dare look around, but his flight leads him forward, deeper inside the house. For a second he glimpses the worn staircase leading up to nothingness. Then his own shadow covers it. The other room is filled with an incredible jumble: a small seeder with its big iron-shod wheel, a fork, a pitchfork, a winch for pulling stumps, even a plough, its share brown with rust, its wooden handles polished. And a host of other smaller things, covered with dust and identifiable only on closer examination.

He goes back to the staircase. It seems to be fragile, and the first step groans beneath his weight. He pauses, his heart beating fast again. But he must go up. The princess certainly spends no time downstairs: it's too accessible from outside, too homely with its old furniture, too vulgar with its tools and machinery. The upstairs, with its two windows so thoroughly blocked that night is eternal there, beyond the flow of time, far from the sounds of life and the noisy world, that's where the princess must be, waiting asleep for her knight to break the spell. Moved at the thought, his muscles tensed, Rémi takes a deep breath, shouting mentally: "Here I come, lovely princess!" One by one he climbs the steps that groan their warning to those above: intruder coming! "I'm no intruder!" Rémi protests. Suddenly a hand strokes his cheek. He draws back, stumbles and barely keeps his balance by grabbing the banister. It was only a spider's web that his head had torn, and now its threads cling to his cheeks and hair. He brushes it off as best he can, slowly to gain time. Then he resumes his march, holding his light in front to burn the other webs stretched before him from wall to handrail. Futile defences that take fire with a tiny puff and disappear.

Rémi's head is now above the upstairs floor. The light shows a short hall leading to three closed doors. No guards, no lackeys, not even lady's maids to stop his progress. Untouched except by his own fear, Rémi steps into the corridor, hesitates a second and decides in favour of the last two doors. The floor speaks and sings underfoot. No possibility of making a surprise attack. For that matter, the whole house must have been aware of his invasion from the start. He thinks how far it is to his exit. So many paces, so many obstacles between him and the window, so many thicknesses of floors, walls, and partitions cut him off from the safety of the night outside and imprison him in this inner night, tepid and stagnant. With a sudden movement he grasps the knob of the nearest door, turns it and pushes inward; a totally empty room, with only the echoes of his breathing in it. He is almost relieved at finding nothing. The second door reveals a room of the same size, but occupied by a wicker baby carriage, a chair with ragged webbing, and a narrow bed with a disembowelled mattress.

Back in the hallway, he is not really disappointed. He had felt from the beginning that the door nearest the stairs was the right one. This was why he had kept it till the last. He rubs his hands, rough with dust and sweat, calling, "Princess, princess, princess!" and touches the doorknob. He doesn't even need to push: the door opens by itself. And the smell reaches him, faint but unmistakable, a whiff of life, contrasting with the stuffiness of the house. The camphor smell of moth-balls, the feminine perfume of the bottles strewn on the dresser with its tarnished mirror – whence a reflection of a pale boy carrying a candle! The intimate odour of a person.

"Princess!" Rémi murmurs softly.

The word snaps the calm and is amplified out of all proportion. Rémi doesn't know his own voice, faltering and hoarse as it is. He takes two steps forward, silently as if he were walking in a dream. His feet are soundless in the dust. He looks around, sweeping the room with the candle's light. On his right, the dresser and an open closet. In front, beneath the boarded window, a large trunk with a rounded lid. To his left, a bed where the pattern of the quilt has almost faded away, a bedside table with a flat candlestick, a rosary, and a dried palm branch in a dry glass. On the wall, sepia photos in frames with fancy gold carvings. Nothing more. The carpet of virgin dust confirms that no one has been here for years. Even the professor had not been in the room during his stay last month.

Rémi goes over to the mirror and stares at his staring eyes. Of course there is no one in the room, but he feels a presence, is certain someone is watching him, but he is no longer afraid. He takes the stopper from a bottle. Only a vague perfume remains. The powder box has scattered its white snow on the grey wood. The closet is still full of clothing hung in an orderly manner, but the dresser drawers are empty. A voice is calling him, weakly, distant. It's Robert.

"Rémi, come out!"

"No, wait!"

But perhaps he didn't hear.

"Come on, hurry, will you?"

In a rage, Rémi gently closes the door of the room and goes downstairs. Robert is just outside the window, not daring to come too close to its black hole.

"Wait for me, just a minute, can't you?"

"No, it's long enough. Pizza and the other guy are walking on the road in front. I can hear them talking."

"They can't see me."

"Come out, Rémi!"

Grumbling, Rémi blows out his candle and stuffs it in his pocket. He climbs out, scratching his back in the process. As he puts back the board without closing the window, Robert peeks from behind the corner of the house to see the newcomers on the road.

"They're walking with a lantern, those dummies. If we try to go home they're going to see us."

"We'll crawl in the grass to the woods just back there and wait for them to go in."

Robert looks after the clubs and Rémi brings his hammer and chisel. On all fours, heads down, they crawl until the small spruce provide cover. There they sit and listen. Pizza and Richard are talking loudly, as if to reassure themselves, but the boys can't catch their words.

"So?" Robert asked.

"So what?"

"Did you find her?"

"Well, I haven't finished looking. You interrupted."

"Look, you were in there a good half-hour, it doesn't take that long to search a house."

"This isn't an ordinary house. It takes more time."

"Come off it, Rémi. You knew you wouldn't find anything in there. Didn't you even see a ghost?"

"Don't laugh. I'll find something."

"It's all very well for fun but you shouldn't have gone so far. As long as you hadn't been inside we could imagine all kinds of stuff. What about now? You know there's nothing."

"I'm the one who went in the house. I know what's there, you don't. Poor Robert, did you really think I'd find somebody flesh and blood?"

"Well, you've got to be able to see your Lady. Like Carmen Martel. I've seen my Lady all right, I even saw her naked. Now, yours there . . ."

"Mine exists. But you can't see her. Not yet. And anyway I don't need to see her to love her."

"What do you mean, not yet?"

"The princess is in the haunted house. I didn't see her, you're right, but I felt her touch me and I heard her breathing in my ear, and I smelled her perfume. She was floating all around me."

"Aw, you just imagined it."

"No, Robert, I told you, she's waiting for me. Even if she's invisible she's alive."

"She's a ghost?"

"You could call her that."

"I don't believe you."

"Listen, she's calling me!"

The house creaks and the wind whistles in the cracks of the boards over the open window.

"That's the wind getting up."

"The wind! You should know by now that you can't trust your senses in the dark."

"You're pullin' my leg, Rémi Simard. You'd like to see me scared."

"Nothin' to be scared of. My princess is good. I'm going back there tomorrow."

"Well, go ahead, you pig-headed mule. Go and listen to the damn wind and its lies."

"You and your wind! Listen, there's no wind now, and you can still hear the house talking."

"Squeaky boards, or a rat. And you'll go back all right. I know you. Okay, suppose you find her. Just say you find her. A ghost, or something like that. What good is that to you? What good does it do you? All you've got is a ghost, not a Lady!"

"Oh, yes I have a Lady. Just like the sleeping beauty. The prince woke her up, and I'll do the same."

"Yeah, but your Lady's not sleeping, she's a ghost."

"I'll bring her back to life."

"Jee-sus, sometimes I wonder if you shouldn't be put away. And me, the idiot, I waste my time listening to your damn foolery."

"You're wasting your time? Well, get out, I'm not keeping you. But you'll stay because you believe it too. But you're chicken, yes, you're chicken, and you say you don't believe, just so you won't be so scared."

"All right, how are you goin' to wake her up, just let's suppose again. You'll do a miracle?"

"I don't know yet. But I'll make it okay, I'll have help. Did you forget the ceremony that kept us here, that made the professor hit the road?"

"You're not goin' to start that business again!"

"I don't want to, but I will if I have to."

"And even if it works, imagine what could happen: I don't know, maybe we'll both die or the devil comes and carries us both off, or we see ghosts, stuff like that."

"I'll take a chance. You don't get a Lady for nothing. You have to win her against terrible odds."

Robert doesn't reply. He's wondering if he shouldn't let the whole thing drop and resign from this fraternity of knights. It seems to him that Rémi's going beyond the limits of what is permitted and reasonable.

"Did you see that, Rémi? A falling star."

"A sign!"

"Aw, don't start that again."

"If you'd seen what I saw yesterday. Dozens of falling stars. Hey, there's another one! Maybe. . . ."

Other meteorites flashed down in the same part of the sky. The boys stared up marvelling for a long time.

"What is it, Rémi? The end of the world, like Godbout said?"

"No. It's the Night's sign to me."

The walking pair were coming back, their voices approaching slowly. They've put out their lantern to watch the meteorite shower. But they soon grow tired of this, and their cabin door slams shut. The night is calm again, with such a calm that Robert feels he must speak very softly.

"Are we goin' home, Rémi?"

"Wait a bit. It's nice and warm here in the branches."

"I want to go to bed and make pictures. Me and Carmen Martel. . . ."

"Shhh! Just listen to that silence! There's the moon with a ring around it, like a picture from a fairy-tale book. People that go to sleep or walk home with lanterns talking loud, they never see a thing like this."

"That's for sure."

"On a night like this anything can happen. It seems to me if we could go away from here walking and walking and never stop, daylight would never come. We'd be kings forever, masters of a night that had no end."

"Did you hit your head on somethin' in there?"

"Robert, you disappoint me sometimes. Don't you find that this night smells of mystery?"

"It smells like spruce gum."

"No, I mean the smell of the moon, the odour of the stars, it smells like burnt falling stars."

"It smells like grass. Sniff! It smells like trampled ferns. That's what we're sitting on."

"You just don't want to understand. On a night like this the fairies dance, flutes play all by themselves, and the dead walk in peace. Everything's possible. Mystery's prowling around making not a sound, just like an animal."

"Well, I don't know about you, but I'm going in."

"Think of the old guy, dead on the road. Maybe he wasn't so crazy after all."

"Lay off, eh?"

"He was no ordinary guy. He's certainly not the kind to stay quiet in his grave. He's goin' to go on looking for gold. At night he'll change into a genie and walk. You can hear his hammer, just listen!"

Robert starts. He clearly hears the sound of hammering.

"You bastard! You're doin' that!"

"No, it's coming from the field behind our place."

It's too dull a sound to be that of hammer on stone and too regular. The earth is ringing like a drum that vibrates long after it is struck, and the noise reaches them as much through their feet as their ears.

"Let's go see," says Rémi.

"No."

"It's moving."

"Let's go in."

"I'm going to see."

Rémi slips off among the spruce seedlings that come to his waist and goes forward in a zigzag as if he were crossing stepping-stones. Rather than stay alone, Robert is following.

"It's coming this way," murmurs Rémi.

"I'm scared," Robert whispers.

"Something's moving over there!"

"I'm scared, Rémi!"

"Me too, but that doesn't matter."

A fantastic beast is born of the darkness, black, with indefinite contours, and a hide that is now invisible, now streaked with silver, innumerable feet and hooves that never touch the ground. Its mane hisses through the air and the monster laughs, as if this cavalcade had no other end than its own pleasure. Skimming the ground, or flying above it, the beast comes toward them fast, catching moonlight as it flies. The boys freeze.

"It's a horse!"

"Look on its back, something white. . . ."

"It's the moonlight."

"No, like arms, and a cape flying behind."

"Rémi, it's death! Death on his horse! Is that a scythe? It's the devil's horse! We're finished!"

"No, he's turning, he's going up the hill. It's not death, he's far too beautiful! There's nobody on his back, just his folded wings. The winged horse! That's a good sign, Robert!"

"It's true there's nobody on his back. And no wings either. It's the light."

"There were wings, I tell you! When he gets to the top he's going to spread his wings like a dragon-fly and take off into the sky. We'll see him gallop through the stars."

"He was just an ordinary horse."

"You dumb bastard! There's no such thing as ordinary. Just eyes that won't see. There, he's disappeared."

"He's over the hill, we can't see him."

"He took off, damn you! Doubting Thomas!"

"Listen, Rémi, you can still hear him running."

"But not on the earth. Up there!"

"A flying horse. Nuts."

"You never believe anything. But what about a minute ago. . . ."

"Well, I thought. . . . uhhh, you'd almost have said. . . ."

"And you were right! Why don't you just believe what you see, not go trying to explain everything?"

"Why don't I believe what *you* see, you mean."

"It comes to the same thing. There's so many things we don't understand. Look up there, see the sparks off his horseshoes?

"Let's go in, come on. I don't like this night."

"We've nothing to fear from anything. Just signs, signs. We saw the fireworks in the sky and the winged horse. Wait and see: that means all our plans are going through."

"I dunno. Come on, go to bed and we'll talk about it."

During the forenoon the boys went off with their mother and little Françoise to pick blueberries. But also, in the mother's mind, to keep her sons away from their new neighbours. Loaded with provisions and with containers for the berries, the boys led the little platoon. They knew

252

the way very well as far as the burnt forest, having actually taken that path at night. Their mother followed, with little sister in tow. Near the poplar that Rémi had vanquished, Dam-Bogga's black stallion was munching twigs and leaves. He whinnied when he saw the humans, and trotted away, halting at a good distance to watch them pass. Robert and Rémi had a slight lead on their mother, who had to wait for Françoise.

"Hee hee," Robert triumphed, "I told you it was an ordinary horse, not a flying one."

"He's black, the colour of night. Who's to say he doesn't grow wings after dark? Did you get a good look at that animal? He's no ordinary horse, Réginald thought he was, but he could never break him in. That horse understands Dam-Bogga's talk. Nobody else on the line can do that. What's more, why did he turn up here, just where we were, and just when we came along?"

"Oh, you! You've always got an answer ready. And you always have to have the last word."

The day was so hot, they could never have picked till mid-afternoon had it not been for a steady breeze that held off the mosquitoes. They came home dead tired, their hands and knees stained purple, lugging their pails filled to the brim with berries. The stallion had beaten them home: his visiting card was all over the steps, and he had gnawed the stair rail, salty from innumerable sweaty hands. Then he had taken off for the meadow across the road, where he was galloping for no good reason except, perhaps, to feel the air slip by his back and hear the earth thunder under his hoofs. He tossed his head, his mane flew and he laughed. A free horse, a wild horse, unhampered by bit or bridle. But when Dam-Bogga came along in slow step with his mare, the stallion forgot his dreams of liberty and joined them on the road without even being called. He followed the rig with no halter or halter shank; and still kept his prancing, dancing, wild-horse air!

Frank and Richard came over to play cards, and the boys, taking advantage of the last daylight, sneaked off unnoticed, their destination – of course – the creek.

"We haven't been in our cave for a long time," said Robert.

"Well, that's where we're going."

They rolled cigarettes with the remains of their tobacco and smoked as they watched the tadpoles wriggling in the pond. To think that so short a time ago they'd been only eggs! Rémi couldn't forget the old prospector who'd died on the road, alone, most likely in the dead of night and maybe the victim of a waking nightmare. A natural death, they'd said. Heart attack.

"Is there any kind of death that's natural?"

"What?" asked Robert.

Rémi had been talking aloud to himself.

"I was thinkin' about the old crazy guy."

"He's dead, what can you do about it? Ha ha! You don't want to try bringin' him back to life, eh?"

"Don't laugh, you darn fool. What's more, he may be all around here, right nearby, listening to us. . . ."

"Rémi, hey!"

". . . especially since there's a chance we killed him."

"Come on, whoa there!"

"I mean it. We gave him such a fright pretending we were genies he must have been on edge the whole time. Heart attack? He was scared! The way he was, he'd hear a squirrel in the leaves or a partridge taking off, or a tree creaking, and he could of been knocked stiff as a board."

"That's not our fault."

"Sure. We killed him as certain as if we'd beat him with our sticks. But that isn't what bothers me. It may be worse: we didn't listen to him. We were the ones who made the big pitch about genies. But what he had to say, even when he was dotty, we were the only ones who could understand. Nobody else. We should have listened to him."

"He was crazy. You couldn't make sense of what he said."

"Maybe he could see things others couldn't. Like dogs can smell what we can't. And birds see things we can't see and nobody says they're crazy."

"We don't know what they see."

"We can imagine. Woodpeckers fly dipping and climbing as if they were on waves. Swallows – you'd say they were dodging big trees when they fly. And the wind! The wind doesn't just blow any old way. It runs down valleys and streams that it's been cutting in the air for centuries. For us the air is full and invisible; it's the same everyplace. If we had birds' eyes maybe we could see that the wind's another world, with pillars of hard air, mountains of hot air, plains of freezing air, and rivers of wind. Just watch birds when they glide and don't move a wing. They're not just hanging there, they're on something solid."

"Even if it's true, what's the difference? You can't see the wind and we can't walk on this solid air."

"Some things can. Dam-Bogga's horse can. Maybe the prospector had birds' eyes. Maybe he wasn't the crazy one. I'm sorry we acted the way we did, the way everybody else did with him. We should have listened to him and learned while we could."

"Well, it's too late now, that's all there is to it. There's no good dreaming like you do, Rémi, that'll never help you fly!"

"Robert, we should have a little prayer for the dead man."

In front of the cracking statue they knelt and composed an orison, asking that the prospector might not rest in peace but continue his search for gold, and that the genies bring him loads of it.

"Robert, tomorrow we're going to give him back what we stole."

"The treasure? It's ours!"

"No, it's his. At least we could bring him back half. Leave it in his cabin."

"It'd be no good to him. It never was."

"He'll be glad anyway."

That night found them back in the grass. Robert wanted to go to Martel's, Rémi insisted on returning to the haunted house. At last they compromised: Rémi would visit his princess for no more than half an hour, and then they'd take the road to the other end of the line. Robert sat down and kept watch, at a respectable distance from the house that Rémi this time entered without hesitation.

Only as he reached the top of the stairs did he encounter the fear he had expected. The door to the room was gaping open, though he was sure he had closed it carefully the night before. He looked timorously around, examining the tracks in the dust. Nothing there but his own. No one had been there, and the door had opened by itself. Or, whoever pushed it had left no footprints. And anyway, Rémi reasoned, an open door is an invitation. And he accepted. He gave only a swift glance to the walls and furniture and went straight to the old trunk. Its rounded cover was heavy, and the rusty catches gave only after many tries. Finally his grazed fingers succeeded in opening it. The strap hinges squeaked and a whiff of odours escaped, the insistent smell of old clothing, the sharp smell of camphor, the evanescent nuances of old perfumes and the sweetness of the cedar lining. Rémi lifted out bits of old finery and adornment, their colours enlivened for a moment by his candle: the lilac shade of lace flowering anew on the black of a blouse, a shiny skirt taking on a violet sheen like the throat of a grackle. Colours, odours, languages of the past. He plunged his hands into the trunk and pulled out armfuls of clothing, which he placed on the bed. Silks, soft cottons, brittle lace, stiff whalebone, yellowed tulle veils, dresses with embroidered trimming: poor cast-offs tidied away with such care, once someone's pride, now, forgotten by all. Once they must have been real treasures in a place of such elementary comfort as this settlement.

Rémi went carefully about his work, mindful of the value that had been attached to these possessions in a more or less distant past. All that now remained was a pair of black patent leather shoes with ankle straps, a crystal vaporizer with a cracked rubber bulb, a powder dish, and an old cigar box of light-coloured wood on whose lid was depicted a woman with a fixed smile on a background of exotic flowers and palm trees beside a green sea. Rémi touched all these things, pressed the bulb of the perfume spray, which emitted a balmy sigh. A little disappointed but still confident, he picked up the box with involuntary roughness and opened it, moving it toward the light. A wedding ring, perhaps gold, a rock-crystal rosary full of glancing rainbows, a horn comb, a necklace of dead pearls, two small lace handkerchiefs, knitted gloves, and beneath all that, almost stuck to the bottom, a yellowed photograph. No, it's a burial announcement. He holds it closer to his eyes. Printed in characters full of flourishes is the prayer for the dead, followed by invocations and litanies. He turns it over: on the other side is the portrait of a woman, oval with its edges gradually fading to the white of the paper, which itself is severely bordered in black. Below the picture, also in black: "In loving memory of Eugénie Ducharme, wife of Léon Savard, born September 24, 1910, and deceased November 16, 1944. May she rest in peace."

Rémi concentrates on the photo. Her fine, regular face is framed in hair that you know is silky and uncontrollable – held more or less in check by a bun for purposes of the picture. Lovely eyes show their vivacity despite the bad print. Despite her death. And her well-defined lips seem about to move. She had been holding back a smile as the picture was taken. She is beautiful, and the grey of the photo gives relief to her features. Looking in her eyes, Rémi studies her face until it becomes as familiar as that of someone known for years. He reads the inscription: wife of Léon Savard. The professor. His wife! She died in this house, maybe in this room. In this bed! Who knows? Everything in the room belonged to her, nothing has been touched. But why were the drawers empty and the clothes in the trunk? Was she getting ready to leave? Maybe the professor had started clearing out the room and been interrupted. In any case, this sanctuary had been preserved, even from the husband's presence. Rémi is sure of that: the dust on the floor must have accumulated for years. Savard, when he came, slept in the room with the battered bed. Not here.

Rémi sits down beside the clothing. The princess, his princess, is here, Eugénie Savard, or rather Ducharme, her maiden name. And she's been dead a long time, since the very year Rémi was born. His Lady is dead! But how could it have been any other way? He had known very well that in this sepulchre-house he would never find a flesh-and-blood woman. A memory, rather. Or something more, a presence, a will; because that's what he feels, all around him, observing him. He inspects the room with a frightened look, but is reassured. She had called, and Rémi came. She wants to stop being a forgotten shadow, she wants to live again in someone's heart. And he is the someone, her knight, prepared for any deed, hurrying toward her. He kisses the picture and puts it gently back in the box, which he leaves in its place at the bottom of the trunk. He kneels down, touches the clothing and shuts his eyes. Inside his eyelids the Lady's image remains intact, and even comes suddenly to life, her eyes move, her lips give him a friendly smile. Rémi presses the perfumed remains to his body and rubs his face against them. These things have touched the loved one's body, a body now dissolved in the ocean of all matter; they were impregnated by her warmth and her woman's smell. Against her cheek that warmth is reborn in the weave of the cloth; these knickers had known Eugénie's intimate places and this blouse had come alive with the movements of Eugénie's body. On the screen of Rémi's closed eyelids the Lady's face flowers in a smile and she gently nods her head.

"Princess! Princess Eugénie!" he murmurs.

And she replies to him! The whole house begins to vibrate, dull thuds become long drawn-out groans, creaking boards become a distant voice calling, "Rémi! Rémi! Rémi!"

He speaks to her as to someone he knows well, praises her beauty, her charm, her intelligence, telling her how happy he is to have found her. He promises to come back every night, and to love her a little more each day. The voice calls him more loudly, again and again.

"Rémi!"

It's Robert shouting. He's beating against the wall, knocking on the pane, sticking his head in the window, shouting, "Come quick! If you don't answer I'm going for help."

Irritated, Rémi has no choice but to go to the stairs and tell him to wait two minutes. Then to the trunk again to put the clothing back as he found it. A garter had been held to a corset by a safety-pin: Rémi fastens it to his sweater.

"A token, Eugénie! I'm wearing your colours now."

He goes back to his brother behind the house.

"God damn, you sure took your time. Almost an hour you were in there. Are you deaf, for god's sake? I was calling you for ten minutes, throwing stones on the roof and rapping. No answer! At least you could have answered. I was gettin' worried."

"I didn't hear a thing. I was talking to the princess."

"Yeah?"

"I'm telling you."

"It's not true. There's nothing in there and you're too proud to admit it. Give in, eh? Say you were wrong."

"Her name is Eugénie Ducharme. Princess Eugénie. She's . . . thirty-four."

"And how did she get in there? Where's she from? There aren't any princesses."

"She was always there. She was waiting for me to set her free. If you could see how beautiful she is, you can't imagine."

"You're pullin' my leg."

"Come and see her if you want to. I'll introduce her to you."

"How does she live there?"

"She's dead, Robert."

"O.K., tell me another one."

"Here, smell my hands. It's her perfume."

"It's true, they smell."

"And look here. She gave me a gage of love."

Proudly Rémi shows him the elastic garter with its shiny buckle.

"Is that a thing for holding up stockings?" Robert asks, surprised.

"Yes, and I didn't steal it like you stole Carmen Martel's brassière. Eugénie gave it to me herself."

"You saw a ghost?" Robert stammers.

"More than a ghost. A woman."

"But she's dead?" exclaims Robert, his eyes popping.

"Alive but invisible."

"Watch it, Rémi, don't do things you're going to be sorry for. You can't play with life and death."

"Scaredy. Come inside with me; you'll see her picture."

"Never. You'll never get me inside that house of the devil."

"Careful what you say, Robert. The princess is an angel. Come with me; don't be scared."

"Sometimes I don't understand you, Rémi. In daytime you're scared of your own shadow, but at night . . ."

"In daytime, in the sunlight you play a part."

"Not me!"

"Sure, you too, Robert. Just like me. I choose to be scared in daytime. It's an image, just like a brand of soap. People like to put a label on you without bothering to know what you really are. You show yourself in some simple way, easy to recognize, and they're satisfied, they think they've got you figured out and they leave you alone. I'm not the only one, everybody wears a mask. You know why? Listen, imagine you're up on the hill behind the house, right on top and it's noon. And you turn around. What do you see?"

"The world."

"What you see is round, like a circus with a blue tent on top. We're all clowns, we're all made up and we're playing a part even if there's nobody around to see. You walk away and the circus goes with you, you're always in the middle."

"Well, suppose you're right, that don't explain why you're not the same day and night."

"Sure it does. We're all clowns in the daytime, but at night . . . there's no more circus. They've taken away the tent and the ring's not there any more. Nobody's watching, and you can only be yourself with your real face, you're not a clown any more. That's why everybody's afraid of the dark. They stick to the light like flies stick to shit. Only knights travel late without lanterns. That's what makes our chivalry important, that's why it's real."

"I'm no clown," Robert protests.

"You and all the others. You're a real gander, a real boaster in daylight. You play the guy who's scared of nothing, believes nothing, has no heart. At night the real Robert comes out, the one I like better, you're scared and you pay attention to things, you're even sensitive enough to believe in dreams."

"O.K., O.K., that's enough brotherly love to make me cry. But that don't settle the haunted house business."

They came out on the road, their own house behind them and the immensity of the night in front. Robert is dragging his feet.

"We're going to Martels," says Rémi. "And on the way I'll tell you about Eugénie."

"Not tonight. It's too late. Carmen's going to be in bed. I don't feel like it anyway. I'm goin' home."

Robert goes to bed, Rémi remains at the window. The midpoint of the night is near, the time when the day's excitement has quite disappeared and that of the morning is still far away, the time when night is at its purest. To go to bed now, and sleep after that first meeting, would be almost sacrilege. In fact he is rather pleased that Robert has left him alone. Rémi needs to be able to think quietly without always fighting unbelief. Robert doesn't like hearing him talk about Eugénie. And Rémi won't do it again. But all this exultation, and he has to keep it to himself! What's the difference? He'll learn to live with his secret. He shuts his eyes and the stars give way to the princess's luminous face. Vague at first, it grows more precise, while keeping the immobility of the photo. What gives it life is the warmth of her eyes and the pulsing blood beneath her delicate skin. Rémi stays for a long time contemplating this face whose lips and eyes express their incredible joy at being alive again. Concentrate as he will, however, Rémi cannot give the face a body. Just a hint of transparent arms, which fade away the moment his attention wavers.

He opens his eyes, and for the fourth night in a row sees the sky in crisis. Nature is celebrating with an extravagance that far surpasses the pleasures princes used to provide with fireworks in their gardens. What kingdom could possess a garden such as this, these celestial fireworks, these thousand fountains murmuring in the distance, these vast, dark lawns and infinite parks with their wild woodlands? Northern lights wrapped the stars in their majestic folds. What monarch could have the power to order such a feast of the elements? The harps of the green world sounded, plucked by the hundred-fingered wind, shivering poplars touched their thousand tiny drums, a solo hare uttered its cry of distress, a vixen and her foxes yelped. And a human voice came from somewhere, singing words that spoke of love and death. Rémi didn't even stop to think who thus expressed his torments of heart and soul; he was content to listen to this tranquil voice that rose without effort and fell without a fault. When the voice was silent the night needed time to recover its stillness. Like Rémi's own heart. He thought sometimes that the outside world seemed to model its behaviour on his own thoughts and echo his own feelings. "A mirror, sending you back an enlarged picture. The world looking at itself in you." Perhaps this was only a game of the mind, an illusion,

262

seeing only what one chose, choosing your point of view. If so, Rémi cared not at all. His joy was too complete.

The next few nights Rémi went back alone to Eugénie's room. Robert didn't even wait outside. Thus he could take his time. Maybe Robert suspected what he was doing, but they avoided talking about it. Every night they went out together, keeping an eye on the humans at the other end of the line, running through the forest beside the creek or holing up in their retreat. Then Rémi would go home with Robert and leave him to visit the haunted house, once more to free the princess from her cedar prison. Sometimes for hours on end he would gaze at her face, so intently that, if he had been gifted in drawing, he could have sketched her perfectly from memory. But he never grew tired of returning to her, of learning more about her, discovering each time new facets of Eugénie's soul.

At first he would stay there, sitting on the edge of the bed talking to her. She'd listen to him patiently, happy in the presence of her knight. But he grew more daring: his compliments, timid at first, turned to passionate declarations of his love. She didn't protest. Her silence itself was encouraging. He would talk to her about the outside world, the night, the cool air upon her skin, telling her of the beauties of the earth beneath the sun and insignificant details about his daily life or the secrets he and Robert had managed to penetrate. The time would pass, and they would be more and more in love. He offered to take her out with him, and she didn't refuse. Soon this became a habit. They would walk in the dark without speaking, communicating with the splendours of the night. A blade of grass with moonbeams on it was an excuse to stop, the shape of a spruce tree would fascinate them, or they would listen long to the sighing of a bush. Eugénie, floating beside him, was now serious, now gay, but always sweet and tender. Patient, she never laughed at the boy's almost childish enthusiasms. He would tempt her into wild antics as they chased among the young growth of spruce like animals in love, she in the lead and teasing, dodging when he came too close, stopping when he was catching up. Then they would walk, and he'd regale her with fantastic stories; in surprise or fright she would open her big, night-blue eyes, and then to reassure her he would stage a show of strength, inventing valiant deeds and tales of tournaments as he jousted with the undergrowth. He would joust with ardour, shouting "Eugénie!" as his war-cry, and the silvered clasp of the garter that he wore so proudly gleamed brightly in the moonlight. The clash of arms and the clamour of battle troubled the silky rustling of the forest, but Rémi would never stop until the enemy lay prone and cloven from helm to groin, lifeless on the ground. Then he would return to his Lady who, charmed by such valiance, would hold out her hand to be kissed. And he would kneel and bow respectfully. But then, on his feet again, he would pick Eugénie up and bear her off at a gallop on his charger's back. They flew at breathless speed across the world, his mount opening great wings of light to bear them through the heights of air. Clouds scudded past as if borne by a storm, and all the elements, stirred by their passing, were agitated and disturbed. Intoxicating flight. . . .

Rémi would have liked to know some of those heroic songs he used to hear by chance on a Saturday afternoon as he was twiddling the dial on the radio. Opera. Arias that he could have hummed or belted out against the wind's own song. Trumpets and cymbals to go with his wild gallops, brass and percussion to imitate the storm, horns to echo in the forest where the horse slowed to a prancing pace. And violins, cellos for the solemn airs to be played on their dignified return. And, of course, flute and piano for their fond farewells within the house.

Rémi felt a desire, almost a need, for music. He was sorry he had never felt this interest before. And now he was here without even a radio. The only songs he knew were hymns and folksongs. And what use was "*A la claire fontaine*" for accompanying a gallop on his courser! It seemed that many kinds of music were about to flower in his mind, perhaps heard somewhere, perhaps inscribed in his labyrinth of cells, but they never reached the surface, remaining, as he thought, "on the tip of his tongue." But the music swelled within him, ready, to burst out as if he had held his breath until his eyes saw burning stars.

After a while Eugénie grew tired and morose and refused to go out. Then Rémi stayed with her in the room. She was pouting, dissatisfied with him. Being a shade, invisible to all, a hallucination, was no longer enough for her, even though he adored her. This love simply did not suit her. Rémi told her of his desire for purity, a relationship that went beyond the flesh, uplifting and forcing him to overcome his senses, a spiritual love full of delicacy and tenderness letting him escape from that sexuality that tries to set its limits everywhere. . . . With her he might hope to attain that ideal. But Eugénie seemed not to understand, and he confided a little further in her. He had never accepted just being a little boy, he always wanted to be older than his age. And then he became a superman, a knight who was master of his destiny. Now he'll never agree to be just another adult like the ones he sees: he wants a life that's out of the ordinary. What better way to achieve it than by this most uncommon love in the margin of the natural order of things?

But Eugénie rebels. She's had enough of being an immaterial shade and sighs for the sweet slavery of the flesh. She is jealous of living women and the effect they have on Rémi's sensuality. She wants to be everything to him, she would like all his joys, all his happiness and suffering to come from her. She demands to be incarnated, to be complete and completely loved. She refuses emasculated love. It's all or nothing. Enough of these Platonic sentiments in the vague unreality of night: she must have the burning sunshine of bodily love.

Then it was Rémi's turn to sulk. For several nights he didn't return to the castle, but when his boredom had driven him back, sheepish and repentant, he had decided to obey her will. Not too certain how to get about it, he first had the notion of spreading Eugénie's clothing on the bed, her shoes at the foot, her slip on the counterpane with her dress on top, and her gloves at the ends of the sleeves. He would then call on his imagination, which he knew to be all-powerful. As he concentrated her head appeared on the pillow, blurred at first, then more precise, taking on volume. He hoped the dress would also swell around her materializing body, but this did not come to pass, despite his invocations and prayers. No matter how he tried, he met with failure. Once, prey to a particularly lively passion, he hurled himself on top of her. He held her beloved face in his hands, her eyes opened, her smile grew broader, but her clothing stayed flat. There was no warmth between Rémi and the bed cover. He kissed his Lady, kissed her on her lips with their taste of earth and death that disappeared as he breathed warmth into them. Her lips became human and full of life. Maybe now . . . Rémi fumbled at the place where her generous breasts should be, but his hand met only the empty sack of her dress. His head fell on the pillow, which was wet with his saliva, and he wept at the futility of his efforts.

Having put the princess back inside her coffin, Rémi wandered aimlessly through the night, filled with a new despair. He was unable to invent a new body for his Lady and doubted if he would ever succeed. Yet he knew the body he wanted her to have, he had sculpted it in clay and knew every detail of it. But the actual creation . . . Even her face was only an image. And time was flying, September approaching. Rémi walked the whole night, unable to think, fleeing, braying aloud, thrashing the bushes and fighting his own languor by running at top speed until he collapsed exhausted, his lungs burning. Haggard and lost, he went home in the pale light of early dawn and slept like a bear all morning.

In their dark room Robert is waking Rémi. He's urging him to get up and prowl around Carmen's house. The night before he'd again caught his Lady at her toilette and seen the splendour of her nakedness, the undergrowth of her pubis, black as the frizzy moss that grows by freshwater springs. And he'd like to go back and peek in at Martel's windows, even though Rémi maintains it's unlikely she would spend that long on her toilette two nights in a row. But there's no holding Robert, and Rémi at last gives in. The bright moon amazes them as they reach the shed roof; it will soon be full. Its light spreads gently across the sky and overflows on the earth, where it lies in thick, milky, stagnant pools. The poplars are effervescent, and tiny bubbles of light burst on their small leaves.

The boys jump into the grass, find their sticks, and are about to start off when Rémi freezes.

"Do you smell that?"

"Yeah, it stinks. What is it?"

"Onions. Toe jam."

"Sweat."

"Psst! Watch out!"

From the corner of the shed a heavy form emerges. The boys retreat along the wall and separate so they can't be cornered together. The form whirls to follow them and the pale light reflects in Pizza's eyes. He smiles, his mouth surrounded by deep wrinkles of shadow.

"So, going out, are we?"

They don't reply.

"Come here."

They don't move.

"Come on, you wouldn't like me to yell and wake your parents? How would they like to discover that you sneak out every night? I've had my eye on you for a while. Midnight raiders, are we?"

The boys are surprised and frightened. Rémi thinks fast.

"And if we do the yelling, my father'll be coming out. We'll say we came out because you called us, that you're telling a pack of lies and we never go out at night. He's goin' to believe *us*, and he'll push your face in. Unless my mother comes out and kills you with the gun."

"Why, you rotten little liar!"

"It's true," Robert said. "Our parents will believe us."

"O.K., O.K., I won't yell, so quiet down. We can talk man to man. Don't be bad boys, we can get along fine, the three of us. Get to be friends."

"We have no friends," says Rémi.

"And we don't want any," Robert adds.

"Sure, friends your own age, I understand. But I'm different, I know about life. I could explain a whole lot of things to you. At your age you want to know everything."

"We know everything."

"But I know funny things, good things, better than anything you could imagine."

As he says this he runs his tongue over his lips in a way that makes Rémi shiver. Pizza approaches slowly, his hands outstretched.

"Don't be afraid, come with me. Just let yourselves go. Uncle Frank likes little boys; he knows how to please them."

A thin line of slobber runs from the corners of his lips onto his chin, and the moon shines on the liquid. Robert clenches his teeth: "For Carmen!"

"For Eugénie!" Rémi replies.

And together they launch their attack.

Taken by surprise, the man has no time to react. The tip of a stave rams at his stomach, a blow from another catches his shin. He goes down groaning, twisting, rubbing his leg, holding his belly, gasping for breath. Robert strikes again, once in the ribs and a second time on the head. Pizza stops moving.

"We've killed him," Robert says, astonished. "It was self-defence."

From afar comes a voice.

"Frank? Frank! Where are you!"

Someone's walking on the gravel road. The boys quickly hide in the shed, where they can see without being seen.

It's Richard, calling in a voice that is more and more terrified.

"Frank! Please answer! I warn you, now, don't you go hiding to scare me. I could just die! Frank! Frank!"

He's getting nervous, running in circles, hesitating to go too far from his cabin.

"Frank, if you don't answer me I'm leaving, I'm leaving you."

A few more paces and Richard stops, tense and ready to flee. Suddenly he drops his affected tone and rediscovers the accents of the tavern.

"Fuckin' Frenchman! God damn slimy bastard. I'm leaving. This is it."

In the field a dark shape moves and groans.

"He's not dead," Robert remarks, relieved.

"Frank! Is that you? What on earth are you doing there? Answer me, will you?"

Richard is running through the short grass with agile little leaps so as not to trip in the tangled stems. He kneels beside his groaning friend, or rather hurls himself on him.

"Frank, Frank, my baby! What's the matter?"

He shakes his friend, gently slaps his face.

"Goodness, you're bleeding! Poor love! Oh, oh, oh!"

He stares around him in the dark. His drawn face grows hard, and it's a veritable fury who stands up, his lips tight and his claws ready.

"Who did this to you? Where is he? I'll kill him, I'll tear out his eyes and his tongue and his balls. I'll tear him to pieces, I'll strangle him, I'll rip his guts out."

As there is no one in sight, and Pizza is moaning, Richard turns back to him. His voice is softer.

"Oh, poor darling. Come on, I'll help you; get up now. I'm taking you home. Come on, you have to help, too!"

With great effort he gets Frank to his feet, pulls one arm over his shoulder and they're under-way, Richard crying and pitying "this poor baby" who is suffering so. Robert and Rémi, when they are sure that Richard and his walking wounded have reached their cabin, climb back to their room. Without even consulting, they decide not to go out that night. From the window they can see the light from the cabin, which burns very late. At the same time they murmur reminiscences of the lesson they gave Pizza. A great victory, but bad business for the future. From now on they'll have to watch their step.

Rémi would go at times to meditate before the trunk in which his dead lover rested, but he was still unable to devise a way to make her flesh and blood. He had no need to open the coffer. He knew her face so well that wherever he was, even in broad daylight, even when others were present, he needed only to shut his eyes to see her. He had modelled that face in clay from their cave, on top of the body that awaited it, so the goddess could make Eugénie's acquaintance. The total effect was most harmonious, so lovely that it hurt. But most of the time Sir Rémi now neglected the haunted house and wandered on the high-road in search of a sign from the unknown. He realized that the solution did not lie with him. Robert, who was privy to his secrets, was terrified that there'd be more black magic hocus-pocus, some blasphemous ceremony likely to break all dams and let invisible forces submerge the world.

At night Robert would try to reason with his brother and in daytime attempted to get him out of his lethargy. Rémi, waiting for his sign, counting the days as they flew past, spent hours on end day-dreaming. Inside his head he made a theatre where the princess and her knight lived through unheard-of adventures, triumphing over fantastic dangers, and loving each other. Robert was in a rage at being neglected during these last precious days, which were being wasted doing nothing. He avoided looking at the calendar, but the colder nights, the poplar leaves that were drying out and rustling, and the air, grown flat, missing its noonday taste of pollen – all these things were harbingers of the end of summer and the start of school.

Robert succeeded in dragging Rémi to Dam-Bogga's place to glean the oats and rye, and split and pile the firewood. But Rémi worked like a zombie. His expressionless face said clearly that his mind was elsewhere. After work, when the boys were enjoying their reward in the kitchen, Rémi cleverly managed to get Dam-Bogga talking about Eugénie Savard. To tell the truth, this was not too difficult. A single question and the old man began silently searching his memory. Another question had him talking, and all you had to do was sit and listen. Dam-Bogga never had a more enthralled audience than Rémi, who was shaking with emotion, and Robert, who was increasingly frightened.

"Was war. Not easy time, damn-bogga. Our children were here, too young to go war. Léon Savard comes here all nervous: his wife dead! I think, that's funny, she not sick. We went with him. My wife wash her and dress her. We put her on the boards. She was beautiful, beautiful. We pray. The light was on her. Light, shadow on her cheek. I cried. It was . . . it was . . . Then service at church. Ground frozen. They put her in cabin at cemetery. Buried in spring. He not there any more. Shutting house before Christmas, went Montreal. Since then, come only summertime."

While Dam-Bogga was catching his breath, his absent gaze directed at the past, Rémi was not at a loss for questions.

"What did she die of?"

"Don't know. Too far, doctor not come. She not sick. People say . . . but that only gossip. Mustn't believe."

"What is it they say?"

"Him bad tempered, her good lady. Him tough man, not talk much. Got mad sometimes, damn-bogga! Village people not like him. Even his neighbour living in your house then, he didn't talk to him. So bad gossips say. . . ."

The old woman rose and began to speak. Her face was distraught. She wasn't speaking to the boys – who couldn't have understood in any case – nor even to her husband, but stared at the wall.

"*Ona nevzemle, net. Doucha ieie po notcham brodit. Ia-to sly-chou, kak ona jalouietsia, zovet pokoinitsa. Molit. Net, net vgrob-bou barynia Eugenie, pokoia iel net. A ia vse molus za neie.*"

She crossed herself, went to her statue and clasped her hands. Rémi looked questioningly at Dam-Bogga, who smiled.

"My wife say, she not in earth, still in house. Not in peace. My wife scared of dead. Me, I put coffin in earth in springtime. Coffin heavy. She in it, Mrs. Savard. I know, damn-bogga. She not free."

"Why would she still be in the house?" asked Rémi, his throat dry.

"That not true. Ghosts, spirits, my wife invent all that. She think like some people, not natural death. Ghost haunting house, can't find no rest, wants revenge."

"And what do you think about it?"

"Oh damn-bogga, I think dead is dead."

He laughed softly but stopped at once when he saw his wife staring at him. He changed the subject and wouldn't say another word about Eugénie Savard. Rémi didn't even hear the talk about the kind of winter they were going to have, or the ones they'd suffered in the past, with terrible storms, blocked roads, families starving because they hadn't laid in supplies. Robert had lost his appetite. The boys escaped as soon as they could, and when they were on the road Robert turned on his brother and blocked his way.

"Did you hear that? A ghost! That woman said it. She died in her bed and not from a natural death. The professor comes back every year: He's repenting. If you ask me he killed her and she turned into a ghost. That's dangerous! Don't you go into that house again."

"Aw, Robert, those are just old women's stories. Don't get scared."

"I'm not scared for me. I never went in that house and I never will. But if a ghost wanted revenge it could take it out on you. I knew all the time it wasn't right what you were doing."

"If she wanted revenge she could have had it long ago, and anyway she wouldn't do it to me, she'd go after the professor. But he's got nothing to fear; she's a good woman; she's not mean."

"So you admit there's a ghost!"

"Aha! You've changed your tune, eh? You didn't want to believe the princess was in the house."

"Is there a ghost or not?"

"She's not a ghost."

"But she's dead!"

"You don't understand. Forget about what Dam-Bogga's wife said."

"She knows it, she saw her dead on her bed, maybe strangled. And she says she's not in the earth. Well, I'm not goin' near that house any more, and I don't want you to either."

"I know what I have to do. Never you mind."

They stopped at Réginald's and didn't come back to the question of the dead woman. But that very evening, as soon as they were outside and had checked to be sure Frank was not lurking nearby, they had an argument. Robert insisted that they should avoid the haunted house and all around it, and wanted Rémi to promise never to go inside again.

Their discussion was cut off by the sound of shouting from the cabin. There was a heated quarrel going on, and the inquisitive youngsters hurried across the road, cut back through the field, and approached a little window, where they could see inside.

His fists clenched, his neck veins swollen and his face lobster-red, Pizza's bulging eyes were rolling. He advanced toward Richard yelling insults and threats. But was this really Richard, this young woman with the terrified face backing away, her arms outstretched in futile defence against the beast? And that pale-blue dress, those spike-heeled shoes! The boys can't believe their eyes.

"No, Frank, no, it wasn't my fault, I swear it."

Richard is cornered, his back to the small table. Pizza stops in front of him, grabs his bodice, and slaps him three times, hard.

"Little whore."

As Pizza relaxes his grip, Richard falls to his knees. His face in his hands, he weeps, and through his sobs asks for pardon, supplicates, implores, and promises . . . Pizza is breathing hard, but is gradually appeased. Next time he speaks his voice is calm at first, but his own words infuriate him again and his voice rises to a scolding scream.

"When I saw you lying beside that fat cow Blanche, so pretty with your white body, stretched out beside that monstrosity . . . How could you?"

"It was her. It was her fault. I was drunk. She dragged me into her room. I don't remember a thing. You know how I am about women, Frank, you've got to believe me, I was unconscious. I'm so sorry."

Pizza is working himself into another rage. He strides up and down, wringing his hands, he strikes the table with his fist and kicks a chair flying against the wall. Still on the floor, Richard follows this performance with an anguished stare, ready to leap for the door or crawl under the table for protection. Pizza drops heavily into the rocking-chair, his shoulders slumped, his eyes staring.

"It just can't be. I can't believe it."

He's weeping soundlessly. Richard goes near him and takes his head in his hands.

"Look me in the eye, Frank. What do you see there? Frank, Frank, my handsome Frank, forgive me and forget the whole thing. I can't bear to see you like this."

Without even raising his head, Frank lets him have a solid left to the pit of his stomach, and Richard collapses on the floor, whimpering. Pizza stands up.

"Don't you touch me, you pig. It's your fault if I'm crying here like a calf. And you'd do this to me! Me! I picked you out of the gutter and did everything for you, gave you everything. You'd do this to me!"

He pulls off his belt, doubles it, and slaps his left palm hard with it several times. Eyes red, teeth clenched, he takes a step toward the fellow cowering on the floor. A kick sends Richard sprawling, and the leather strap descends again and again, on his back, his ribs, the arms raised to protect his face. Richard looks for an escape, crying and screaming, trying to crawl under the bed. Pizza thrashes away like a madman, laughing and jeering. Suddenly his arm is tired, and he notices that Richard isn't moving. Then the big man lifts his victim onto the bed, tries to waken him, calls him, loses his nerve, runs to get a wet rag and washes the inanimate face, gently slaps his pale cheeks and rubs the limbs marked by his whip. Pathetically, Pizza begs Richard to come back to him, tells him how he loves him, asks his pardon. He forces a few drops of alcohol between Richard's lips, and takes a few prolonged swallows himself. Richard opens his eyes and moans softly. Pizza consoles him, holds him close, picks him up like a child, and carries him around. He rocks him in his arms, and Richard cuddles up small. Robert snorts with laughter.

"Christ!"

"Not so loud."

"Have we had enough of this?"

"Those guys are crazy. Pizza's a maniac. They'll be at it again tonight, just you wait. When I saw him whip the other guy I thought about the time we gave it to him with our sticks. Served him right."

"Seems to me Richard kind of likes being beaten. They say there's people like that."

"Women. And Richard almost is one."

"Yeah, did you see him in that dress? You'd swear he was a woman."

"Oof. He looks like a girl even when he's got pants on."

They were soon back in their room, and went straight to bed. Rémi, waiting for sleep to come, had a vision of Richard in his blue dress. You'd think it was a different person.

Blows on the door, cries, shouts, a terrible racket in the middle of the night rouse the Simards from their slumber. The boys wake up and Françoise starts to cry. Below, their mother, all excited, is exhorting their father to go see what's the matter. Light is dancing on the ceiling, and over the shouts of their father and Pizza, Rémi can hear a roaring sound. He rushes to the window: the cabin's in flames! Great tongues of fire lash out through the windows and door, licking the walls and meeting at the roof to form a vertiginous column of twisting flame. As it rises higher the wind whips and bends it, and the air is full of sparks and firebrands. An enormous cloud of smoke has formed, its base lit up with orange light. Robert is full of admiration.

"Now that's a fire! In Montreal, all you got before the firemen came was a little smoke and flame if you were lucky. But look at that! Look at the colours!"

"Purifying fire!"

At one point Rémi had feared for the princess and her chateau, but the wind is forcing the heat and flames in the opposite direction, toward the hayfield with its green aftergrowth.

"I'm goin' to have a closer look," says Robert.

He picks up his little sister, who is awake and still crying, and goes down to the kitchen, where a lamp has been lit. Rémi stays at the upstairs window to watch the fire. The haunted house is gilded by reflections with great violet gaps between them. Rémi thinks the princess might be afraid. He calls up her face, and it appears in the flames. No, she's not afraid, she's smiling a little. She's probably just as happy to be rid of the undesirables. "They'll have to leave," Rémi thinks. "The cabin's past saving and they're not the kind to build a new one." His father and Pizza are out on the road. They can't go much closer, the heat is too intense. They stand there, helpless against the fire's fury. Rémi wonders if Richard is in the pyre. That'd be a fine sacrifice! Soon the whole cabin is swallowed by the flames and loses its shape. The roof caves in. The flames, almost blown out for a second, come back with renewed vigour, then settle down to a steady burn.

In the kitchen their mother is preparing a snack. Rémi suddenly feels hungry but resists the temptation to go down at once. He has to wipe the happy look off his face first. The men's presence so close to his castle was becoming a menace. Sooner or later curiosity would have driven Richard or Pizza to explore the solitude of the old house. And Pizza, after his beating at their hands, was a constant danger. The fire is providential. Who knows: perhaps it's not of natural origin! Threatened, the princess defends herself! And the night protects its cavaliers!

Robert was in a corner, and when Rémi came down Françoise, delighted at this unforeseen midnight celebration, was babbling happily. Frank was telling for the tenth time how the lamp had fallen off the table and the oil had caught fire, and the trouble they'd had escaping from the spreading flames that had almost blocked the way to the door. They had saved nothing but the clothes on their backs. Far from the table, Richard was rubbing his bruises. He'd tripped, so the story went, escaping from the flames. Rémi could imagine the scene as it had really happened: a rough-and-tumble. Pizza, his rage fuelled by some new development – perhaps a bottle of booze – had beaten the younger man again, bumped into the table and upset the lamp. Or perhaps he had simply tried to incinerate Richard.

Rémi's father offered to drive the disaster victims as far as Méo's place, but Pizza refused, asking permission instead to spend the night at the Simards. In the morning Mr. Simard could drop them off in Amos on his way to work. They had nothing to keep them out here. The mother was not keen on this notion, but how could she refuse? She laid a bed for each of them on the floor. Rémi slept badly, waking constantly to listen for a heavy footstep on the stairs. He feared a visit.

In the morning Rémi and Robert woke early, but came down only when the sound of their father's car had faded down the road. They ate a hasty breakfast and ran to examine the remains of the cabin. Rémi had taken the precaution of wearing rubber boots, but this was in vain because the blackened ruins were still smoking, and the embers, smouldering under thick ashes, gave off such heat that exploring the debris was obviously out. They circled the place with caution. Here was what had been the door, there the remains of a beam. The back wall had fallen inwards, protecting a piece of floor. Shrivelled objects littered the scorched grass. The opalescent masses of molten glass panes shone in the grey of the ashes.

With the cabin gone, the house opposite was more lonely than ever. Only fields lay before it now. You could see it from farther, and it could see a greater distance. The closest neighbours were the Simards. No more Frank and Richard, no more old prospector. As if the house had known how to defend itself from the curious. There was the professor, of course, but he probably came back on a kind of pilgrimage, unconsciously obeying a malediction or spell that had been cast upon him. And Rémi? He was protected by the powers of night; and, what was more, his presence was welcome in the house and by the princess sleeping there. Rémi shivered at the thought of how the house could have done away with him as it had certain others. But now there was nothing to fear. He had been chosen, he was the elect.

"You're not talkin' very loud," says Robert, who's been watching his brother for a while.

"I'm thinking."

"I bet you're like me: you have a pretty good idea what went on here."

"I can imagine."

"A little heap of black, that's all that's left. Just think, it was a cabin yesterday!"

Rémi is rebuilding the roof and walls in his mind, he can see the room, and above all, the scene that was played out there. Without quite knowing why, he is searching for a meaning in all this that would transcend appearances.

The whole afternoon there was a procession to the ruins. All the inhabitants of the line, even Godbout, came to see the sight. And they all stopped off to visit the Simards. Except for Godbout, who left as he had come, on foot, speaking to no one. Rémi would have liked to keep him company part of his way, just to hear him spout. He might have had an explanation for the fire and how it happened: the vengeance of Jehovah on Sodom, or a trick by Father Ricard to get the settlers to move off the line. Going to Godbout's house was too compromising. Dam-Bogga arrived on his horse-drawn hay wagon with his wife in tow. Sitting at the back with their feet dangling above the road were Diane and her brother Albert. Méo and Blanche came with Réginald and Sonia in their latest acquisition, a secondhand Buick, its body as full of holes as an old boot.

Everyone went first to meditate for a few minutes over the ruins, making guesses, passing judgment on the former occupants, then proceeding to the Simards' kitchen for refreshments. It was just like a wake. Glad to have company, and despite her lack of sleep, their mother put herself out to entertain her guests. There were coffee and tea and drinks and snacks. Just like Sundays. People hung around, doing nothing but sip and eat, glad to see each other. Everybody recalled a fire he or she had seen, trying to top the previous story. Méo told the most dreadful one. He explained with all the gruesome details of screams and smells, how in France he and his company had turned their flame-throwers on a haystack and the Germans hidden in it. But everyone just laughed at him. For the last long while no one had given any credence to his tales of the front. This was the case ever since he had, in a sober moment, admitted that he had shot himself in the foot to get out of crossing the Channel to the firing line. Méo swore up and down that his story of grilled Germans was the truth. He didn't worry about contradicting himself. Each day his truth was a different one, and each was more true than the last.

Midday came and no one wanted to leave. Outside the sun was strong, and the air had a dusty bite to it; but inside in the shade a refreshing breeze blew through the open windows. Everyone felt like skipping work. The women made sandwiches and plates of cold meat, and people ate as they pleased, with no fuss or bother, crowded around the table or with a plate on their knees. Somebody said "cards" and no one refused to make that effort. That was it for the afternoon. Rémi went up to sleep but his mother stopped him.

"Mind your manners, now, we've got company. You have to keep them amused," she said, pointing at Diane and her brother.

"Time you moved away from here, auntie," Réginald jeered. "They're turnin' into little savages, those kids of yours."

"Why don't we go out," Albert suggested.

"That's right, you snot-nosed little fuckers," said Méo. "Get the hell out of the kitchen so we can settle down to business. Come on, there, Rachèle Simard, fetch the cards and get a move on. And you, Reg, you great tub o' shit, bring your beer in here."

Réginald went to fetch the bottles from the trunk of his car. Diane and Albert followed him. Rémi and Robert stayed behind the house and followed its walls so they could sneak away to the creek. Diane was keeping an eye on them from the corner. She mimicked their mother.

"Mind your manners, you've got comp'ny. You're to keep them amused!"

"We have things to do," said Robert.

"You leave and I'll go in and tell your ma. She's not goin' to like that."

"You'll never change," said Rémi.

The boys had stayed close to the wall to be in the shade. The girl marched straight over to them and stopped just an inch from the fist Robert was shaking in her face.

"You've got a nerve, you little bitch, comin' to dare me like this, after all the rotten tricks you played."

"All you gotta do is behave like everybody else. Wanta make peace?"

"Never!" said Rémi, shocked at the idea.

"A truce? Like 'time out' in tag?"

"Trust you? We don't know you, Diane," said Robert.

"We know her, all right," shouted Rémi.

"You don't know me at all, Rémi."

Robert hesitated.

"You know, Rémi, mother said . . ."

"I say no. Nothing doing, I'd rather be punished."

Rémi was determined.

Diane said calmly, like a reasonable person, "Seems to me we could try and be friends, or at least not fight all the time. We never took the trouble to talk."

Rémi shrugs. He's about to leave.

"We could go the four of us and play in Dam-Bogga's barn while he's here with his wife. The dog knows us."

"Sounds good, eh, Rémi?"

"No."

Diane doesn't give up.

"I got tobacco."

"And we could pinch some beer from Réginald," says Robert, going her one further.

"Cigarettes and beer and hay. Think of the fun we'd have, Rémi."

Diane does her best to be convincing. "I ain't goin' to eat you alive. And Albert here won't tell."

"Once and for all, no!"

And Rémi adds for his brother's benefit, "Come on."

Robert doesn't budge. He is torn between his allegiance to Rémi and the prospect of playing in the hay with Diane. Rémi is surprised at his attitude, and stares down his brother, who gives in first. Diane follows the scene with interest.

"Aw, come on, Rémi?" Robert begs.

"No."

"Always have to have your own way. I'm going."

"Go to it! But if that's how it is, you know what it means between the two of us."

Diane comes close to Robert and takes his arm.

"Come on, you. You won't be sorry."

Robert allows himself to be led toward Réginald's car, but casts a woeful glance back at Rémi, who, without a word, turns on his heel and crosses the road. He hears Robert shouting to his mother that he's seeing the Martels home. Diane has one last try.

"Rémi! Come on, eh?"

He doesn't reply, but goes on toward the creek so that Robert will know full well where he's headed. To tease him, no doubt, the others are laughing and singing louder than normal. His brother's treason puts him in a rage, and for a moment he even thinks of destroying the breasts of clay. The burnt cabin attracts his attention. To forget his anger he inspects the ruins. He picks up a strap hinge, its rust turned scaly with the heat. He turns over a plank with his foot, blows the ashes off a jewel made of melted glass. Then Rémi decides to go to the cave by a short-cut through the fields. In the grass behind the remains of the cabin he discovers a chair escaped the fire. A splinter of glass is stuck in the woven seat. Suspicion confirmed! Pizza in a rage. . . . He must have thrown the chair through the window, and some plates after it that landed intact, then upset the table, breaking the lamp and starting the fire. Something else catches his eye: one of Richard's shoes. Pizza must have thrown it out with the rest. Rémi picks up the shoe and holds it tightly as he walks toward the creek. He had no idea why he bothers with this object.

In the field: a nest of field mice destroyed by the mower. Crickets fleeing in desperate leaps. Above, a hawk circles on the updrafts of the air. Rémi goes down toward the stream bed through brush and alders. The stream is there, like a trickle of blood in a vein. He takes off his clothes and holds them in the air as he crosses the water. The current whirls around his legs and rubs against his stomach. It's really like blood running, full of wilfulness and blind forces. He climbs the far bank and walks to the pond paying no heed to the raspberry bushes that scratch his naked body. He lays down his clothing at the mouth of the cave and wriggles like a worm into the interior, dark and filled with the stagnant odour of mould in the clay and the sharp smell of sap of tiny roots. By candle-light the goddess is smiling her doll's smile. Rémi kneels and tells her of Robert's desertion. He feels that he's emptying out his anger. He then shows the shoe to the divinity and tells her what purpose it had served, and how Richard metamorphosed himself into a woman. And as he speaks he suddenly sees the light. He sees the meaning of the fire and the departure of the intruders. He holds the shoe up before his eyes and again sees Richard transformed into a woman by the magic of a costume. That was the solution! All he'd have to do was dress Robert in Eugénie's clothes. In the haunted house and the magic of darkness, the operation would succeed, and he would know the softness of his loved one's body, and it would feel his warmth. But first he'd have to persuade Robert to play his part in this mummery.

He tried for a while to imagine the scene, and above all to find arguments that might convince his brother. On his way home he knew that the castle was giving its ligneous consent and approval to his plan. As if the house were also the princess.

Robert was home, wearing a shamefaced expression. Rémi gave him a chilly glance and said nothing. Let him stew a bit. They went early to bed, still without exchanging a word. In the dark, waiting for sleep to come, Rémi said dryly, "I hope you had fun."

"Not a chance. As we got closer to their place I saw Godbout coming out of Martels'. I saw red, and I said some bad things about Carmen, and then I had a fight with Diane. I pushed her in the ditch. Imagine! Godbout coming out of Martels' house."

"Serves you right!"

Rémi rolled over to sleep.

All next day Rémi avoided his brother, made no response to his attempts to make up, and tried every means of arousing his jealousy and curiosity. After supper, figuring that Robert was ripe for his plan, and partly because of his unhappy face, Rémi spoke to him.

"Don't worry. It doesn't mean a thing, Godbout going to see Carmen."

"But he did go and see her."

"So what? He wanted to talk to her, maybe he even likes her. What's the difference? She doesn't love him. Anyway, there were kids in the house. You're worried over nothing."

"One thing sure, I'll never get her. Specially after I punched Diane. And I never believed I would anyhow."

"Diane won't tell. She's pigheaded. She'll try and get back at you, but she won't blab. Your only problem is you, you've got no confidence."

"All that stuff about Ladies . . . Carmen Martel barely knows I'm alive. Even your Eugénie's better than that."

"You mustn't doubt, Robert. By the way, about Eugénie. . . ."

"Eugénie nothing. I don't want to hear it."

Robert went away, and Rémi decided to let him sulk until he came around on his own accord and made his apologies. It took two whole days. Taking advantage of having the upper hand in this situation, Rémi explained how he intended bringing the princess to life. Robert's surprise gave way to anger. Never would he be a party to such a masquerade. Rémi was patient. Convinced himself, he was able to be convincing. He got his brother to accept the principle of the transvestite disguise, beat down his last reservations, replied to his objections, and insisted on the importance of the operation. But when Robert discovered that the ceremony was to take place in the haunted house, in the very room where Mrs. Savard had died, he went back on his decision. An uncontrollable terror possessed him. First of all, there was the ghost; but most of all there was the fear that it would all turn sour, that the dead woman would be reincarnated and he himself would disappear. He kept recalling scenes from Saturday afternoon horror movies in Montreal: tombs that cracked open, skeletal hands, the monster with its hideous face. Rémi doubled his patience and persuasion and, at the end of a week, Robert agreed to go with him into the house in daylight. Then, afterwards, maybe. . . .

The sun was beating down on the window sill. A broad sunbeam, thick with dust, lit the kitchen. Rémi went in first, followed by Robert, who was ill at ease and clumsy.

"You. . . . you don't think, Rémi, that the princess. . . ."

"No! She loves company. Anyway, she sleeps in the daytime."

"Yeah, but at night. . . . Even downstairs! I told you I'd never go up to the bedrooms."

"Sure, sure, that's O.K."

"Would you look at the junk! What's it all for? Hey, look at those big pinchers. They look handmade."

"Nice, eh? Nice round lines, and shiny metal. Looks like an animal when it's open, the screw's its eye. And it's all going to waste here."

They picked up the tools, weighed them in their hands, tried them out, blew off the dust, and in many cases, wondered what they were for. There were anonymous tools that had come from a factory, and others less perfect but with more personality because of their defects. Tools invented to answer momentary needs, fashioned with patience and love: drawing knives, pruning hooks, pliers, a plane, tongs, a mortise gauge, a grindstone, an axe for squaring timber. And things made with those tools: wooden pails, a kneading trough, a wash-tub, a churn, a bench for stripping bark. In the front room the boys found farm implements: hoes, shovels, rakes, scythes, dead tools from which the hand of man had been withdrawn. They spoke eloquently of a hard-working past. Robert was uneasily aware of the staircase that sloped up to disappear in the darkness of the next floor. He wanted out. And there they were, outside, in the bright sunlight, leaning against the wall.

"Well?" said Rémi.

"Well, it's a house."

"Nothing dangerous about it. You can see that. Couldn't you feel the princess there, all around us? She was glad you came."

"I didn't feel a thing."

"So you didn't feel danger either, eh?"

"You're right, you know. Say, that house is full of things you could use. If we were staying here I'd take some."

"They're old things. The past is no good. People always think the past is better and finer and more useful, and it's not true. People don't want to forget, it's easier to stay with things they know. Look at Godbout and Ricard: they're fighting over old crap, old ideas. And what do they teach us in school? Old crap. Everything about yesterday, nothing about today."

Somebody was calling them. Françoise wanted to play. Rémi held his brother back for a moment.

"Well?"

"Well what?"

"What I asked you about last night."

"I don't know."

"You saw the house. Nothing to be scared of. Say yes. If you only knew how important it is for me."

"I'll see. I got to think about it."

They're at the window. Robert's still hesitating.

"I'm not so sure."

"Don't let me down, Robert, don't let me down!"

Rémi is begging. His brother follows him, grumbling. In the house, chock-full of a dense obscurity in which every movement echoes, Rémi, who knows the place by heart, leads his brother along.

They feel their way up the stairs, which creak underfoot. Robert is terrified and unable to speak, and his brother pulls him with a most unusual strength. Poor Robert, prisoner of the dark, can only go along. On the landing Rémi at last lights his candle. He moves familiarly in the place, as if he were at home. If he realizes how threatening their situation is for his brother, he doesn't show it, nor does this worry him. The bedroom door opens quietly and Rémi goes in with the light. Robert, to avoid staying alone in the dark, quickly follows. The perfumes in this room! And the presence you feel! Maybe it's all in Rémi's imagination, in his desires. Robert knows only that he must resist, must not believe, above all must not be afraid. There's no such thing as ghosts. But he goes forward, tensed to avoid the furniture, his head down, shoulders hunched, as if something were going to pop up behind him. The heat of day is still strong within the walls, making the air still more acrid. His throat feels hoarse and his saliva is grainy with dust.

"Take your clothes off," Rémi whispers.

"I don't want to. I want to go."

"Don't be scared, if you stick with me nothing's going to happen to you. But if you go, I'll put the light out and hide. And she'll be mad and you can make your peace with her. It's a good ways from here to the window."

Filled with hate and a rancour that he dares not show, Robert undresses and drops his clothing on the floor. The candle sets the shadows flickering, beating on the walls, and causing the bed to tremble. The whole room has come alive, and, through its bluish mirror like a horse's eye, it is staring at the boys. Robert weeps silently but Rémi pays no attention. He has opened the trunk, and his passion rises as he takes out the dress. He holds this and other tawdry finery out to Robert, who pulls back his hand and draws away. Rémi is forced to dress Robert, who's paralysed by fear. He's like a plaster mannequin. When Rémi puts the corset around his waist his skin shrinks away from it and he stiffens as if the material were icy or burning hot.

"Lift your arm, put your hand through, pull the sleeve on."

Each piece of clothing brings the same reaction of disgust and terror. When he's finished, Rémi steps back and delightedly contemplates his creation.

"Turn around."

From behind the illusion is perfect. From the front Rémi quickly manages to impose Eugénie's face on this borrowed body. He shows Robert the photo.

"Look! Admire yourself."

But Robert turns away. Rémi touches his arm, caresses it, nearly swoons, goes mad, hugs his waist, lays his cheek on the shoulders where the black dress smells so good and murmurs.

"Eugénie, Eugénie, my love, here you are in my arms at last. We're united in a life beyond death."

Robert defends himself weakly while Rémi pushes him toward the bed, but as soon as his leg touches the mattress he leaps and shouts, "No! No! Not on the bed where she died!"

"Where *you* died, my dear," says Rémi softly.

Robert struggles, but his strange clothes hamper him and his brother, having pushed him over, hurls himself upon him.

"No! I don't want anymore!" howls Robert.

"Quiet, not another word or you won't get out of here alive."

He had shouted, but now his voice is calm.

"Love has vanquished death. I woke you out of your sleep to love you, sweet Eugénie. Do not refuse me, you yourself called me to you."

Blinded by passion, Rémi caresses and hugs the heaving body. He takes these convulsive, panicky motions for bursts of passion. His voice is transformed as he gathers all the fine words he knows.

"Night is our home, my love, our kingdom where all is ordered to delight us. You called me and I came to you. Sweet lady, yield at last to your knight who has faced a thousand dangers. I want to love you till the end."

Robert, stiff with fear, tries to react. He does not want to make his brother's madness worse. He murmurs, "I'm Robert. I'm Robert, your brother, Robert!"

"Eugénie! You're Eugénie! Eugénie Ducharme! Savard killed you, but I'm bringing you back just as you were, free, beautiful and wild!"

Robert curls up, shuts his eyes, and lets the fury of the storm go over him in kisses, caresses, embraces. The knight is subduing his Lady. His hands lost in the rustling fabrics, he touches, explores, takes possession. Robert has disappeared, on the pillow lies the smiling face of Eugénie. Her cheeks have lost the frosty look of death, warmed by the living heat of her body. Robert is weeping. He tries to shut out the outside world, to concentrate on his tears and his own body. And he struggles not to become Eugénie, tells himself repeatedly that he's Robert, Robert Simard, and fights desperately to keep death from emptying his being. He struggles, because his brother's words and gestures are persuasive.

"Oh, my princess, we must be together in spite of death and time. No one will ever take you from me."

In Rémi's ears the protests and complaints are transformed into words of passion and sighs of expectation. Suddenly Robert breaks free, howling. The spell is broken, Rémi is crushed. Eugénie has disappeared and under him Robert is struggling in women's clothes. His passion dead, Rémi drops on the bed, which he beats with fists and feet. He groans and sobs. Robert sees his chance and gets up, strips off the clothes in a hurry, picks up his own and makes off with the candle, still naked. Rémi is left in the dark, weeping out his despair. Stricken by his failure, he curses himself, accuses his brother, and scolds Eugénie. He threatens her, reproaches her, would like to destroy everything, burn down the house with himself in it. Then he weakens and begs the Princess to appear. She is deaf to his appeals.

It took him a long time to grow calm and pull himself together. It was all over. Everything he'd done had been in vain. He got up, piled the clothing back in the trunk, and went out. He took the precaution of closing the window. He would never enter this house again! Robert emerged from the shadows at the corner of the shed.

"You god-damn fool! I'll never forgive you for this. You were the strong one in there, but now. . . ."

And he gave his brother a sound thrashing, against which Rémi put up not the slightest defence.

The tension between the brothers diminished gradually, but they spoke only when it was necessary. Robert was unforgiving, and he avoided Rémi when he could. Rémi, for his part, asked for nothing better than this solitude. He had to learn to live with the extent of his failure. His last hope had vanished: the Lady would never be his. She had wanted to be more than a shadow, to be a woman of flesh and blood. He hadn't known how to transform her and now she resented him and fled his presence. Despite his resolve he went back to the haunted house, which now seemed empty to him. In vain he called her, opened the trunk, touched the bed: nothing happened. The house had no message for him.

Yet the more she fled him the greater was his desire. He thought only of her, of all the promises, of what could have been. If his eyes closed for a moment, her beloved face appeared in its mysterious beauty, a fragile illusion that could be broken by a beam of light. Rémi languished, spending long hours daydreaming, inventing adventures in which he, a demi-god, rode beside a Eugénie quite palpable and lively.

Like the haunted house, Night itself slowly grew deserted, drained of its mysterious forces. Rémi began to see it again as it no doubt appeared to everyone else, and soon gave up his excursions after sundown. The knights were a thing of the past.

They had to rise early, drive more than twenty miles on the stony road to get to school, and lunch on sandwiches that tasted stale from waiting in the box, the same taste every day, no matter what the filling was. In the afternoon they often had to wait more than an hour till their father finished work, then take the same road back.

Between being the only ones to eat at school and taking the daily ride together, Rémi and Robert were finally forced to speak, the more so as they had to put up a common front against the crowd of strange kids who had known each other all their lives. The newcomers stood out and were not about to be accepted yet, let alone integrated. The town children merely observed them for the time being. They nicknamed them "the settlers." And to think that in Saint-Gérard they'd been "the ones from Montreal!" Robert and Rémi again learned to think of each other as brothers rather than knights in the same Order. Rémi had lost the special powers night had given him, and Robert regained his usual ascendancy. After a week school had become routine, and the boys knew who would be their friends and who their possible enemies. They eavesdropped discreetly on the other boys' conversations, and the daily life in Amos, it turned out, was not unlike their life in Montreal. Soon they would get to know it. For the moment their evenings brought a different reality: chores to do, wood and water to be brought in, lamps to be filled with oil.

Their daily rides to and from Amos saw painful reminders of settlers' failures fly past on both sides of the car: felled trees that had never been burned and never would be, fields of unpulled stumps standing like the wooden crosses in some abandoned cemetery, houses without doors or windows, inhabited by the wind, stables with roofs grown sway-backed under the snows, cultivated land gone fallow. Desolation, and bankrupt dreams! Here and there a farmhouse still alive, or barely so, only accentuated the feeling of desolation. What a contrast with Amos! That's not true either, said Rémi to himself. They're just the same. There was a similarity between the stump graveyards and the little houses lined up between the church and the sawmill, with the hotels on one side, where you could drink and forget that the "new land" had never been born. The failure suggested by the abandoned houses on the sideroads was written in neon letters all along the main street. Amos was Montreal and Montreal was the forsaken sideroad of Saint-Gérard half-emptied of its dreams. Rémi felt that he had come across a great truth: The settler's never far away in us. The settler, screwed out of the hard work he's done, who'll never get the deed to his lot. His property. Someone else would reap his harvest. I don't want my sandwiches always to taste like the tin in the lunch box. Those guys that go to work at the sawmill, do their sandwiches taste like mine? Stale. Like grass for sheep. Son of a sheep.

The thought of failure obsessed Rémi, and he told himself he'd lacked perseverance in his quest. In class he felt nostalgia for the summer, especially for the nights that the two cavaliers had peopled with fantastic fauna of which no zoology text would dare to write. Those long runs, always new and different, from this distance took on the dimensions of epic adventures, and present everyday life became duller by comparison. Sometimes, when he closed his eyes, he could still see Eugénie's face. But the visions were brief. In the middle of a class, staring at a blackboard whitened with symbols, among all these sleepy heads and despite the flow of knowledge passed on in the most monotonous of tones, the love of a young boy for a dead woman became as absurd as the terrors of the night recalled in the first reassuring light of dawn. Rémi had to try hard to remember all the things his love had driven him to do. Those were like happenings in another life, a world of fable, but still not far away. It was good to think that at any moment you could swim out of the current and regain its shore.

His desire to repossess the night grew stronger during religious hour. The chaplain would explain the mass, its rites, and their meaning, and Rémi compared them to the savage ceremonies celebrated under the complacent eye of the Black Goddess. The elementary forces and the power of the knightly priest of darkness seemed more grandiose and terrible than those of the chaplain with his feeble mumbojumbo. His mealy-mouthed talk of graces and indulgences were pallid beside the memory of Rémi's own virile and blasphemous incantations. The religion the chaplain proclaimed was a thing of the past, going through the motions of what no longer made sense, like all traditions. Like Ricard's religion, the call of the shepherd to his flock. Like Godbout's, too, a religion for the English that allowed a black sheep to think it was a wolf. Another relic of the past. But the Black Goddess and her cults! Rémi thought, I must go back to the cave and pray or celebrate some new rite to keep from getting caught again in the webs the priest is weaving and the others that lie in wait in books. He didn't want to march in step and be taken in like the others, or bend his knee on command before a pale plaster god. The Black Virgin, her body varnished with the blood of sacrificed frogs and field mice, was so much more real and true!

On the Friday night a great storm broke over the countryside and Rémi had to postpone his projects. He stayed up late in the kitchen and imagined the ceremony he'd invent before the cave. The chaplain's teaching gave him ideas. He'd say nothing of this to Robert. It would all remain between himself and the Night.

Their mother was undisturbed by the bad weather. She was beaming with joy because she had only three weeks to wait before their move to Amos. With this in sight she could easily put up with her solitude, and the whole family benefited from the mother's joy. Their father was relaxed and made jokes. Rémi thought it would be an interesting evening, that when Françoise was in bed they'd talk about something less banal than usual. When the usual chatter about the line and Amos was exhausted, he'd try to get his father to dig up old memories and tell tales of his youth. But the parents felt like sharing their joy with other adults, and as soon as Françoise was asleep they went off to party at Réginald's, leaving the boys to watch the house.

So it was that Rémi found himself with Robert in the kitchen, in the midst of a silence woven of many tiny sounds. He closed the vent on the Coleman lantern and it went out. The silence was growing heavier. The light of the remaining lamp yellowed the room, leaving great patches of dark. The stove snored steadily, roared for a second as a gust of wind went by, then slept again. A stick of wood slipped and fell inside, resin crackled, and the fire seemed about to die when a great gust came down the chimney and blew smoke out of every crack. The fire began to die again, but caught and gurgled, imitating the whirr of partridge in springtime.

Rémi is tired of listening to the stove, and looks outside. Whipped by the rain and whetted by the wind, the house is complaining. Lightning flashes, thunder rolls behind it. He can feel the night infiltrating the house, hiding in the corners of the room and under furniture. Suddenly he has an urge to be submerged in darkness. He blows across the lamp chimney and the dark flows in every window and floods the room like a tide. Its waves subside and the blackness stagnates. There's a smell of oil and burnt wick. He has to step comically in the dark to reach his chair. Robert didn't protest when the lamp went out. He allowed himself to drown in the wave without a struggle. Rémi thinks that Robert too had needed such a bath. They're sitting there, like two drowned men at the bottom of a lake. A bluish flash or a reddish glow from the stove give depth and volume to the dark and make its presence more immediate. Robert gets up go to the cupboard.

"It's better like that."

Rémi doesn't need to answer. Robert brings him a glass and some brandy, and they savour the fire in their throats and the heavy perfume after they swallow. Then Robert begins to talk, recalling the great storm early in July, when he'd calmed the elements to reassure Carmen Martel. Rémi in turn evokes memories of their nights, transfigured by the passage of time. They relive their struggles and devilish tricks, their fears and their desires. Everything comes up, even the mad night when Robert almost disappeared for Eugénie's benefit. In a trembling voice Robert tells of his struggle with the spirit of the dead woman.

"I'm not mad at you now. I think I understand a bit."

Everything leads them back to the cavern of clay, sanctuary of an obscene goddess, place of strange rites, of celebrations with ever-changing rituals, a den where lambs went to grow pointed teeth and claws!

"Godbout and his wolves and sheep!"

"Oh, he's not wrong. But he's not a wolf!"

"We're wolves, aren't we, eh, Rémi?"

"I don't know. I'd like to be."

"Yeah. Look at Father Ricard, we beat him at his own game. And Pizza, we beat him for real. And think of Diane in the shit puddle and then in the ditch. We always won. We were the strongest."

"But we didn't always succeed. Especially the most important time."

Rémi's voice is trembling with emotion. Robert fills their glasses again and begins to talk. He describes the school and Amos, boys at school, their move. Rémi feels that his brother is experiencing his own nostalgia, the same anguish at losing their night-time kingdom.

"Rémi, I want to stay on being a knight. Maybe we could keep it up in Amos."

"It wouldn't be the same. You couldn't even do it."

"You could if it was true."

"But we didn't succeed when we had everything going for us. Just imagine in town. . . ."

"You said we'd get our Ladies. You said so! It didn't work. We're going away from here like all the others, with dreams that didn't work."

Robert sniffs and goes on drinking.

"I believed in it, Rémi."

". . . ."

"Now it's too late. We lost. We aren't wolves!"

". . . ."

"You told me . . . Now give me an answer."

"I believed, too. I still do, Robert."

"You're just tryin' to make me feel good."

"No, maybe we gave up too soon. We have to search some more, start going out again. Since last time at the haunted house the knights haven't been out. That has to change. Anything's possible, but you have to have faith. We're doubters, Robert."

"We hardly have any time. Goin' out at night . . . and then getting up for school."

"Tomorrow night. At least once more. We'll have a ceremony, a midnight mass. We'll go the whole way, with monsters and demons and genies, and we'll wake the dead. We'll make the night shake and tremble, even if we die for it. At least it's better than being a sheepish follower and beaten before you start. We sinned through laziness; we have to get our pardon."

Rémi grows excited as he talks, he gets to his feet, gesticulates, and Robert is fascinated. He feels his enthusiasm returning.

"We'd forgotten our Goddess. We neglected her. Tomorrow we'll go and worship her; we'll do evil in her honour."

They compete in describing excitedly all the bloody sacrifices, inventing all the litanies and perverse prayers they'll need, all full of blasphemies and horrors. You can't start from nothing: first you have to destroy what exists then build on the débris. They can only worship the Black Virgin after breaking the other idols. Profanation comes before adoration.

Rémi tries to think of a particularly vile sin to commit right away, just for a warm up. The alcohol stimulates his imagination and he envisions fabulous but impractical varieties of indecent assault, sadistic murders so outrageous that they might be considered sacred. He searches his memory, tries to imagine historic atrocities and biblical horrors, the Canadian martyrs, Christians and lions, the holy Innocents, mere allusions that had awakened powerful impressions. Suddenly he gets the notion of a frightful sin, something to sully what is most precious to him, a sin that will destroy and likewise liberate.

In his parents' bedroom he lies down on the bed in which he was conceived and touches himself. Rémi feels strings bursting inside him. He had thought of them as sensitive, like guitar strings, now he realizes they were merely fetters. In the shadows around the bed he imagines the smile of the Goddess and the slim shape of Eugénie. He must defile, deny, reduce all to human proportions. Refuse to be dominated. Be free that he might grow. "Have to find something worse for tomorrow, something even better." Now he can straighten up as if a weight had been lifted from his back. No one will ever again be superior to him. "I'm not born to be a failure. I haven't got a sheep's soul. Fuck the past. I'm not bound by something that happened before. Knock down the cathedral in Amos, you've got enough stone for a castle or a bridge, or a wall, or a great tower for seeing far away." He takes some more brandy and sits rocking. "Later I'm goin' to change my name. Simard! Hell! A name for me, a new name as if I had no ancestors. Why should I live with their mistakes? I want to make my own, shit! New mistakes. And Robert will help."

That Saturday the sun seemed rejuvenated and ready to wipe out all traces of the storm. The family went to Val-d'Or to Réginald's brother's place and others vaguely related to them. The boys were left somewhat cold by relatives, and Val-d'Or was a depressing place. But they couldn't get out of the compulsory visit. With their mother looking on critically, they smiled and put on their best manners for the old great-aunt. The family reached home only as night was falling, dog-tired by the miles of driving through country where the grass was already turning down. The boys had to pretend to sleep and at the same time struggle against their desire to do so. It seemed to take an interminable time for the house to settle down.

The sharp September air whipped their faces and awoke them fully. The night made them want to run, take advantage of their rediscovered freedom. Rémi had wanted to make a long outing of it, perhaps even the whole night. Rucksacks on their backs, off they go toward civilization. Robert has knotted Carmen's brassière to his staff and carries it proudly. They have no idea just where their run will take them. They must, however, find offerings for their sacrifice and somehow make up for lost time. Not a word is exchanged. There's nothing to be said, each of them is searching. Méo's house, silent and dark in its clearing, brings them back to reality.

They go over to it, sniff around the place without finding a sign of life, and prudently go inside. If the occupants are asleep, they'll give them a scare. If no one is there, they'll make the best of that. Robert feels beneath the sink where the bottles are usually kept and comes up with a full one, its seal intact. Without bothering to identify its contents he puts it in his bag and, just for fun, the boys tip over the table and chairs and throw the mattress off the bed – and lay the plates on the floor without breaking them.

The Martels have only a night-light on, but Réginald's place is all lit up. The evening ritual of cards is in progress. "Want to spy?" asks Robert.

"I'd kind of like to go to the village."

"The village?"

"I've got a reason."

They try to melt into the brushwood along the ditch until they are far past Godbout's. Then it's nothing but dark night with its agitated, twinkling stars. The way finally comes out on the access road. They turn right toward the confused cluster of lights that is the village. They are no longer alone. The humming of power lines accompanies their passage. Once they have to crouch in a wet field pitted by the hoofs of cows, to wait for a car to pass. Then the village houses are close by, flooding the road with light. Voices: the general-store-restaurant-billiard-hall is still open and some young people are chatting on its front stoop. Behind the first house, in a junked car abandoned to its rust, glows the red of two cigarette tips. Perhaps a pair of lovers. The boys leave the road and angle off into the field through a dark grove of trees. Dogs bark. Past the bushes lie the cemetery, the church, and the priest's house.

They make their way toward the parochial buildings. There's a light on in the presbytery, and great animation in its dining-room. Muffled echoes come from there: children crying, lively conversation, reprimands from parents. The little white car is not in its parking place. The boys take a chance on peeking through a window. Luggage and boxes stand in one corner and clothing is piled on the table. On the floor a dozen people are trying to sleep on mattresses. "That's right," Rémi remembers, "Ricard is sheltering this family that was burned out." The kitchen smells and family life in his immense home, usually so quiet, must upset the priest. Robert, as if he had the same idea, jeers, "He must have gone to the women to get some peace."

"The women . . . or something," Rémi whispers.

No, Ricard is making a tour of the farms to organize a bee. He puts up with the small annoyances of the invasion of his house with resignation, almost with joy. The fire and the building bee are welcome: after a series of failures and the opposition to his projects, the priest had become a recluse. But events had forced him to open his heart again to others and reawaken him to his mission. The building bee will be a way of bringing his flock together and making them share in a common task. Later. . . . He dreams as his Volkswagen brings him back to the presbytery. At the top of the fifth-line hill, which overlooks the village, he stops and turns the engine off. Below him are the lights of Saint-Gérard. Darkened houses make the village look smaller, but he knows it so well that he can even locate the houses drowned in darkness. For a moment he amuses himself by identifying each yellow patch and giving it a family name. His village, where he, God's farmer, must cultivate their souls. A laboratory in which he, an alchemist of mankind, may find the true philosopher's stone: happiness on earth through social harmony. In the expectation of eternal joy. Oh, if he could only share this exaltation! But he is as lonely and isolated as all his predecessors.

Rémi leads Robert nearly to the sacristy, to a darkened corner. They look around: no one has seen them.

"What are you going to do?"

"I'm going in," says Rémi.

"Are you crazy? What if he comes back? Ricard, I mean."

"Look, when you finish school for the day, do you go back there at night? No? Ricard neither."

"You know what we're risking."

"*You're* asking *me*?"

Robert tries the door. Locked. But he climbs on his brother's shoulders and succeeds in opening a small window, through which he slips inside. Reaching down for his accomplice, he hoists him up and helps him through. They risk a few steps on the waxed parquet. Their hearts are beating overtime: there's a delicious fear of being caught in the act, exultation at law breaking, and the joy of acting in secret, in the dark, of being . . . a threat!

Ricard takes a last, long, panoramic look at the landscape. He knows that in daylight he would see the chequerboard of fields, the sea of spruce, the clumps of yellowing aspen, the big barns of well-to-do farmers, and the poorer ones, barely bigger than the settlers' houses. Far away, over the tree-tops, would rise the steeple of Saint-Dominique in Béarn. Still farther, on a clear day, he would see the sun glint on the Harricana and Lake Obalski. There's nothing comparable to the softness and tender greens of Temiskaming. On the other hand, nature here is rough, unrefined, half-finished. But he had wished for this exile, wanted it, chosen it against all good advice. The land where his mission lay! A great emotion moves him. He won't return to the village just yet; he'll take a little walk in the brisk air. The clumps of alder and hazel are singing. Ricard goes toward them. The need to touch and caress the dying leaves . . . It will be a long winter. The need for memories of summer. His foot slips on something. Intrigued, he picks it up. Before ever seeing it, he knows. Disgust rises in his throat at the feel of the thin, supple rubber. He throws the safe as far as he can and turns back hastily. "Satan is always nearby, watching for the moment propitious to temptation. Struggle and pray." Ricard folds his hands together and walks up and down, his head bowed, reciting a Hail Mary. He walks near the trees. His eyes, now accustomed to the dark, discover on the moss, in the grass or on the lowest branches the most unspeakable sights, crumpled handkerchiefs, empty beer bottles, and even a pair of girl's panties hung on a bush, like a landmark or a rallying flag. He rips it down and tears it in pieces. The banner of evil! So this was the place where the young met. He had suspected there was a place where they did what was known as "parking," but here! In plain sight of the village, on the hilltop, nearest to heaven! So many

301

bits of garbage, so many sins never confessed to him! In addition to vice itself then, there are an incredible number of false confessions leading directly to sacrilegious communions.

Lord Jesus, what kind of shepherd am I? he wondered. An innocent dreaming of Eden, while Evil gnaws away like a cancer. Who else can wipe it out? Sexuality! The root of all evils, downfalls, and defections. Make this a forbidden place? The police? The young would go elsewhere. It is within themselves that Satan must be fought. First, identify them. Accuse each one at confession, force them to admit their sin? Would he not risk shocking and upsetting those who were innocent, and even give them ideas? Ah, but Satan is a subtle one! Yet he, Ricard, would triumph through prayer and mortification.

Ricard weeps silently and kneels to pray. But this brings him close to the orgiastic remains. This handkerchief embroidered with a J, whose can it be? Julie? Jacinthe? Jocelyne? Josée? They are all of a susceptible age. Their mothers, then, are negligent! Perhaps there is even complicity, perhaps they close their eyes to these escapades. Escapades! Is the evil truly so deep-rooted that this sexual debauchery is now considered mere escapades, bagatelles? Does he, in fact, know his village, his faithful? Julie, Jacinthe . . . He can see their faces, apparently so innocent. Only yesterday, their solemn communion. Now he imagines them stark naked, the hands of boys pawing their budding breasts. He sees the couples coupling, hears their groans and laughter. Ricard weeps his heart out. He crawls forward on all fours, feeling, exploring among the rubbish. He imagines all the youth of the village here in a writhing mass of fornication. Sex for its own sake! Rejection of the family, the child: man reduced to his animal propensities. A short while ago, he recalled it was the great settlement crusade, building for the future, hope that was planted the length and breadth of the fields. Was this the harvest? Hard-hearted youth thinking only of fleeing to the city, and meanwhile forgetting their boredom and the emptiness of their lives without ideals in this artificial paradise of drink and sex! Damned sex! Original ineffaceable sin. Sex, sex, sex!

Rémi bumps into the table. His fingers find the model. The priest's projects, the dreams that his saintly naivety wants to make concrete. "Failure, failure!" murmurs Rémi as he tears out the trees and grass represented by mosses and sponges. Robert comes to help, crushes what he can and demolishes all he can touch. Rémi opens a cupboard and takes out a chasuble and stole, which he rolls up and stuffs in his rucksack. His eyes have grown used to the dark and he ventures into the church. In the choir he hesitates, words pass through his mind: sacrilege, profanation, simony. This is against his belief and against the teaching he has received. What if it were all true? What if the statues encircled him and crushed him in their plaster arms? Or Christ flattened him with a lightning bolt? Or the tabernacle opened on a horror, with the face of the crucified sadly smiling? It seems to Rémi that the tabernacle lamp is swinging up there, though the air is still. Despite this he lays his hand on the latch. Nothing happens. He opens the tabernacle. Still nothing, no noise or thunder or blinding light, still less an other-worldly voice. Nothing but the faint squeaking of the hinges. He returns to the vestry.

"O.K., well, let's get a move on."

Robert emerges from a corner:

"Is this the pascal candle?"

"Looks like."

"I'm takin' it."

They clamber out the window and land on the crunching gravel. They run behind the presbytery where the lights are now out, climb a small board fence, and drop to the ground out of breath.

The shapeless moon, rust-red, peeks over the crest of the spruce forest. In the distance, on what seems to be a hill, headlights are switched on. The moon grows pale as it rises, and in its light they see the crosses around them.

"Damn! We're in the graveyard!" says Robert.

Rémi examines the crosses lined up like trees in an orchard. But, he notes as he observes them more closely, they're not really in line, or no longer so, as if the wood had come to life again and was growing according to its tree-like logic. Each one is crooked at its own angle. Three stone monuments break the harmony. Monuments is perhaps not the word. They're slender steles, but rich in comparison with the wooden crosses.

"Christ! Let's get out of here," says Robert, uneasy to find himself in such a place.

Rémi doesn't answer. One of these crosses must bear Eugénie's name and, below it, her bones are mingled with the soil. He wants to touch her cross. He gets up and begins to explore each inscription, standing a little to one side so as not to obscure it with his shadow. Occasionally he has to brush off the dust or dig out letters with his nails. Names after familiar names . . . dates, ages, crosses for women who raised big families, the same crosses for lazy women or children who died in the budding. Crosses, nothing but mouldy crosses! And beyond the cemetery what might have testified to courage and hard work no longer counts: the children forget or leave, and brush grows on the cleared land. Just a cross, like the stub of an old movie ticket. Nobody remembers what the film was about.

Robert keeps close on his brother's heels: he's too uneasy here to stay alone. He can't forget that the dead are sleeping underfoot. They must wake when they hear steps, angry at being disturbed, jealous of the living . . . then fight their way to the surface and stretch their bony hands toward his ankles . . . Robert panics. He takes off at a run, his rucksack clanking behind him. The crosses whip by on either side, they seem to be getting closer. They're hemming him in! He dodges and tacks without looking down, his eyes fixed on a cloud for a landmark. Something's coming behind him, it's after him, touching him, arms try to grasp him as he passes. He never ran so fast in his life; without slowing down he leaps the fence. Outside, he no longer forces his legs, but lets the impetus take him far beyond the dead. He sits down, out of breath, searching for pursuers.

Rémi has found Eugénie's grave. He caresses the cross, cleans it, and sets it straight. A car drives in at the priest's house and its headlights sweep the cemetery. Rémi drops flat on the ground. The lights go out and a car door slams. The boy stays still for a moment, listening, his ear to the ground. Nothing. Rémi, on the grave, realizes that his face is above the skull of the dead princess. He shuts his eyes and calls to his beloved. He knocks, softly, with his fist. Nothing happens, the earth is as tightly closed as a stone wall. Rémi had hoped that Eugénie, fleeing the abandoned house, might have taken refuge among her own remains. What is under him is the glacial earth of Abitibi. Parting the grass, he scratches up a little of that soil and puts it in his pocket.

Muffled by walls and the distance, a great cry comes from the church, a long, drawn-out cry as of a man falling from a high cliff. Rémi gets up and runs to join his brother. To warm themselves they open the bottle stolen from Méo.

"Did you hear a scream?"

"No."

"You were too far away. I think the priest went in the church."

They laugh, proud of their power, and drink again to get courage for the long walk to the Creek of the Curse. On the way their feet grow light and their gait supple. They are princes of the road and masters of this night from which others are excluded. Gradually the barking dogs grow silent and the village is left far behind.

Ricard is weeping, moaning, complaining. How can this be possible? This vandalism in the vestry, his model destroyed. Broken dreams! A punishment? Tribulations allowed by God, not so much to test his servant as to remind him of his wretched human fate and prevent the undue swelling of his pride. Well, God succeeded! Ricard feels lucid about the carnal shackles that limit him. He is not entrusted with some glorious mission: he is the humble and imperfect instrument of the divine will. This thought he finds comforting. He goes to collect his thoughts in the church before the body of Christ and to find strength in prayer and mediation; and what does he find but a desecration, the sacred hosts scattered on the altar! And some are missing. Missing too is the lovely chalice with its harmonious lines and polished silver, his mother's gift on his ordination. God is testing him beyond reason because he loves him and expects much of him.

The moon makes a collage of shadows on the cross raised at the corner of their line and the access road. Robert climbs up and tears off the spear which comes away without breaking. He brandishes it, laughing, threatens his brother with its harmless point until Rémi takes it from him. Its dry wood is brittle, aged by the weather. Will anybody notice tomorrow that the sacred monument has lost one of its attributes? Nobody looks closely at this sign of other days.

"This will make an offering. Hang onto it."

All is quiet among the humans. Dam-Bogga's dog comes over to the fence without barking, takes a sniff and goes back to sleep. They walk fast to be quickly rid of the danger of these inhabited places. A lamp burns low in Méo's kitchen.

"They're scared, Robert. Sure as hell it's the devil turned their house upside down."

"That gives me an idea. Hold my stick, Rémi, and walk on."

Robert moves in on the house and risks a peek in the window. Méo, his face haggard, is drinking straight whisky. Blanche is on her knees picking up the plates, stopping frequently to make the sign of the cross. Robert draws back, takes aim at the bright window and throws the spear with all his strength. Screams and curses follow, as the pane smashes and the weapon disappears inside. Robert hides. The two come out, she holding the lamp and leading the way as she waves a palm branch and cries to the four winds.

"*Vade retro satana*, get thee behind me, Satan, thou who hast lost God for all eternity. *Vade retro*. And look out, I have a blessed palm leaf."

Méo follows brandishing a bottle by the neck, looking around fearfully.

"Don't play crazy games! I'm on your side, look here, I brought you somp'n to drink, for Chris' sake."

Blanche is brandishing a dried palm branch, from which the wind blows the dust away. Her lamp is giving a fainter light but her voice is still strong.

"*Vade retro satana. Vade retro satana*. God damn it, Méo, stop pushin'."

"March! And let me be. Satan, you an' me's buddies."

"Shut yer trap, Méo! *Vade retro satana*."

Rémi laughs till the tears come. Robert has joined him. He had gone in the house to recover the spear and liberate another bottle. He chases his brother, waving the spear. Rémi, feigning terror, takes off, shouting in Blanche's voice, "*Vade retro. Vade retro!*"

But they are silent as they pass their own house. As soon as they are far enough Rémi starts talking loudly again. Suddenly he utters a shout of surprise. Robert raises his cudgel, ready to defend himself.

"What's wrong, Rémi? What is it?"

Without replying, Rémi sets off at a run toward the abandoned house, and Robert sees that it's standing wide open: someone has taken the boards off the doorway, and removed the door itself. In the grass he notices two broad tracks, left by a truck, running from the road to the house. Looters! "Wait for me," he shouts.

He catches up with his brother and lights the great candle from the church. Rémi goes inside.

"Oh, no! I don't believe it!"

The place is empty. Nothing is left of the jumble but a few bits of scrap iron. No more tools, no furniture, no machinery. Could the professor have emptied his house? No, he wouldn't have torn off doors and windows or taken away the cupboards. It was looters, sure enough. They must have come while the Simards were away. Rémi rushes to the stairs and goes up four steps at a time. Robert is close behind and still uneasy, though the house, washed clean by the wind of its odours from the past, is no longer menacing. A sob comes from the bedroom. They've taken the furnishings, even the trunk. The clothing, deemed worthless, has been dumped on the floor. Rémi is lying on it, embracing it, weeping loudly. Robert is motionless, contemplating his brother's distress. What can he do to console him? He can almost share his sorrow.

Gradually Rémi grows quieter. He searches anxiously among the clothes until he finds the little box, which he holds tightly to him. Then he collects the clothing in a great bundle and rolls it in the coverlet. He is still crying, and his voice is cracked: "It's all right, I'm going to save you. I'm taking you with me to our cave. Nobody can hurt you there."

Robert is suffering along with his brother. To help him he hangs the bundle on his staff.

"Here, take one end. She'll be fine in our hide-out. Come on, let's go."

Rémi can't bring himself to leave.

"Come on, Rémi. She's not here any more."

They walk slowly, unable to see where their feet are going to land. The heavy package swings on its pole. Robert is forcing the pace: he's in a hurry to rid himself of these clothes that remind him of a night in the dead woman's bedroom. They set down their burden at the entry to the cave, Eugénie's belongings on one side and the Church appurtenances on the other, with Rémi sitting in the middle. Robert gathers wood and stacks it high, adding bits of bark and dry twigs. Rémi seems to be regaining control of himself.

"This was Christ getting back at us. Ricard's god beat us to it because he knew we were going to rob the church. He was avenged from the start."

"Wouldn't surprise me if it was Martel."

"Could be. Him or some other sheep. It's all the same. It's the god of the sheep that's behind it all. We're getting back at him, Robert. It's our turn to strike."

"What if. . . ."

"You're not scared, are you? The Black Goddess is on our side. Take a slug and pass me the bottle."

They take turns drinking.

"Don't let it bother you, Rémi. I know, it's awful that they broke into the princess's castle, but you saved her at least; she's here with us."

"No, I don't know where she is now. All we have is her clothes. She'd left the house even before the robbers got there . . . and she wasn't in the graveyard either. Gone. I don't know where. Nothing's any use now."

In his discouragement Rémi drinks like a madman, and after every swallow he is more depressed. Around them the night is silent, stilled by the cold. The moon, small and motionless, shrinks still smaller. Robert, put in the mood for action by their walk, the sacristy, and alcohol, doesn't want to see this escapade fizzle out to nothing: he wants a celebration, a ceremony to help forget this first week of school. He tries to shake Rémi out of his despair, touch his pride, whip up his aggressiveness.

"You're a loser, Rémi. The princess is right to leave you."

Rémi is expressionless and goes on drinking as if he hadn't heard. Robert finds Eugénie's dress and, without Rémi's noticing, puts it on and taps his brother on the shoulder.

"Rémi, it's me, your princess!"

Rémi reaches out and feels the smooth cloth of the dress. The familiar odour of it awakes him.

"Eugénie! It's you!"

"You're a coward, Rémi, I'm disappointed in you. At your very first trial, the first obstacle, you leave me in the lurch and crawl away like a whipped dog. And I was so proud of my knight! And what about me, poor Eugénie, chased out of her castle, wandering in the dark and pestered by the shades! I looked for you and called, and waited and waited. And you sat on your ass and let me suffer. Coward! Coward!"

"That's not true! I'm no coward. But I have no power. Send me a sign."

"A sign! You should send me one! Show me where you are."

Now that Robert has awakened his brother's interest he stops playing princess and drops his ceremonial voice. He grabs Rémi's arm.

"Do something, damn it! Get her to come, make her come back. Do something, even if you're not sure of winning. It's like the school yard: you've got to hit first, even if you're not the strongest. The others'll hang back, just from seeing you make the first move."

"It's not the same thing."

"Sure it is. Imagine you're strong and powerful, order the princess to come, scare her if you have to. You're a knight, a high priest of the dark. You can do it."

310

Rémi stands up. His legs are wobbly but he holds his head proudly as Robert's words reverberate in his brain.

"You're right."

While Robert takes off the dress and lights the fire, Rémi dons the chasuble and lays the stole around his neck. They hang Eugénie's clothing in the branches of a rowan tree so that the princess can watch the ceremony. In the light of the growing flames the bits of clothing fill out with the flesh of darkness. The officiating priest takes the Black Virgin from her retreat and, holding her at arm's length, starts a one-man procession with great pomp. Robert joins him, bearing the pascal candle. They march as far as the stream, circle the tranquil pond, stray in the alders for a moment, then return to the place of the great fire. They set up their statue against the slope, her belly and breasts caressed by the heat. Her body, its skin as scaly as a reptile's, soaks up the night and the fire like a thirsty sponge and fattens upon them. And on top stares the doll's angelic head with its gentle eyes and timid smile. But Rémi, kneeling before the goddess, is not duped by this appearance. The black scars in the pink plastic cheeks are dark rivulets remaining from the blood of other sacrifices. They speak loudly of her appetite for death and blood, her greed for sacrifice.

Strengthened by his meditation before the idol, Rémi the high priest approaches the fire, which serves as his altar. Robert kneels and waits. Rémi wets the fringe of his stole in alcohol. He visits the choir and sprinkles the goddess, blessing Robert as he goes by. Then Rémi invokes the Night and calls on the spirits of the elements, summons the dead to answer his call. His voice grows stronger and the words come by themselves, surprising the boy himself.

When he stops, the spruce forest organ groans solemnly. The saucy sounds of the stream join the chorus. Drawn by the heat, juices leave the roots, ooze up, and hiss beneath the fire. The earth heaves, the sky looms darkly. Everything moves and breathes in this amphitheatre. The nocturnal nave fills with observant faithful. Rémi knows now how the ceremony must go. He can draw on the teachings of the school chaplain. After the offertory, the consecration and communion, come the prayer of thanksgiving and a frantic dance around the fire. The boys drink, and their bare feet slap the earth. Howling, Robert repeatedly stabs the flames with his spear. Laughing, they chant, "They pierced his hands and his feet; they counted all his bones."

They are both drunk now. They see the night and its inhabitants joining them in their circle dance. They hear the earth and the forest speak and answer, hear the crackling of the air. Rémi feels Eugénie nearby, hesitant, trying to escape but imprisoned by a conspiracy of higher powers. So that she can recognize him, he removes his sacerdotal costume, hurls it in the fire, and whirls around, calling her sweet name. The beloved face is floating above a bush, with a diaphanous smile and shadowed eyes. Rémi rushes to her but his arms close on empty air. The vision has retreated. He follows it, in hot pursuit of Eugénie through the forest.

Despite the weariness that stiffened their muscles and weighed on their eyes, the boys suggested going to mass in Saint-Gérard. The mother was pleased at their initiative. In recent weeks the family had neglected mass because of the boys' misadventure with the priest. This, and their un-fettered summer, had made her fear they were becoming little savages beyond faith and fear. It was reassuring to see them volunteer for mass. It must be the good influence of the brothers' school in Amos.

Impatiently the boys watched for the celebrant to appear. They wanted to see Ricard's face, see what he would do and say. He made his entrance according to the usual ritual and prayed before the altar as if nothing had ever gone wrong. But Rémi had caught a glimpse of his distraught face and reddened eyes. He noticed the missal leaning against the tabernacle door to keep it closed. When Ricard approached the pulpit he seemed more stooped than usual. But as he began to speak all his energy returned. His own words awoke his spirit at the same time that they jolted his audience. The orator took on a grave and trembling voice as he abandoned himself to the eloquence of his emotions.

"Dearly beloved brethren, it is with a broken heart that I speak to you this morning. My affliction casts me down, but indignation raises me up again. If I am trembling, it is from the rage inspired by a sacred anger. My brethren, I must tell you that impious creatures, or perhaps one only, have sullied, pillaged, sacked, violated, and profaned this temple of God. Not satisfied with leaving unspeakable remains in the sacristy, the sacrilegious monster stole sacerdotal vestments and the pascal candle. These misdeeds did not, however, satisfy this damned soul. In its demoniac madness the vicious beast forced the door to the tabernacle and carried off my chalice. At the same time he stole the Eucharistic species, the sacred hosts, which will now serve God knows what satanic ends."

He paused to allow his words to penetrate. He saw the anger on their faces.

"I see your indignation, and I understand it. It speaks for the nobility of your hearts. But we are Christians, and thus charitable men. We must forget the lust for vengeance and ask God to forgive the miscreant. Yet charity is not laxity. We must act as soldiers of Christ to protect our possessions and defend our faith. The enemy is among us, threatening our souls and attacking our holy religion. The enemy is Satan, and he is incarnate in a face that we all know. Need we name him, this hellion through whom evil comes about? No, you all know who he is. Satan is at home in his house. He is a pampered guest there. And already full of confidence, he begins to manifest himself elsewhere. Last evening, no doubt at the moment when the sacrilege was being committed in our temple, Satan and his cohorts of devils were attacking the house of a fine family at their hour of prayer. To prevent them from honouring their creator! Obscure and supernatural forces were turned loose, breaking windows, overturning tables."

Ricard pointed to the first pew where Blanche and Méo sat with bowed heads in an attitude of piety and dejection. "Hypocrites!" Rémi laughed to himself. It was too comical, and the two brothers nudged each other. The priest resumed his tirade trying to hold the interest he had aroused in his flock.

"And it is not the first time this fine couple has been victim of the intrigues of the Evil One. And there will be others – perhaps yourselves! Those whom he cannot charm or vanquish, he will crush. His power is terrible. Do not forget that he is a fallen angel, a spirit. Christ on the mountain was able to repulse the Tempter, but we poor humans, what can we do against the powers of evil? Fortunately we can pray, and we have holy water and the crucifix as invincible arms. And Satan knows this. Which is why he shows himself only as a last resort. He prefers to be forgotten so that he can act without our knowing, taking advantage of our natural penchant for what is pleasant and easy. Do not wait for extraordinary events to recognize the works of the Evil One within your life. He is working daily for your ruin. And now that he has his temple within our parish we must expect him to become more insolent. Insidiously he will lay siege to our village, to our houses, to our lives. When I think of the doubts and the impiety he can sow in the hearts of our young, inexperienced as they are, when I think of their weakness that he exploits to encourage innumerable vices, I tremble for them, I fear for them. I weep for these souls in peril. The Evil One, settled so close to us!"

He caught his breath for a few seconds, and started again, emphasizing his words with resounding slaps on the wooden railing.

"We must clean out this cursed sideroad, clean out this ante-room of hell, isolate the disciple of the Old Nick, prevent him from spreading the word of evil and, finally, amputate it from our parish. Let him go hang elsewhere!

People along that line have realized it, families are moving out. And so much the better! I said, we must clean out this ante-room of hell. It would be more accurate to say WE SHOULD HAVE cleaned it out, for now it is too late. The Evil One has other places in our parish dear to him, places he calls his home. He draws our people there for unimaginable orgies. Do not look so sceptical! I tell you, Satan has his faithful in our village, he lives hidden here among us."

The priest's voice grew shrill. "Satan inhabits this land that you or your fathers tried to tame to found a settlement of dignity! A land where we would recapture our dignity through work, and learn to cherish freedom. It was land we dreamed of, simple but honest; and now it grows corrupt and, if we do not put order in it, it will be the new Sodom. Pioneer fathers, your seed germinated in sin and gave an ill harvest: our ripening fruits are scabbed. Look at our youth! The youth for whom all this was done. Remember, fathers, we made the cleared land bigger than was needed, thinking of the race to come. Remember the suffering, the privations, the trials, remember the mud, the heat, the flies in summertime, the cold, the solitude and hunger in the winter? Was all this done in vain? Perhaps. Where is this young race we were working for? Yes, we may well ask, for it is not embodied in the young we see around us. Your sons turn up their noses at your clearings, they turn their backs on the land, and go off to hire themselves out to masters in the city or the mine. And your daughters, do they want to take up the torch and be fruitful and multiply our race in abnegation? No, they are giddy and flirtatious and bored with work. The race of strong, free men has not come to pass."

He was growing more calm. In the congregation some were blushing. Some older men were downcast, thoughtful. Boys looked at each other, grinning discreetly. The priest's voice grew more friendly.

"But we mustn't blame them too much: we made these young people what they are! Did we do all we could to instil our ideal in them? And the ones who gave up the settlement, weren't they a poor example, preaching despair by their actions? Yet we must admit the fact: our young people, the grain we sowed, are not up to our fond hopes. They have a servile heart unworthy of our high plans. Worse still, many of these young folk are rotten through and through with high living, drunkenness and laziness. To satisfy their vices and avoid hard work they are ready for any compromise. I am not exaggerating. A single example: young boys and girls come together at night in a certain sanctuary of Satan, where they give themselves up to debauchery. And the place is not far from here, in plain view of the village, beside the fifth line. I will not go into details, but let those whom the shoe fits wear it. They should confess it and repent!"

The priest paused, his index finger pointing to the heavens. He allowed a dense silence to descend on the congregation. It was easy for him to read the embarrassment on certain faces. He would remember their names. That would be useful later. Did the handkerchief with the embroidered initial belong to Julie? Sixteen, she was. And there she sat beside her mother, her body stiff and her face expressionless. But she was wringing her hands nervously. And what about Joseph Tremblay's eldest boy? Did he use the family car for his vile pastimes? The silence dragged on, broken only by nervous coughs and the shuffling of feet. A churchwarden ostentatiously consulted his watch so that Father Ricard would get the message. Oh, he got the message, all right. But they weren't going to get off that easily. He would say what had to be said. And just too bad if they were late for lunch.

"This land, where the future was to rise like the sun, more beautiful than even in our dreams: are we going to let it die? Are we going to let it bleed to death like a wounded warrior? Can we submit to our village being wiped off the map? To all our sufferings and hopes wiped out with it? And our labours and our pains? Shall we let the grain die in the furrow or be carried off by the wind to farther fields? No, no, and again no! We must react, give roots to our dreams and make them real. There are ways to change the course of history. First, we must create jobs here to stop the exodus. We must make life better here to counter the mirage of far horizons. We have enough good elements still to create the race of men we desire. But only a common and concerted action has any chance of success. I have ideas on this subject, which I shall impart to you soon."

The faces of his flock began to show boredom and fatigue, and their attention wandered. The priest understood that he had reached his limit. He had exhausted even himself by his eloquence. And he had so much still to say! But that could wait till next time. He ended his sermon with an exhortation to prayer and hurried through the rest of the mass.

The Simards gave Blanche and Méo a ride home. Méo told in great detail how their house had been shaken and perhaps even lifted from the ground, how the plates had sailed through the air of their own accord and landed upside down. Grimacing faces had appeared at the windows, they had heard whimpers and groans inside the walls along with rattling chains. And he had almost been killed by the spear that pierced the roadside Christ. It had crashed through a window, grazed his shoulder and stuck in the wall. And this morning when they came back to the house it had disappeared. Blanche told the whole story over again, elaborating on Méo's account. She and Méo were chosen victims of the netherworld. On the priest's advice they were going to move out, leave the place entirely. And right now. Tomorrow. They would stay at the hotel in Amos until they found a place to live.

They stopped to let the couple off at Réginald's. Everyone had to go inside for a minute, just long enough for a drink. Around the table, the tale of the devil's attack was told again, in a new version more horrible than the last. Réginald got a big kick out of that, teasing the story-tellers, saying they must have had one too many and then seen themselves in a mirror.

"Anyway, Blanche and me's goin' away. We're goin' to town tomorrow with René and never comin' back. Goodbye this road!"

"That's a good reason to go. You been lookin' for an excuse to get out of here for weeks now. Eh? Am I right?"

"That's my beeswax. What's more, we're not ready for winter. Nobody out here's ready for winter. Dam-Bogga told me you can't imagine what it's like here in winter."

"Sonofagum," Réginald exclaims, "it's not 1930 any more. Dam-Bogga don't know it, though. He spends the whole summer gettin' ready to lock himself in the cabin for the winter, packin' provisions in like a squirrel. He lives like he did in those days, but times has changed. The roads are open, there's stores, you can buy everything. Poor Dam-Bogga, what a life he leads! He just gets by from one year to the next."

"And what do we do?" asked Sonia roughly.

"Jee-sus!"

The single word is her husband's reply. But it is punctuated by a blow of his fist on the table and followed by a look of near hatred. The two syllables are loaded with meaning. Sonia knows it, and relapses into silence. There is an uncomfortable moment in the kitchen, which dissipates as Réginald goes back to teasing Méo.

Sonia is thinking of the coming week when Réginald will be away, working with Martel trucking pulpwood. Six nights of terror, what with this tale of devils, six days of boredom with only a child for company. Sonia begins to weep softly, ignoring the others. She begs her husband to stay.

"It's no life here, me alone with the kid. An' think of winter coming. We agreed our three families would start out here on the same line so we could help each other an' have a bit of social life. The others are leavin' so let's you and me go, too!"

"You want to leave? Sonofagum! An' go where? We're well off here, no rent, we got firewood an' a cow. An' after the holidays I'll take my unemployment money and work here on the lot. It's a great life!"

"Sure, an' it's not you has to stay out here alone."

"Alone? You got Carmen next door and Dam-Bogga just down the road. An' even Godbout, though we don't know him."

Réginald makes fun of his wife's fears. She insists, and grows aggressive.

"I know it suits you just fine to be away most of the time. You'll feel free. You can go an' play the young bachelor and drink an' chase the broads with Martel. And Sonia, crazy bitch, stays home and sticks it out!"

The visitors are embarrassed. Some try to look busy, pretending not to have heard what was said. All but Méo, who sneers, and Blanche who gets up red-faced, her eyes bulging with anger. She pulls at Méo's arm.

"You think that's funny, you god-damn heartless bastard? You're just like the others."

Blanche stares down the males in the room, even the boys.

"You're all the same! No-talent, heartless bums, and all you think about is havin' fun and being waited on hand an' foot. If it wasn't for the women . . ."

"If it wasn't for the women," Réginald cuts in, "we wouldn't have to work. We wouldn't even need underwear."

"Oh, you damn fool!" says the fat woman, and sits down.

"Woman owes respect and obedience to her husband," Méo chuckles.

Blanche takes umbrage, "I'm not your wife. A good thing, too!"

"God, no, you're not my wife. If you was. . . ."

Méo turns toward Réginald.

"Show you're a man, Jee-sus. Show who wears the pants around here!"

Blanche squeezes Méo's neck until his feet beat a jig on the floor.

"Shut yer ass and mind yer business. Another word an' I'll smash you, you worm."

Mrs. Simard makes a sign to her husband: they should leave now. Standing in the middle of the room, hanging, Sonia looks dazed. She no longer reacts, she's indifferent to what is going on around her. She only feels a great despair welling up inside her, rising like a flooded river. Then it overflows: she begins to weep and groan and gasp. And she runs and hides in her room while her legs can still support her. In the kitchen there's a moment of stupor. Mrs. Simard goes after her. Réginald starts talking again in a voice that is uncertain for a second, then grows indifferent, as if nothing had happened.

"You'll all stay for dinner. Take pot luck. Our last meal together for a long time, maybe. Sonia'll get over her childishness in a minute, she'll be glad if you stay."

"There's nothing childish about it," Blanche thunders, pounding her glass on the table. "You guys don't understand nothing."

"What I do understand is, you scared the hell out of her with your demon stories. She's a sucker for that stuff, Sonia is."

"She's right to be scared."

"The devil! Hey, it's you two's the devil."

Méo backs up his companion. He is deadly serious.

"Listen to me, you tub of lard. The devil has taken over our house. This isn't the first time he showed up. Just come and see the shape the place is in, doubting Thomas!"

"Oh, you just had another fight. Don't try and scare me, Méo. It's hard enough to keep yourself alive without makin' up stories into the bargain, eh?"

"There's nothin' made up, god damn it!"

"Méo, you promised the priest you wouldn't swear no more," scolds Blanche.

"Lemme alone, you old fool, we're talking man to man here, can't you see? Réginald, the devil exists. The priests have always said so."

"You an' your priests! Why don't they solve our problems if they're so smart? Then we'll have time for their devils and hell."

"Pagan!"

"Ha ha! Look who's talkin'! Is that you, Méo? Sonofagum, the old devil did scare the hell outa you!"

"I'm not scared. I'm no scaredy cat. I went through the war in them trenches, I saw death up real close and I wasn't scared. But there's things that are too much for the powers of a man."

"You and your war! Don't make me laugh! Pissed up in some barracks or in the digger in England. You're shittin' yourself, Méo!"

"Méo empties his glass and lets the insult pass. Réginald looks around the room, proud of his verbal triumph.

"You don't think it's funny, uncle?"

Mr. Simard shakes his head, "Well. . . ."

"Hey, you don't believe those stories, do you?"

"You never know. 'Pears all that exists."

"You're kiddin'!"

Réginald isn't laughing now.

"Oh, I'm not scared of the devil," the boys' father hastens to add. "But something must have happened at Méo's place. Something not normal."

"Uh huh. . . ."

Réginald scratches his head and combs the hair back in place with his fingers. He goes on talking but has changed the subject. Now it's his projects with Martel and how much money he's going to earn. As long as you keep your nose clean there's work to be had. As he describes his working week and the hotel where he intends to stay, he leaves small gaps filled with grins and winks. "Sonia's right," thinks Rémi. "Her husband's on the make." Robert had got a great kick out of the tales of demons, but Rémi is a little shocked. Their joke had taken on unforeseen proportions, even forcing Méo and Blanche to leave. And Sonia's terror is another consequence.

The women come back from the bedroom. Mrs. Simard has a hand on her niece's shoulder as she pushes her along. It's been decided that Rémi is to sleep here during the week, his father will stop in the morning to pick him up and at night to let him off. That's for the next two weeks. Sonia won't be quite alone and she can get used to her husband's absence. And Rémi could look after and milk the cow.

Rémi cannot refuse. For a moment he's speechless. This upsets the plans he had for these last weeks on the line. And he'll be far from Robert, just after making up. Rémi sees that everyone is waiting for his reply. His hesitation goes on too long. His mother is looking at him quizzically, with little nods to force him to agree. Sonia's eyes are begging. Now she's getting scared again, thanks to his indecision. He nods his head.

"It's O.K. by me."

"Perfect, if that'll patch things up," says Réginald. He turns to Rémi. "You're not scared of the devil, Rémi? What'll you do if he comes along?"

"The devil? Oh, I don't believe in him. If he comes I just refuse to believe in him or pay him any attention. What can he do to me? Kill me with a spear nobody's going to find?"

"Spoke like a man, sonofagum! Have a hair of the dog, Méo!"

Méo sets down his glass and after three curses grumbles, "He'll not be such a hero when he's got the devil starin' at him."

That Monday morning they left earlier than usual, because they had to stop at Réginald's to pick up Méo and Blanche, who had spent the night there. Their luggage filled the trunk of the car, and they had to hold suitcases on their knees as well. Rémi left a bundle of his things with Sonia.

"We'll expect you for supper."

There was a Provincial Police car stopped at Godbout's house. They'd been at Sonia's earlier to question her. It seemed they suspected Godbout of having robbed the church. Rémi felt a twinge of conscience. He felt something like friendship for this despised and rejected man. But what the heck! They wouldn't find anything at his place anyway! And who was going to start searching along the creek or discover the cave and the chalice in it? There was no clue to lead them there, and the parish was a big place.

At noon hour the boys talked for a long time about what was happening to them: Rémi staying at Sonia's, the impossibility of going out at nights – that was the end of the chivalry of the dark. Last Saturday's ceremony had brought no results. Nothing could change the course of events now. Robert was saddened, Rémi somewhat less, though he took care not to show it. His new situation pleased him, and he thought about nothing else that afternoon, forgetting to pay attention to the teacher. It would be like taking a trip: his first separation from his family! He thought of Sonia, her femininity, her eyes, the way she walked. It would be great to live near her.

His moving in turned into a celebration. All afternoon Sonia had watched the sun go down and felt her anxiety grow. In this house alone with a child and all the shadows that settled in as the day's end approached. Sophie didn't understand, but she felt her mother's nervousness and lost interest in playing, loitering peevishly near the lamp, which Sonia had lit much earlier than usual, long before daylight ended. Sonia thought of November, December, when the night would begin in mid-afternoon and last well after she was up in the morning. . . . She shivered, despite the warmth of the stove, which obliged her to keep the door open. But Rémi's arrival drove her fears away. Though he was only an adolescent, Sonia would have someone to talk to besides Sophie with her childish prattle. She merely asked him about school and how it was in Amos, but her joy was obvious. Rémi felt that he was being received as a distinguished visitor, and he was aware of the almost imperceptible transfer of power. He was the man of the house. Sonia led him into Sophie's room.

"This is where you'll be. Sophie will sleep with me."

Alone, he took off his school clothes and put on some overalls.

"I'll go do the milking."

It wasn't a suggestion or a request for approval. Just a statement of fact.

It was dusk already, a chilly dusk with hardly the sound of a bird to be heard. The fallen leaves of the aspen had lost their golden glow and were tarnished and rust-coloured. High overhead the faint cry of passing wild geese swelled and faded. A kind of melancholy, its origin unknown, settled in him. But the stable smell improved his spirits. That good, strong animal smell! There was more life in the stink of a single cow than in that of a classroom full of boys. Who had robbed man of his odour? Rémi tended the cow, fed her, let her drink, milked her, changed her bedding. Motions, a series of motions gone through mechanically, which could be repeated ad infinitum. Rémi thought he would be happy this way. The motion of the hand on the teat, the stiffness of his unaccustomed fingers; or his arms wielding the pitchfork, the slight ache in his shoulder. When he had finished, Rémi wondered what he had been thinking about. The cow smell? He couldn't have been thinking about that the whole time. He must have been dreaming about something else. He couldn't remember, but he had an impression of well-being.

While Sonia strained the milk and poured it into other containers, Rémi brought in armloads of stove wood. His chores completed, he washed in the basin under the pump, while Sophie looked on. He touched her nose with a wet finger.

"It's ready. Come and eat," she said.

The table is set as if for a Sunday feast. The lamp stands at Réginald's place, at the end of the table, drawing reflections from the pots of gherkins and pickles. Sonia sits with her back to the fire so that she can reach everything and pass it. Rémi sits down across from her.

"Not too much, eh?"

"Eat up, Rémi. A man's supposed to have an appetite."

He sits there like a king. Sophie is delighted to have her "uncle" there. For Sonia, he is the one who stands between her and the terrors of the night. He stares at her unembarrassed because there's no one there to notice. He is even obliged to look at her, because they are the only two adults! They say nothing. The little girl bears the burden of the conversation, asking questions and answering them herself. Sonia has a good appetite, and when she leans over her plate Rémi can stare at her as he likes. He sees that time has marked her face. When she stops smiling the wrinkles don't go away, but change to fine crows' feet at her lips and the corners of her eyes. There's a faint wrinkle on her forehead and black circles under her eyes. Her cheeks are not yet slack but in places the make-up seems to flake about tiny fissures. Her neck is a little fleshy. She looks up and smiles at her observer, and at once age disappears, life takes over.

After the meal Rémi doesn't offer to help with the dishes, as he would have done another time or even yesterday. He spreads his books on the freshly cleared table and appears to be absorbed in his homework. He's the man now, and behaves as he has seen men do. The ceremony that will rule his stay in this house is being set. Above the rattle of the dishes he hears Sonia singing softly. Then she stops.

"It doesn't bother you?"

"No, no."

And she goes on with her work. From behind the book Rémi watches her full hips swinging to the rhythm of the *chansonnette*. The kitchen is peaceful. Sophie has gone to sleep in the rocking-chair petting her doll. Sonia puts her to bed and finishes tidying the kitchen. She's cleaning the stove with salt, which sizzles on the metal, when Carmen Martel arrives. She's come for milk.

"What's your hurry, Carmen? Have a cup of tea. Come on, eh?"

"I guess I got time."

They sit down at the table. Rémi forces himself to look studious, though he's finished his lessons and is tired of books. The women chatter like young girls, joking and laughing. Quick surreptitious glances allow Rémi to glimpse the neighbour woman's impressive curves to Sonia's supple gestures. He is more and more conscious of their odour, which comes in waves. With joy he recalls the atmosphere when he first discovered women and began to watch out for manifestations of femininity. Soon he can no longer pretend to study. Down goes his book.

"Would you like some tea?" asks Sonia.

Carmen Martel looks at him.

"It must be nice to have a man in the house, eh Sonia?"

"That's for sure. I'd be scared silly alone."

"Didn't take you long to replace Réginald."

The two women laugh.

"Aren't you scared when you're alone?"

"Not so bad now we've got a man in the neighbour-hood."

Rémi knows they're joking and that Carmen's making fun of him, but he feels that there's a grain of truth in what they say just the same. Sonia pours liqueurs, and Mrs. Martel protests she has to put her children to bed. But there she stays at the table. Rémi goes over to the other side of the stove, in the warm half-light. Pretending not to pay attention, he listens to them chatter about their daily lives, what they did today and what they have to do tomorrow, their little worries and the latest accomplishments of their children. They forget Rémi's presence and, without thinking, go through a host of harmless gestures, fingers smoothing their hair back from their temples or moving on their drinking glasses, a tongue that licks deep into the alcohol, or a play of eyes and eyebrows that follows and comments on the other's words.

Mrs. Martel leaves and Sonia bars the door.

"I'm glad I have her for a friend. She's always got a little joke or some story to tell."

"I always thought she was more serious."

"Sure, when her husband's there and there's company. But you should see the two of us alone. Sometimes when she comes over she makes me laugh till I cry."

"Well, I'm goin' to bed now."

"You're right. Time flies fast and tomorrow. . . ."

"Oh, yeah, I have to get up at six for the cow."

"I'll give you a call. Good night."

"Night."

In the bedroom he undresses quickly and slides under the cool, almost icy, sheets. He stills the sound of his breathing and listens. Sonia blows out the lamp and feels her way, bangs into a chair, and swears softly. The sound of the stove is reduced to a murmur, and Rémi's hearing grows more acute; his ears can see through the board partition. The bed creaks; the springs squeak under her weight. Sonia is sitting, she's taking off her shoes and stockings. He can't hear that well, of course, but imagines her motions and invents the swish of nylon. Now she stands up and bed springs squeak again. There's the quick purr of a zipper, the snap of the elastic belt of her skirt slipping between her fingers. She pulls her night-shirt over her head. When at last she's lying down, the bed complains for a long time as she tries to get comfortable. She clears her throat, then, a little later, sighs and is silent. A stick of wood tumbles in the fire and Rémi gives up listening for signs of life. He imagines sounds – all the sounds the woman would make if she got up and made her way through the dark house to come to his side. His imagination is so successful that he has to listen attentively to be sure his inventions are not real. All he hears is the regular breathing of Sonia asleep.

Then Eugénie's face appears, her mouth stern, her eyes reproachful. She stares at him coldly. Eugénie! He's astonished, paralysed, unable to react or think. No use closing his eyes; the image stays printed on his eyelids. Sleep comes slowly, with Eugénie still staring at him.

Sonia was leaning over him, touching his shoulder and calling him. His eyes, still squinting, saw Eugénie's smile and her living body! She was near him, alive. He murmured, "Eugénie. . . ."

"I'll bet you were thinking about a girl!"

He seemed embarrassed, and she laughed. Leaning a little farther down she kissed him lightly on the cheek and went out.

By the time he had finished his chores in the stable breakfast was ready. Sophie was still sleeping. Sonia, in a heavy dressing-gown, sat warming herself near the stove and watched him eat. The sun was rising, and with it Sonia's spirits rose. As Rémi ran out to meet his father's car at the road, Sonia came to the door and stood there a moment despite the chilly air. The sun was just above the tree-tops and its light was dazzling on the frosted grass. The sound of the car died away. Now you could hear the barnyard sounds at Dam-Bogga's place, the dog's bark, the baa-ing of the sheep. She thought of other mornings that had been accompanied by the ritual sounds of a big farm awakening. That was far away. She had even thought it was forgotten. Her face grew sad, and she went inside.

The trip to town was a silent one, though Rémi felt the quizzing looks his brother gave him. When they were alone, walking the last stretch to school, Rémi had to tell all about his evening. He did so, but went no farther than the bare facts, unable to explain his situation in the house. And if he had been able he wouldn't have wanted to. He made a lot of Mrs. Martel's visit.

"Lucky bum, I wish I was in your place!"

Rémi was glad to be "alone" in the class-room. He withdrew to his desk and pretended to listen, leaving his mind free to wander until the voices turned to distant murmurs. He'd have liked to live last evening over again, but it was the princess's face he saw. It erased everything else, enthralled his imagination and even prevented him from inventing epic adventures for Eugénie and her knight. There was her face, nothing but the face, the texture of its skin, its shadows, her eyes, her lips. There wasn't even the flicker of an eyelid. The immobility of death and print. And the face took on density as if it were going to submerge the present, envelop everything, and imprison the boy in its fixity. Rémi struggled to keep afloat, forced his ears to listen and clung with his mind to some word of the teacher's. But the words whirled around him faster and faster until they all were meaningless, or too filled with meaning, then broke up into mysterious letters.

Recess was his salvation. He played football, ran, played all out, spent his energy so he wouldn't have time to think. But the bell rang and called him back to class. Frightened at his previous visions, he paid almost frantic attention to the teacher's explanations and went so far as to ask a question. At noon, to please his brother, he went over Carmen Martel's visit once again. Then they began hatching projects for after their move. Robert talked about a possible expedition for the knights the following weekend. Rémi shivered: how could he ever meet the night and master it when he was barely in control of what happened in broad daylight? He was afraid that he had gone out of bounds and unleashed forces too powerful for him, which were trying to precipitate his downfall. He had tried to bring the dead to life, had failed, and was ready to forget.

But what if she didn't want to? He would have liked to flee, but where was he safe from Eugénie? When she disappeared he had searched everywhere in vain to find her. And all the time she was ensconced within him, waiting for the right time to show herself. She had never wanted to be incarnate again, knowing that she could only survive in the mind and heart of her knight. She could live no life but his. An image flashed into Rémi's mind: a bloodsucker! She was a leech sucking away his life, a kind of tapeworm in his brain. He felt a wave of nausea. Robert touched his shoulder.

"Rémi! Rémi, are you sick? Have you got a fever? You looked real bad just now."

All afternoon Rémi's mind wandered. He thought again about the bloodsucker. Eugénie had lived and was still alive with the life he had lent her, but now he wanted to forget, and she was struggling against this second death. The stubborn image floated before his vision. He hated his princess now. He opened and shut his eyes, tried to switch his attention to a hundred subjects and cling to the presence of the others in his class. But Eugénie's portrait seemed engraved in him. His whole relationship with her, his chivalry, the Black Goddess – had all these been nothing but a trap used by the dead woman to take possession of him? He was afraid, he wanted to cry out, to run and run and never stop, just to escape from that image. Throughout the afternoon he struggled without a move, without a sound, in the midst of his class-mates who had no notion of the combat that was in progress. Rémi lost: on his way home she was still with him.

As he went in Réginald's house he felt less anxious. Eugénie relaxed her grip and retreated from the carnal presence of another woman. For Sonia, it was her own fear and the dark itself that drew back when Rémi arrived. And so they smiled at each other stupidly for a long time, with the joy they felt at being together, a joy that neither would have liked to explain. Sophie, seeing their faces, began to laugh, and they laughed with her.

Rémi changed, drank a cup of tea, putting off the moment when he would have to go to the stable. The evening darkened fast. He had to go sometime and did so holding the lighted lantern high. The wind was whispering in the aspen branches, tearing away their few leaves. "She's here," he thought. He walked quickly, hunched and tense, trying to close his pores against her. The dark was thick and hostile. Relief! – he was in the stable, which was so small that the lantern could light every corner. The dark was held outside, and the warm, heavy smell was reassuring. The cow's hide was a tangible reality, and her teats, which he squeezed hard. To exclude sounds from outside, Rémi concentrated on the small noises in the stable. The pail rang with the first spurts of milk, which soon foamed up with a silky, rhythmic whisper, the cow chewed and swallowed, her hoof scraping the wood of her stall, the dung fork grated on the concrete gutter and the manure piled up with a dull flop. The lantern was flickering. If it went out Rémi would be defenceless. He hurried back to the house careless of the milk that slopped from the swinging pail.

They made supper last a long time without planning it or knowing how. When the dishes and other chores were done and the child in bed, they went back to sit at the table. The Coleman lamp whistled and gave off its hard, white light that made the dark window panes even more opaque. They drank tea, then a liqueur, and smoked cigarettes. Sonia waited in vain for a visit from Carmen. Bedtime was approaching, and Rémi dreaded the thought of the dark house. Eugénie would take advantage and attack. Walls, however thick, were no hindrance to her. She would get inside him again and he would have to live with her all night and keep her alive the following day. Rémi thought of a movie about Count Dracula: the vampire lurked around his victim's home, awaiting the moment to strike.

He tried to make the evening last forever. Afraid? Rémi, the knight of darkness? Yet it was fear, sure enough, that was tying knots in his innards and choking back his breath. The window, which he glanced at surreptitiously and much against his will, held a threatening night at bay. He felt it all around as it breathed on the house, licked at it with tongues of wind, and sharpened its claws on the roof. A night as dark and strange as the first. They'd been leading him on for two months to believe he was master of the night. Hunched in his chair, Rémi wondered how he had ever dared to venture with such confidence miles from the nearest light, like a nocturnal animal. And he trembled as he thought of his battle with the tree-monster or the ceremonies at the cave or lying on the earth in the grave-yard. And he had never, never been master of the night. The princess had tamed the dark so that he could live in it. Now she was stirring up the shadowy forces against him.

Somehow Sonia guessed at Rémi's anxiety, and his fear rubbed off on her. The later it grew, the less easily she laughed. Her smile became pitiful and sad, and finally disappeared entirely. To prolong the evening she made coffee. She tried to be jolly, but it was a clumsy attempt. The wind shifted to northwest and began to blow hard. She stared at Rémi.

"I'm scared."

She was sorry at once that she had said it, pulled herself together, laughed at herself and twisted nervously at a lock of hair.

"Crazy, eh? At my age! Forget it, I'm not scared. You're here; the door's locked. You did lock it?"

He nodded.

"What was there for me to be scared of?"

She shrugged and poured herself another cup of coffee. But by the time she had returned to the table her frightened expression had reappeared. She touched Rémi's arm and looked wide-eyed at him.

"Did you hear that?"

"It's just the rain."

The pelting drops whipped the roof, rolled down the panes, and broke, rattling, in the eavestrough.

"It's stupid, being scared of the dark, but all of a sudden I feel the way I did when I was a kid. There's all kinds of things outside."

"There's nothing outside, Sonia, it's no different from daytime."

He's trying to reassure himself at the same time.

"I feel that there's something all around the house."

"It's the rain, nothing but the rain, Sonia."

"But I can't help thinking about Blanche and Méo, and that devil that attacked them. They're gone, but he's still hangin' around."

Rémi broke into uncontrollable laughter and she was scandalized. She, a grown woman, confided her fears to a young boy and he was making fun of her. It was crass rudeness. She'd never have thought it of him. She had a good notion to go to bed, just to show him what she thought, but he excused himself as he recovered from his fit.

"Sonia . . . I'm not . . . laughin' at you, it's because. . . . Oh, it's too funny."

He was off again, laughing so heartily that she found it contagious despite her anger.

"If you swear you won't tell, I'll let you in on a secret."

"I promise."

"Well, the devil was Robert and me."

"What?"

"Yeah, it was us scared Méo."

He was laughing again. She looked at him curiously.

"It can't be true."

"Sure. We went a little too far, maybe. We didn't want them to leave, we just wanted a little fun."

"But . . . that was in the middle of the night!"

"Keep it to yourself, eh? We sneaked out and went down to their place."

"How?"

"We walked."

"At night, all alone?"

"Yeah."

"I really can't. . . ."

And so, Rémi told her the whole story of the trick they'd played, explained the face smeared with firefly phosphorescence, the stones on the roof, and the shouts and reactions of their victims. Sonia had a good laugh. Every time the laughter flagged Rémi would add a new detail to start it off again.

"You're a pair of little demons. Pulling a stunt like that, you should be paddled for it. They could have died!"

"We didn't think about that, just the fun."

"You weren't scared, going all that way in the dark?"

"I'm not scared of the dark. I was a. . . ."

He almost gave way the greater secret. In vain Sonia tried to re-awaken their laughing mood. In the renewed silence the pounding rain made the dark seem closer. Then the Coleman lamp began to fizzle and its flame turned orange.

"Even after what you told me, I'm scared just the same."

"You mustn't be scared, Sonia. What's to be scared of?"

"I don't know. What about you?"

"Me? Not a bit."

"Just the same, I can feel you're anxious. Maybe it's just me getting you worked up with my crazy ideas."

"No, come on!"

The Coleman lamp was growing darker. Sonia lit the oil lamp and their combined lights piled shadow upon shadow in the corners of the room.

"More coffee?"

He shook his head.

"Tea? A cigarette? Come, have a smoke. Here."

He took the cigarette from her trembling hands. He was forcing himself to be calm.

"It's gettin' late. You must be dead tired, and you have school tomorrow."

"School. . . ."

Suddenly he remembered the day he'd had.

334

"But if you're not too tired," she went on, "I'd like to stay up a little longer."

He touched her arm.

"Don't you be afraid. I'm here."

Feeling needed, having to play the protector, reassured him. And she must find him very understanding, putting off his bedtime when he was so tired. The fact that he himself was in no hurry to lie alone in the dark was another matter. She didn't have to know that.

The Coleman lamp went out and continued hissing air. They turned it off. Outside, the rain grew heavier and thunder rolled. Sonia was in despair at this noise and talked to fill time, telling about her adolescence in the east end of Montreal, her first dances, her job sewing in a sweatshop, her boy-friends, meeting Réginald, getting engaged. She stopped the story before her marriage. Ah, there she could have told a tale, but she remembered that her listener was a young boy. She built the fire up to a good blaze again. The clock said one. Time for bed.

"Would it bother you if I left the light on in the kitchen? Would it keep you awake?"

"No, it wouldn't bother me."

Rémi lay down in the half-light where the glow of the lamp mingled with the shadows. He forced himself not to think, and went to sleep before Eugénie's face could appear.

He breakfasted with Sonia looking on. She only had a coffee.

"I'm sorry about yesterday. I was stupid, afraid for nothing."

"Forget it."

"But I kept you up late. And you didn't get a good sleep. You were dreaming. I heard you talking in your sleep. You even screamed."

"I know. It woke me up."

"Who is Eugénie?"

He froze.

"Look, you said her name over and over."

"I don't know. A dream's a dream. You can't control it."

As he seemed annoyed she teased him gently.

"Your girl-friend, eh? Aha! The cat's out of the bag!"

"No, heck, no!"

"You don't want to tell me about her? You can, any time. I won't tell."

"Next time you're scared I will."

"You think I'm a baby, eh? Réginald would have laughed at me."

"No reason to laugh. Everybody's scared sometimes."

"You were scared, too, yesterday."

"Maybe. Not for the same reasons. But that doesn't matter. The nice thing was being scared together."

She looked at him for a moment.

"You're a funny one, you are. Sometimes you talk like a man or better, and a person could almost forget your age. It makes me feel good to have you here."

He put down his knife and fork, brushed away his crumbs, very deliberately, and stared at her in turn.

"Ain't I the man in this house?"

She gaped at him. Her expression was indescribable. She looked down and her fingers fiddled with the table-cloth, then smoothed it nervously. She started to speak but the words didn't come. Sophie awoke and called her. Sonia quickly rose and went to her. Rémi prepared for school and left.

No sooner was he outside than Eugénie made her presence felt. Despite his resistance she had slipped into him before he even reached the car. He lived all day in her company, paying no attention in class, and twice the teacher caught him out. Noon hour brought him some respite. Robert, with his questions and conversation, kept Rémi from struggling in the net of Eugénie's image. But the afternoon was still to come, and the thought of it was gruesome to him. "Am I going crazy?" he wondered. Dream was becoming more real than reality. Rémi was afraid he would never return from this voyage. He was alone, no one could understand him, not even Robert. People would laugh at him or send him to a doctor. But it was no laughing matter. This parallel world, a world with no attraction for him, just an immobile face, was encroaching more and more on his day-to-day reality. Distressed, he wondered who could help. Sonia would be terrified. Ricard might grasp the subtlety of the danger, he might even be able to break the spell, the curse as he would call it. But asking his help meant putting yourself in his power, becoming his dependent, at the mercy of his beliefs. Worst of all, it meant admitting defeat. Head bowed like a sheep. The priest would be only too glad to triumph. No, never! Rémi would go it alone, he'd exorcise himself. He wouldn't even have the help of the night, as he would have had before. But he'd fight! Anything was better than going down meekly.

"Robert, when you get home go to the cave and bring me the photo of the princess and the token."

"Are you nuts? It's dark already when I get there."

"Not very dark. And you know the way. Maybe you're scared?"

"Hey! You mean me? Well . . . maybe a bit. Alone, like. . . ."

"Do it for me Robert. Please. It's important."

"Yeah. You're still thinking about her."

"Sometimes."

"You miss her?"

"A bit. Go there, do it for me. You can do it. You've done a lot worse."

"I was a knight then."

"You still are."

"Ha ha! What's that worth now?" Robert scoffed. But seeing his brother's desperate mood, he gave in, grumbling, "You know, god damn it, you've made me do things nobody should have to do."

Rémi had no idea what he would do with this death notice, nor why he had asked for it. But anything was better than sitting down and waiting for the end. In class he leafed dully through his books, knowing he would find no refuge there. And in fact he spent the afternoon rejecting the dream face.

The ritual was established now; the milking, bringing in firewood, a wash, a change and then the table, set for a feast. And the feast was for Rémi. Sonia's greeting, and even Sophie's, made him realize how welcome he was in the house. As evening approached, Sonia's fears came back with growing intensity. Rémi's arrival brought some relief. She had been waiting impatiently for him, almost enjoying her fear as soon as its end was in sight.

This morning she had mused about last evening, touched by the thought that tonight would be the same. Then she had a pang of guilt. The intimacy of their shared fear seemed indecent in broad daylight. For hours this idea obsessed her: she was Réginald's wife, and a mother as well. Rémi was a young adolescent. That they should feel so close was somehow abnormal. And it was assuredly a sin that Réginald's absence should turn into a daily celebration. That shook the whole foundation of the household. "For better or for worse." The better had been rare and the worst had been frequent, with a man who liked the bottle and chased every skirt he saw when her back was turned. But that was her lot. Sonia had been resigned to the fact that her life would always be like this; and here the presence of a young boy raised sudden questions and endangered the precarious balance that, for her, had been the only possible way of living.

Sonia had often dreamed – and still did sometimes – of having adventures. A handsome man she'd see at church or elsewhere, the hero of a dance on some special evening would become for weeks the central figure of the stories she told herself. When she was cooking or doing dishes or housecleaning, she would imagine a whole romance, seeing herself living happily at its centre. These fantasies had been her greatest joys, and she had often been impatient to be left alone to her domestic tasks so that she could be alone with her admirer of the moment. This secret life was a guilty one, of course, but harmless, really, since her infidelities were nothing but dreams and imaginings that came to nothing. But this was different, now, with Rémi. Oh, she didn't imagine any kind of romance or adventure, nor did she want it. The very idea was ridiculous. But he was there. And she enjoyed his presence and waited for his return, cleaned house, set the table, fixed her hair, and made her face up as she no longer did for Réginald. Sonia was almost ready to accuse herself of infidelity. Rémi preoccupied her and despite his youth he was doubtless sensitive and intuitive enough to feel the ambiguity of their situation. Had he not said, "Ain't I the man in this house?" These words had stuck in her mind and bothered her since morning. Silly. She was twenty years his senior; he could have been her son. She was old in experience, much of it unhappy and full of disappointed hopes; he was rich in promise. They had nothing in common, nothing they could share. Then why this delicious familiarity with its hints and complicities? Her face clouded a little as she reflected that he was not unaware of her charms, that she secretly excited him.

By three in the afternoon, Sonia was determined to change direction and behave like a reasonable woman who respected her wedding vows, ready to send Rémi home and put up with her fears; by four she had put off this step until the following day, giving herself that much respite. Rémi found her day-dreaming. Embarrassed, she stammered out an awkward greeting. He sat in the rocking-chair with Sophie on his knee and closed his eyes, gradually relaxing.

After supper Sophie wanted a story. He lay down beside her, thinking, "This is Sonia's place." He made up a story about the knight on his white horse who defended the princess against the dragon and finally carried her off to a far country in the land of dreams. He spoke loudly enough that his cousin could hear as she did the dishes. When he came out to the kitchen again she was sitting at the table.

"That was a long story, you have some memory!"

"No, I made it up."

For a while they found nothing more to say. Then Rémi looked at the window, dark and opaque, in which the lamplight was reflected as in a mirror.

"It's dark."

Sonia's eyes narrowed. Was he trying to renew yesterday's fears? Were these words supposed to mark the beginning of a ritual? It's dark. You should be afraid. But I'll be there, at least to share it if I can't reassure you. But Rémi had made the remark mechanically. He was calm, knowing that Eugénie would watch him from outside but not come in. Reprieved until tomorrow. He listens, but hears no sound from outside. The night, full of life and noises in summertime, was strangely empty in September. The insects had been put to sleep by the cold, the frogs no longer sang, the birds had gone south and the grass, soaked with rain and worn thin, was too soft to whisper. This was the desolation that said winter was on its way. Suddenly he heard a door slam in the distance, and a dog bark farther off. Then he saw a swinging light.

"Comp'ny coming, I think."

"Who?"

"Must be Mrs. Martel."

"Oh!"

Her exclamation is enigmatic, but as she prepares a place for her friend at the table, Rémi wonders if it hadn't a shade of irritation in it. As the visitor comes in her eyes sparkle and her voice is teasing: "Got your new dress on, eh Sonia?"

Sonia blushes and her answer starts with a stutter.

"Er, well . . . ah . . . if . . . if I never wear it what's the good of having one?"

Carmen returns to the charge.

"But a different one every day! And your hair's done as if you were goin' out! And all made up, too!"

Sonia tries to be evasive.

"If I was to wait for a big date . . .!"

And she notices her friend's red nail polish. It's Sonia's turn to tease.

"You're all dolled up too, eh?"

"I'm like you. If I waited to be asked out my clothes would rot."

They smile at each other.

Rémi admires the visitor, her smart appearance, her tight black sweater, her grey skirt stretched over her hips. She sets her glass down and turns mocking eyes on Rémi.

"And you have to put on the dog a bit when there's a new man in the house."

He feels helpless with these two women who share their friendship, their confidences and their age. He's a little boy again, uncertain of himself. Pretending to do homework, he settles down in the rocking-chair with his history book. He reads two lines of it, just enough to cut himself off from the women and their conversation. This is an ideal time to think things over: he's free from Sonia's charm and Eugénie's power. He can reflect at leisure.

He recalls his day at school, totally taken up with the dead woman. How come the others didn't notice his distraction? It must have been plain to see. Maybe they're saying behind his back that he's a weirdo! Eugénie's face, her features: an obsession he had to get rid of. An obsession? And what if it were vengeance from the beyond, for troubling the last rest of a dead girl? Or Ricard's god punishing him for his sacrilege and blasphemies? But that would mean Ricard was right. No, his god was no more true than the Black Goddess he and Robert had created with their hands, or all the other man-created gods. Rémi is sure there's no vengeance from the outside. It's in his mind that something's going off the rails.

A burst of laughter brings him back to the kitchen. He turns a page and pretends to read. Believing that he's absorbed in study, the women are talking freely. Their chat is not as trite as you might imagine. They're not talking about their small troubles or their children, but about their life as women, and about their men. He had imagined them to be docile, submissive servants with an intellectual level somewhere between infancy and that of an adult male. Suddenly, as he hears them talk, he realizes that they are the discreet, almost cunning guides of the household, letting the man think he is king. Rémi has an uncomfortable feeling of insecurity. He had thought he was on the side of the strong and dominant, a man in the making, already superior even to grown women. And here are these two wives for whom their husbands are no more than rash, impulsive children, spoiled children that are given their way just to keep them quiet. His system of values crumbles. His theories on life do not apply.

Not only do women not envy man his penis, they actually dare to call it by mocking diminutives. When Rémi hears Sonia tell how she convinced her husband that she had "trouble with her organs" to cool his bedtime ardours except when it pleased her, he finds this shocking. Especially as it's humiliating to be on the same side as that idiot Réginald. Carmen says she refuses to be like her mother, "tyrannized by the man and obliged to perform her wifely duty." Laughing, she explains how a few drops of iodine allow her to pretend she's "not well," as her husband understands nothing about the cycle.

"You know, Sonia, getting into bed and pow! No! Sometimes I feel like it in the afternoons, then I get ready just thinkin' about it. And he'll come home and give me shit about something and pay no attention to me all evening. Then, just as we go to bed he's all on fire. Well, I put his fire out for him. I don't know how often I've told

him, get me ready, take your time. But he never understood."

Rémi, listening, understands and approves. You have to
pay court, and better more than less. As he had done for
his Lady. He knows, indeed, and he won't be like the
others.

"They're all the same. Before they get married they're
real Don Juans, buying flowers and holding the door. Then
that's all over from one day to the next."

"That's for sure."

In vain Rémi tries to read some history. Will he too turn
out like Martel or Réginald? Or like his own father? Better
never marry! For a moment he pictures himself coming
wearily from work, finding a grumpy wife and screaming
children, and complaining that supper isn't ready or the
way he likes it. A nightmare. But he won't be like the
others. He'll love her all his life like a true knight.

Sonia is talking about an ideal life with a man who
would be her companion, friend, and equal, and who
would treat her as such.

Carmen says, "The Dam-Boggas?"

"Something like that."

They have lowered their voices, which now have a
confiding tone. A quick glance shows him their heads close
together and their eyes sparkling. Rémi perks up his ears.

". . . something exciting, adventure . . ."

"You don't really mean it, Carmen!"

Sonia looks shocked.

"I feel I could give in."

"You couldn't!"

"Just once. Why not? I won't always be thirty-five. Time
flies."

"Sure, for everybody. But that's no. . . ."

"I expected. . . . I thought you'd have more understanding. . . ."

"Oh, I understand! If anybody can, I can! But did you
think I'd encourage you?"

"I hoped."

"You hoped I'd decide for you?"

"No. But it's not easy. If you were me. . . ."

"But I'm not. And I never will be."

"You don't know that. You're . . . Sonia, if you encouraged me it wouldn't mean it was your fault."

"I'd be your accomplice."

Sonia is on the defensive. Carmen is desperate. "I've no more strength. I'm weakening, Sonia."

"Think what you've got to lose."

"You think what I've got to lose. Think about it. Put yourself in my place."

"I'm against it, Carmen, I really am. But if it happened I'd understand."

"That's some help anyway."

"Not for me! It's catching. I'd be less sure of myself."

Carmen insists, "Be my accomplice, then."

Sonia touches her friend's arm and shakes her head, smiling sadly. Carmen shuts her eyes and sighs. Her face, tense before, grows calm. Sonia notices Rémi's intense gaze. She quickly withdraws her hands from Carmen's arm.

"I think Rémi has finished his homework. He's staring at the bottle."

Her tone is light, but Rémi makes no mistake: something important was just decided, and he feels excluded, like a child left out of grown-up decisions. His curiosity is aroused, as well as his pride. He joins them at the table and lights a cigarette. He's still trying to understand, imagining impossible things but nothing plausible. Does Carmen want to run off and leave everything behind? Is she going to do away with her husband? Or is it one of those things where the baby is killed with a knitting needle before it's born, things that Blanche tells about with veiled words? Nothing fits, and he knows he can't question Sonia later. He'd like to show that he knows Carmen's secret, that he's not a dupe like other men, that he's different from them. But how can he, without appearing silly? He'd like to touch them both on the arm and say, "Aha! I know all!" But he can hear them laughing now.

"Ha ha! This young man's daydreaming. I'll bet he's in love," says Mrs. Martel.

"It's true our Rémi's a dreamer," says Sonia approvingly.

He smiles, happy to be noticed.

"Well, tell us about her! Is she pretty? Do we know her? Is she an Amos girl or did you leave her in Montreal?"

"Her name wouldn't be Eugénie, by any chance?" hints Sonia.

"Eugénie! Sonia! What kind of a name is that? Maybe it's a nickname he uses because he doesn't want us to know his sweetie's real name."

"Is she a real pretty little girl?" Sonia asks, trying to catch his eye.

"Or a grown woman?"

With these words Carmen Martel sketches in the air a silhouette with voluptuous proportions.

"I bet that's it! At that age they like mature women, even if they're spoken for already. Eh, Rémi? We don't worry about those things. We just love in silence and dream away."

Rémi blushes and feels stupid because he has nothing to say. Mrs. Martel is triumphant, sure of being on the right track.

"It's a woman with real attractions, not a green girl. A woman with experience, who knows about love. But tell me, Rémi, what can you offer a woman like that?"

She takes a sip while waiting for his answer. If you say nothing, you'll go down in the esteem of these women, you're nothing but a kid they can make fun of. You have a chance to show off, to let them know you understand lots of things. But it's a big risk. Rémi's glass trembles a little, and he hardly recognizes his own voice, it comes out so hoarse.

"It's funny. . . ."

A stupid way to start. He can see Carmen's lips already curling in derision. Hurriedly he adds, "Dreaming. . . . It's not only when you're fourteen that you dream about impossible things, things that aren't allowed."

The words reach Carmen like a slap in the face and her smile freezes. Rémi is horrified at the effect of his little speech. Carmen is flustered. He accidentally touched a sensitive spot. The silence weighs heavily around the table. He tries to remedy the harm.

"Sometimes dreaming is the best. And the most real."

But this only makes things worse. Finally Sonia clears her throat and says with forced gaiety, "The kettle's whistling. Like some coffee?"

Mrs. Martel shakes her head.

"I have to put the kids to bed."

"You've got time. Just ten minutes."

"No, I already left them alone too long."

"It's really too bad that you can't spend a whole evening with me!"

"I have no sitter."

"Seems to me it would do us good to have a real chat for a change. Come on over tomorrow when the kids are asleep."

"I can't, Sonia. There's the fire. And what if they wake up? No, I can't do it. Unless. . . ."

"What?"

"If Rémi would come and look after them. Seems to me he stays up pretty late. There was still a light on here when I went to bed last night."

"Why yes! That's an idea! Of course Rémi will go! He's good and reliable and he'd be glad to do us a favour!"

"Sure?"

"Of course!"

Rémi is in a rage because it all happened without a by-your-leave. The women's conversation was so fast there hadn't been a single gap, as if it were planned. He tries to find a connection between this plot and the murmured conversation he had overheard before. A lot of pieces are missing. Carmen puts on her jacket and leaves, her skirt swinging.

When they are alone again Sonia feels a little guilty and tries to make up.

"Now you get a coffee. It's good of you to go to Carmen's place tomorrow night. We don't often get a chance to talk, her and me. There's always the kids . . . You know, women have their little secrets, little private things. It may seem childish, but we've no other way of having fun. It's real nice of you to do this."

His voice is flat as he answers, "I'll go."

"But it doesn't make you very happy."

"Oh. . . ."

He thinks, "They're sending me off with the other kids."

"You wouldn't be scared over there?"

"No! Of course not!"

"And the kids will be asleep. It won't be very long anyway. Just this once."

"It's O.K. I said I'd go."

"There's something you don't like about it."

"Oh, the responsibility. Fire, or a kid gets sick."

"The house is just over there. You can get us if anything happens."

"And I don't like the Martel kids much."

"Even Diane?"

"Especially her. She's a cock-teaser."

Sonia's eyes open wide. Rémi regrets the expression.

"She's a little sneak, that's true. And her mother's so nice! But never mind, she'll be in bed."

"Yeah, but will she be asleep?"

"Are you afraid she'd assault your virtue?"

Sonia's in a good mood again.

"She could be up to anything. To get at me she could say I raped her or set fire to the house. That's her type."

"Don't worry, her mother knows her. She'd believe you first. You know Diane smokes and drinks in secret?"

"That don't surprise me. I could believe worse."

"There *is* worse!" Sonia leans toward him, like a gossip, and lowers her voice to play the part. "She's a vicious little brat. Last year some things happened at school – not very nice. And she started it all. She dragged the others into it, even older ones. And it reached the priest's ears. Poor Carmen, she cried when she told me. Diane is her crown of thorns."

"Hey, it's only nine and I'm sleepy already!"

"Yes, we went to bed late yesterday. I'm sleepy too. And I have a feeling I'll sleep well. I'm not as anxious as yesterday."

Rémi was well aware of the fact, because there was no more of the intimacy their shared fear had brought about. Rather a kind of indifference. Sonia was not as close to him, and he no longer felt like a king in his domain.

Robert had felt unsafe as long as the death notice was in his possession, and gave it to Rémi with obvious relief. He also brought the garter that Rémi had once worn as a token. He told Rémi later how he'd had to fight off his fear to fetch these objects from the cave. He hadn't been able to run his errand before supper, and it was hard to find an excuse for going out afterwards. Finally he had gone to bed, having failed in his mission; but he couldn't sleep for thinking of Rémi's trust in him. And so he had climbed out the window and ventured into the dark, where he heard all kinds of invisible creatures creeping and walking. He had followed the creek to their cave with all its memories. Robert made a long story of his courage and determination. Rémi told him how he appreciated all this and talked about Mrs. Martel to reward him.

Rémi, in the privacy of the toilets, felt free to contemplate the photo on its wrinkled, worn card. It was good to hold Eugénie's portrait in his hand, to have her outside of him. He concentrated on memorizing this imperfect likeness so that it might replace the lively beauty in his mind. Alone in the washroom, he began talking softly to her.

"You're nothing but an invention. I imagined you. You're a memory of nothing. Understand? Nothing! You don't exist. It was the past I tried to bring to life. See this token? I'm putting it down the bowl. Look! There it goes! I was in love with lies, with my own dreams and foolishness, not with you, dead girl, and your dust and earth. You're no more real than the Black Goddess is or the ceremonies I made up, or the knights. That was all lies! My own lies, and I believed them. The ceremonies and religions, the dark forces don't exist; they're powerless. There's only the will and the ideas. And now I want you to disappear forever. I'll never think of you again except as a half-rubbed-out image, like a small pile of bones. You were dead and never rose."

He went back to class and a while later, when the obsession returned and his mind fixed upon the princess as it had done on previous days, he had only to think of his monologue and glance at the black-edged photo held in his cupped hand, and he was liberated. Finally he was able to follow the course and listen to the teacher's explanations. Rémi was happy. He was driving his madness back, and each time he succeeded he felt stronger. Eugénie was going to space her visits and soon would come no more.

He had expected to find Sonia cool and distant, as she had been that morning, but this was not the case. She was wearing a dress he had never seen and was very attentive during their meal. Later, torn between haste and nervousness, she sent him off to baby-sit at Martel's with a present of two cigarettes in his hand. Mrs. Martel wasn't ready yet, and he sat in the sheepskin-covered rocking-chair while she carried their only lamp into the bedroom to finish her make-up. He heard the puffing of an atomizer, the click of jewellery and her voice humming a song. She reappeared with a swish of her green dress, set the lamp on the table near him, and went off with a sprightly step, saying she wouldn't be gone too long.

Rémi was still puzzled. Why were the two women so excited? And both dressed up as if for a big occasion? In Sonia's case it might just be for him; but Carmen? Just to call on Sonia? What could they do together? And Rémi started imagining them in love with each other, holding hands and making passionate declarations. He smiled at this absurdity, but the pictures he had created were so beautiful that he pushed them to extremes. He saw them looking into each other's eyes, flattering each other, hugging and kissing. Arms around each other's waists, they walked to the bedroom and undressed, caressing each other and lying down on the bed where Rémi slept. He was excited. He would have liked to go into Carmen's room and touch himself while continuing his mental peep-show.

"What are you thinkin' about?" He jumps. Diane is halfway down the stairs. "Mm? What are you thinking to make you smile that way?" His face hardens.

"Not about you, that's for sure."

"There you go again. And I was being nice."

"If you want to be nice, go to bed."

He rocks and looks at the stove.

"I can't sleep."

"Do what you like. This is your place."

"Don't get mad. We could have a chat."

"What about? Nothing."

"You can talk with your hands, first."

"Pffff. . . ."

"We could go an' lie down together."

He shrugs.

"I'd be nice. Don't be scared."

"I'm not scared."

"What's the matter? Aren't I your type? Too young? I could show you a few things."

"I'd rather learn somewhere else."

She laughs.

"You're scared, that's it. You're a scaredy, Rémi Simard."

He stares at her. Slowly, she's fingering the hem of her night-gown.

"O.K., I'm a scaredy."

His voice is weary, not even aggressive.

"Rémi, Rémi, I could cure you of that."

"Go back to bed and leave me be."

"You think I can sleep knowing you're in the house?"

"You've nothing to fear from me."

"That's the trouble," she says and heaves a great sigh.

"That little bitch," thinks Rémi. Silently they try to stare each other down. She looks old, he finds. Her eyes are old, her features hardened by life, her skin is wrinkled like parchment. She's old in spite of her youth.

Old at twelve! She had looked like that even when she was little. Never was a child, never pure, never innocent, never carefree. As far back as she can remember she was bad and everyone told her so. As long as she can remember, she had been playing with herself, exploring boys' bodies, fascinated and sickened at once. She always knew that she disliked herself and was disliked by others, and that she was destined to be unhappy. Everything had started wrong: she'd been conceived by accident before marriage; her mother had had to have a Caesarian and had made a slow recovery; and Diane had caught every childhood disease in the book: a difficult baby. Wrinkled, dried-up, skinny. After their church wedding the parents hadn't even had a fat, healthy baby to show off. She was a capricious and crabby child. She began to walk too early, in a hurry to rummage everywhere, always getting into trouble. The very first words she strung together were used to cheat or lie, and as she discovered the power of words, she practised lying with a passion. She hated the children that followed her, detesting them systematically, one after the other, and leading them into trouble for which they were punished in her stead. This was her greatest pleasure. She was detestable and nobody hesitated to tell her so. And so she maintained her reputation by fostering quarrels in the family.

"Rémi. . . ."

She said his name in a whisper. But he continued to stare at her in silence.

The first person to show her any affection, tenderness or interest was a stranger, a man her family took in for several months. He would laugh at her mean tricks, showing that he didn't take them seriously. One Sunday he even brought her some ice cream! Of course she fell deeply in love with him. She was five and beginning to behave like a woman with her alluring ways, dressing up for him, learning how to smile and trying to be kind. She tried to seduce him: she wanted to be his forever. Surprised and shocked, he pushed away her tiny hand, rebuffed the minuscule woman, slapping her face and calling her all the hateful names he knew. She was stunned, and stood there, feeling something in her shrivel.

Remembering this intense love, Diane feels the tears come to her eyes. Has life any meaning, any value at all? Her world is upside down. Why not put an end to it, once and for all? People hate her more and more, and she doesn't know how to change the pattern. Her clumsy attempts at tenderness all turn sour and her cries for help turn into clawing matches. Despair. That first wretched love: the end of everything. What could she cling to?

"Rémi. . . ."

Her voice is begging.

He's afraid of her. He may even be thinking all the words she has heard so often: monster, vicious, liar, mean.

"Rémi, Rémi. . . ."

Puzzled, he studies her. Her eyes are swollen and filled with tears. Another trick? He's afraid of her. And she's looking so intensely at him. If only he'd hold her hand, just for a second. She should go to him now, right away, before he has time to react. She'd sit on his knees, cling to him so hard he couldn't push her away. She'd shut her eyes and stay quiet while he rocked her, thinking of nothing, desiring nothing. Not saying a word. Just being tender with somebody, being rocked till the end of the world.

But she sits where she is and weeps softly. She thinks of all the beings she's invented, known in dreams, with whom she has lived in harmony. These ghosts, more real and human than her family, exist no longer. She killed them off after she discovered that they were ineffectual against despair. Even her dreams hate her now. She looks back on her twelve years as on a great, arid desert, glaring and empty. Twelve wasted years.

Diane bursts into tears and runs away upstairs, her bare feet padding on the wood. Rémi is nonplussed. What's going on? At the same time he's glad she's gone.

It takes him a while to regain his calm. There is no sound from upstairs. Diane has silenced her tears, if she's still crying – if she ever really cried! All he can hear in the house is the soft purring of the stove, and this near-silence becomes intolerable. He goes to the sink and works the hand pump, less out of thirst than to hear the pump handle squeaking, the gasping of the leather valve and the stomach sounds of the water rising in the pipe. He pumps far longer than he needs to, and fails to hear Mrs. Martel's arrival. It's the sound of the door latch that warns him at the last moment. She is out of breath and her clothes are rumpled. Her face looks tired, but her eyes are bright.

"I was long, wasn't I?"

"No. Anyway, I'm not in a hurry."

"The kids?"

"They didn't wake up."

"Thanks for watching them for me. That was real nice of you."

"It was a pleasure, Mrs. Martel."

Walking past her to the door he thinks he smells something strange among the perfumes: strange and yet familiar. Outside, his alert nose picks up the odour of damp earth. Dam-Bogga was ploughing today. Rémi stops at the aspen and leans against it. Light is flowing out of the house where Sonia is waiting for him. But he takes his time. He wants to be alone. And he is really alone: Eugénie has not come to trouble him even here in the dark. He has won that battle. The princess has disappeared forever, killed by his will, as it created her. From now on the night will be devoid of marvels, but empty, too, of menace and unseen enemies. A shadow darkens the window of Réginald's house. Sonia's watching for him. She's alone and probably scared again. He lingers a moment more, and, when he finally goes in, finds a woman toying nervously with her finger-nails. She seems relieved and at the same time anxious to hide the fact. He fancies there is a reproach in her eyes: you took so long! He is happy to imagine there's also a touch of jealousy: was it Carmen held you up?

"The children didn't give you any problem? And what did Carmen say? Has she been back long?"

Seeing Rémi's astonishment Sonia becomes confused. Her hand makes a helpless gesture as she searches for an explanation. Rémi is baffled by her question. But he comes to her rescue.

"I stopped on the way back to look at the night."

"Oh, that's it? I thought you were late. I was starting to get scared."

She pokes the fire.

"There's water on. Would you like a bite to eat as well?"

"Maybe, a bit."

She pokes at the wood, lifting one stick, then the other.

"I'm a big stupid, you know? Scared of the dark, at my age! You were late and I was getting jumpy."

"Did you have a good chat?"

"Oh, sure. We rattled away like a couple of old gossips."

"Old gossips of thirty-six."

"You know it's good for the morale."

From the cupboard she brings the dishes.

"You don't know what it's like to be shut up in this cabin the whole week long, on this sideroad where nothin' ever happens. The mailman hardly ever stops, and apart from him nobody comes. At least you get to go to town every day."

"Town! I could do without it. I didn't mind a bit staying out here this summer."

"Summer's different, Rémi. You go outside, there's work to do, it's lively; the men are here. But now, just imagine how dead it is here in daytime. I'm lucky to have Carmen Martel."

They take their places at the table.

"This is a pie I made today."

"What do you talk about, anyway, you and Mrs. Martel, if nothing ever happens?"

"Oh, we talk about the time before we came here. The town or the village. There were people around, relatives, we visited neighbours, we got around. There were stores and things to do, movies and parties, special occasions for getting dressed up, going to the hairdresser, trying things on. We were real women then. But here. . . ."

She cuts a bit of pie with her fork, then lets it fall.

"Here! With winter coming, I'm caught here like in a grave."

Rémi eats away and lets her talk.

"When I think about it, it's . . . horrible!"

She bursts into sobs, and then begins to talk through her hiccups.

"Snow. Damn snow. Snow everywhere, nothing but white and the dirty green of these damn spruce trees. Prisoner in this house, in this damned settlement. If only I'd known."

She cries a little more before going on.

"There's the night that starts at four o'clock and lasts till eight in the morning. Then there's the daylight white like a different sort of night. Chimneys blocked, snow banks, blowing snow. Damned winter . . .! Ever since I was little it's been the same . . . snow, and cold. Sitting by the fire for months at a time."

Rémi keeps his head bowed, uncertain what to do. She blows her nose and sobs twice.

"And Réginald won't be there all week. And sometimes he won't even come on weekends the roads are so bad. Damn god-forsaken country, I shouldn't ever have come here with him. Him and his crazy ideas. Always hopes, always promises. And getting in deeper every year. If he'd only listened to me. But no, he knows better than anybody. Whadda *you* know, Sonia? Shut up and go where you're told!"

Sonia has been talking without thinking of Rémi's presence, and he has kept quiet as a mouse to stay out of her monologue. When she stops he looks up at her. Her made-up face with its rivulets of tears would be comical if it weren't for the reddened eyes filled with despair.

"And you won't even be here, Rémi. I'm goin' to be alone an' that's it. Daytime, that's not too bad, but the nights! Endless nights beside the lamp, and nights when I can't sleep. Lying awake for hours listening to the house creak and the nails squeak, and shaking. And the stove starts to go out and I'll be cold an' I won't dare get up to stoke it. And the pump'll be frozen in the morning and the house like ice. God-damn misery! I was brought up that way, but I thought there was an end to it. I've seen better, you know. Comfort, electricity, oil furnaces, T.V. I never thought I'd end up in a hole like this."

She bites at her nails as she weeps. Rémi is an uneasy witness. She has no right to tell him her troubles like this. He's too young to be burdened with other people's problems, especially those of a woman who could be his mother. But he waits, fascinated, for further revelations. She starts in again.

"And then the wind in winter-time. That's the worst. For days and nights it's goin' to whistle around the house, I'll hear nothing else, I won't be able to forget it for a minute. That's the wind that cuts you off from the rest of the world. Rémi, if I had any sense I'd pack my bag and take the kid and get out of here before the snow comes. I'm scared! I'm scared I'll go crazy. Just thinkin' about winter I get cold, cold, cold!"

Hunched together, she begins to tremble. Rémi brings a blanket and puts it over her shoulders. She pulls the edges around her and sits there exhausted. Rémi makes more coffee.

"Here, drink this. It'll warm you up. Why don't you sit by the stove?"

"No, I'm all right. Thanks."

Rémi stays behind her so he can't see her eyes.

"I'm crazy, is that what you think? Eh? I'm sorry. Forget what I said."

"That's O.K."

"Whatever you do, don't tell anybody."

"It's between us two. But I won't be able to forget it."

"I didn't believe the half of what I said."

"Oh, yes you did. And I understand."

"You know, Rémi, it's not that I don't love Réginald, but sometimes. . . ."

"You don't have to explain."

"Sometimes men think of nobody but themselves. The wife don't count. I'm the man; I make the money and I make the decisions."

"Yeah."

"Well, that's just not right. Women. . . ."

She can't find the words to express what she has held pent up all these years, resentments, the memory of events that she suffered rather than experienced, frustrations, the feeling of being a second-class person, while knowing. . . . Rémi lays his head on her wool-covered shoulder.

"Women have a soul, you know."

She thinks over these words for a long time, while the wind rises outside, heaving at the northwest corner of the house like a steer rubbing against a tree. It roars down the chimney and the fire replies. Rémi gently withdraws his hand. Sonia bends her cheek toward it and holds it there.

"Leave it, it's warm. Listen to that wind. God it's a short fall here. There could be snow tomorrow! What am I goin' to do?"

"Tough it out."

"That's right. Stick to it. What else?"

"It'll be O.K., just wait. Something will happen."

"You don't believe what you say. Nothing ever happens."

"Make it happen."

"What."

"I don't know. Give your life a kick in the ass."

It's the first time anybody ever suggested she should act instead of preaching patience and resignation! But it's easier said than done. With his other hand Rémi strokes her hair, timidly at first, fearing her reaction. She lets her head fall back and he plays with her waves and curls. Sonia is breathing noisily.

"Sometimes I can't believe you're only fourteen."

"Me neither."

He draws back, and to cover up his feelings, goes and shuts the draft in the noisy stove-pipe. Sonia, standing now, hands him the blanket. She looks at herself in the mirror on the wall.

"Oh, I look hard! Like an old woman."

Passing the sink, Rémi notices there's only one cup and saucer in it. Carmen Martel was never even here! If she had been, there'd be two cups and some glasses as well. He says good night to Sonia and goes to his room. Alone, he rubs his cheek on the wool where her warmth is still present. The perfume of her make-up persists where her tears washed it down. Rémi has trouble sleeping. He puzzles over Carmen Martel's strange actions but comes to no conclusion. Where could she have gone? To Dam-Bogga's? But she wouldn't have had to invent a lie with Sonia just for that. No, she got herself dressed up to meet somebody. Maybe out at the road. But Rémi hadn't heard the sound of a car. One sure thing, she hadn't sat up with Sonia, or Sonia wouldn't have been so impatient for him to get home.

After the milking, Rémi had a shock as he was cleaning the stable. In the gutter, under a wisp of straw, something caught his attention. He fished it out with the fork. A handkerchief! And not just any handkerchief. The one Carmen Martel had stuffed in her sleeve before going out yesterday. What was the odour he'd smelled on Carmen when she came home? A whiff of stable! This explained everything, even the mysterious conversation the day before yesterday. Carmen Martel had met a man here! Rémi gazed around the stable, trying to imagine the scene. There, in the corner under the trapdoor to the hay loft? Or here, in the stall where the horse used to be, where the cow's fresh bedding was kept? Or there in the corner, standing against the wall, so they wouldn't get dirty? Carmen had met a lover here! She'd come in all trembling, still hesitating, tempted a dozen times to go back while she could. She had called softly, someone answered, and the rest happened without light and almost without words: just a few whispers. . . .

Rémi forked out the manure while continuing to invent Carmen's adventure. As soon as they finished she had fled. She stopped at the tree to catch her breath and stayed there a long time, feeling the bite of remorse. Then she smoothed her clothes with the flat of her hand to remove the clinging chaff. She gave her hair a touch in front of an invisible mirror, and walked slowly to the house. She was imagining the scene as she went inside. She went over and over it, trying for the pose that would seem most normal and finding answers to possible questions. She was about to go into her husband's house, the house where her children were sleeping. She felt a painful confusion, which must have shown on her face. Was her guilt so easy to read there?

Rémi was jubilant. It was so simple. Her phrase to Sonia: "I'm weakening." But who? Who was this mysterious lover? He couldn't imagine. Somebody from the village? How would she get to know him? She hardly ever went there, and then with her husband. Somebody on their line? Rémi smiled as he eliminated Dam-Bogga. And it couldn't be Robert, though he was the one who deserved the lady's favours. "I'm weakening." That presupposed a continuing or even assiduous courtship, with declarations, propositions, follow-up. . . . Godbout! There he was, just down the road, within reach as it were, lonely and at loose ends. Carmen, so close by, is a temptation to him. Perhaps it started with his wanting to convert her, and desire took over from missionary zeal. No need to meet her often, he starts writing ardent missives, which he drops in her mailbox at night. Does she answer him? In any case he lets time and her imagination work for him. He suggests meeting times; she refuses. He pursues her with his advances, she hesitates. He begs her and she gives in at last. But where should they meet? At her house? There are the children. His is facing Dam-Bogga's, too risky. Réginald's stable is there, half-way between their two houses and far back from the road, and its very discomfort adds to the excitement of their tryst.

Rémi is uncomfortable at being so close to such a mystery, but delighted to have discovered this illicit love. He finds it less pleasing that Godbout should be the chosen man. He'd have preferred the lover to have more style. This liaison is too unpoetic, and Rémi can't allow it to continue. There are several ways he can throw a monkey-wrench into it: refuse to baby-sit; hint that he knows all; intercept their correspondence. In front of the stable he finds the trail going diagonally up the slope. The grass has preserved the footprints intact, and in the field a series of broken clods interrupts the furrows' crests in a path that passes close to the stone pile and heads straight for Godbout's house. Rémi smiles. He is the one who knows, the one who can call the tune.

In the car Rémi hears his father giving the latest news of the family. Robert's eyes ask silent questions as if he knew that Rémi had a secret. Right now, Rémi thought, Sonia has rushed over to Carmen's place, or is thinking about it. Or waiting for her friend to come. She's burning with impatience: to participate, if only indirectly, in the adventure, to feel close to the mystery and, as Carmen's accomplice, to share her feelings. And most of all to know what those feelings are, whether remorse, anxiety, regrets or joy. And how it was, and what happened, and what he said. All these confessions would later feed Sonia's daydreams.

When the boys were alone Robert asked question after question. Rémi could not reveal secrets that weren't his or talk about events about which he only had a hunch. He concealed more from his brother than he had ever done, and felt he was creating a gap between them. He was growing more independent, and no longer wanted to share his inner life. The summer's friendship, the result of sharing everything, was growing weaker. They'd stay good chums, that was all. As he had to provide something to satisfy Robert's curiosity, he invented gossip that contained insignificant crumbs of truth.

At noon hour Robert ate with a classmate. Rémi took the opportunity of reviving the memory of Eugénie Ducharme. Not only did she not appear to him during class, he had trouble even imagining her face. Secretively, he took her photo from his pocket. It was getting more and more wrinkled, grey as a barn door and just as full of cracks. Cheeks like old boards. The boy had an inspiration: what if it was the house he had loved, not a dead woman? Trying to give a new body to Eugénie had been a mistake. Wasn't the house her body, her dwelling-place? A kind of mutual completion of spirit and wood. The house that loved me! That was what called me, invited me in, invented this princess to lead me on. And now the house has been raped and looted, it's trying to invade me and live on inside me. He had to laugh at this idea, and saw his classmates looking strangely at him, for his laughter had been audible. Embarrassed, he walked away. Stupid! It was all in my head!

This was the last night of his week with Sonia, and it was a dull one. The table was set simply and Sonia, dressed in everyday clothes, was morose. After supper Rémi sat in the rocking-chair and missed his family. For the first time. Sonia was playing solitaire. Rémi thought they were like two children who feel guilty and are afraid of being caught out, probably because Réginald was coming back next day. Sonia was getting ready to be a wife again and hide her real personality. Right now she probably regretted indulging in such familiarity with her little cousin. She had stayed faithful. Réginald had no cause for concern: she would never give in to the attraction of the unknown as poor Carmen had. Yet Sonia was not unruffled. She had opened up to a stranger as she never had to her own husband, and was suffering from this moral infidelity, this adultery that was so subtle Réginald himself would laugh at it, never understanding its depth or its importance.

She was getting confused in her game and cheating to win.

"I guess you're glad to be going back to your own folks."

"What about you? When does Réginald get here?"

She shuffled the cards for a moment before replying.

"Yeah, I'll be glad to see him here. He promised me a battery radio."

Rémi remained silent.

"We're going shopping tomorrow. Anything special you'd like to eat next week?"

Her tone said that she did not deny their evenings together. She'd rather not linger over them and certainly not talk about them, but she was giving him to understand that next Monday it would all start again.

"You don't need to soften me up, I'm not mad. Why should I be? And you don't need to cover up, it's natural you should be glad Réginald's coming home."

Sonia looked surprised.

He went on, "And if it makes you so happy to have him back, you don't have to be ashamed in front of me."

She looked at him, horrified, her jaw gaping. Her hands were trembling. He bowed his head, ashamed. What hateful impulse had impelled him to destroy the delicate balance in his relationship with Sonia? He didn't dare look up. She must still be staring at him, trying to understand. She whispered, "Why? Why?"

No doubt other words would have followed, but she was interrupted by a knock at the door. She ran to her bedroom and Rémi opened the door. It was Dam-Bogga and his wife come for an evening visit, which meant a game of cards. The old man slapped him on the shoulder and laughed for no reason. Sonia came out hooking up the collar of her dress.

"Well, that's a nice surprise. Look, I just changed! I had a feeling we'd have company."

She became the charming hostess everyone knew, and put her guests at ease. Rémi was relieved at the interruption, even if he had to play five hundred. The tension between him and Sonia gradually relaxed. The evening went on forever and Dam-Bogga, in his passion for the game, failed to notice that his partner and his adversaries were tired. He never stopped talking, recounting bits of gossip picked up in the village, speculating about the coming winter, and telling how he was preparing for it and what remained to do. He had received a letter from Professor Savard asking him to tear down the house and keep the wood. Rémi thought for a moment to explore its mysteries. Now all that would disappear. Just as well, after all.

The Dam-Boggas at last went home.

"Listen, Rémi."

He was apprehensive. Her voice grew more gentle.

"Nothing was said tonight. On the weekend we'll forget it and we can go on being friends. You mustn't say horrible things. Words can hurt. I'll know you understand or guess everything. But I'll be able to pretend not to see it. O.K.?"

"Yes."

Rémi's home-coming was the occasion for endless effusions by Françoise.

"Funny," said his mother, "you seem different, more grown-up."

Rémi felt different. He now saw his family from a fresh viewpoint and thought of himself not as a member of this group but as an individual with his own life. One day, very soon, he would leave for good and take charge of his own destiny.

"Did you do a good job? You didn't give Sonia any trouble?"

"I did the milking, I brought in the firewood, and filled the Coleman."

"I'm proud of you, my big man."

"He's only a year older," said Robert, offended. "I'd do just as good as he did."

"Sure you would. You'll get your turn to prove you can act like a man."

Their mother had already packed many of their possessions, and the boxes were piled up in the living room. Rémi spent his morning putting his personal things in a carton. When he had finished, the pile of what was to be thrown away was as big as the one of things he kept: souvenirs of no importance, a stone picked up by the St. Lawrence river, an apple blossom that no longer evoked the smile of the girl who had given it to him, toys, a collection of airplane cards, rockets and other useless baubles, plastic soldiers and animals and a tiny submarine. Robert greedily sorted through this heap, and rescued a good part of it. Rémi saw that the gap between them was widening.

Supper with their father, who was happy to have ended his week's work, was pleasant. One day's reprieve, thought Rémi. Tomorrow he'll be wearing his old expression of a worker afraid of losing his job. Tonight they could talk to him, listen to him. It was the last Saturday evening they'd spend in this house! It would surely be a special evening! But the parents went off to play cards at Réginald's. When their little sister was asleep the boys sat on the stoop despite the chilly air. Rémi offered his brother a cigarette.

"Where'd you get them?"

"Stole a pack from Sonia."

He wasn't about to admit that she'd given him the cigarettes, Robert wouldn't have understood.

"It's dumb, you know, but I was bored this week."

"I know. Me too."

"School's no fun. And I'm fed up drivin' there and back every day."

"Nearly an hour!"

"Eating god-dam sandwiches."

"Won't be long now. Just one more week."

"Yeah. It's not so great havin' to move. It's nice here, you get a great view and you're all alone. In town there's just a little yard, you got neighbours. . . ."

"It's funny, eh? Now it's all decided I'll be glad when we're there."

"What? You're kidding, eh, Rémi? Hey! We had the best summer here we ever had. Too bad it's over."

"It'll never come back."

"Yeah, but wanting to leave. . . ."

"We'll go on to something else. I'm starting a new life in Amos. Something different. When you move you turn into somebody else. Just think how you were in Pointe-aux-Trembles and then how you are right now. I'm not goin' to fight change. I'm goin' to push it along faster."

"You changed already. Always reading, even at noon hour. And you never play with the other guys."

"Books are full of things. Stories, characters, life. . . ."

"Come on, we've got enough reading for homework. Go and read more? No way."

"You've got other kids to play with now."

"Yeah, but they'll never make up crazy things like you could. The knights! You know, it was stupid in a way, but we had a lot of fun. I was scared sometimes, but we sure saw a lot of things!"

"It wasn't stupid. We believed in it, so it was true."

"Then it's still true?"

"No. I don't believe any more. But when I did believe, it was true."

"The only thing I regret is not getting my Lady."

"That was part of the game."

"Well, I believed in it, anyway. . . ."

Robert went inside and Rémi opened his senses to the night, attentive to every sight and sound. Night bathed him, cool and limpid, making visible her most distant stars. There was a trace of northern lights, and Rémi marvelled to think he was seeing the twisting, mixing, and dilation of gasses whipped by solar particles. These were no dancers or mysterious nudes, what he saw was the beauty of a natural phenomenon. Deprived of the fantastic beings with which Rémi had peopled his night, the dark, having lost its own will-power, was no longer the divinity he had imagined, but was still fascinating and beautiful. As he went back inside the house he reflected that the world had no need of gods to be miraculous, only an attentive man. Robert was building a tower with a Meccano set he had found in a box of old toys. He unconsciously rejected change and clung to the past. Rémi settled down by the lamp to read. He had just discovered with delight the characters of François Mauriac.

Réginald came over on Sunday afternoon. He drank two beers in a row and talked about trucking and the problems he and his partner were having, their hard work and long hours. He had to get back to Rouyn that very night to start work at six in the morning. He came to fetch Rémi. Disconcerted at first, the boy quickly decided it would be nice to see Sonia a day earlier than planned. He was, in fact, glad to leave home, as his father had put on his weekday face. This morning as they hunted partridge he had treated the boys as companions. And he had smiled. Now the smile had changed to a resigned grimace. Rémi vowed never to get that way. He'd rather be an incorrigible dreamer, like Réginald. In ten minutes, his mother had packed his bag and he went off with his cousin, who drove too fast, and the body rattled.

"You don't mind comin' over?"

"Your place or my place, it's all the same. Milkin' a cow's not a big deal."

"You're a great help. I'll pay you back somehow. Hey, why don't you come out with us for a week? That'd do you good, working for a change."

"I've got school."

"School! It won't hurt if you miss a week. You'll learn about life with us guys. You know, we don't work all the time. When the truck's loaded we drive a good spell, we have a smoke and a beer, and we talk a bit. We have fun. And at the hotel at night we don't get bored."

"Maybe."

"I'll talk to your dad. He'll let you go. How old are you anyway? Fourteen?"

"Yep."

"Sonofagum! There's some young chicks there, they won't run away. You ever have fun with a girl?"

Rémi blushed and hesitated.

"Well, a bit. . . ."

"You come along with us. Réginald's goin' to see that you lose your cherry."

Listening to his cousin talk, and even allowing for his blowhard tendencies, Rémi imagines that he doesn't stint himself. Drink and women must certainly drive up the little company's expenses. They arrive at the house.

"Rémi!" Sonia is astonished.

"I went to get him," her husband explains.

"I thought you'd gone to Martel's!"

"That's the point, Martel told me we have to leave early. We gotta go to Malartic for two new tires."

"Leaving Sunday! What's the sense of that, for heaven's sakes! And the garages are closed anyway."

"It's a guy Martel knows. We gotta change them tonight to be on the road bright an' early tomorrow morning. Payin' for the truck and the gas and repairs an' board at the hotel, we can't afford to miss a trip."

"Réginald! And your supper's just ready!"

"Aw, don't gimme that stuff."

"Réginald. . . ."

She began firmly, but her husband stopped her with a gesture.

"Never mind that crap. I gotta earn money! It don't grow on trees, what I bring you. I earn it god-dam hard! You should be glad you never married a bum that'd let you die hungry. Sometimes a person would think you're too dumb to get that through your head!"

She follows him into the bedroom and there's an exchange of words, so low that Rémi can distinguish nothing. Réginald comes out with his haversack. He kisses Sophie, grins at Rémi, and leaves. With his long, healthy stride he walks to the truck and tosses in his belongings. Martel joins him a few minutes later and the truck is on its way.

In the bedroom Sonia is weeping loudly. Sophie, distressed and seeking consolation, turns to Rémi.

"Why mamma crying?"

"Maybe she's sick, or she's afraid she'll miss your daddy."

He rocks her for a moment, singing "*la Poulette grise.*" Her worries gone, the child slips to the floor and begins looking after her dolls, which are behaving themselves in a row on the stairway. The dishes from noon are soaking in cold, soapy water. Rémi washes and dries them, careful not to make a sound. He doesn't want to draw attention to his presence, dreading a little the moment when he'll be face to face with Sonia. She'd been humiliated, dragged down to the level of a servant before a stranger – or worse, her friend! What can he do? Pretend not to have noticed what happened, or show by his expression that he's on her side? Or say nothing, as she would surely prefer. Finished he takes his suitcase into the bedroom, hangs up his clothes, and lies down. On the other side of the partition the sound of weeping has stopped. Rémi decides to stay where he is and give Sonia time to get up and regain her composure. She'll appreciate his tact.

"My uncle Rémi's lying down."

Sonia must have replied with a gesture.

"Are you sick, mummy?"

"A little bit. I feel better now, darling."

"Does it hurt? You're crying."

"No it's all over. See, I'm smiling!"

"Ha ha! You're funny! All dirty."

Sophie goes back to her dolls.

"My uncle Rémi did the dishes."

"Your uncle Rémi's very nice."

"He rocked me, too. I'm hungry."

"The chicken's in the oven. It won't be long."

"I'm hungry right now, mummy."

"It's true, you didn't eat much at noon."

Sonia makes her a little snack. The child eats in silence.

"Sophie, wake up! You're going to sleep! You'll fall out of your chair."

"Can I go and lie down with my uncle?"

"Yes, but don't wake him."

Rémi shuts his eyes. Sophie climbs up on the bed and slides under the covers.

"Rémi, are you asleep?"

"Yeah."

"Me too!"

And after wriggling for several minutes she actually goes to sleep. Rémi gets up without disturbing her.

"She's asleep," he says.

"No wonder. Last night she was awake till eleven. And this morning she was up at seven."

"Something smells good."

"Chicken. It'll be ready in a minute."

"I'd like to get the milking over now. It's a bit early, but . . ."

"The cow won't mind an hour one way or the other."

When he comes back the table is set, as he expected. And Sonia has taken pains about it.

"Want some wine?"

Without waiting for his answer she uncorks the bottle.

"Even if we're settlers of a backwoods colony, we still know how to live!"

There's something like rage in her tone.

"You'll see how good I make chicken."

They eat, washing the food down with copious servings of wine. By the end of the meal Rémi is so full and sleepy that he just wants to enjoy his bliss complacently. Sonia takes the last of the bottle. The boy's silence makes her think of her quarrel with Réginald. She chokes back her resentment.

"At least there's somebody likes my cookin'!"

"And your company."

She grows pale. Seeing that the wine bottle is empty, "No wonder I'm drunk! An' I'm still thirsty."

"Go on, you're not drunk."

"An' why shouldn't I be drunk for once? He don't have any scruples."

Rémi doesn't want his digestive calm disturbed. He tries to change the subject.

"Hey! I see you got your radio."

"Yeah. Tell me about it. He forgot the batteries! You know, it's only for Sonia, no problem."

Rémi frowns. That's a bad start.

"You saw the way he treats me, like a child. And yet. . . ."

She hiccups.

"An' it's been like that the whole time. The gentleman has his whims and he satisfies 'em all, ev'ry one. But when I try to get a word in, shut yer mouth, enough of your nonsense. I've had it."

She clenches her teeth to keep from crying, and her features grow hard. Suddenly she looks old. Uncertainly, she goes to get the crème de menthe and fills two glasses.

"He didn't even stay for supper. That stuff about tires, that's a lie. I know him, you better believe it, after ten years! An' Martel's another like him. They're gonna pass the night at the hotel drinkin' with the sluts. That's what they do every night."

"Maybe not. . . ."

"Oh, yes. Réginald's a skirt-chaser. I know that."

She stares angrily at Rémi, as if he were responsible for her remark.

"Just as well he left."

She pours another glass.

"Yeah. An' I want to cry. I'm fed up cryin' over that heartless man. I didn't come into the world to cry. I didn't."

"Don't you think . . ."

"Don't you start reproachin' me, eh?"

"No, Sonia."

He is determined to keep his mouth shut from now on.

He stirs the fire. She approaches the rocking-chair. As he is picking up the blankets: "Leave all that. Tomorrow. . . ."

The kitchen has grown dark, and Rémi takes the lantern off its peg.

"No, I don't want you to see me like this. Bring the bottle and sit down."

He brings a chair near the stove.

"I'm drunk. Look crazy, don't I?"

"I can't see you. It's too dark."

They remain silent for a moment. The shadows grow deeper.

"I don't judge you. Here, have another glass."

"I don't know if you can understand."

"I can try."

"What a weekend! He came back after dinner, yesterday afternoon. A nice dinner I got ready for him and it was ruined. He smelled of drink. Of course they'd stopped at the hotel on the way. We went shopping in Amos. I did, that is. His honour had people to see. At the hotel, of course. All alone like a real turkey I went, with the kid and all the parcels. I even brought his cases of beer. I'm used to it. We come back here and, before I've even unloaded the car, Martel's there again. They're at the table guzzlin' beer and I'm makin' supper. Then we have company, Dam-Bogga and his wife and Carmen and your folks, I like them all, specially your parents, but last night I could have done without the visit. We played cards. Everybody drank and yapped and smoked. Then I made a snack. It was after two when I got to bed an' I was dead. Réginald was plastered. He hadn't said five words to me the whole night, nor a dozen since he got back, an' all of a sudden our gentleman's horny! He don't care if I'm dead tired, or that I'd like to talk. Who wants to hear what I have to say anyhow? Come on, there, Sonia, do your job, gimme some ass. I'm the guy that keeps you."

She's sobbing. Rémi would like to run away. All this suffering!

"Shit life, shit drink! I'm sick of it all."

He is devastated, and almost angry at Sonia for inflicting her troubles on him.

"He got up at noon today and ate, then he went to Martel's. From there he went and got you. I hardly saw him all weekend."

She drains another glass. Rémi is no longer counting.

"Just as well this way. At least he can't treat me like dirt when he's gone. I'll be O.K. for a week. I won't have to put up with him and I won't be bored. He's never bored, he has his good times. Sometimes I wonder what keeps me from . . . What kind of a life is this? Did I deserve it? Skirt-chaser, liar. And all because of the bottle."

Saying this, she filled her glass. Rémi hasn't the heart even to smile at this incongruity.

"I'll tell you, this isn't the life I dreamed about. No sir! You know, when I was young . . . I wasn't too tall, I was slim, I was well built, with just what I needed where I needed it. Men told me I looked like a doll. Did I have admirers! Dozens of them! Some good catches, too. Some of 'em turned out real good: Damas Roy has a store and Irénée Goulet got to be an M.P. I coulda had a doctor. I turned him down, I was in no hurry. My mother told me, make the most of your good years. I did, all right. And then I met Réginald at a dance. He was handsome and tall and well dressed, and he had the blarney. He coaxed me, he dazzled me with his dreams and promises. But I still hesitated. I hated the thought of getting married. One night he had me. Then I didn't get the curse, there we go, I'm pregnant. It don't take long to get married. And then, god damn it, I wasn't pregnant at all! To I think I got married for nothin'!"

She was still for a moment. Rémi is thinking about going to bed. Maybe she wouldn't miss him, she's so drunk.

"Rémi, get me my cigarettes from the table."

The flame of the match reveals a drawn face with frightening eyes.

"Then it all came: the disillusionment, promises not kept, dreams that go nowhere. I had saved some money, and that went down the drain. And ever since we've been going lower. To end up here!"

She weeps for a long time, then slumps in her chair. He rushes to her and keeps her from falling, succeeds in keeping her on the seat. But she seems unable to control herself. She murmurs unintelligible words and scraps of sentences, snatches like "You understand me . . ." and "you're my friend . . ." and "what kind of life is this?" Her body is limp and heavy.

"Give it a try, Sonia. Stand up. Up, Sonia. That's right!"

He has to let her lean on him as far as her bed. She flops on the mattress, her legs dangling. He gets a direct noseful of her breath redolent of crème de menthe, then she rolls onto her back and lies there motionless. She's breathing heavily with the occasional snore. He shakes her, trying to tell her to cover herself. No use, she's too sound asleep. He sits down on the edge of the bed, takes her hand, caresses her calloused palm, and lies down beside her.

Hands behind his head, he stares at the ceiling, which he can't see in the dark room. He should get up and join Sophie, but just the thought of the effort makes him tired. And what's more, there's a woman sleeping beside him; he's lying beside a woman! Rémi remembers that he has already imagined this woman naked, and the thought disturbs him. He feels sudden desires, wild projects. Dead drunk, she would never resist and would remember nothing in the morning. Could he take advantage of a friend that way? No: he'll get up and go to the other room. But he stays. Finally, holding his breath, he lays his hand softly on her belly, without pressure and watching out for a possible reaction. She's sound asleep, and her belly rises and falls regularly. After a moment he slides his hand up to her stomach, then to a breast, and cups his palm around it, barely touching. She's still asleep. Whatever he does she'll never wake. He caresses her breast more firmly as his desire grows infinitely strong. The dark allows every intimacy. He kneads her other breast. Suddenly a phrase of his cousin's, heard that afternoon, rings in his mind: "Réginald's goin' to see that you lose your cherry." Rémi suddenly feels sober. He pulls back his hand. He's not really sober, and he staggers on the way to the kitchen, bouncing off the door frame in the process. He gropes around the table-top until he finds the bottle. He tilts it high and pours a burning gulp down his throat.

Rémi is sorry that the recollection of Réginald's words interrupted him. That great lout deserved to have a stranger satisfy his wife. But . . . what would be her pleasure if she were taken while unconscious? Wouldn't she be happier to know that Rémi's friendship was reliable? His contradictory thoughts and desires chase around in his brain. One minute he's ready to go back to her, but a second later he repents and hates himself. He drinks again. It's hot in the house. He opens the door and stands in the doorway, looking out into the starless night. His friendship for her . . . it may be over tomorrow in any case, she'll be mad at herself and ashamed. She'll never again let herself go with him, never feel at ease. Might as well seize the opportunity. On the other hand, she has confidence in him and thinks he's different from the others. And any one of the others would be after her in bed right now. She's unhappy enough already. Could he risk disappointing her as Réginald had always done? Oh, what a burden friendship was!

He takes another slug from the bottle and lights a cigarette. He's thinking about Sonia's tears and recriminations. People have no right to confront him with these problems. Learning about life? Ha ha! If that was life . . . But he wouldn't have a life like that, mere appearances, saving face before company and the neighbours and children but hating each other and breaking their hearts in private. Did all couples have such troubles? The Martels? Maybe, since she didn't hesitate to take a lover. Or rather, she hesitated, and then jumped the fence anyway. His own parents? Hidden arguments from time to time. He had had an inkling occasionally, some hints of . . . But nothing serious, nothing like Sonia's troubles. Eugénie? No doubt she'd been secretly unhappy. Her husband was not the prince she had wanted as a girl.

He tossed his half-finished cigarette into the grass. There was a distant rumble of thunder. Sudden gusts also warned of a coming storm. Eugénie. The night. He finds the dead girl's photo in his pocket, pulls it out, crushes it in his hand and, on the point of throwing it away, changes his mind. The first drop of rain falls and Rémi goes inside. Sonia is still snoring. The door had been open too long and the room is freezing. Rémi stokes the fire.

Grown-ups! He's one of them now. Almost. And after waiting so long it's with a certain sadness that he takes note of his new status. He had thought he would be able to apprehend this new world with his reason, his intelligence, analysing and unmasking it at leisure, but it has revealed itself through the heart, through sensuality, evanescent and subtle in its manifestations. Beneath the small visible edifice of this world Rémi is amazed to discover immense underground structures, an infinite maze of vaulted cellar rooms. Having made this discovery he would very much like to draw back from it a while. But this would only put off the day, he'll have to face it sooner or later.

A series of flashes ruptured the dark and draws Rémi to the window. A single flash reveals the house next door. Carmen Martel – another adult with a false facade. How had she taken her husband's hasty departure? Certainly better than Sonia, and without tears. Perhaps with relief. As an adulterous woman her husband's presence would be a constant reproach. What if she used the wrong name when speaking to him, or talked in her sleep, or betrayed herself in a careless phrase? Her weekend would be two days of alertness, watching her step. Now that he's gone she can relax and indulge in her guilty thoughts, daydreaming of her lover, talking to herself as if he were there. Will she want to see him soon and ask Rémi to look after her children? He had wanted to prevent their liaison. Not any more. Carmen certainly has the same wretched fate as Sonia. "I'm weakening," she had said. Rémi imagines the resistance she put up before giving in to her passion. She must have fought herself for a very long time, have overridden barriers, forgotten religion and her upbringing. He catches himself wishing her happiness.

He can't sleep. Too many ideas are bouncing about in his mind. He sits rocking in the dark, which is broken occasionally by lightning. Rain is falling hard. Rémi continues to drink, and in his drunkenness he rejoices in the fury of the storm. It's good to be sheltered and warm, floating in your own skin and tranquil in the midst of all that fury. Exultant, he goes to the window and with extravagant gestures orchestrates the thunder, the lightning flashes and the rain, moulding them into a sublime symphony. He has almost regained the powers he had as high priest of darkness.

Sonia makes a sound. He goes to her.

"What is it?"

She's still asleep. He shakes her gently.

"What's wrong? Are you thirsty?"

He pats her face. A flash of lightning reveals the quick grimace.

"Get undressed and cover up."

But it's useless to shake her, she has sunk again into her deep torpor. From the way she is curled up she must be cold. He tries to free the sheets and cover her. The bluish light of the storm gives a surrealistic gleam to her motionless features. Her hair looks raven-black and her skin, in the brutal light, like marble. Rémi is frightened and touches her face with the back of his fingers. He is almost surprised not to find her skin turned cold. Her pretty dress is going to be all mussed. Rémi thinks, "I should take it off." No. Yes. A favour. But he has no right. She'll never know in any case. The idea of undressing her excites him. What if he stripped her naked?

"Wake up, Sonia. You have to go to bed."

He makes a last try but she doesn't even react to his rougher handling. He turns her on her belly and with trembling hands searches for the little hook that fastens her collar. At last. Now the zipper. With a single swoop, right to her waist. Lightning shows her graceful back and the horizontal of her brassière. He succeeds in extracting her arms from the sleeves, pulls off the dress with some difficulty and folds it as best he can. He has only to roll her to the foot of the bed, turn down the covers and finally get her beneath them. He hesitates a moment. The scene is magical in this strange light and he wants to preserve the spell. His head confused, his eyes intoxicated, his body on fire, he is exultant. The moment is worthy of his craziest dreams. No, he's not going to deprive himself of it right away. In fact, he's going to turn her on her back to see his fill. He pulls on her shoulder and her hip. How hot her skin is! Sonia remains inert, her arms flung back. In invitation, he thinks. But her expressionless face and her snoring clearly say that he's not invited. Rémi marvels at the volume of her breasts and the bronze lights of her flat belly. And those fleshy hips! Her blues, her mauves! Her thighs marked by the garter-belt. He's ecstatic, torn between the pleasure of his mind, which savours the uniqueness of the sights, and his desiring flesh.

Snow White awaiting her prince. He stoops and kisses her. She doesn't flinch; her lips are warm and alive. Rémi withdraws abruptly, feeling that he is losing control. Swiftly he covers her and runs to his room, where he lies down beside Sophie and falls asleep in a second.

Knocking, loud and repeated, at the door. Rémi half opens his eyes, trying to remember where he is.

"Rémi's not ready?"

It's Robert.

"Rémi . . . er . . . he's sick."

"He is! Hey, you don't look too well yourself!"

"No, we all got sick. Upset stomach. I think the chicken I made yesterday was no good."

"Nothing serious?"

"No."

Their father is leaning on the horn.

"We'll stop by tonight and see how things are."

"Fine. Have a good day, Robert."

He leaves and Sophie awakes.

"Did I sleep with you, uncle?"

"Yes."

"Yippee!"

Sonia is standing in the doorway.

"Come on, Sophie."

"Was that Robert?"

"Yes. Was that O.K., what I said?"

"Fine."

"I slept in this morning."

"Anyway, my dad couldn't have waited for me."

Sonia is poking the fire. Sophie is with her in the kitchen.

"Did you go to bed very late?"

"I don't know. Don't remember."

"Funny, I don't remember much either. I don't even remember goin' to bed."

"Nothing to remember, I guess."

"That's true."

He's lying on his back, his eyes closed. There's no rush. He's thinking about the preceding night. He, at least, has forgotten nothing. In a way he regrets not taking advantage of the situation, but he knows his mind would not be easy as it now is. It would have been rape. Good smells drift in, making him want to get up: burning firewood, coffee perking, sputtering bacon. Then he remembers the cow. And yesterday he'd milked her early.

"Up already?"

"Yeah. The cow. She's goin' to wonder what's going on."

When he returns every trace of yesterday's disorder has disappeared. The table is set and Sonia is humming as she fries the eggs.

"I've gone and muddied your floor. Got a rag? My feet are bigger than my head."

"Leave it."

"No, no, I clean up my own mess."

"Still raining?"

"It's not pissing any more, but I wouldn't be surprised if it started again. The sky's low and black."

"A real fall day."

"There's sunlight inside."

She doesn't understand, and he has to point at the bright yellow dress she has on. Then she smiles and starts singing again, a song about birds and springtime and flowers. He secretly watches her as she works. To think that a few hours ago he touched that body! But he's happy: he was able to control himself, and for the first time he didn't blindly obey his instincts. Just like an adult – and better than those he knows.

All day he hung around her, discreetly noting and marvelling how she kept her smile and her good humour even while doing the roughest or most disagreeable chores. Maybe because he was there to help her?

"Are you always so good humoured?"

"Yes. Well, not always."

"I mean, with all that work."

"Oh, the work don't scare me. I like it. When I feel bad it's because of the other things."

That Monday night Carmen Martel came around. Sophie was barely asleep and Rémi was annoyed that their neighbour should destroy their growing intimacy. She asked him to take care of her children Tuesday evening and he agreed. She chattered away about everything and nothing, then went home. Sonia seemed bitter.

"Another night alone," Rémi blurted out.

"Oh, yes," she answered, sighing.

They both noticed their slip at the same moment, and froze. They looked at each other incredulously. But a second later they had burst out laughing at the ludicrous situation. Sonia quickly grew stern.

"You know?"

"Of course."

"How?"

"I'm not dumb. I feel all, know all."

"So I see."

"Anyway, so what?"

"Exactly what *do* you know?" She seemed anxious.

"Everything. Godbout, the stable, adultery."

"What nice words you use," she remarked icily.

"There's other words too. Dreams, passion, boredom, risk, adventure, not wasting your life completely, showing that you're still a woman. Forgetting all the shit. Dreaming . . ."

"How old are you?"

"Twenty-four."

She laughed a little. Then her face grew sad. "Listen, Rémi . . ."

"You don't have to tell me anything."

"When you discover other people's secrets you have to keep them."

"Don't worry, I can keep my mouth shut. Anyway, why should I care? It's none of my business."

"It means the happiness of so many innocent people."

"I'm not crazy, I know that. And you saw I was ready to baby-sit. I kind of like the whole business."

"You like it?"

"Sure. I'm not goin' to throw the stone at Carmen. On the contrary. It serves Martel right."

"Hey, Rémi. . . ."

"Sure! It's up to him to pay attention to his wife. She's a real pearl, smart, sensitive, good-lookin'. It's fine if she thinks about herself a bit."

"If everybody followed your ideas. . . ."

"Yeah, eh? There'd be a lot of people doin' just like her."

"Yes, and I think she's wrong."

"At least she's brave."

"She's crazy. She's got everything to lose. I told her so."

"If she's careful she has everything to gain."

"So you approve?"

"Sure, like I'd approve of any woman in her place."

"You've no morals, Rémi."

"If it's moral to waste your life and make it unhappy, I have no morals. Anyway, it's not morals that stops people. It's fear."

Sonia went to put water on and get cups, trying to steady herself with these familiar gestures.

"Don't you think, Sonia, a lot of people hold back out of fear?"

"I know you're thinking of me when you say that."

"If it wasn't for fear wouldn't you have had an affair?"

"Well, maybe, if I was in love. Even then I'm not sure. You can't just. . . ."

"Lots of people do."

"Just because somebody breaks a leg I don't have to."

"But you dream about other men. You told me."

"Let's change the subject."

She poured the tea and sipped it slowly, dreamily.

"But it bothers you, don't it? You think about it even if you don't want to talk about it."

His voice was friendly, his eyes wide open. She felt she could confide in him.

"A person can't hide a thing from you."

The silence was long. They found nothing to say, or didn't dare say it. At least he smiled.

"You don't look like the missus with a house and family anymore. Look at you – you're like a girl that her mother caught in some kind of hellery and she's expecting a scolding."

"A girl! It must be the lamplight."

"The lamp doesn't change your eyes."

"I've got young eyes?"

"Now, yes. And your smile too."

Sonia's voice was hesitant.

"How . . . how do you mean . . . young?"

"As young as I am."

She looked away, tapping a finger-nail nervously on her cup. Then she laughed with faked indifference.

"Well, that's because you've been here all day. I'm influenced by you and Sophie."

"I'm not a kid, you know."

"You're not an adult either."

"I see more than lots of them."

"You read too much."

Their tea was cooling off.

"We sang today and we laughed and teased each other. You splashed me with dish-water. A real missus doesn't play like that."

"Yes, we laughed. It reminded me. . . ."

"Go on, say it. Are you scared to?"

"No, I'm not scared!"

"Yes, you're pulling back. You're acting like a missus again."

"I am a missus, as you put it."

"Not all the time. When you tell me about your problems and troubles and when you cry in front of me you're not a missus anymore. A missus doesn't cry in front of a boy and tell him stories about an unhappy woman."

"Rémi! I thought we agreed to. . . ."

"Why do you only have confidence in me and let yourself go when you're scared or sad?" She tried to answer but could not. He went on: "I don't just want to be your friend when you're in trouble. I want it when you're in good humour and sober."

"You know, the words come easier when you've had a drop or you're scared. Circumstances, sort of. But some words, just to say them cold, like that . . . Aren't you scared of words?"

"Not any more. If you knew the things I've said! But we shouldn't be scared of words between friends. Am I your friend?"

"Yes."

"Like you never had before and never will have?"

"I never opened up like that, it's true. With Carmen we don't need to talk. Things are so much the same. Will I never have another friend like you?"

"I don't think so. Do you know many people who would have carried you to bed and taken your dress off and covered you and then gone and slept with your five-year-old daughter?"

She turned red and hid her face in her hands.

"Was I that drunk? I don't remember. That's horrible!"

"No! You drowned your sorrows; you needed that. Look at you today, you're in good shape!"

She shook her head.

"I'm ashamed."

"What of? Nobody saw you. I don't count."

"I must have looked like a crazy old hag."

"No, there was a storm, and lightning. You were lit up blue. It was fantastic."

She laughed.

"If we could see ourselves! More of that and I'll take myself for a beauty."

"You should have seen yourself yesterday."

"How was I?"

"Lying on your back with your arms out wide, your face was quiet. You were asleep. Some light came in past the door curtain and some direct from the kitchen window and the reflection from the mirror shone crossways. That gave you skin like stone, blue and golden and mauve. You looked like Sleeping Beauty."

"I don't believe you but it's nice to hear. You sound like a poet."

"Maybe I'll be one some day."

Sonia stared at him.

"Rémi, you're really something."

"I've just been reading a poet. Leclerc. It's so beautiful I could cry sometimes."

"You know, I used to. . . ."

"You used to what? The words won't bite you."

"It's so silly. I never mentioned this, not even to Carmen. When I was young. . ."

"Well?"

"I used to write poems."

"You did!"

"Don't laugh. I kept a diary and I'd write verses in it. That surprises you, eh?"

"No."

"I don't look it, though."

"You think so? I bet you still do it, in your head."

"Almost, yes! The other day, it was in the morning, and I was looking at the aspen all turned yellow, and all of a sudden a poem came to me. I said it out loud. Don't ask me to tell you what it was, I've forgotten."

"That's great!"

"Imagine! At my age!"

"Your age! Sure, sure."

"I guess you don't know what it's like to get older."

"I'll find out, like everybody else."

"But enjoy your life before you do. What is it you're reading."

"It's called *Andante*."

"Hey, why don't you read me something from it?"

He went to get the book and sat down near the lamp, which was smoking a little. As he read he sought for intonations appropriate to the verses, binding the words into their relationships. He read one page, feeling some stage fright, as if he were at school. The second page came more easily, and his self-consciousness was lost in the music of the words. And then read on for half an hour. When he stopped, dry mouthed, his jaw sore and his head bursting, there was a silence that lasted an eternity. Sonia opened her eyes, which she had closed to see the poems' images. She was smiling, and seemed a little breathless.

"That's beautiful."

"Yes. I think things like that help you to live."

"You know, that's what was on the tip of my tongue; that's what I had in my head and couldn't say it."

"And wouldn't have dared if you could have."

She made more tea.

"I think I'll start keeping my diary again tomorrow. Not every day, just when I feel like it."

"And making poems, too?"

"Maybe."

She was standing in front of him with the cups. Her eyes were shining.

"I left some years behind tonight."

He took his cup and Sonia looked at him, undecided. Then she set down her own cup and went quickly to her room, rummaged in a drawer and came back with three black notebooks.

"I must really have gotten younger!"

It was her turn to read, timidly at first, apologizing in advance for the foolishness of her poems, in which she sang of the love she had not yet known, describing her excitement at a snow-filled landscape or an autumn forest. She also read him passages from her diary, explaining the context and laughing, or touched at the thought of herself as a young girl, seeing herself again in those days. She also read a description of a summer morning on a Gaspé farm: the sounds and smells, and the feeling that time stood still and this happy morning was eternity. Rémi was moved, and when Sonia had stopped reading he heaved a sigh.

"Thanks."

"It's not up to much."

"It's priceless."

She gathered her notebooks with care.

"Do you know what time it is? Ten to midnight?"

"Late. Well . . . good night."

Rémi hesitated, unwilling to move. As he passed in front of her, Sonia stopped him and kissed him on both cheeks. He held her, grasping her shoulders, and kissed her in return, but long and on the lips. Their eyes were open. Then she pulled away and went to her room, leaving him to blow out the lamp.

He lay in bed, listening for a while to the sounds of her preparations for sleep. Rémi was exultant: he had a friend, and accomplice, even in the sphere of words. And he too would write a poem tomorrow. He thought of doing something on "night" and was already searching out his images. He barely heard the sound of Sonia's feet as she came to join him.

On the Tuesday evening Rémi went to look after Carmen Martel's children. During the day he had hesitated: why not change the game and let Robert accomplish his knightly dream? He'd tell him to take to the road with his weapons. Robert would be afraid, but the idea of battling for his Lady and possessing her would buck up his courage. His weary muscles would hold him back, but his mind would drive him on. He would crouch low beside the stone pile and, when his rival's shadow approached the stave would go into action and his adversary would quickly collapse without a cry.

Carmen warned by Rémi, blackmailed perhaps, would not refuse her young pretender. Rémi would know what to say to ensure her co-operation. He almost choked at the thought of her hate-filled glance as she listened to him. She might even want to kill him for destroying the last vestige of her pride. But he went off baby-sitting without breathing a word to Robert. Nothing must trouble Carmen's adventure nor further tarnish a pleasure that doubtless bore its own burden of remorse.

Diane came down to the kitchen, where Rémi was reading to pass the time. He was anxious to be back with his cousin. He was thinking of her, in fact, when Diane arrived, thinking Sonia was no older than he was, that she didn't dominate him. Since they were equals, he also had no more wish to dominate her than to be dominated.

Diane's voice was conciliatory: "Wouldja mind if I sat here for a while? I won't bother you. You don't have to talk to me."

He smiled at her and nodded. She was a kid! There was such a distance between them! How could he have feared her?

"Just pretend I'm not here."

He closed his book.

"That wouldn't be very polite."

"Oh, nobody bothers about me. You look happy."

"Yes, I am."

"I guess 'cause you're going away."

"Partly."

"Amos. Or anywhere! I'd like to get the hell outa here."

"Why?"

"Make a new start. Never see anybody I know, ever again."

"As if you'd been through it all!"

"Through too much. I want to change."

"You don't have to go away for that."

"I think it'd help. How can I change myself here? You know what people think of me?"

He shrugged.

"Sure you do. People musta told you. But you're too embarrassed to say it. They say I'm a whore."

"Oh, come on!"

"You knew it."

She was in a rage now, her eyes had grown mean.

"What you don't know is, it's their fault. I was only ten and I'd have done anything to have them make a fuss over me. I was dragged into it. And now the same ones treat me as if I had the itch. There isn't a one of them wants to be seen in public with me. In their gang they call me the old slut. Not just the ones at school, the ones that are already workin' as well. They turn up their nose, at me, but as soon as they get me alone in a corner it's let's go, Diane, show what you can do. I'm no whore! Christ, no! An' that's the end of it, they can go jerk off in their corners, I won't be there. It's the end! Everything's finished!"

"Nothing's finished, Diane, you're only twelve! Nothing's even started yet."

"But it's awful bein' stuck with the same life. The same people. I'd like to love, I'd like to be loved."

"Don't be in a hurry, it'll come."

"I been waiting a long time."

"Just have patience."

"When you . . . when you came here I thought, maybe it's him. You didn't know anything about me, I'd be able to start again. But . . ."

He shrugged, with a woebegone air.

"I'm in a jam, eh? It's their fault. I'm all mixed up now." She looked pitiful.

He lied, "It could have been O.K. Yeah, I think I could have loved you, but you see, I was in love already. I still am."

"In love. . . ." She day-dreamed a moment, then grew curious. "Does she live in Amos? Is that why you're in such good humour? You'll see more of her when you move."

"That's right."

"Luck-y. What's it like?"

"What's what like?"

"Bein' in love?"

"It's . . . good. It makes you happy."

"What do you do together?"

"Oh, we go for walks, we talk, we hold hands. And we laugh. We feel good together."

"And do you kiss?"

"Sometimes. Not all the time because just being together makes us happy."

"You're lucky, Rémi. Oh, I'd like . . ."

"It'll happen to you. You're not ugly. You're O.K. when you want to be."

"What do you do to make it happen?"

"You mustn't seem in a hurry, don't scare people off. And . . ."

He stopped. There was a footstep, no, a shoe scraping on the edge of the stoop. Diane stood up, waved goodbye and, with a contrite smile, hastened upstairs.

"Good luck!" Rémi whispered after her.

The week went by too quickly for Rémi's taste. Every evening he and Sonia read a few pages of the book, exchanged memories, talked about the past and present, but not at all about the future. They talked mostly of dreams and ideas, things over which the passage of time has no control. She showed him how to dance, humming the songs to mark the beat. Rémi felt changed. He felt as if a long time had passed since Sunday night, and every day as he met Robert he could measure his own progress.

Supper on Friday was a leave-taking, a sad occasion despite the candles placed on either side of a bouquet of dried grasses Sonia had brought in that day. As Sophie was there, they spoke with their eyes. And at last were alone. He helped with the dishes and, now that they could talk without restraint, found nothing to say. His hand touched hers a few times, that was all. Then they sat up by candle-light, and the first words were still long in coming.

"Sooo," sighed Sonia.

"I'm not going to the end of the world."

"But you're going."

"Mustn't be sad."

"I have lots of reasons, though. Not only are you gone, but winter's here."

"You can beat fear, Sonia."

"What about boredom? And what can I do against the snow and the desolation of this road? I'd like to leave too, like you. Like the ones who built this house. But I can't."

He stood up without replying and fetched a book from his school-bag.

"It's for you. I bought it because I know you'll like it."

"A book for me?"

Her face lit up.

"I didn't dare write anything in it, 'To Sonia' or anything like that."

"*Dialogues of Men and Beasts*. Félix Leclerc. The same one?"

"Yes. I didn't write anything, I just underlined a bit. Look on page seventy-one."

She flipped through the pages and read from the underlined portion, first softly, then aloud.

"I shall be myself. If I have a song in my soul, it will rush forth one day, because no one can kill what shall live, or make live that which should die."

She repeated the two sentences, then, "Being oneself."

"Staying here, that's not you."

"What else can I do?"

"Leave."

"Leave?"

"Move away, or leave everything."

"You don't mean it!"

"I don't know. It's up to you to decide what you'll do."

She pondered for a long time, then gestured impatiently and, with a quick shake of her head, rejected or postponed some idea. She looked down at the book again.

"Thank you for this. The only other book I ever got as a present was a prize in school. 'If I have a song in my soul, it will rush forth one day.' That's beautiful!"

"What's going to happen to young Sonia?"

"Well, when you're gone I'll be doin' what you call 'playing the missus.' I won't kill the young me, I'll just keep her inside and let her out to write her diary once in a while. But her friend won't be here to encourage her."

"And love her."

"Rémi!"

"Why not? There's not much time left. No time to mince words."

"I like you, too."

"Like?"

"My friend."

She watched the straight, unflickering candle flame.

"I'll think a lot about this week, and all the things we talked about."

"And our nights?"

"Shhhush!"

"We'll see each other again, but it'll never be the same."

"And it mustn't be the same, Rémi. What's he say in the book? Not to make live what should die?"

"Something like that."

"Do you understand, Rémi? Even if it hurts us, tonight's the end. We must only think about it in the future, never talk about it, and above all never try to start again."

"Not tonight. It finishes tomorrow morning."

"All right. Tomorrow morning." She acquiesced with a smile.

"Don't worry, Sonia, when I move it's a new life starting. What we did this week will be a memory. A beautiful thing, but a thing of the past."

She slept with him the whole night, going back to her daughter just shortly before dawn. Réginald arrived at nine and took Rémi home in Martel's truck, which would do the move for the Simards. When the first load was aboard, the family left in the car. The boys stayed behind to keep an eye on the baggage until the truck returned. After the excitement, the house was strangely silent.

"Robert, would you mind waiting here while I go to the cave?"

"What for?"

"Just to see."

"Don't be too long, eh?"

"The truck won't be back for three or four hours."

Professor Savard's house has been transformed by Dam-Bogga into several neat piles of boards. Only the crumbling chimney shows that a building had been there a few weeks ago. Behind it, the cleared forest with its rotting wood. Never to be burned. The forest would repossess it all, crushing the dreams of men. The kingdom will never be, but Rémi doesn't care a fig about that, indifferent as he has become to the successive failures of the sheep-people. He doesn't feel he's a quitter like the others, even his parents. Was his knightly quest a failure? No. He feels that he met the only real challenge in it all: becoming an adult, a wolf among the sheep. That's been done. Nobody's going to stuff him like a suitcase. Priests, teachers, counsellors, establishment – let them all come: he'd be ready.

Despite the brisk air there is still a breath of sunlight. Zigzagging among the small clouds above the hill, a hawk glides slowly. Jays are calling in the dogwood bushes by the stream. The prospector, the genies, the knights, the dark and its magic: it seems to Rémi an eternity has passed since all that. And the distance makes those things, so important at the time, become insignificant. He sees himself three months ago, still a kid, paddling in the muddy water. Barely three months ago!

Near the pond the cat-tails unravel in the wind. The cave gives off a powerful musty smell. He goes inside despite this deterrent. . . . A whole jungle of roots has pushed through the roof, causing small landslides. The smell comes from the clothing Robert scattered when he came to look for the mortuary photo. The princess's clothing! The Black Goddess! The idol is cracking, and when Rémi lifts her, the legs fall off and her waist crumbles in his hand. Her head rolls on the floor of the cave and as he pushes it aside his hand strikes the chalice in its hiding place beneath a dress in rags. Better get rid of all that. With a stick he starts filling up the entry by knocking down walls and vault. Perhaps other children will come here some day. Let them dig their own cave!

Beside the stream, Rémi digs a ball of paper out of his pocket: Eugénie's photo. He hurls her in the creek, watching her drift away and sink just as the water loops around a bend.

The Abitibi region of Quebec, spring 1959. The Simards, a working-class family from Montreal, decide to try their luck and settle on a scrub farm. As they travel north, they pass derelict farm buildings and overgrown fields – it is apparent that others have failed to do what they now set out to do.

The novel focusses on the Simard sons, Robert and Rémi, and is told from their point of view. Just entering puberty, they react to the tedium and seeming hopelessness of the life of the adults around them by creating a fantasy life. In quest of this, they often slip out of the house for nocturnal rambles, spying on neighbours and seeking an ideal woman to fall in love with. They create their own cult – complete with ceremonies, an idol, and a shrine in a cave – in opposition to the power of the church, represented by the arrogant and bigoted Father Rivard.

In *Knights of Darkness*, Soucy portrays adults with limited resources leading stultifying lives, relieved only by drinking, card-playing, and sexual misadventures. At the same time he captures the coming of age of two imaginative and determined boys as they move into adulthood and personal independence. And in lush style, he recreates the mystery and isolation of the Abitibi as it exerts its influence on all the characters.

A novel of social realism, adolescent imagination, and political allegory, *Knights of Darkness* will delight all readers of fine Canadian writing.

JEAN-YVES SOUCY was born in Causapscal, Quebec, in 1945, and grew up in Montreal. His first novel, *Un Dieu chasseur* (1976), was published in English, under the title *Creatures of the Chase*, in 1979 by McClelland & Stewart.

Cover design by Marque

ISBN 1-895246-29-6

01999

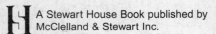
A Stewart House Book published by
McClelland & Stewart Inc.

9 781895 246292